Pandora's Girl

By the same author

Daughter of Darkness

Pandora's Girl

Janet Woods

ROBERT HALE · LONDON

ISBN 0 7090 6942 1

Robert Hale Limited
Clerkenwell House
Clerkenwell Green
London EC1R 0HT

2 4 6 8 10 9 7 5 3 1

Typeset in 10/13pt Garamond
by Derek Doyle & Associates in Liverpool.
Printed in Great Britain by
St Edmundsbury Press, Bury St Edmunds, Suffolk.
Bound by Woolnough Bookbinding Limited

For Sandra, my in-the-middle daughter.
You're the tops!

CHAPTER ONE

The phone rang.

'Pandora Rossiter.'

'It's me, your grandmother.'

The silence lasted almost a quarter of a minute, then Pandora proceeded with caution. It might be something completely different from what she feared. 'Why have you called?'

'I need you. I'll expect you after the weekend.'

Pandora's breath expelled in a sigh. Typical Emily Dysart. Straight out with it and with no regard for another person's convenience or sensibilities. She ignored the emotion churning in her chest. Her grandmother wouldn't welcome it.

'I see.'

'You'll come then?'

'That goes without saying.'

'The will's written up. You'll inherit everything.'

Pandora didn't ask about her Aunt Lottie and grandmother didn't mention her. There was no need. She would never leave the estate to poor Lottie.

After she replaced the receiver she stared unseeingly out into the garden. At last she'd been forgiven for disgracing the family name. She felt like crying, but didn't. Emotional outpourings had always been frowned upon when she'd been growing up. She gave a faint smile. Even if she'd decided to cry, the tear-ducts would probably have atrophied through disuse by now and all she'd cry would be dust.

Dust to dust. Ashes to ashes.

Emily Dysart was dying. She'd told Pandora a little while back, but it

7

had taken her three years to get to the actual point of inviting her grand-daughter to visit her. She must be close to the end. With her passing Pandora's life would change – and so would Gerald's.

She pressed her face against the cool glass pane. Today was her husband's fiftieth birthday. The predictable surprise party had been arranged – the cake with candles, the champagne in ice-buckets and the barbecue in the garden.

The neighbours had arrived, eager to make an occasion of it because most of them were retired, and the village of Cedarbrook in the county of Gloucestershire offered little in the way of excitement except for an eagle's nest high on an outcrop of rock, and the dubious and infinite drama of other people's lives.

Friends weren't noticeable by their absence. Gerald didn't have any and had discouraged her from forming any close friendships herself.

There had been the usual elaborate charade that morning, pretending the postman was late, forgetting to wish Gerald a happy birthday before he left for the office, and making out a shopping list to delay his arrival home whilst the guests assembled.

The boys were already home from school for the weekend. They were almost men now. Adrian was captain of the cricket eleven, and destined for Oxford next year. Michael was in his penultimate school year and set to follow in his brother's footsteps.

They were Gerald clones. Tall, their hair light brown, they were quietly well-mannered and already showing signs of stuffiness. Both would become accountants and join the family firm. It was hard to believe she was their mother, or that enough passion had been generated in her to conceive them.

When Gerald's car edged into view she pasted an automatic and dutiful smile on to her lips. She'd miraculously produced his heirs from their sporadic copulation; now that part of her marriage was temporarily shelved.

Gerald wouldn't dream of having sex with her when he was in the middle of an affair. She was his wife, and relegated into the pending basket until it was over. Then she was serviced out of a sense of guilt and duty, as if Gerald was charging the battery of the classic car in the garage – which he took for a spin now and again just to keep it ticking over.

He'd just started an affair with his latest secretary. Pandora had consid-ered divorcing Gerald several times over the past few years, and for exactly the same reason – until she'd realized she just didn't care.

She watched him alight from the car. He was handsome, with just the right shades of silver in his hair to make him look distinguished. Then there was the touch of boyishness in the curve of his smile – and smugness too, the smile of a man who knew his worth, his rightness, and his place in the world.

His glance wandered to where she stood at the window, his ego needing the reassurance of knowing she was waiting for him to come home.

She was perfectly groomed, as always, as he expected her to be. Her hair was fashioned into a chignon, her straw-coloured linen dress was immaculate, her feet were encased in brown leather sandals with small heels.

His smile expanded with practised ease and confidence, and he raised a hand in greeting.

She returned the smile, the curve of her mouth a perfected exercise. Her green eyes feigned a welcome. What hypocrites they both were!

She was thirty-eight years old. She'd stood at this window every weeknight for nineteen years. It was the last time she'd do so.

There was an air of secretive excitement about him when he approached the house – like a child who knows he's won a prize, and pretends ignorance. Stupidly childish really, for a man who'd passed his prime.

His lips brushed her cheek. She could smell his secretary on him. Duty-free Chanel from the trip to France. Each time he started an affair he took them to the same hotel in France for the weekend, and bought them Chanel.

She always did rather better than them with her conscience gift.

'Darling, they're perfectly lovely,' she said, clipping the diamonds into her ears. She tied a silk scarf around his eyes and led him towards the garden – part of the charade.

'Surprise!' everyone shouted – and Gerald managed a perfectly unbelievable, totally amazed smile, which faltered for a moment when he set eyes on his secretary.

Pandora didn't usually invite his secretary, but she thought it might prove to be fun this time. It was going to be more so, on this, the last time she would host Gerald's birthday party.

His secretary's mouth was a tangerine gash, her hair was a smooth, hennaed bob, her body angular. She looked frighteningly efficient and fit – not one to settle for being the other woman.

The secretary's eyes ran speculatively over the house, then lit on

Gerald. His eyelids flickered as he consciously avoided her gaze. The tips of his ears turned red and he sucked in his stomach.

As the evening progressed he became slightly over-animated – like a youth trying hard not to show off, and nearly succeeding.

Pandora's eyes flicked from one to another, watching, assessing, trying not to give the game away by letting her amusement show.

The secretary's smile was brittle, her eyes adoring and possessive of Gerald. She looked about eighteen, was actually twenty-two. Nothing of the bimbo in this one, though.

What was her name ... Anne ... Jean? Something short. Pandora smiled apologetically at her.

'So sorry, I have a terrible memory for names.'

'Mare, without the I.'

Mare-without-the-I couldn't meet her eyes.

'As in female horse? It must be a nuisance, having to explain the pronunciation all the time.'

She felt a twinge of conscience when Mare suddenly looked unsure of herself.

'I don't, usually. Gerald ... Mr Rossiter said it's better not to.'

Pandora knew what it was like to be in love with Gerald, she'd been in love with him herself at that age – and still loved him, in a sanitized, habit sort of way, because she'd learned to ignore his faults over the years.

She decided not to tell him today. Today was his birthday, today the boys were home. No – today was not the day to tell Gerald about the property she was about to inherit. Or that she was going to leave him.

She told him about the inheritance on the Sunday night, after the boys had gone back to school.

'Let me get this straight,' he said, buttoning up his blue-striped pyjamas. 'You're going to Dorset to look after your grandmother.'

'That's right.' She applied moisturizing cream to her neck and massaged it in. 'Will you mind?' *Say you do, and I'll forgive you the secretaries and I'll stay.* She could see his face in the mirror, his brow wrinkled in thought. Her mind jettisoned a second, contradictory thought. *Say, go!*

'The alternative would be a nursing home, I suppose?'

Her fingers strangled the neck of the cosmetics jar, and she slowly screwed the lid on tight. Did he have to deliberate when the fate of their marriage hung in the balance?

'She doesn't want that ... there's Lottie to consider as well.'

'Ah yes, Lottie.' He sighed rather heavily, as if Lottie was his burden to bear. 'I've got no objection if that's what you want to do.'

'It's not that I *want* to, Gerald. It's my duty.' Gerald understood words like duty.

'Yes . . . yes, of course. And once it's over, you can put Lottie in a home somewhere.' He yawned, closed his eyes and turned on his side. 'That's settled then.'

Not as far as she was concerned. 'I asked you if you'd mind.'

'Of course not. The boys and I will be all right,' he said sleepily. 'And it won't be for long. As soon as you get the inheritance we can sell the house. Marianna must be worth quite a bit. The money can be . . . invested . . .'

She stared at the mound under the covers. Gerald always fell asleep swiftly after he took his sleeping pill, and started to snore exactly thirty seconds later.

The second hand on the crystal mantle-clock ticked off the seconds, *five . . . six . . . seven . . .* How could she have ever married a man who wore blue-striped pyjamas? *Fifteen . . . sixteen . . . seventeen . . .* How could she stay married to a man who invested her money without consultation, and before she'd even got it? *Twenty-three . . . twenty-four . . .*

'I'll never sell Marianna, and if I go, I won't be coming back,' she whispered. *Twenty-nine . . . thirty. . . .*

A snore gently burrowed into his pillow.

'I gave birth to a daughter when I was fifteen,' she said aloud. 'If she hadn't died she would have been twenty-three years old now.'

He kept snoring. It was odd how used she'd become to carrying on a conversation with herself. Perhaps she was going mad!

'Her father was a family member. He didn't hurt me. He made me enjoy it, even though I was under age.'

Sparks flew from her hair as she swooshed the brush through it. 'Grandma wouldn't believe he was the father, and I didn't understand then that he was just a dirty old man. I hope you're not going to be a dirty old man too, Gerald.'

He mumbled something that sounded like a name.

She stared over at him, eyes narrowing. 'How long have you been screwing your secretary?'

The snoring stopped and she grinned. 'You didn't think I was capable of such language, did you? You think I'm made of plastic, that you wind me up with a key and I perform for you. Well, not any more, Gerald.'

A series of bubbling snorts danced from the side of his mouth.

'I know all about your affairs.' Throwing the brush amongst the various pots of cosmetics littering her dressing table, she strolled across the room and slid into bed beside him. 'Poor Gerald. You're such a fool.'

He sucked in a deep, shuddering breath and started snoring again, deeply and evenly.

Her lips brushed against his cheek in a goodbye kiss.

'Sweet dreams.'

Emily Dysart watched her granddaughter through lowered lids.

Pandora was sitting in a cane chair gazing out over the garden, her eyes dreamy and retrospective, as if she was remembering the past.

The girl was a paradox. To anyone who didn't know her, she had an air of unruffled serenity. They didn't sense the churning undercurrents of wilfulness. Pandora bestowed the sweetest smile even when she loathed the recipient. She disguised her insults, the victim left unaware – though it might occur to them sometime afterwards that they might have been insulted.

Emily had loved her to distraction once. But that was before Pandora had driven her grandfather into his grave. She should have kept her counsel.

'I'm not going back to Gerald,' Pandora suddenly said, and turned to smile at her. 'He has affairs.'

'No one has ever been divorced in the Dysart family. One puts up with things and turns a blind eye.' Emily might as well not have spoken, and wished she hadn't when an accusatory glance was flicked her way.

Pandora folded her hands in her lap. 'I'm going to live here. If I go back to Gerald he'll sell Marianna and put Lottie in a home.'

Pandora had always had a soft spot for Lottie, and she loved Marianna. Emily had counted on that, but she hadn't considered the girl might leave her husband. Her frown was intercepted by a level gaze.

'The boys don't need me now – and they'll love visiting me here.'

Emily didn't want to be fussed with problems – and she didn't want to quarrel. She didn't have the strength. Pandora would do what she wanted to do – she always had.

The breeze coming through the window was perfumed with lavender and sunshine. It wasn't the sort of day one should talk about such things. It was a day to drift, something she'd just learned to do.

A musty, decaying smell wafted up from her body, which was as dry and as folded as old flannel. Death was a step away, waiting for her to trip – waiting to catch her. She made a strangled sound in her throat, refusing to take that step.

Her granddaughter came to place a wrap round her shoulders. Pandora's fingers drifted gently over her hair and she sighed. 'Why did you send me away?'

'Oh, God, why rake that up?' Emily whispered, when what she really wanted to say was, *Why dredge up the guilt I've been living with all these years?*

Pandora's eyes were as green and as brilliant as emeralds when she turned, and her smile was serene. 'It was cruel to send me away when I was grieving for my baby.'

She should have known Pandora wouldn't let her die without punishing her. Emily rallied her remaining strength. 'How could you grieve? You hardly saw her.'

Pandora's eyes softened. 'The nurse let me hold her. Her skin was like silk and her hair was a wisp of gold. When you told me she'd died I felt as if my heart had been ripped out.'

A tear gathered at the corner of Emily's eye, a tiny, crystalline drop. Although she tried to stop it, it was followed by another, then another. Embarrassed by this show of emotion she gave an anguished cry.

'It's all right, Grandma.' Gathered into Pandora's arms, she was rocked gently against her chest, as if Pandora was the mother figure, she the child. It felt comforting.

Why hadn't she ever rocked Pandora in her arms and comforted her when she'd been troubled? Why hadn't she taken her side when it became obvious she'd been telling the truth and why had she closed her eyes in Lottie's time of need?

Because she'd mistaken her own stubbornness for strength and her stupidity for pride. She'd loved her husband too much to see his faults. As a consequence, she'd allowed her own beloved daughter and granddaughter to suffer.

There was no time for pride now. She should tell Pandora she loved her, tell her she'd lied.

And although the words trembled on her lips they were too hard to say and were pulled back into the knot of misery lodged tight in her chest.

It was too late – too late to tell her the truth. She couldn't jeopardize Pandora's love now, and ignorance wouldn't hurt her.

Yet she needed to be forgiven. Her chest constricted around her sob, as though it was being squeezed in someone's fist.

'I'm so sorry, Pandora.'

'I know, Grandma,' she said soothingly, 'I know. . . .'

But Pandora didn't know – and death was just a tiny step away. . . .

CHAPTER TWO

The difference between the two counties had been nakedly apparent to Pandora's eyes as they'd walked down the winding lanes towards the church.

The forests and lush, multihued greens of Gloucestershire were slightly claustrophobic when compared to the gentle, green-gold landscape that was Dorset. She appreciated it more because she'd been away for such a long time and the delight of nostalgia had not yet left her.

Her hand reached for Lottie's as the vicar eulogized.

'Emily Dysart was a valued member of the community, always ready to help others and espouse family values. . . .'

The description of Emily was a flattering one. Keeping a tight grip on her boredom Pandora glanced at Lottie. Sunlight streaming through a stained-glass window had caught her attention.

Lottie didn't seem upset by her mother's death. Her preoccupied blue eyes were unclouded by grief, or any other emotion for that matter. Yet something showed in the depths of her eyes, some elusive spark of intelligence Pandora had noticed on rare occasions before. She briefly wondered what Lottie was thinking as she allowed her glance to wander over the congregation.

Only a few people had attended the service, and she knew hardly any of them. There was the interfering and inquisitive Mollie Jackson, who helped clean the house, and Emily's sister – the coquettish Joy, who'd already buried two husbands and whose third looked as though he would make it a hat-trick.

Joy's lipstick had bled into the lines round her mouth – her hair startled people with its brightness and her eyelashes were caked with mascara, which had spread like marmite on bread under her eyes.

15

When Pandora had been growing up, Joy had been held up as an example of what she shouldn't be. Yet, she'd always had a sneaking regard for Joy's spark of individuality, and her bohemian style of living.

The reality had fallen short of Pandora's expectations when she'd briefly lived with Joy between her fall from grace and her marriage to Gerald. Joy's individuality became self-indulgence, and the bohemian lifestyle translated to semi-squalor.

Joy and Emily hadn't spoken for several years, though they'd continued to exchange Christmas cards – usually of the cheap variety as an expression of their continuing disapproval. Pandora hadn't expected Joy to come to the funeral. She hoped she wouldn't make a fuss, afterwards.

When the vicar began a prayer she stifled a yawn. Thank God the service was nearly over! Why did churches always smell so dusty and sour?

'Lottie wants a pee,' her aunt whispered, sliding her rear back and forth on the pew.

Gerald turned his bowed head and his frown slid disapprovingly to Lottie's face.

'Be quiet.'

Lottie's eyes flared with embarrassment, her face closed up and she withdrew into herself.

Why had he done that? Lottie couldn't help how she was. An accident had left her with the mind of a twelve-year-old.

From a distance, Lottie didn't look fifty. She looked like an adolescent with her petite, girlish figure. Up close, she had an open face with guileless blue eyes. Grey threaded her brown hair. Her vagueness was endearing, and those who met her for the first time didn't realize she was anything other than normal.

'Come on, I'll take you.'

'She can wait.'

Pandora stood, shooting Gerald a challenging look and gaining immense satisfaction from the surprise in his eyes. She hadn't often bothered to contradict him over the years.

The priest looked up and frowned. Aware she was an atheist, he probably thought she'd disrupted the service on purpose. It would be more disruptive if Lottie peed on the floor.

Several pairs of eyes surreptitiously followed them when they left the church. Pandora's heels cracked on the faded black-and-white tiled floor, the noise allowing an opportunity for a couple of people to clear their throats without being too conspicuous.

Hardly anyone was praying for Emily's soul, just paying lip-service by bowing their heads and looking pious and suitably solemn. Rituals made uncomfortable situations comfortable, but whether the mourners believed in the prayer they intoned was a different matter altogether – most of them were reading from a common-prayer book held on the lap.

Somebody had forgotten to unlock the lavatory door. Pandora took Lottie behind the hedge, where she squatted to relieve herself, her sensible boiled-white knickers cuffing her slender ankles together. By the time Pandora had got Lottie sorted out the service was over.

At least they didn't have to bury her grandmother. Her body had been dealt with in private at the crematorium the day before. Her ashes were enclosed in a grey marble urn and a plaque to her memory had already been viewed in the Garden of Remembrance by the mourners. It was hard to imagine Emily Dysart reduced to dust.

Gerald had a sulky look when they joined him. He'd be more annoyed when she told him their marriage was over. She would tell him after the funeral lunch and she hoped he wouldn't be too tedious about it.

It was late afternoon. Mollie Jackson had just departed after clearing away the lunch leftovers and whispering a warning in her ear.

'That actress is poking about in Mrs Dysart's things. You want to keep your eye on her.'

Joy held the delicately painted vase up to the light. 'This didn't belong to the Dysart family, it used to belong to my mother.'

'I believe it belonged to Emily.' Pandora took the vase from Joy, and placing it gently back in the cabinet, locked the door and slid the key into her pocket. 'I don't think she'd like you touching it.'

Joy's mouth curved into more of a smirk than a grin. 'It was left to me in our mother's will.'

'I believe you agreed to accept its value in cash, instead.'

The glance Joy gave her was almost calculating, certainly a measure of some sort. 'The value has risen considerably since then.'

Joy was nothing like Emily, who'd been short and neat. Upright and angular, she looked older than her sixty-five years and her mouth was a mass of lines puckered around nicotine-stained teeth. The black shirt and pants she wore had seen better days and looked as if they'd walked straight off the opportunity-shop shelf and on to her body.

Pandora smiled at her. 'Emily knew a bargain when she saw one.'

To which Joy shrugged. 'In my book it's called taking advantage of someone less fortunate.'

'It wasn't her fault you married the wrong men.'

Joy looked annoyed at being reminded. 'Ah, but it was. Emily introduced me to my previous husbands – both of them gamblers. One was a bully, the other an alcoholic, and both of them much too old for me. Marrying older men seems to be a family trait.'

Pandora's glance went to Gerald. He was talking to Joy's third husband in the garden. Brian looked thin and tired.

'Brian's dying, you know.'

Joy's grief hit Pandora like a tidal wave. Her face was haggard and vulnerable when she turned to face her, an unspoken question in her eyes.

'He has about six months.'

She didn't know quite what to say. Joy would see right through a platitude. 'Is there anything I can do to help?'

'Not unless you can perform miracles.'

'Would that I could. How are you off for money?'

Joy inserted a cigarette into a holder and lit it. Her finger ends were yellow, her nails shocking-pink to match her lipstick, and bitten to the quick. She squinted through the smoke. 'If you could manage the difference on the increased value of the vase . . .'

'Perhaps you'd like to take the vase instead. It could be sold at auction.'

Joy's eyes flew open in shock. 'Uh . . . I don't think so . . . you know what my place is like with people coming and going, it would probably get broken. Actually, I'd never consider selling it. It's an heirloom.'

'Of course.' Why hadn't she realized that the vase – always a bone of contention between the two sisters – was an object which enabled charitable transactions to be conducted, whilst leaving their pride intact. 'I'll ask Emily's lawyer to post you off a cheque.'

Lottie came into the room, carpet-sweeper in hand. She smiled vaguely at them, then proceeded to make a run at the crumbs on the carpet.

'What are you going to do about her?' Joy whispered.

'Nothing. Her life will go on as usual.'

A thin, pencilled eyebrow rose in surprise. 'You're staying on here?'

'Yes.'

'By yourself?'

When she didn't answer Joy swooped in a deep breath. 'I've just realized why you married Gerald. He resembles Robert Dysart.'

Something thumped against her diaphragm. 'Does he? I hadn't

noticed.' Which was a downright lie, she'd noticed about five years after her marriage to him, when the disenchantment had begun to set in.

'Like hell you hadn't.' Joy's fingers dug into her arm. 'It was true what you said at the time. Your kid's father was Robert Dysart.'

Pain stirred in Pandora's chest. 'Isn't it a little late to start believing me now?'

There was pity in Joy's eyes. 'Emily must have come to believe you, otherwise she wouldn't have changed her will back to favour you.' She began to laugh. 'The vicar must have thought he had it made. Can you imagine Emily leaving everything to the church when she has family to inherit?'

'Let it drop, Joy.'

'Emily blamed you for the death of your grandfather. She adored him. She'd never have forgiven you if she'd really believed—'

'Shut up, will you? It's none of your damned business.'

Pandora didn't usually lose control, but Joy had always seen through any pretence and knew how to bring out the worst in her. She hadn't even realized she'd raised her voice until Gerald and Brian gazed towards the house.

Joy's eyes narrowed in on Gerald. 'He doesn't know, does he?'

'There was no point in telling him when the baby died at birth.'

'You've been married to him all these years, and you haven't told him you were raped by Robert Dysart and gave birth to his child?'

Pandora tried to keep a grip on her temper, and in doing so gave away more than she intended. 'I wasn't raped. I loved him.'

'Talk about father figures,' Joy said in disgust. 'You should consult a shrink.' She spun around when something crashed to the floor behind them. 'Oh, my God! What have you done, you clumsy fool.'

Lottie hid her face in her hands.

Pandora's glance took in the crystal fruit-bowl upturned on the floor. She crossed to where Lottie stood and slid an arm around her thin shoulders. 'Don't be upset. It's not broken, it fell on top of the fruit.'

'Joy shouted at Lottie.'

'She didn't mean to . . . did you Joy?'

'Oh, for God's sake!' Joy said, obviously exasperated. 'I didn't mean anything by it.' She fished in the voluminous black bag she was carrying and brought out a bag of liquorice allsorts. See what I've brought for you, some sweets.'

Lottie's smile came back.

'Take them to your room and watch television whilst I talk to Pandora, there's a dear.'

'There's really nothing to talk about.'

'What do you mean there's nothing to talk about? What if Gerald finds out about your daughter?'

'Unless you tell him, he's hardly likely to. Stop meddling in my life, Joy.' She smiled to take the sting from her words. 'Shall I ask Gerald to run you to the station or will you stay for tea and catch the later train back to London?'

Joy sighed. 'You won't get rid of me that easily. I need to stay the night. Brian's tired out and the morning train would suit him better.'

It didn't fit in with Pandora's plans, but she couldn't turn a dying man out. Gerald could wait. 'You're welcome, as long as you don't talk about the past. I'll prepare a room.'

'Obviously, you're made of stronger stuff than Lottie,' Joy muttered as she began to walk away.

'Lottie?' She turned, puzzled.

'At least Lottie didn't have a baby,' Joy said.

'I don't get you. I thought Lottie—'

'Fell over and hit her head?' She gave a short, sharp laugh. 'That was Emily's story. Lottie was got at. It was all hushed up.'

'Emily told you that Robert Dysart did it?'

'No, but did you see the way she reacted when he was mentioned? It makes you think, doesn't it?'

'I don't know if I want to think about it at all.'

'You will eventually. You might look like a Dysart but you're like your mother. She always wanted to get to the bottom of things. Much as she tried, Emily was never quite able to dominate her. She couldn't stop Grace marrying your father, and she couldn't stop her killing them both.'

'That's a perfectly horrible thing to say. It was an accident.'

Joy flicked ash into a pot plant. 'The truth usually is horrible. Your parents were about to split up when Grace drove the car into that tree. She was doing a ton. There were no skid marks.'

Pandora could feel her eyes smouldering as they met Joy's. 'Why are you always such a bitch?'

'Pandora?' Gerald gave her a puzzled look from his position at the doorway. 'That's no way to speak to a guest. Apologize.'

As if she was a schoolgirl deserving of reprimand! Even Joy gave a chuckle at his tone. This was her house, not his. She'd talk how she damned well liked in it. Hell, Joy was right! Robert Dysart had been a father figure and so was Gerald. She felt disgusted with herself – disgusted with him.

Then a sense of freedom enveloped her. Striding to the hall stand with Gerald behind her she grabbed up her jacket. 'I'm going for a walk along the beach. I need some fresh air.'

'I'll come with you.'

'I need to be alone.'

'But, Pandora—'

She felt like screaming. 'Stop smothering me. Go home, Gerald. Leave me in peace.'

'Wait, you're upset,' he called out as she strode off through the front door, leaving him on the doorstep.

She turned and smiled at him. 'I'm not upset. For the first time in my life I feel independent.'

'You can't be independent. We're a couple.'

She stared him straight in the eye. 'Not for much longer. I want a divorce.' How stupid he looked, like the donkey from *A Midsummer Night's Dream*. Only she'd woken up from the dream, knew he was an ass and had fallen out of love – not the other way round.

She felt dangerously, deliriously happy. 'Goodbye, Bottom,' she yelled and began to dance over the grass in the direction of the sea.

He watched from the doorway, his mouth open with astonishment, looking definitely ass-like. She wouldn't have been surprised if he'd hee-hawed as he faded from her sight.

The beach was deserted, the shadow of the cliff lay long and grey over the sand. Seagulls dropped from the sky to circle hopefully round her, their wings a soft whirr of sound.

A cool breeze skimmed salt smells off the sea – the same breeze that became a gale in winter. Between the sea and Marianna a long, low hill muscled out of the earth like an arm to protect the house, though the shrubs and trees were still whipped into a frenzy in winter.

Pandora shrugged into her jacket, half-closed her eyes, breathed in the smells of her childhood and listened to the evening hush of the sea.

She recalled the good things, like picnics on the beach with Lottie and her grandmother. Emily had always packed a little basket with a lid at both sides and filled it with slices of homemade egg-and-bacon pie, fruit, and tart lemonade made from real lemons.

Emily had taught her to cook in the large kitchen with its scrubbed wooden table and old-fashioned coke-burning stove. 'Nourishing English food,' she'd said. 'None of this foreign rubbish that leaves you feeling hungry half an hour after it's been eaten.'

Everything had to be measured in exact amounts, something Pandora had always enjoyed – adding the ingredients spoonful by spoonful until the brass scales balanced so perfectly in the middle that one grain of sugar could weigh it down.

'A true Libran,' Joy had said once, when the sisters had been speaking. To which Emily had retorted, 'Don't fill her head with such rubbish.'

Yet, with the sky purpling to dusk and the earth exhaling the fragrance of a summer night, Pandora felt at one with the beauty of the world and knew nature had balanced it perfectly.

Tomorrow, the lawyer would arrive from town and she would know exactly where she stood regarding money. Having gone through the accounts with her grandmother, she was aware the house cost a great deal to maintain.

She might have to find herself a job. But what? She'd practically gone from school to marriage, except for a stint in Harrods when she'd lived with Joy, and she didn't have any qualifications. She'd met Gerald there when he'd been shopping for a tie.

She tried to think of some hobby she could utilize, but failed. Her life had consisted of socializing, motherhood and housewifery. Gerald wouldn't have had it any other way.

'I don't want you to work,' he told her. 'You have an important role looking after the family.'

Gradually, the ideas in her head had been replaced by the trivia of domesticity. She felt resentful – as if she'd missed out on something. But then, she only had herself to blame. She'd spent nineteen years in a static state of her own choosing, instead of growing.

Now she was fully awake, and responsible for Lottie and herself.

Her jaw tightened when Gerald crunched across the sand towards her.

'I was worried about you,' he said when she frowned at him. 'I've decided to stay a couple of days and take charge of things. The lawyer has to be dealt with, the real estate people contacted.'

'I'm not selling.'

'Don't be silly, Pandora. Marianna is too big for a holiday home.'

She avoided his eyes, not enjoying what she was doing to him. 'I'm going to live here, Gerald. I've decided to leave you, now the boys are old enough. In fact, I wrote and told them so this morning – told them we'd grown apart.'

'You're overwrought,' he said soothingly.

'I didn't tell them about your affair with Mare. Or about the other affairs you've had over the years.'

He shifted from one foot to the other, an expression of injured innocence wiping the guilt from his face when he spluttered. 'I don't know what you're talking about.'

She began to stroll back towards the house. 'You can live in the family home. My half of that and the investments can be transferred into the boys' names.'

His hand fell on her shoulder and spun her round. He looked like a wounded Labrador. 'Darling, what is this? You're talking nonsense.'

It would be easy to give in to his persuasion, pretend it hadn't happened. Life would go on as before, comfortable and familiar – and a lie.

Nineteen years of suppressed anger was a tight, aching knot inside her.

'I want half the income from the investments. Adrian and Michael can spend the weekends with you and I'll have them for the holidays. They're grown up now, so the choice really should be theirs. We'll ask them what they'd prefer.'

'For God's sake, Pandora, I won't have this.'

'If you agree, I won't press for more.'

'And if I don't?'

'I'll go for the jugular. Investments, house, business, cars. I'll hire the best divorce lawyer in England and have him subpoena all of your secretaries. Wronged wives do quite well in the courts these days, I believe.'

His face suffused with colour. 'You bitch. How long have you been planning this?'

She'd been married to him for nineteen years and for the first time saw anger in his eyes. It made things a little easier. He had no right to be angry, only she did. 'Probably since your first affair, eighteen months after our marriage.'

He forced a mildly reproachful look to his face. 'I can't recall—'

'I can. Her name was Amanda Foster. I believe she was seventeen.' She aimed a tight smile at him, enjoying the power of having the upper hand. 'Your call, Gerald.'

'What about the investment jewellery I bought you?' he spluttered.

She began to laugh. 'Is that what it was? I thought it was a conscience gift. Fine French perfume for the girl-friends, diamonds for the wife.'

'It cost me a fortune.'

She slanted her head to one side. 'I'm entitled to it – a gift of love from my faithful husband. Consider it a bribe for keeping quiet.'

A tic worked in his jaw as he stared at her, his eyes were wounded. Gerald didn't have a spontaneous sense of humour, so the tic must have been a sign of tension. He'd soon figure out he'd be better off doing things her way.

When he realized his wounded expression was not going to work, the anger returned. His fingers dug into her shoulders, making her wince.

'If you bruise me, I'll make sure I visit a doctor so it's on record.'

His grip loosened and he flung her away from him, so she nearly fell. 'Ask your lawyer to contact mine,' he said, then turned and stalked rapidly away from her.

She let him go ahead, waiting until her racing heart returned to normal. By the time she reached the house his car was pulling out of the drive.

Joy handed her a glass of white wine when she went inside, her eyes were filled with a bird-like curiosity.

'You look upset.'

'I really need something stronger. I've just told Gerald I'm leaving him.'

'There isn't anything stronger.'

Pandora gazed around her. 'Where's Brian?'

'Gone to bed. I've made us an egg salad for dinner, and there's some chocolate cake left over from lunch for dessert.'

'Thanks. It's been quite a day.'

She was surprised when Joy caressed the side of her face with her knuckles. 'Poor you. If I'd known what you intended to do, I would have made myself scarce.'

Tenderness from another woman she didn't need. She fought a sudden urge to cry.

'Thanks, Joy, but it doesn't matter, now. It's over.'

Joy's eyes displayed concern. 'You're all right?'

She nodded. She would be after a good night's sleep. It would be safer to stay on generalities at the moment though. 'I might get a dog.'

'Lottie would like that. She always wanted a dog, and Emily wouldn't let her have one. She said they shed hairs all over the furniture.'

'Gerald said that when I asked him for a cat.' She experienced a sudden rush of adrenaline. 'I might get a cat as well. I might get a hundred cats and a pack of dogs.'

Joy chuckled. 'Which would make the house smell, and the noise would drive you insane. Handle freedom responsibly, or it might become your master. One thing at a time, OK?'

'OK.' Tears pricked her eyes. She snatched a wad of tissue from her pocket and aggressively blew her nose. 'A dog for Lottie, then.'

A kiss landed on her cheek. 'Now you're thinking sensibly.'

Linking arms, they wandered through to the kitchen and joined Lottie at the table. She gazed from one to the other, her eyes clouded with worry.

'Who's going to look after Lottie now?' she said.

It was Joy who answered her. 'Pandora is. But you've got to help look after her, too. You're not a child any more.'

'Lottie has always looked after her,' she said, and the secretive smile she gave made Pandora gaze at Joy in puzzlement.

CHAPTER THREE

There was something elusively familiar about the man standing on Pandora's doorstep. Tall and in his late thirties, his dark hair displayed a rather dramatic and premature grey streak at one temple.

He gazed steadily at her through warm, brown eyes, a faint grin tugging at his mouth.

'Simeon Manus,' he said by way of introduction, and stuck out his hand. 'Nice to see you again, Pandora.'

First name terms. When? How? His grip was firm, and she couldn't quite remove her hand from his without making it too obvious.

'Simon Manus? I feel I should know you.'

'Simeon.'

'The only Simeon I can recall . . .'

'. . . attended the same class at Ashford primary school with you.'

Her eyes widened. 'Simeon Woods? But he was an obnoxious little squirt who—'

'Dropped garden worms down the back of your dress. My name was changed when my mother married again.'

'I'm glad we've sorted that out.'

'Actually, we met several times after that, at the church youth club. I believe I beat you in the table-tennis tournament when we were thirteen.'

'Then Dennis Hopper beat you in the final.' They both laughed. 'Did you know everyone called you Woodworm behind your back?'

'That figures.' He gently squeezed her hand and let it go. His grin was a mile wide. 'I apologize for the worms.'

She laughed and threw the door open. 'What on earth are you doing here?'

'Representing Teague and Frapp. He's my uncle, on my mother's side.'

'Who? Teague or Frapp?'

'Teague. Frapp died over twenty years ago. He was Teague's uncle, on his mother's side, too.'

'I see ... I think. Actually, I was expecting Mr Teague.' Slanting her head to one side she noted his quizzical lift of the eyebrow and wondered how Simeon had grown up to be so attractive. As she recalled, he hadn't had many friends at school. The boys had bullied him and called him a sissy and the girls had regarded him as a nuisance. 'Tell me, when did you exchange worms for legalities?'

'Are you sure you want me to go into that?'

'Perhaps not. We all change.'

'Some less than others. You look exactly the same as you did at thirteen.'

She smiled and stood to one side. Somewhere, he'd learned the art of gentle flattery, and wore it like a second skin. 'Please come in. I'll fetch us some coffee.'

Pandora led Simeon into an airy sitting-room overlooking the back garden. Dappled sunlight streamed through the open french door, bringing with it the smell of honeysuckle.

She left him in a chintz-covered armchair whilst she went to make the coffee. When she returned, he'd pulled one of the occasional tables towards him. A manila file was set in the middle of it.

She gazed curiously at it. 'Emily Dysart's life story?'

'And Lottie's, and yours.'

'Ah, I see.' She exhaled in a series of stops and starts, her eyes flicking up to his. 'Will I find this uncomfortable?'

He fiddled with a thick, red rubber band holding the folder together. 'I can't see why. There's nothing personal in it. Just copies of deeds and certificates and such. If you'd prefer Mr Teague—'

'No. I'm sorry. It wasn't a personal remark I made earlier, and I certainly didn't mean to suggest Mr Teague was more qualified to handle my grandmother's affairs than you were. I just assumed he still handled her affairs.'

'I've been dealing with them for the past five years, and entirely to Mrs Dysart's satisfaction, I might add.'

He seemed a trifle over-sensitive. 'You don't need to explain, Simeon. Would you like sugar and milk in your coffee?'

'Both, thanks.'

She handed him a dainty cup, immediately wishing she'd used mugs when she saw how awkward it looked in his large hands. 'Look,' she said. 'I don't know why I'm playing lady of the manor. I don't know if I'm making you nervous, but I'm making myself nervous. Would you prefer a mug? I would.'

His laugh went a long way to allay her nerves.

'I'm sure I can manage without spilling it all over myself, this time. Why are you nervous?'

'I don't know. I'm not used to dealing with lawyers, my husband usually does all that.'

'Would you rather we wait until he was here?'

'Oh, no. I've left him.' She bit her lip. Saying it out loud seemed to make it suddenly real. 'It's only recent, you see. I'm not used to it yet . . . being single, I mean.'

'I know what you mean.' He picked up the file, curved it lengthways in one hand and slipped off the band with the other. He laid it on his lap and flipped it open, suddenly all business.

'Your grandmother has left you comfortably off. However, there are matters she'd discussed with us concerning the house—'

'I won't sell Marianna. It's Lottie's home and I love the place.'

His eyes flicked up to hers, brown and astute. 'Mrs Dysart didn't expect you to sell it, but she was worried about the considerable amount needed for its upkeep. Her accountant did a projection. Within fifteen years Marianna will bankrupt the estate.'

'I'll get a job.'

'It's doubtful you could earn enough to cover the maintenance.'

With her singular lack of qualifications, Pandora knew that was doubly true. 'So, what was the plan?'

'That the house be divided into four apartments – one unit to be retained by the family, the other three sold on life leases – or rented out.'

'I have no intention of selling a chimney pot – let alone three-quarters of the place.'

'Good, because your grandmother favoured letting them. The apartments would bring in a high rent, which would cover the maintenance and give you an income.'

'I don't know if I want to become a landlord.'

'The business end could be handled by a rental agency on a commission basis.'

She thought about it for a moment. 'I'd lose my privacy.'

'The sort of people who could afford to live here would value their own. I don't think they'd bother you.'

'How much would it cost to convert the place?'

He drew a folded sheet of paper from the file. 'It's already been costed out and money set aside for it. The interest the money's been gathering should cover any inflation discrepancy.'

'You mean, my grandmother was going to go ahead with it?'

'Had she not become ill she would have.' Simeon shrugged. 'It's your house now. It's entirely up to you.'

'Can I think about it?'

'Of course. I'll leave the conversion blueprint with you – though there should be one in your grandmother's file.'

'I haven't had time to look for files.'

'She kept her personal file in the desk in her sitting-room upstairs. The key's hanging on a hook under the desk.'

'I haven't been in there since she died.'

Simeon's expression softened. 'If you'd prefer someone with you when you clean it out, I'll be quite happy to help.'

Pandora didn't want a man to lean on. She wanted to be independent and do things for herself. 'I'm sure I can manage.'

His eyes shuttered over and his voice cooled. 'As you wish.'

She felt guilty. By rebuffing his offer of help she'd probably lost the chance to make a friend. 'I'm sorry, I didn't mean that as it sounded. It's just . . . it has personal memories attached, and having someone else there is a little bit inhibiting if one wants to cry or something.'

'I understand,' he said.

'What will happen to the invested money if I decide not to go ahead?'

'Whatever you want to happen. It's your money once the will has gone through probate. All we need to do is lodge the signatures.'

He went on to other business, making everything easily understandable to her. Finally, he stood up to go.

'Do you handle divorce?' she said as he was about to get into his car.

'I'd rather not.'

'Why?'

'Because it's not something I'm good at, being stuck between warring parties.' He smiled and started the engine. 'I can recommend someone who specializes in divorce, and who won't see you off.'

'Thank you.'

'I'll ask her to ring you.'

'Her?'

'Her name's Carol Stringer.'

It was on the tip of her tongue to ask Simeon if he was involved with the woman – then she thought: he's probably married with a family, and besides, his private life is none of your business.

Having sorted that out, she inclined her head. 'Fine, thanks.'

Lottie was coming in through the gate when he drove off. She waved at Simeon. He pulled to a halt, leaned out of the window and began to chat to her.

Pandora frowned. She'd never seen Lottie so talkative. Usually, she rarely spoke unless spoken to. Then she remembered she'd never observed Lottie relating to people outside the home . . . and in fact, had spent several years living apart from her before her grandmother died, so she was making an assumption.

Lottie's face was shining with happiness when she reached her, her smile was wide.

'Where have you been this morning, Lottie?'

'Walking. Lottie forgot the time.' The smile faded and she hung her head like a naughty child.

Pandora sighed. It was obvious Emily had been too strict with her, not allowing her to stretch herself to capacity.

'That's OK. When you go out could you just let me know? Or leave me a note. You can write, can't you?'

Her head bobbed up and down. 'Lottie can write. Lottie can do lots of things.'

'I know you can. You're just hiding in there, and one day you're going to pop out and surprise me.'

'Lottie likes surprises.'

Which reminded Pandora about the dog. 'That's good because I've got a surprise for you. Get in the car, we're going into town.'

They were back within an hour. On the back seat an animal regally reclined. He'd been the best the pound had to offer, a whiskery brown and grey, matted creature, with long legs. He stank to high heaven.

The dog unfolded from the seat and stuck his head out of the window when they rolled to a halt, surveying his surroundings with a look of complete disdain.

'You needn't think you're going to lord it over us,' she warned him. 'And you're going to have a bath before you come into the house.'

'Lottie will bath him,' her aunt said, draping her arms possessively round his neck.

A little while later a different dog emerged from the outhouse. He raced around the lawn with Lottie after him. He shook himself several times, then between that and rolling on the grass he lifted his leg against every available tree and bush. Having thoroughly marked his territory he allowed himself to be caught, and stood patiently whilst his coat was brushed into bristling, hairy splendour. Pandora grinned. A pack of dogs was definitely out of the question.

Any stray thought the dog might have harboured of freedom fled after he'd scoffed a dish of leftover stew and vegetables. He settled himself on a couch with a pleased expression on his face. Clearly, life had never been so good.

Pandora handed Lottie a book. 'This shows you how to train him. Teach the commands one by one and keep repeating them until he's learned. OK?'

By the end of the week, Sam had learned the basics of acceptable dog behaviour, which demonstrated that he wasn't as stupid as he appeared – and that Lottie was more intelligent than she let on.

'Well done, Lottie,' she said. 'What else can you do that you haven't told me about?' Lottie tossed her head in that shy way she had, smiled a little secretively and said nothing as she walked away.

Pandora decided to make it her mission in life to find out.

'Lottie has led too sheltered a life,' she said to the people from the disabled society over the phone the following week. 'My grandmother wouldn't let her go anywhere by herself, or train for an occupation.'

They insisted on a psychiatric report and made an appointment.

The doctor's name was Bryn Llewellyn. He was large and sure of himself, and he gazed at her steadily and said nothing whilst she repeated what she'd already said over the phone.

Pandora found him uncomfortable. A psychiatrist should be middle aged, have a wise face and wear glasses. He should not be young and large and be oozing with sex-appeal, like this one. Nor should he wear a maroon waistcoat over his shirt-sleeves, like a singer in a barber-shop quartet, or pleated pants the colour of clotted cream. As if his appearance didn't go against him, she was inclined to dislike him when he said he preferred to see Lottie alone.

'I'm afraid I can't allow that.'

He gave an unbelieving growl of a laugh, rose from behind his desk and loomed over her. 'Can't allow it?' he said, and his soft, Welsh-accented voice was full of menace as he shovelled his hand under her elbow and lifted her to her feet. 'Decorative as you are, Mrs Rossiter, you will wait outside. My consultations are private, unless I decide they're otherwise.'

Against her better judgement, and gathering her dignity together, she stalked outside to the waiting-room, where she sat and fumed for an hour or so.

'Well?' she said, when Lottie finally emerged, looking pink and pleased.

Bryn Llewellyn smiled serenely at her. 'I haven't drawn any conclusions yet.'

Which was annoying to say the least. 'Well, when you do, you have my number.'

'I most certainly have,' he drawled.

Bryn Llewellyn stayed infuriatingly in her mind, so she felt compelled to question Lottie about what had taken place between them. Lottie got so upset that she disappeared into her room for the rest of the day and not even Sam could entice her out.

Pandora rang the psychiatrist. 'What the hell did you say to her?'

His voice was puzzled. 'Actually, we got on like a house on fire. Come in and see me tomorrow. I'd prefer to discuss this face to face.'

Which was a complete waste of time as far as Pandora was concerned. A man who upset Lottie was *persona non grata* in her book. Despite her feelings, she intended to go, anyway, curious to find out what he had to say.

'Her problem stems from a childhood trauma I should imagine,' he said the next day. 'We must get to the bottom of it.'

Pandora thought it safer to stick to Emily Dysart's truth than Joy's suspicions. 'Your imagination is way off course. Lottie hit her head when she was a child, that's the basis of her problem. Why are you trying to make more of it?'

'She doesn't appear brain-damaged to me. Has she had a scan?'

Two could play at being confrontational. 'Have you?'

'Why are you being so defensive?' he countered, and leaned over his desk, his spiky dark hair and flecked hazel eyes making him look attractively eccentric. Even his name was eccentric, sort of pointed and threatening. Bryn Llewellyn, nearly all angled consonants.

'Because I love her, and she's been placed in my care.'

'And you think I'd do something to hurt her?'

'Somebody did.'

'Ah . . .' He leaned confidently back in his chair and smiled encouragingly at her. 'Did that somebody have to be me? I bet you quizzed her as to what went on and then she got upset.'

She blushed a bit, remembering what she'd said to Lottie about this man . . . but of course, he would try and twist things, because that was his job. Then her blood began to race because his expression had become a bit too personal for comfort, which was annoying and flustered her, so she dropped her bag and had to scramble around on the floor to pick things up, and every time she looked up he seemed to be examining her from a different angle.

'You're making me annoyed,' she said.

'Why should my admiration for you be annoying?'

Pandora didn't answer. She wasn't about to engage in a bout of sparring with such a devious man, not until she knew him better, which of course, she never would, because she didn't like him enough to want to.

She made a further appointment which she conveniently forgot to keep, and though it crossed her mind he might just phone and smoulder a bit, she really thought nothing more of it until she received his account.

She rang him straight away. 'The amount is outrageous. You work for a charity – they don't send accounts.'

'I donate my time to the charity. If you're too lazy to cancel an appointment someone else could have used, you get to pay.'

Anger surged through her body. 'And what if I don't?'

'OK, I'll pick you up at seven and you can take me out for dinner, instead.'

'Listen, you arrogant—'

'Tsk, tsk, tsk . . .' He hung up on her, and when she rang him again she only got his answering machine.

'Don't bother turning up,' she shouted crossly into it. 'I'm going out.'

But only to the beach with the dog.

The August evening was perfect. Sam loped on ahead, the trail marked and familiar to him now. He'd turned out to be a good dog, amiable and not too boisterous if he was walked twice a day.

Adrian and Michael would love him. They were coming down at the weekend, their first visit since she'd left Gerald. After the week with her they were going to Cowes for a week of sailing with friends and then on to Tuscany, where they'd join their father for the remainder of the holidays.

'The Tuscan holiday was your idea,' Gerald reminded her, 'and you're quite welcome to join us.'

She'd been tempted to say yes. It would be easy to go back, to let Gerald take charge of her life again and to overlook his infidelities.

But the divorce was under way.

Pandora hadn't really taken to her lawyer. Carol Stringer was whip-thin and touching thirty, her sharp-featured face made to look more so by a cap of cropped, jet-black hair. Electric blue eyes glowed from a pale face – making her look as jittery and restless as Pandora found her to be. She thought the mistrust might be mutual, but it didn't affect the woman on a professional level.

She lifted her face to the cool kiss of the breeze. Freedom came at a cost, but it was worth it. Her sons were men. In a few short years they'd be married and would probably make her a grandmother.

She'd like a granddaughter – one who looked like the daughter she'd given birth to. A pain of such sharp poignancy twisted into her chest that it stopped her in her tracks.

She'd never asked where her baby had been buried. The shameful incident, as it had been labelled, had been placed in the never-to-be-discussed basket.

There was a sudden, urgent need in her to find her baby's grave. But not this evening. In the morning she would be fresher and less sentient.

Since she'd moved back to Marianna, she'd been up and down emotionally. In her marriage Gerald had been the sun around which she'd revolved. Now she was cast off and drifting, and at the mercy of her feelings. It was a little scary, but deep down she knew there could be no going back.

Giving a sigh, she reluctantly whistled for Sam. She'd better get home before Lottie set fire to the kitchen.

At Lottie's insistence, she'd left the preparation of dinner in her hands, but couldn't help wondering what sort of mess she'd make of it. A packet cake was one thing, a whole meal, another.

She saw him when she was half-way across the lawn, standing at the sitting-room window, a glass in his hand. He waved to her.

He was either thick-skinned or had a giant-sized ego. She guessed it was the latter.

She entered the house through the french door, not bothering to smile at him. Sam gave the visitor an inquisitive sniff, then headed off towards the smells coming from the kitchen.

'You really are annoying. What are you doing here and where's Lottie?'

'I said I was coming—'

'I left a message telling you not to.'

He was infuriatingly relaxed, his eyes almost intimate, as if they were old friends, or even lovers. 'I haven't checked my answering machine today, and Lottie's in the kitchen. Did you think I'd murdered her and thrown her body down the well?' He chuckled. 'Are you always so bloody hostile to guests?'

His effrontery took her breath away.

'Why are you being such a pest?'

His mouth stretched into a grin, the effect being piratical rather than pleasant. 'The last person who asked me that was my mother.' He waved a hand over the drinks tray. 'Would you like a drink?'

'A sherry, thanks – just a minute, you can't walk into my home and take over.'

'I know.' He turned away from her, picked up the decanter and filled a small glass. 'I'm probably the rudest man you've ever met . . . right?'

She gazed warily at his back. 'I can't recall meeting anyone quite like you before.'

He turned to place the sherry in her hand and grinned. 'That's being diplomatic. You dislike me, right?'

She took a deep breath, steadying herself. She wasn't going to bite.

'Is there any reason why I should?'

'I've formed the impression you feel threatened by me.'

'For a shrink, you jump to a lot of conclusions. Why are you here?' In control of herself, she went to move past him.

His fingers closed lightly over her wrist. 'Isn't it obvious? I wanted to see you again.'

They had eye contact now. His were a peculiar greenish hazel, black-flecked and confronting. She knew hers reflected her curiosity.

'Subtlety isn't one of your strong points,' she suggested.

'You seem to bring out the latent adolescent in me.'

She gently disengaged her wrist. 'I refuse to be blamed for your lack of social skills. Go home and grow up.'

He chuckled, his eyes filled with an irrepressible mischief that brought a smile to her face. 'Lottie has invited me to dinner. Do I have your permission to accept?'

She shrugged. 'If you feel like risking it. I'd better go and see what she's up to.'

'Why don't you just leave her to it?'

She felt herself bristle. 'You think I should?'

He sighed, then subsided into one of the wicker chairs, looking as if he had every right to be there. 'Whatever I say, no doubt you'll do the opposite.'

She took the chair across from him, realizing, too late, that he'd manipulated her into doing exactly that. She began to laugh.

'Have I made a total ass of myself?'

He steepled his hands together under his chin and gazed over the top at her.

'Do you want my professional opinion?'

'Not at the prices you charge.'

'Ouch.' He dropped his hands to his lap. 'Let's forget my professional calling for the time being, shall we?'

'Okay. Why did your mother call you a pest, Mr Llewellyn?'

'I hypnotized her two chickens, and they didn't lay any eggs for a week.'

Her eyes widened. 'How do you hypnotize chickens?'

'It's a trade secret. Would you scream if I kissed you?'

She moved her head in an uncertain gesture, because she thought she really shouldn't encourage him. On the other hand, she was thinking how very much she'd like to be kissed by him, which was quite disconcerting and unlike her.

He took it as a negative. 'In that case, I won't.'

She didn't know whether to be glad or sorry. His sensual bottom lip positively invited attention, and the deep, growling octaves of his voice were a turn-on. When her hormones gave her a nudge she stood up, acutely aware of the on-going scarcity of sex in her life.

'Excuse me, I'll just go and see if Lottie wants me to set the table.'

'I've done it.' He rose as well, and sliding his hand to the nape of her neck gently pulled her face to his. How tender the gentle exploration of his kiss. There was nothing demanding or threatening about it.

When he released her she was trembling and felt like crying. The eyes gazing into hers were liquid and enigmatic.

'Not bad for a Welshman, huh?'

'I haven't had any previous experience with Welsh men, but no, it wasn't bad.' Coolly, she nodded, then turned and walked away from him, every molecule in her body flaming with awareness, certain that one day she'd go to bed with Bryn Llewellyn – but not today. He was too sure of himself.

She shouldn't have worried about Lottie's cooking. Tender lamb chops were accompanied by steamed vegetables, followed afterwards by a dessert of rich, chocolate mousse. She'd picked up her mother's cooking skills.

'That was wonderful,' Bryn said, leaning back and patting his stomach.

Lottie beamed a smile at him and bustled off to make coffee.

'Can I get you a brandy?'

'Not this time. I've already had wine with the meal, and I have to drive home.'

She ignored the tiny query in his eyes, smiling at him impersonally. He was already too self-assured,

'Thank you for being so nice to Lottie. I was worried about her when she disappeared into her room. Now, I think it might have been something I said to her.'

'You overreacted. It's understandable.'

'She's a gentle person. I don't want her hurt.'

His eyes became a conflagration of alertness. 'Are you telling me something may have happened in her past that will hurt her if it's recalled?'

She felt her jaw tighten. 'I said nothing of the sort.'

'But something *did* happen?'

'How would I know? I was only a child – an accident I was told.'

'It might be on record.'

'What might?' she said warily.

'Her accident.'

The Dysarts' doctor had retired, and had left town shortly after she'd given birth to her baby. Pandora remembered her grandmother grumbling about them having to sign on with a new one.

She smiled at him. 'It's possible.' And it was more than possible that all the records were in her grandmother's file – but she wasn't going to tell him that.

At least Bryn didn't overstay his welcome. A decent interval after finishing his coffee he stated his intention of leaving.

'I hope I can visit again, some time. Perhaps you'd like to help out with meals on wheels, Lottie. They're always after volunteers.'

Lottie nodded, a shy smile on her face.

'I'll explain the situation to the organizer, and ask her to ring you,' he said when Pandora escorted him to his car. 'Thanks for this evening. I enjoyed it.'

'Good-night, then.'

He chuckled when she turned and walked back towards the house. 'Coward,' he taunted.

'Don't push your luck,' she warned, and going inside, shut the door behind her and leaned against it, a smile on her face.

CHAPTER FOUR

'Was it because of Mare?' Michael asked.

It was the last day of Pandora's week with her sons. They were on the beach, resting after lunch of sandwiches, cake and fruit.

Her boys, tall and bronze, didn't seem like her children, but more like the modern, handsome young men on hoardings who advertised after-shave or underwear. They drew the eyes of women and carried with them an air of self-consciousness only the very youthful and aware of themselves had.

'We agreed we wouldn't mention it,' Adrian said, throwing a piece of dried seaweed at his brother. He bestowed an apologetic glance on her, and she registered that his voice had deepened to a permanent manly tone since she'd last seen him. 'We don't need to talk about you and Dad, do we? I mean, it's not really our business.'

Only it was their business. She and Gerald were their parents. As gently as possible she said, 'I didn't realize you knew about Mare.'

'Oh yes, and about the others,' Michael said, looking awkwardly earnest.

'The others?'

'Oh, for God's sake,' Adrian exploded at his brother. 'Did you have to mention the others? I told you Mum wouldn't have known, otherwise she would have left earlier.'

The smile she gave them was almost a grimace. 'Of course I knew, but I didn't intend to break up the family, for your sakes.'

'I don't suppose it would have hurt,' Michael said, his voice sounding deceptively off-hand, despite the pain displayed in his eyes. 'Other chaps at school hardly ever saw their fathers.'

'I wanted you to grow up with your father. He loves you both very much . . . we both do.'

'Then, why. . . ?' Michael blushed bright red when Adrian kicked him, and mumbled, 'It doesn't matter.'

Pandora knew exactly what he'd been about to ask. 'I don't know why your father was unfaithful, and you mustn't let the fact that we've parted influence you in any way. Some men just have different needs. Since you're almost adults, you shouldn't need me to tell you that. You'll have to ask him.'

Adrian nodded, the expression in his eyes both secretive and know-ledgeable, as if he'd experienced the release of that need – which he probably had, she thought with a shock. And Michael? Michael with the downy blush to his cheek, his eyes avid and shifty with the thought of it, also seemed aware of the way one went about the accommodation of a woman's body.

She experienced a sense of unreality to find herself seated on a sunny beach discussing the facts of life with her two grown-up sons.

She wanted to ask how they'd known about Mare. She wanted to ask if Mare had moved into her former home, was sleeping in her bed, her thin muscular thighs accommodating Gerald's pelvic thrusts. But she didn't.

Both of them were moving towards the water now, towels held in front, to be dropped at the water's edge as they ran into the sea – two young men in a thrash of foam and over-loud shouts to conceal their mortification at the unwanted result of the conversation.

The subject of Mare was brought up again, just as Pandora put them on the train.

'Mare's pregnant,' Adrian blurted out.

It was unlike Gerald to be so careless. Pandora felt a bit sorry for Mare, because Gerald had invited her – his wife – to go to Tuscany with them. He wanted them to be a family again, and Mare and her baby didn't really count.

Gerald was a creature of habit, the others were just a convenience. Now, he'd have to take responsibility for Mare and her child. Pandora wouldn't allow him to wriggle out of it by becoming his family again.

'Do you mind about the baby?' she said gently.

'It does rather change things.'

Adrian's sullenness was unexpected. He was really too old for it. 'But it's not the baby's fault, and you'll have a new sister or brother.'

He threw a careless arm around his brother's shoulder, making them one. 'We don't need one, do we, Mike?' Michael shook his head, willing to think as Adrian directed because that's what he was used to doing as the younger brother.

They looked relieved when the whistle sounded. When they leaned out of the train window and kissed her, and she felt the sting of inexpertly shaved upper lips against her face, she knew the time was fast approaching when they'd need no one.

Simeon Manus called on her the following week – just as she'd intended to clear out Emily Dysart's room.

'I wondered if you'd thought any more about the alterations to the house.'

'Not really in depth.' The frown drifting over his face surprised her. 'But I've looked over the plans and can't see any reason why they shouldn't go ahead. I intend to have the back garden fenced off if they do. It's not needed for access, and I don't want strangers wandering in front of my windows.'

'They won't all be strangers. I hope to rent one of the apartments myself.'

She laughed as she led him into the sitting-room, enlightened by the admission. 'So that's why you're pushing me?'

'Partly,' he said, unabashed by her teasing. 'Also, the sooner it's done, the sooner you'll have an income from it. Within two years the alterations should be covered and you'll be making a profit.'

'You give good value for a family lawyer.'

'My uncle wouldn't have it any other way. Its an old-fashioned firm.'

'It's too old-fashioned. When I meet Mr Teague, I shall tell him to remove Frapp from his brass plate, and put your name up there. Teague and Wormwood.'

He grinned. 'You do that, but I think I'd prefer Teague and Manus.'

She made them tea, and she found some little iced cakes Lottie had baked to go with it. Afterwards, they looked over the rest of the house, trying to imagine it divided into apartments.

'They'll be a decent size,' Simeon muttered, as they stood at an upstairs window and gazed down through the dip in the hill to the horizon with its glimpse of the sea. 'This is the one I've set my heart on.'

He'd chosen well. The windows of the other two apartments would overlook the front garden, the road and the distant town. But the assumption that she wouldn't want the sea view herself rankled a bit.

'I'll let you know when I've decided,' she said.

He glanced at her, his eyes wary, and slightly probing. 'I'm in no hurry, but do you have a problem with having me move in? If so, you must say now.'

She was being bloody-minded, finding fault where there was none. She had no intention of moving upstairs. A niggle of guilt made her sound more conciliatory than she'd meant to be.

'Why should I have? I'll have to clear out all the old furniture and go through the attics before any conversion goes ahead – but I guess you can have first choice of the apartments.'

A small tenseness of mood in the atmosphere just disappeared, leaving her wondering whether she'd imagined it being there. Simeon was clearly a man who didn't let an opportunity pass.

'I wouldn't mind buying one or two pieces when you've had it valued.'

'I never considered anyone might want it. Most of it's heavy and ugly.'

'When you grow up with furniture it tends to merge into the background. I'm not an expert on antiquities, but some of this looks as though it might be valuable. I'll recommend someone to value it, if you like.'

'I know someone who's in the business.'

He glanced sideways at her, looking not altogether pleased, his voice bristling with affront. 'As you wish.'

It was more a matter of asserting her independence than lack of trust. Simeon had the same deceptive air of authority as Gerald, and if she wasn't very careful she'd be agreeing to everything he wanted. He was also more sensitive than she'd thought him to be, though he hid it well.

'Will your family be living here?' she said, suddenly curious as to whether he was married or not.

His eyes veiled over. 'I'm divorced. My daughters live with their mother.'

She moved on to what she hoped was more solid ground. 'How old are they?'

'Sarah's twelve and Emma's ten.' He took out a photo, smiling in the way fond fathers do as he held it out to her. Two blue-eyed princesses, with long, fair braids, smiled shy schoolgirl smiles into the camera.

Her own baby daughter had never blossomed into a little princess, had never smiled for a school photograph to be flourished with pride under someone's nose. Her baby had been a shameful family secret; her death had been greeted with relief. She'd been disposed of as quickly and as quietly as possible. She felt a sudden, swift surge of grief, and anger at the unfairness of it. *Someone should have loved and wanted her besides me!*

'They're beautiful.' Her hands were trembling when she handed it back.

'They're doing well at school.' He shuffled the photograph back into his wallet and his proud smile faded. 'I miss them.'

Because he so obviously loved his daughters, she felt compelled to tell him about her guilty secret, somehow knowing he'd be sympathetic.

'I had a daughter once. She died.'

His face took on the mixture of guilt and embarrassment people get when they've unwittingly chosen the wrong subject. 'I'm so sorry. I had no idea.'

She engaged his eyes. 'Of course you didn't. It was before my marriage, and all hushed up. Look, I didn't mean to embarrass you, Simeon. Seeing the photograph of your beautiful daughters made me think about her, that's all. I'm sorry I mentioned it.'

His head slanted to one side, his eyes were bright with interest. 'I'm not. I'd like to hear about it. Your grandmother never said.'

'Well, she wouldn't, would she? I was only fifteen at the time. The father was ... a ... family member. I only saw the baby once. She was beautiful, and I bonded with her like a mother should with her baby, even though I was still a child myself.

The lawyer in him escaped from its leash. You were under age. You could bring charges, you know, even now. There must be records.'

'For what reason? The man's dead.' She smiled up at him, feeling better for mentioning the unmentionable out loud. 'This is the first time I've told anyone about it. It's odd, but after all this time I can still remember the baby's face.'

Simeon took her hand in his as they made their way downstairs.

'I'm pleased you felt you could trust me. It explains why your grandmother sent you away.'

'The shock was too much for my grandfather. He died not long after. Grandma never forgave me.'

'She must have. She changed her will.'

'I think she realized I was telling the truth about who the father was.'

Curiosity was burning in his eyes. 'Are you going to leave me guessing?'

She'd told him everything, so she might as well tell him that, as well. His reaction would be interesting. 'He was my grandfather's brother, Robert Dysart.'

Curiosity turned to shock and he blurted out: 'The bishop?'
She nodded.

His lips pursed around a long, silent whistle. 'I can see why it was hushed up.' A kiss briefly touched against her face. 'Poor little Pandora.'

His pity was uncomfortable, even though she'd invited it.

'I thought I loved him, you see . . . he always took my side against my grandfather and was affectionate right from the beginning. My grandparents were strict, and I needed love. He provided me with it.'

'You must have felt betrayed.'

'I didn't know quite what to do when he denied being the father. I rather think he convinced himself nothing had happened between us. He rarely spoke to me from then on, and used to hurry past me with this martyred look on his face when we met – as if I'd accused him unjustly – which, in the family's eyes, I had. And of course, that made me feel guilty, exactly as it was designed to do.'

'You should have had some counselling.'

Bryn Llewellyn infiltrated her mind, his potent presence there annoying her. She couldn't imagine consulting him with a problem of any sort. He was too confrontational a man, too clever by half and too attractive. Or was he?

Better not to dwell on the personal, she thought hastily. There were better-looking men in the world to fall in love with; more charming men, men easier to be with and less obvious – like Simeon.

'Would you like to stay for lunch?' she said.

Regret clouded his eyes. 'I'm afraid I've already made arrangements.'

She didn't allow her disappointment to show. 'Another time, then.'

He drew an electronic organizer out of his pocket and fiddled with the buttons. 'I'll be away until after the weekend,' he murmured. 'How about I pick you up on . . . now let's see . . . Monday and Tuesday are out. Would Wednesday suit you? I'll book a table at the Carrington.'

'I'll look forward to it.' Although she hated being slotted into his appointment schedule, and would rather he had asked her, it had been ages since she'd been to a decent restaurant. 'I might have some news about the furniture then. You must let me know when you've decided on the pieces you want. Everything outside our personal living area will be going.'

His eyes touched on hers, as guileless and as honest as brown eyes could be. 'I made out a list when I originally made an offer to buy them from your grandmother. I expect it's in her desk.'

Grandma had obviously decided not to sell them to him. Pandora wondered why as he drove away.

Later that day she told Lottie about the plans for the house.

'Turning Marianna into flats will bring in some money to maintain the building. It's your home as well as mine. What do you think?' She smiled when Lottie nodded. 'I don't suppose you understand all this, but the place will be a mess once the builders move in. Most of the furniture and stuff will have to be sold, because we can only keep what we'll need. So if there's anything special you'd like to have, let me know. Someone is coming to look at it the day after tomorrow.'

'Lottie understands everything. She would like the pretty Chinese box her mother keeps in the secret place.'

Which was the longest sentence Lottie had ever said to her. Pandora gazed at her in some surprise.

'Grandma had a secret place?'

Lottie's eyes slanted suddenly, so she looked almost sly. She laid a finger over her mouth. 'Shsssh,' she said gently, 'it's a secret.'

Distracted by an agitated phone call from Joy, with the news that Brian was failing fast, and could she please borrow some money, because their income didn't cover the special things he needed – Pandora pushed Lottie's statement to the back of her mind. She scribbled out a generous cheque, shoved it in an envelope and hurried off with it to the post-office.

It was Mollie Jackson's cleaning day. Mollie was the type of person who had to be seen to be efficient, and the house was noisy with the sound of the vacuum cleaner and the voice of the quarrelsome, bustling woman, who popped her head round the door when least expected to furnish Pandora with the latest titbit of unwanted gossip.

She wished she could swap Mollie for someone quieter and less familiar in her manner, but she had no excuse to get rid of someone who'd almost become part of the furniture over the years. Mollie had taken over the cleaning when her mother had retired. Although she was excellent at her job, Pandora found it a relief to get away from her and escape to the sea-shore.

The leisurely summer seemed to have transformed itself into a facsimile of winter overnight. There was a bite in the wind coming off the sea, and pointed grey crests fingered upwards from the water's surface when she and Lottie took Sam for his morning walk.

The tide was half-way in. The waves reached for the cliffs in a long dragging motion scooping grooves of sand and shells into the water with wet, raking fingers. The sea hissed and slapped, the wind keened through the sea grasses, peppered sand into their faces, whipped their hair into strands and snatched the air from their lungs.

Experiencing a mad sort of exultation, Pandora observed the clouds boiling up on the horizon.

'I think we're in for a storm. We'd better go back.'

With the wind at their backs they were almost blown up the cliff path. Sam bounded ahead, the flaps of his ears flattened against his skull and his mouth snapping at the wind when he turned to check their progress.

The sky darkened and thunder began to rumble. The rain started just as they cleared the hill, small drops borne on the wind. They ran pell-mell, two women, and a dog barking with the joy of the game, reaching the shelter of the porch in a pother of breathless laughter just as the sky opened.

The house smelled of polish and disinfectant. Mollie had obviously not expected them back quite so soon, because her three hours weren't up, and she'd gone. She wouldn't have done that if Emily Dysart had still been alive, but the work had been completed in its usual efficient fashion, so Pandora had no reason to complain.

They took a while to get their breath back. Slumped in armchairs, and with mugs of tea in their hands, they watched the storm playing havoc across the sky for a while from the safety of the sitting-room window.

They rose together by some unspoken agreement, going upstairs to Emily Dysart's rooms. The task of clearing them out could be put off no longer.

Emily's clothes were placed into plastic bags. Everything had been repaired, cleaned, and neatly ironed. It struck Pandora that it had been arranged deliberately before her grandmother's strength fled, leaving everything easy to dispose of – and with no intimacy.

The clothes would be dropped off at the charity shop, except for the underwear. Her grandmother would not have liked her sensible under-garments to go on public view, however anonymously.

Pandora turned to the desk in the small, adjoining sitting-room. The key was where Simeon had said, and inside were several little compart-ments containing stamps, a bottle of ink for the gold-nibbed fountain pen her grandmother had always used, and various other bits and pieces like paper-clips and receipts.

There were no private letters and the writing compendium was unused. An address book recorded business contacts, Joy's address and the home address Pandora had shared with Gerald for the past nineteen years.

If Emily Dysart had ever cultivated friendship with anyone, she'd gone to great pains to cover her tracks in the years leading up to her death. There was nothing of a personal nature in the desk – not even the file Simeon had mentioned.

The top drawer of the dressing-table yielded a few toiletries, headache tablets, a Bible and a purse containing some loose change, a driving licence and a wedding photograph in a perspex window.

She stared at the youthful version of her grandparents, trying to see the people behind the serious, sepia poses. They seemed stiff, uncomfortable with one another. Yet they'd lain together, writhing in the throes of their passion, and had given life to two children.

One was her father, Leander Dysart, who'd married beneath himself and died as a consequence. The other was Carlotta, or Lottie as she'd always been called – who'd become strange after a blow on the head. *Or something worse, if Joy was to be believed.*

She removed the photograph and placed it on top of a box of loose ones she'd found in the wardrobe, thinking it was strange how so staid a couple had named their children so exotically – and that it had carried over to her own name. Perhaps she could make up a family tree for the boys.

The second drawer held a small crowbar. She stared at it, wondering if her grandmother had kept it there as a weapon.

She glanced over to where Lottie sat, staring blankly into space. What went on in her head? Had Joy told the truth about the reason for her illness? If Robert Dysart had taken her own virginity by seduction and stealth, he might possibly have taken Lottie's by force.

There was something disgusting about it all. He'd been a priest, he'd been a married man. *He'd been a paedophile, and she his victim. He should have been able to control himself. They should have believed her.*

'Why, Robert,' she whispered, picking up a photograph of him standing with his brother. 'Why did you do it?'

She became aware of Lottie's gaze on the photograph, of a deep-seated expression of horror and disgust in her eyes. She placed the crowbar on the dressing table, crossed to Lottie's side and hugged her tight.

'Did Robert Dysart do something terrible to you, Lottie? If he did, and you can't handle it, you must talk about it to someone and get help. That doctor at the centre, perhaps.'

When Lottie put her hands over her ears she pulled them down. 'Robert Dysart can't harm you any more, Lottie. He's dead. The only Dysarts left are you, me and my boys.'

Lottie shook her head. 'And Trinity.'

'Who's Trinity?'

Lottie didn't answer. She left the bed, picked up the crowbar and knelt in front of the boarded-up fireplace. She inserted it into a hole in the board, and used it like a lever. The board lifted upwards on hinges, revealing a shelf.

Set squarely on the shelf was an exquisite black lacquered box inlaid with mother-of-pearl. It matched some Chinese lacquered pieces upstairs, which had been brought back from China on a trading expedition by one of her ancestors early in the century.

Lottie lifted it to the bed, opened the lid and tipped the contents out in a heap. 'Secrets, secrets, secrets,' she whispered and, smiling broadly, bore the box away, leaving a small hill of papers on the bed.

Here were her grandmother's files. Here were the family certificates, the house deeds, the historically important letters and the myriad other papers essential to prove a connection – a claim – a passing acquaintance or even an existence.

She stirred them with her hand. Piles of yellowed papers, all important to her grandmother, important enough to be hidden away in a chimney. Perhaps Emily had intended to set fire to them before she died, but hadn't been able to find the strength.

Perhaps I should burn them myself.

But even if the past could be burnt, someone in the present would soon find it again if they tried hard enough, stored in the files of some computer. Diseases, inoculations, overseas trips, mercury-filled cavities in teeth and DNA, all compressed so that hundreds of thousands of records fitted on the head of a pin, as if they'd disappeared into a black hole. Strange how a stroke of a key could retrieve the exact information when it was needed.

She placed the papers on top of the photographs and stripped the covers from her grandmother's bed. There was a grey hair on the pillow. She picked it up and twisted it around her finger. It was impersonal, like thin wire.

Her grandmother hadn't died in her bed. She'd died in the sitting-room downstairs, resting in her chair and gazing out over the garden. There was an infinitesimal moment in time when everything had stopped for her, like a tiny noise in the centre of another noise, suddenly ceasing.

Pandora hadn't noticed for a little while, just carried on talking to her, until some subtle change in the rhythm of the room had alerted her subconscious to change. The change had been the departure of a life.

Emily's hands had been folded one over the other on her lap, her head inclined a little to one side. Her eyes had been wide open, and had rolled partially up into her head so the whites could be seen at the bottom.

It hadn't taken Pandora long to get used to the altered rhythm in the house, though now and again the reminders of family – or the love the Dysarts had never been able to express – brought her a moment of private sorrow.

She gazed around her. This was a big room, and would be part of their apartment. It would do for when the boys visited. They could paint it themselves, and she'd take them out to choose the furniture they wanted. She'd make it a family thing, so they would be involved and think of Marianna as home. After all, they'd inherit the place one day.

She spent the rest of the afternoon going through the papers. There was no birth certificate for her daughter, just house deeds, family birth and death certificates, and a copy of the coroner's report on her father's death.

How sad it was, Pandora thought. Her daughter's short life had never rated a mention as far as Emily Dysart was concerned. It was as if she'd never existed.

The storm abated about five o'clock, blowing back out to sea, and leaving a leaf-strewn landscape, beaten-down flowers and a capricious breeze that carried the scent of early autumn. A watery sun broke through the clouds, layering long brush-strokes of misty, pale-ochre light over the garden.

Lottie had started planning the dinner, and Pandora was happy to let her. Cooking was something Lottie had proved to be good at now she'd been given the chance, and she wanted to encourage anything her aunt was good at.

Instead of the beach, she decided to go to the churchyard and find her child's grave. She wondered if her baby had been given a name. She should have broken right through the wall of silence and asked her grandmother whilst she was still alive.

There were several Dysart graves in their own little corner, amongst them, Marianna Dysart, for whom the house had been named when it was first built. Then there were Pandora's parents, her grandfather, and her grandfather's brother, Robert. It was strange that Emily, who'd married into the family – who'd become more Dysart than those born with the blood – had elected not to join them in death.

Robert Dysart also had a window in the church, dedicated to him by the parish. It struck her as ironic that the window depicted the virgin Mary with a child – though it wasn't the usual Catholic image, for the Dysarts had always been staunch Anglicans, until Pandora had discovered one day that she was an atheist.

Robert Dysart's memorial window showed a modern woman in a calf-length blue dress. She had a thick, defiant mouth, stout, country legs and a robust child straddling her hip – who looked as though he'd grow up to be a rogue instead of a saint. The woman held a fisted hand aloft, giving the window a Stalinesque appearance.

Pandora kicked some leaves from the graves, looking for a plaque of some sort. There was no child buried here, and nothing in the memorial garden. Perhaps her baby wasn't in hallowed ground because she hadn't been christened.

By some stroke of luck the church was open. The vicar gave her a slightly sour look, which might have been something to do with the fact he'd missed out on the bulk of her grandmother's property. The church had received a small bequest, which might have been an entry fee for Emily into heaven, she thought irreverently.

The vicar's face was pinched and porridge grey, as if he washed it in cold water, and not too thoroughly at that. Wire-framed glasses left red marks each side of his nose, and short strings of white hair dangled from his bald head.

'I wonder if I could look at the parish burial register from twenty-three years ago.'

He sniffed and glanced at his watch. 'It's choir practice shortly.'

'Tomorrow then, if it's not convenient now.'

He hesitated, his glance going to the memorial window – and remembering, perhaps, that she was related to his former bishop.

He shrugged and led her to a dusty office, where a bare light-globe hung three metres down from the ceiling on a length of black flex.

A woman was taking hymn books out of a box. She didn't look up.

A grubby diamond-paned cabinet held the registers. He found the correct one and left her to it. 'Put it back where it came from, shut the door behind you and let me know when you leave,' he said.

There were no entries of burials at all for the month in question. The christenings yielded only one. Trinity James. She stared at it, puzzled.

Lottie had mentioned the name. *Trinity*? She scribbled down the details, then hunted down the vicar, who was by the choir stalls.

The woman had followed her out, lingering nearby to place the hymn books on the stands.

'A baby, you say?' The vicar's brow wrinkled in thought. 'We don't get many babies. I would remember burying one, however long ago it was. A traumatic business, the death of a baby.' His voice took on an unctuous tone. 'Suffer little children. . . .'

'You might not find much comfort in those words were it your child.' She turned to go, remembering the trauma only too well.

'Whose child was it?' he said when she reached the door.

'A relative's.'

'The diocese covers more than one parish,' he offered. 'Bishop Dysart might have arranged the burial at another church.'

'Thanks for your help.'

'You should make an effort to come to church on Sunday, Mrs Rossiter.'

'Why?'

'Because you're a Dysart and should set an example.'

'An example of what, hypocrisy?' she said as gently as possible.

He stared bleakly at her for a moment, then dismissed her with a nod and shuffled off towards the altar.

CHAPTER FIVE

Despite scrutinizing every piece of paper from the lacquered box a second time, Pandora found no mention of her daughter's birth or subsequent death.

She came across the offer Simeon had made to her grandmother for the furniture amongst the papers, and handed it to the valuer she'd employed – the nephew of one of her former neighbours in Cedarbrook.

His fleshy face registered a faint smile when he looked at it.

'The serpentine-fronted walnut desk will fetch much more at auction, so will the table. Take my advice and make him bid for them. The break-front bookcase is a reproduction. By all means let him have it at that price.'

'You mean, cheat him?'

She was the recipient of a calculating look. 'He made an offer – which you may accept or not. If the bookcase was genuine, you'd be way out of pocket. Then again, advertised as a repro it could still bring in more – or less – than the offer. The remainder of the estate will bring in useful sums and the oriental pieces should sell well – especially since you still have the original bills of sale, which are curiosities in themselves.'

She led him up to the attics. Once again that faint smile of his came, but this time it had a rueful edge to it.

'I can't put an estimate on this. Everything will have to be catalogued.'

She shrugged. 'It's only junk. I should just throw it away.'

Alarm chased across his face. 'You'd be surprised how little actually is junk from a sales point of view. The smaller antique dealers will be down here in hordes once the word's out. I'll bring a couple of assistants down next weekend, and we'll catalogue everything.'

She gazed dubiously along the length of the attic. 'Will that be enough time?'

'It's surprising how quickly it can be done on a computer. You won't mind if we camp here for the night, will you? We'll bring our sleeping bags and be as unobtrusive as possible.'

'As long as you let me feed you all.'

His cheeks wobbled when he chuckled. 'I was hoping you'd say that, Mrs Rossiter. We'll hold the auction in six weeks' time, mid-November. Will that suit?'

She took a deep breath and nodded. Selling off her family history felt a bit odd, as if she were cutting away the umbilical cord that attached her to Marianna – but it was no use hanging on to stored junk.

She was honest with Simeon on the phone, which was more than he'd been with her.

'You can buy the bookcase if you want. It's a copy. The other things on your list are genuine, and worth much more. You'll have to bid for them.'

There was a moment of silence, then his voice creamed against her ear. 'Believe me, Pandora, I had no idea of the value when I made the offer.'

His answer disappointed her. There was no doubt in her mind that he was lying, and she'd thought him better than that. If he'd shrugged it off, laughed, and said it had been worth a try, he'd have risen in her estimation.

'I'll let you know about the bookcase tonight. I might get it cheaper if I bid for it.'

'You might.' He wouldn't. If he didn't buy it she intended to withdraw it from the sale. She wished she hadn't pushed him into dinner, but she'd appear churlish if she backed out now. Besides, she wanted to pick his brains about her daughter.

Pandora wore a floaty, flowered chiffon tunic over a pale pink, ankle-length dress for dinner with Simeon. His eyes swept over her, as if appreciative of her femininity, but in a distant sort of way – then his smile came, warm and intimate, *and practised, like Gerald's.*

'You look exquisite.' He consulted her over the menu, but chose the wine himself and ordered for them both. He was putting on a performance, trying too hard to convince her of his worth.

'Why did your marriage split up?' she said.

He looked taken aback for a moment, then the urbane mask slid into place. 'There was another man involved.'

'I'm sorry. Do you miss your wife?'

His glance attached to hers, his eyes limpid, like dark glass. 'On occasion.' The fine, mocking curve of his mouth appeared almost feminine as he twirled the stem of a wine glass between his long fingers. 'Do you miss your husband?'

She smiled a little ruefully. 'I keep forgetting you're a lawyer.'

He chuckled. 'I can understand that you'd want to get back at me for the offer. I've decided to buy the bookcase. I'll bid for the rest.'

She stared at him. 'You did know their value, didn't you?'

'Nothing I could say would convince you otherwise. Actually, I'm a little put out that you think so little of me.'

'The concept of which is all in your mind, Simeon. You have about as much idea of what I think of you, as I do of what you think of me. You're good at hiding what you think.'

'That's true,' he murmured, and didn't buy into it further. He made a show of tasting the wine the waiter brought them, then nodded his approval before turning his attention back to her. 'When's the auction to take place?'

'November.'

'Good, I'll be there. Now that's out of the way, let's forget about business and enjoy the evening.'

If she'd hurt his feelings in any way, Simeon didn't show it. He was a charming companion, guiding their conversation through books, plays and music. It was surprising how much they had in common – and surprising how he managed to control the conversation.

It wasn't until she was on the doorstep that she realized she hadn't had a chance to bring up the subject of her daughter.

'Would you like to come in for coffee?'

He stooped to kiss her cheek, his eyes brimming with regret. 'Unfortunately, I've got an early start in the morning.'

'It was a lovely evening. Thank you, Simeon.'

'I'm glad you enjoyed it. We must do it again sometime,' he said, committing himself to nothing before heading for his car. She waved as it crunched away over the gravel drive.

'Never mind,' a voice growled from the shadows. 'You can invite me in for coffee, instead.'

Heart sprinting, she turned, and drawing her wrap around her for the scant protection it offered, said. 'Bryn! What are you doing here?'

'Waiting for you.'

Relief came with the ebbing of adrenaline. 'Behind a bush? You're not going to flash at me, are you?'

He chuckled and stepped into the porch-light, a great, black-haired bear who was swaying slightly. 'A man has his pride. It's too cold to flash effectively.'

The scenario made her laugh. 'Are you drunk?'

'I shouldn't be at all surprised. I was celebrating my birthday.'

'Alone?'

'"Secret, and self-contained, and solitary as an Oyster", as Dickens put it. That's why I'm drunk.'

'Haven't you got a home and family to go to?'

'I'm an orphan.'

Which wasn't exactly the answer she'd expected. She glanced at the empty driveway. 'How did you get here?'

One step brought him within a few inches of her. He gazed down at her, his eyes an onyx glitter. 'Stop asking so many damned questions, woman.'

He was too close for comfort. His body was too powerful, his voice too deep, his eyes too astute – even if he wasn't quite sober. There was a split-second of danger when he pinned her against the wall with his body, and lightly bussing his mouth against hers, gazed down at her, grinning like a devil. 'If you don't open the door I'm going to fall over.'

She pushed him aside and let them in; then, leaving him sprawled in a corner of the couch with a pleased grin on his face, went to make him some coffee. He was asleep when she came back.

She removed his shoes and his tie, dragged his jacket off and straightened him out. The couch was large. With the addition of a couple of pillows and some blankets he would be fairly comfortable for the night.

She sat and watched him whilst she drank his coffee, a smile on her face. The Welsh bear looked vulnerable with his defences down, like a big baby.

'Happy birthday, Bryn,' she said, and after planting a kiss on his unresponsive mouth she went to bed, leaving him to slumber in private.

He was gone when she rose the next morning, leaving a short, but exquisitely penned note of apology on the kitchen table.

Dearest Lady,

Oh, God, that men should put whisky in their mouths to steal away their brains! Can you forgive me?

Bryn Llewellyn, feeling like Othello this morning.

'Shakespeare would turn in his grave,' she said when she rang him later that day. 'How's your head?'

'Is this my head on my neck? Good God! I thought you'd replaced it with a pumpkin as punishment.'

She choked out a laugh. 'Be serious, Bryn.'

'Okay. Who was the fancy dude who brought you home last night?'

'Serious, doesn't mean you can intrude on my personal life.'

'Funny how I've become slightly deaf this morning.' He cleared his throat. 'How personal is he?'

'Why do you want to know?'

'It should be patently obvious why I want to know.'

Laughter filled her voice. 'Spell it out for me, Bryn.'

'You're purring, like a cat with a mouse,' he said. 'You've got me trapped under your paw and you're playing with me because you're not hungry enough yet. All you have to do is extend those claws and ...' A sexy growl shivered into her ear. 'Thanks for the good-night kiss.'

Thank God he couldn't see her blush. 'You must have been dreaming, and I think you've got the wrong idea about me.'

'Have I, Pandora girl? We're so hot for each other we're destined to end up in bed together, and will probably spontaneously combust. That's what I want, and so do you.'

She gave a light laugh, not sure how to cope with this direct approach now she'd got it. 'Spontaneous combustion sounds a bit uncomfortable.'

'You wanted me to spell it out and I have. Come away with me for the weekend.'

Desire tongued at her body. 'I can't. My sons are visiting, and I have some people coming to value the furniture.'

There was a drawn-out moment of silence. 'I just happen to have some free time coming up. How about we go to a hotel?' he growled.

Delicious quivers of shocked excitement raced through her. 'A hotel ... when?'

'Now.'

Her body began to burn at the thought of an illicit affair – only it wouldn't be illicit now she was practically single. One could only be unfaithful in marriage, as Gerald had been.

'I ... I don't know.' She picked up a magazine and tried to fan the heat from her face. Deep down she did know – she just needed a little bit of persuasion. *So persuade!*

'The Arrowsmith's Arms. It's off the beaten track. Do you know it?'

'Yes, but—' *Stop butting!*

'One o'clock.' He hung up.

Which gave her enough time to prepare and depart without prevarication. *Clever Bryn, he must have read my mind!*

Only she did change her mind, even though she'd perfumed and satined herself up like a tart on parade, and was on her way to the door.

The phone rang.

For a moment she was tempted to ignore it, then she snatched the receiver up 'Pandora Rossiter.'

Somebody coughed. 'It's Flora Selby here.'

Flora Selby? She sounded like an older woman. 'If you're looking for my grandmother—'

'It's you I want. Pandora Dysart, that was.'

The name, Flora Selby, meant nothing to Pandora despite the vaguest of feelings that it ought to. 'Is it important? I was just about to go out.'

'Depends, don't it? It's not important to me. Might be to you though, seeing as you was enquiring about a baby at the church the other day.'

Pandora's heart began to boom. 'You know where she's buried?'

'Don't know nothing about no burial, do I? I do remember you, though. I was Robert Dysart's housekeeper. He was right fond of you when you were a lass – right fond, if you get my drift.'

Something churned sickeningly inside her. 'Why have you phoned me?'

'To pass on a bit of information. Might be somethin', might be nothin'.'

'And it's going to cost me, I suppose.'

'Don't be like that, dear.' The whine in Flora Selby's voice set Pandora's teeth on edge. 'Just a little donation for my old age. It's hard managing on a pension, and you won't miss it.'

Pandora sighed. 'What's the information?'

'I'd be a fool to tell you now, wouldn't I? I'll be in the café in the mall. I'll wait for half an hour. Should be enough time for you to get here, but no skin off my nose if you don't come. Won't get another chance, though.'

Pandora gave a fleeting thought to Bryn as she made her way into town. She grinned. He'd been too confident, so it would serve him right.

She recognized Flora Selby as soon as she saw her, feeling surprised that she hadn't at the church. But then her back had been turned towards her, and Pandora hadn't really been taking any notice of the woman with the hymn books.

Flora's hair had turned iron grey, but was still pulled tightly into a bun.

Her wrinkles swept back from her eyes and mouth in strands to disappear into her hair. She was one of those women who'd always looked like a grim old maid – and nothing had changed. Pandora could have sworn she was still wearing the same double-breasted, navy-blue coat she'd worn all those years ago.

She collected a cup of muddy-looking coffee from the counter and joined Flora at the table with a pleasant, 'Good-afternoon.'

'Let's not waste time on niceties,' Flora said straight away. 'Do you have something for me?'

Pandora slipped an envelope across the table, the contents, courtesy of a hurried stop at a cash point. Flora slowly counted it, restarting the count when she lost her place half-way through. Eventually, she nodded, seemingly satisfied with the amount.

'Twenty-three years ago, Bishop Dysart brought a baby girl home with him.'

Pandora's heart jolted. This was definitely not what she'd expected. 'Can you remember the exact date?'

'No – but it was half-way through May. "Look after her, Flora," he says. "Her parents will come to collect her tomorrow".'

'Did the bishop often bring babies home?'

'Now and again, if their mothers were ill or something.' Her eyes narrowed. 'But not babies as young as this. It were newborn and came with feeding bottles and a tin of milk, all new. Could hardly suck, it were so young – and his missus wouldn't have anything to do with it, either. She locked herself in her room, she did, and wouldn't come out until it were gone from the house. Poor soul, she died in the looney bin, or so I heard.'

Pandora faintly remembered Robert's wife as a pale, quiet wraith of a woman. Guilt washed over her – but there was nothing she could do to put things right now. Her heart began to bang painfully in her chest. 'Go on.'

'The baby's parents came the next day. The mother didn't look sick to me. She was awkward with the baby, too – not natural, like, but smilin' and cuddlin' her all the same. The man was an earnest-looking young chap. Talked posh, like the bishop.'

Pandora stared at her, not trusting herself to speak.

'Then that old lawyer fellow turned up. Andrew Frapp, I think his name was. Dodderin' old bugger, he died not long after. They all went into the office together for a while, then took the baby through to the church and had her christened. The vicar was none too happy, what with him having to fit it in between services at such short notice. But with the bishop being the boss, and him actin' as godparent and all, the vicar couldn't say much. He had plenty to say afterwards though, he never did like the Dysarts.' She gave a sly smile. 'It struck me as odd, the bishop being godparent – especially with him actin' as if he hardly knew the parents.'

Pandora's mouth had grown so parched she didn't care that the coffee tasted as bad as it looked. 'What was the baby called?'

'Trinity. Trinity James.'

A long sigh left her mouth. 'Thank you, Mrs Selby.'

'I ain't saying nothin's wrong here, and I wouldn't swear to it in no court – but I kept my ears and eyes open, and there's nothin' wrong with my memory. With them all gone now, and me retired, there's no profit in keepin' it to myself.'

It sounded as though she *had* profited by keeping it to herself in the past, but Pandora didn't push it.

'I don't suppose you know what happened to the James family?'

Flora Selby stood up, her mouth a thin line. 'Had no reason to enquire and it ain't my business. That's all I've got to say. Good-day, Mrs Rossiter.' And she was gone, leaving behind her a faint odour of disapproval and mothballs.

Feeling soiled, Pandora wandered out into the car park. Her head could hardly cope with the questions and answers it was demanding of itself.

Why did Flora Selby think this would interest me?

Because Trinity's your child.

My daughter died.

Then why are you digging the past up?

Okay. Deep down, right at the genesis of my intuition, I feel she's alive.

Logic tells you otherwise. Why would the Dysarts lie to you?

It was a shameful secret. Robert Dysart was a pervert. Look what he did to Lottie. My grandparents knew Robert was sick, but rather than face it, they turned a blind eye and let their own child and granddaughter suffer.

Loathing for them surged through her. They'd given her daughter away without a qualm. Where was she now?

'Trinity?' she murmured, tasting the name on her tongue. The irony of it suddenly occurred to her. Robert must have regarded his daughter as a holy creation, not a carnal act. He would have given her to believers.

Her involuntary laugh had a bitter ring to it. *Bloody hypocrites! Baby snatchers!*

Calm down. You're getting steamed up over conjecture. She took a couple of deep breaths, wishing they were stiff brandies.

She drove home in a daze, collected Sam and took a long, bracing walk along the seashore. It was dark when she got back. Lottie was home from her voluntary job with meals on wheels, and dinner filled the house with mouth-watering smells.

She gave Lottie a hug, then looked up Bryn's number in the book and punched in his number. The answer-phone cut in. She wanted to scream. He was in, she could sense his presence waiting for her to speak – so he could say something cutting, or clever, or both.

'I couldn't make it, OK? And what's more, there was a damned good reason.' The tape rolled on, the silence nearly deafening her. She sighed. 'OK, so I should have phoned, but it was important and I forgot.' Silence still, and she'd had just about enough. 'I know you're there, Bryn. Next time you want a couple of hours in a country hotel don't summon me as if I was some eighteenth-century serving wench you wanted to tumble.' She banged the receiver down.

He'd probably come over, all fuelled up to give her a piece of his mind. OK, if that's what he wanted, she was ready for him!

The front doorbell rang. 'Shit!' she muttered, striding to the door. 'Why can't people leave me alone when I'm frothing at the mouth?'

'You have three minutes in which to convince me with an excuse,' Bryn said, staring pointedly at his watch. 'And it had better be a good one – or at the very least, an undetectable lie.'

She felt all sorts of fools. 'Someone rang with news of my daughter, who I thought was dead all these years. It seems as though she might have been given away for adoption.' To her disgust, she laid her head on his shoulder and burst into tears. What the hell had happened to her new-found independence? 'I don't know what to do.'

His arms came around her in a bear hug. 'It sounds like a good excuse to me.'

'And I left a horrible message on your answer phone,' she snuffled into his coat.

'S'all right. It's used to horrible messages. Last week someone said to it. "Doc, I weigh twelve stone and my testicles weigh six. Do you think I'm half nuts?"'

'Sometimes you're a pain in the arse,' she muttered, giving a watery laugh, 'and your jokes are abysmally adolescent.'

He chuckled. 'You sound impressively toffy-nosed when you're being rude. Flatten your a's if you want to give your arse more impact.'

'Aaaaarse,' she said into his waistcoat, which was a rather splendid black-and-white striped affair.

He tipped up her face and gazed at her, grinning irrepressibly. 'Your eyelashes are running down your face. Go and sort yourself out. I'll tell Lottie there'll be an extra one for dinner.'

'You've got an in-built bossy streak.'

'That's what happens when you grow up with five sisters,' he shouted after her. 'You've got no idea what a handicap it is.'

'You said you were an orphan the other night.'

'I was lying. I wanted you to feel sorry for me.'

'Tell me about your sisters,' she said when she came back.

'They're not very interesting. They're all married, and have handfuls of brats, who are convinced I'm a set of climbing bars when I visit.' His hazel eyes shone in the light. 'My sisters' names are Olwyn, Bronwen, Mary, Cordelia and Glenda. What's your daughter's name?'

'Trinity?' she said without thinking, then made a face at him. 'At least, I think it is. I'm not sure – I'm not even sure she is my daughter.'

'*I know nothing except the fact of my ignorance.*' He smiled at her. 'Socrates. I can quote suitable platitudes all night, or we can cut corners. The latter would suit me better. The fancy bits trip off the tongue to con my private patients into thinking they're getting something for the exorbitant fees they're required to pay.'

She came straight to the point, telling him everything as simply as possible. He listened, speaking only when he needed to clarify something. She finished by mentioning her meeting with Flora Selby.

'People are such fools,' he said with a sigh. 'The good thing about the lie they foisted on you is that you didn't collect any adoption scars. You've got no idea of the on-going trauma associated with adoption.'

'I can imagine. At the moment I feel totally cheated, and furious enough with everyone concerned to spit out long tongues of fire.'

'Like a Welsh dragon,' he said with a faint grin. 'You have some very real problems ahead of you now. First, you have to establish if your daughter's birth or death is registered and whether she's still alive – then discover if Trinity is actually your daughter. That might need to be proved by DNA testing if it comes to the crunch. One thing you have to realize,

Pandora. Even if she survived, and you discover where she lives, she might not want contact with you.'

'I can't think why, when I'm her mother.'

'If you imagine she's got some magical emotional tie with you, forget it. The first few hours after birth would have made an indelible impression on you, but wouldn't have registered with her.'

That was something she hadn't considered. 'Put like that—'

'You should have counselling first. She may not know she's adopted. If she does, she may be damaged from that. It depends on her upbringing – whether she was raised with siblings, her adoptive parents, whether they had any natural children. There are hundreds of traps.'

Dismay filled her. 'The obstacles sound insurmountable.'

His eyes were uncoloured by emotion. 'Not if it's done step by step – and not if you accept the outcome might not be what you want. First, establish whether her birth or death was registered, then I'll put you on to an organization dealing specifically with adoptions and reunions.'

'What if there was a cover-up by the lawyer?'

'You said there was a doctor and midwife present. It's hardly likely they'd collude in falsifying the records.'

She hadn't thought of that. 'Thanks for the advice, Bryn. I'm most grateful.'

His fingers stroked against her hair. 'You've got guts. Most people would want to leave this mess buried.'

'It's been buried long enough. If my daughter's alive I want to find her. If she's not, I'll accept it – and if you think I need counselling, would you . . . would you consider. . . ?'

A quirky smile touched his lips. His eyes were as calm as a forest pool. 'Call me if you think you need any and I'll recommend someone. I can't afford to become professionally involved when I intend to pursue a more personal relationship.'

'Tricky,' she murmured, unable to make up her mind whether she was flattered by his declaration or not.

'I've got the dinner ready,' Lottie called out.

They were on their way to the dining-room when Pandora stopped in her tracks.

'Lottie usually starts sentences with her name, as if she's talking about what someone else is doing.'

'She's been kept fairly isolated all her life. Now she's mixing with people on an almost daily basis, she's much more confident with herself.'

His eyes were glowing with deep compassion. She formed the impression nothing could shock this man – but he cared. She stared up at him. 'You know, don't you?'

'I guessed as soon as you told me about Robert Dysart. When he was young he wouldn't have been able to control himself and would have hurt her. There would have been other victims, especially if he had anything to do with children's homes.'

Disgust churned uneasily inside her. 'I don't want to think about this too much at the moment, Bryn. How on earth do you manage to distance yourself?'

His hands closed around her shoulders and he turned her round to face him. 'It isn't easy, but I wouldn't be much good to anyone if I couldn't dissociate, though I must admit I experience the odd moment of disgust and anger.'

He kissed her – so very tenderly that her lips clung to his, enjoying every intimate moment. He smiled at her afterwards. 'I just wanted you to know what you missed out on this afternoon.'

'There will be other afternoons.'

'Yes,' he said, looking as if he knew as well as she that the ultimate intimacy between them was unavoidable. 'I'd say you've got enough on your plate at the moment. We'll wait until the timing's perfect. That way there won't be any regrets.'

'And which of us will decide when the timing's perfect?'

'One or the other,' he said, his eyes enigmatic again.

It turned out to be a simple procedure to obtain a copy of the birth certificate. In fact, the whole affair turned out to be simple.

The birth had been registered by Robert Dysart. Pandora was named as the mother, Robert as the father. His occupation ambiguously stated: clerical. Her daughter had been named Trinity. There was no death certificate.

She rang Simeon, explaining the situation regarding Andrew Frapp. 'I need to know if he had anything to do with the adoption.'

Dubious at first, Simeon got back to her the next morning.

'I'm going to ask for your word that the source of this information will remain confidential between us.'

He seemed satisfied with her spoken promise.

'As you were under age, Robert Dysart applied for custody of the child as her father, and immediately put her in the children's home. Andrew Frapp represented him in court.'

'Why wasn't Robert arrested?

'It should become clear in a minute. Your grandfather signed the adoption papers as your legal guardian. The adoption process seems to have been speeded up. An order was issued by the same magistrate the day after, and once again, Andrew Frapp represented the bishop. Thirty days later, Robert Dysart and your grandfather signed the final consent form, and Trinity Dysart became Trinity James.'

'So my grandparents knew I was telling the truth?'

'Your grandfather certainly did. The four men and the doctor present at the birth made up the board that administered the children's homes. The business was hurried through for expediency's sake. The whole thing stinks.'

'And the sad thing is, I can't bring any of them to justice.'

'From a purely selfish point of view, I'm not sorry about that. Any revelation of this type would damage my prospects of a partnership – and probably ruin your life and hers.'

'Now I know for sure what happened to her, I'm going to try and find her, Simeon.'

'I imagined you would. If I can do anything more to help. . . ?'

'Thanks, you've done enough.'

His chuckle was ironic. 'I hope it redeems me for the misunderstanding about the furniture.' Which was as near as he'd get to admitting he'd tried to take advantage of her ignorance. 'Take care, my dear. These things are not always as straightforward as they seem, and daughters are tender little souls.'

And, for some reason, she liked Simeon for saying that a whole lot more than she'd ever liked him before.

CHAPTER SIX

The weekend had a chaotic feeling to it. Upstairs, things banged and scraped. Dust filtered through the house and the odd mouse or spider scuttled about.

The sky was overcast, and rain beat ceaselessly against the window. The boys were filled with a restless energy that seemed to have no outlet. In fact, Pandora had the feeling they'd rather be somewhere else.

When she introduced the subject of their decorating a room to their own taste they didn't seem at all interested, so Pandora dropped the idea.

Engaging them in conversation was hard going.

'How's school?'

There was a grunt from Adrian, and a barrage of complaints about the food from Michael.

'Is your father keeping well?'

Synchronized grunts this time.

'What about Mare and the baby?'

Both of them stared at her, their eyes peculiarly mask-like, then Adrian said with a guarded casualness, 'What about them?'

'Are they keeping well?'

'I dunno.'

She could have shaken him. 'What do you mean by, "I don't know"?'

'Dad doesn't want us to talk about her to you, that's what I mean.' He picked a magazine up from the table and began to leaf through it.

The ferocity of anger she felt sent tremors through her body. She hadn't expected Gerald to be so underhand as to try and alienate her from her sons. Scooping in a jagged breath, she counted to ten. 'I get the picture.'

'Mare's a . . . a bitch,' Michael said, his face turning a dull red. 'She threw away the wedding photograph of you and dad from the mantelpiece. I found it in the dustbin.'

Adrian stared into space, a dreamy smile on his face. 'Mare's OK.'

'That's because she wiggles around the house with hardly any clothes on,' Michael taunted. 'You've got the hots for her.'

Adrian's eyes blazed scorn in his direction. 'You can talk. She and Dad were laughing because you were making cow's eyes at her the other day.'

'At least I don't write drippy love poems about her,' Michael sneered.

'You sneaky toad, you've been prying in my desk!' Her elder son's temper erupted so quickly that Michael was sprawling on the floor before Pandora had time to react.

'Adrian! What the hell's wrong with you?'

He stared down at Michael, tight-jawed, and with his fists clenched. Her son was suddenly a stranger to her.

'Nothing's wrong with *me*. I'm just sick of being in the middle of your marriage troubles.' Thrusting his hands in his pockets he slouched towards the door. 'Why can't you all leave me alone? I'm going out.'

'Come back here at once! It's pouring with rain.' The door slammed shut. 'Adrian!'

'Let him go,' Michael said offhandedly. 'A bit of rain will cool him off.'

'My God!' She couldn't believe what had happened. 'Are you all right? I don't know what's come over him. You used to be such good friends.'

'Yeah, I'm all right.' Michael scrambled to his feet. 'He's right you know. We *are* in the middle. Why don't you and Dad just ask each other what you want to know?' He looked hopeful for a moment. 'I think Dad would send Mare packing if you wanted to come home. The atmosphere is awful with her around. I thought she was nice at first, but she's just a tart. Adrian's running around after her when Dad's not there, and she encourages him.'

'Michael!' she said, shocked, 'That's an appalling thing to say.'

'Well, he does and she is. Everyone's at everyone else's throat because of her.'

She put her arms around him. 'I'm sorry you and Adrian are suffering, but I'm not going to go back to him.'

His body was taut with disapproval and he wouldn't be comforted, but pulled away, mumbling, 'I'm not a kid any more, you know.'

Dismayed, she watched him head out after Adrian. Her sons were seething with adolescent resentment, growing up – growing away from her.

They came back soaked to the skin. They apologized, but the incident had introduced a sour note. The atmosphere didn't seem to lighten, and she was glad when the weekend was over.

'Testosterone,' Bryn said when she told him about it. 'Potent stuff at that age.'

'But what can I do about Mare walking about half-naked?'

'Let them enjoy the fantasy without embarrassing them.'

'But they're only boys,' she wailed.

Bryn's mouth curved upwards into a smile. 'Men are always boys to their mothers, and besides, Michael seems to be clued up to her. What's the worst thing that can happen to them in this situation?'

Ignoring Bryn's teasing smile she struggled to find something credible, besides the obvious – which in Bryn's eyes would most likely be the best thing. 'Mare might play one off against the other. Perhaps I should warn Gerald.'

'She's already doing it, and unless your husband is entirely stupid he'd have noticed he has two young lions as rivals. Believe me, he'll take the appropriate action.'

Which he did – showing Mare who was in charge by moving her out of the house and into a rented flat. A week later, she packed her bags and disappeared from the scene.

Adrian went with her.

'I blame this on you,' Gerald shouted down the phone. 'If you hadn't left a perfectly good marriage—'

'I don't consider you constantly racing all your secretaries into bed to be a sign of a perfectly good marriage!'

'If you'd been half the wife you should have been, I wouldn't have needed other women.'

Which stung, even though it was totally unfair. She'd expected her marriage to end in a civilized manner, not degenerate into a screaming match.

'Stop shouting, Gerald. Mare has obviously done this for revenge.'

'A damned nuisance,' he grumbled almost to himself. 'It's hard to get a decent secretary this time of year.'

Self-centred sod! 'Try a middle-aged one this time, not one young enough to be your daughter. You must have known Adrian was of an age to fall in love.' She rubbed it in a little. 'Especially when Mare walked around the house half-naked, and the pair of you ridiculed Michael behind his back for making eyes at her.'

'He told you that? Oh, my God, I thought it was a harmless crush.'

'At that age, a crush can be pretty intense,' she said, picking up on Bryn's comments.

'What about Adrian's exams?'

'He's already sat them.'

'Then what about his place at Oxford? The boy's ruining his life over a cheap piece of skirt.'

She bit down on her tongue. Sarcasm wasn't going to help matters. 'I expect Mare will ditch him before Christmas. He hasn't got much money of his own, and she doesn't strike me as the type to rough it.'

'Do you think he'll come back?'

'Adrian's sensible. He'll think things over and decide what's best for him once the excitement has worn off and reality sets in.' Which was quite easy to say, but harder to believe at the moment. It rather depended whether Mare decided to let him off the hook. She crossed her fingers. 'I expect he'll come to me, rather than face you, first off.'

'I expect you're right.' Gerald sounded utterly miserable. 'Pandora. You know I still love you. The others didn't mean a thing. Everything's such a mess. Why don't you come home?'

She steeled herself against the self-pity in his voice. 'You brought the mess upon yourself – and I *am* home.'

'Perhaps I could come down at the weekend and we could talk it over.'

'That wouldn't be a good idea. The contents of the house are being auctioned and I'll be busy. Besides, I have no intention of coming back. Our marriage was a farce. I only stayed with you because I thought it would be better for the boys.'

He gave an over-heavy sigh, designed to work on her conscience. 'You will let me know if you hear from Adrian?'

Her voice softened. 'Of course. Try not to worry, Gerald. If he's anything like you, he won't allow his personal life to ruin his career.' Which was a jibe below the belt she just couldn't resist.

Predictably, Gerald regarded it as an ego-stroker. 'Yes, he's always been sensible.'

Over the next week she jumped every time the phone or doorbell rang.

The auctioneer's helpers came back to arrange everything from the attic in lots, on long trestle tables they'd brought with them. The better china pieces were locked in a couple of glass cabinets – the oriental artefacts displayed in one room.

'It looks good now it's displayed,' she said, surprised by the effect they'd achieved.

'A professional display attracts better prices than the flea-market look.'

'Is there anything I can do to help on the day?' she offered, and expecting a negative answer was surprised when one of them said:

'It's hard to stop pilfering at these house auctions. You might like to wander round and keep your eye on things. Report anything suspicious to us, and make sure your living quarters are secure.'

'Sort of like a store detective?' The idea appealed to her. 'My son will be visiting this weekend. I'm sure he'll enjoy helping out, too.'

But Michael rang her, begging off and saying he was going to a friend's place and wouldn't be down until the evening.

Bryn bid against Simeon for the walnut desk. Each sent the other challenging looks across the room every time they made a bid. They lost out to an antique dealer, against whom Simeon duelled and won for the table. He paid an outrageous price for it, and she thought he only bought it to save face.

She hadn't realized Bryn had decided to play detective too, until he took a drooping false moustache from his pocket, stuck it to his upper lip and prowled the rooms with a fierce scowl plastered on his face. Even so, some of the smaller items drifted off tables and into pockets.

The main auction was over very quickly. Furniture was humped downstairs and strapped precariously to the tops of cars or loaded into vans. The few pieces left over were knocked down at bargain prices. Stragglers turned over the remaining bundles of lots, like crows on a rubbish tip, buying anything that looked as though it could be sold for a profit at car-boot sales. Then they were gone too, and all that was left was trash and dust.

'We've done well,' the auctioneer said, a smile on his face. 'I'll give you a ring when I've sorted the accounting out, Mrs Rossiter.'

Bryn gazed down at her after he'd gone. 'I've enjoyed today.'

She eyed his disguise and grinned. 'So I noticed.'

'Your boyfriend was here?'

'Was he,' she said, her grin becoming a smile. 'Is that why you bid for the desk?'

'Could be! It's the old male challenge thing. We like to thump our chests a bit on occasion.'

'You look more like a Mexican bandit than Tarzan.'

The moustache jiggled when he sighed. 'You're not going to tell me about him, are you?'

'His name's Simeon Manus. He's my lawyer.'

'So, I did that ape act for nothing, and all my male displays were an utter waste of time?'

She laughed. 'Not entirely.'

He slanted his head to one side and stared at her, his eyes half-amused, half-serious. 'Well . . . were they a waste of time or not?'

'I do like Simeon, but where's your sense of adventure? You're rather nice as well, and sexy and sweet.'

'*Sweet?*' The eyes that caught hers glowed with a lazy sort of menace.

She got in first, slipping under the guard of his drooping moustache to kiss him, long and hard. His hands slithered down her back to cup around her buttocks and bring her hard against him. This was one sexy man who wasn't going to let an opportunity pass.

'Mum?' The yell came from a distance. 'Where are you?'

'Sweet,' she repeated. Gently she peeled the moustache from his lips, threw it aside and slid her hand into his. 'Come and meet one of my sons.'

'Just at this moment I wish your son was on the moon,' he said. 'You're full of surprises.'

'Mum!' Michael's voice had a strange urgency to it.

'Up here, Michael. We're on our way down.'

He met them half-way, his face frantic.

Her smile faded. 'What . . . what is it?'

'Adrian. He's in the car. Something's wrong with him.'

Some nameless dread glued her feet to the floor. 'What do you mean . . . something's wrong?'

Calmly, Bryn took control. 'Take me to him.' Half a minute later he was carrying in her barely-conscious son from Michael's car.

Bryn sniffed Adrian's breath, felt his pulse then gently peeled back his eyelids. He made a satisfied humming noise in his throat, then slapped Adrian sharply back and forth across the face.

She gasped.

'What have you swallowed?' Bryn shouted into his ear.

Adrian mumbled something unintelligible.

'Go through his pockets,' Bryn said to Michael, who obeyed with alacrity, a few seconds later holding up a blister back containing a couple of pills. Bryn popped one out with his thumb, then tasted it. He nodded to himself.

'How many have you taken?' he shouted into Adrian's ear, and held up his fingers, stabbing them in front of Adrian's unfocussed eyes. 'One – two – three – four. . . ?' The number got larger and larger.

Adrian finally grunted.

'How long ago? Half an hour – one hour. . . ?'

Another grunt.

'Have you got to subject him to an inquisition?' Pandora shouted frantically at him.

He ignored her, and heaving Adrian over his shoulder carried him through to the bathroom, where he hung him over the edge of the bath and stuck his fingers down his throat.

As a treatment, it was messy, but effective – and was followed up with a blast of cold water from the shower hose, which flooded the bathroom and nearly drowned them all.

Adrian regained full consciousness, coughing and spluttering, to become the object of another inquisition from Bryn – who, not satisfied with his assurances, examined his arms and thighs for needle marks.

'For pity's sake,' Pandora shouted, determining she'd never forgive Bryn for being so rough with Adrian. 'He said he isn't an addict.'

Bryn's eyes met hers, as hard as tourmaline. 'Addicts lie. If he has to go to hospital the police will be involved and it will be on record. Is that what you want?'

She shook her head and bit down on her lip to stop herself from crying. 'Adrian can't be an addict ... he just can't. Things like that only happen to someone else's sons.'

His expression softened and he brushed his knuckles gently against her cheek. 'He'll be OK, I promise. Trust me. Give me ten minutes, then bring me some ice cream if you have any.'

An hour later her son was tucked up in bed, his stomach full of the ice cream Bryn had shovelled into him. There were dark rings under his eyes. He looked totally exhausted and sorry for himself.

Bryn turned to Michael, a smile on his face. 'You keep a cool head in an emergency, young man.'

'He'll be all right, won't he, sir?'

Bryn draped an arm round Michael's shoulders, leading him from the room. 'Enough of the drug leached into his system to make him sleep until morning, and his cholesterol and sugar levels will be sky high after all that ice-cream, but he's out of danger, thanks to you.'

'I didn't do much.'

'Don't underestimate your contribution. Perhaps I should introduce myself. I'm Bryn Llewellyn, a friend of your mother and a shrink by profession. You must be Michael. I've heard a lot about you and Adrian.'

There was a proud glow around Michael, and more – a touch of hero-worship blossoming in his eyes. He was trying hard to remain modest, and his shrug was self-effacing. 'You saved his life, not me.'

Bryn patted his shoulder. 'Let's say we managed it between us.' They disappeared through the square of light filling the doorway.

Michael's voice floated back to her. 'What does cholesterol mean, sir. . . .'

Adrian's fingers clutched at her wrist. 'I'm sorry, Mum. Promise you won't tell Dad.'

She kissed his clammy forehead. 'I'll have to let him know you're all right. He's frantic with worry.'

Tears trickled from the corners of his eyes. 'Mare went to a clinic. I would have looked after her and the baby, but she just laughed at me and told me to grow up. I hate her now, she's a bitch.'

Half of her wanted to kill Mare for trampling on her son's tender feelings, the other half was relieved she had. It might have hurt, but at least he harboured no illusions about her now.

'Where did you get the pills from?'

'I found them in her bathroom. I didn't intend to harm myself . . . I just wanted to sleep for a long time and forget . . . about her . . . about what she did.'

'Now you *can* sleep, and you must promise me never to do anything so stupid again.'

But he'd already drifted off. She kissed him again, knowing it was the last time she'd be able to treat him as a child. He'd learned a hard lesson and would be different in the morning.

Lottie had prepared a meal of stew and dumplings, but Pandora wasn't hungry. Michael and Bryn scoffed hers between them. The three of them went out with Sam, leaving her to phone Gerald in private.

She side-stepped his queries and assured him Adrian was safe, lying when he asked to speak to him by telling him Adrian had gone to see a film with Michael, and she'd make sure he'd contact him the next day.

'I suppose you blame this on me,' he said quietly, 'and I'd deserve it if you did.'

The last thing she wanted was for Gerald to unburden his guilt. He could stew in it.

'I don't blame anyone. Adrian's an adult and must take responsibility for his own actions. So must you. If it's any consolation to you, Mare has disposed of the pregnancy, so you won't be liable for child support down the track.'

When she heard a quick, relieved intake of breath, she hung up.

'I'm sorry I shouted at you,' she said to Bryn when he was about to leave. 'I'm really very grateful for what you did. Adrian didn't intend to kill himself.'

'It was a cry for help, that's all. If he'd really intended to kill himself he'd have succeeded. What was it all about, his father's woman?'

She nodded.

'Is that why you left your husband?'

'Not really. He's been unfaithful for years. I used his infidelity as an excuse, this time. I left him because I didn't love him and the time was right.'

He slid into the driver's seat without touching her, his expression curiously bland. 'You have two fine sons. Why do you need to find your daughter?'

'Because I gave birth to her, because she was part of my body, because I need to know if she's happy.' She closed her eyes against the pain. 'I wish I'd believed she was dead, because I'll never be content now until I know she's well and happy.'

Bryn was smiling as his hand briefly caressed her face. 'I hope she is, for your sake. When will you tell your sons they have a sister, or do you intend to leave them in the same state of blissful ignorance you were in?'

She struggled out of her self-indulgent cocoon and turned to the confrontational reality of his eyes. 'You can be an utter shit at times!'

'You said I was sweet earlier on.'

'It must have been the coating on the pill that fooled me. Go away, Bryn.'

He laughed as he started the engine. 'Do you want me to darken your doorstep again?'

She couldn't quite bring herself to be cut off from him entirely. 'Not until next weekend. Apologize, and you'll get an invite to dinner.'

'Sorry, but I'm going to Wales next weekend.'

Which was a bit of a let-down, and she felt miffed. 'Have a nice time.'

He slid the car into gear. 'I'll have a better one with you along. I'll pick you up on Friday evening.'

He was too arrogant for words. 'What about Lottie?' she yelled after him.

He reversed to where she stood, his smile an ironic sliver. 'Haven't you noticed? Lottie looks after *you*, not the other way around.'

He was gone before she had time to take his statement in, but she was thinking about it when she stalked back indoors, everything in her fizzing with annoyance.

Lottie was clearing the table. She looked up and smiled, her eyes bright and happy.

'I'm thinking of going to Wales with Bryn next weekend,' she said to her. 'Will you be all right by yourself?'

'Yes,' Lottie said simply, and Pandora knew Bryn had been right.

Trinity's adopted family had once lived in a semi-detached house in Dorchester. They didn't live there now.

Pandora's knock was answered by a woman in her late sixties, who gazed suspiciously at her from behind a grille. 'We bought the house from Mr and Mrs James twenty years ago.'

'Do you have any idea where they went?'

'Sorry.'

'Could you tell me . . . did you notice if the Jameses had any children?'

The woman thought for a moment, then she smiled. 'A toddler. A solemn little girl with blonde hair and big eyes. I remember feeling a bit sorry for her.'

Pandora's diaphragm contracted. 'What do you mean?'

'They corrected her all the time. It didn't seem natural at that age, I mean, children that young can't be expected to sit still all the time and remember to mind their manners, can they?' The woman caught herself, and frowned. 'Why do you want to know?'

'I'm related to Bishop Dysart. He brought me to meet the Jameses once. Now I've moved back into the district I thought I'd look them up.'

The door was suddenly opened and her smile became warm. 'I remember the bishop. His wife chaired one of the committees I was on. He was such a lovely man – they were both nice. It was a shame when she was . . . taken ill.'

'Yes,' Pandora said, and squashing the twinge of guilt she felt at the mention of his wife, turned to go. 'Thanks for your help.' She fumbled in her bag, took out her notebook, scribbled down her phone number and handed it to her. 'If you think of anything else, perhaps you'd give me a ring, Mrs. . . ?'

'Young . . . Audrey Young. And you are?'

'Pandora Rossiter.'

'Grace Dysart's daughter?'

Pandora gazed at her. 'You knew my mother?'

Audrey Young was smiling broadly now. 'We were at school together and I attended her wedding. I think I've got some photographs somewhere. Would you like to come inside and look at them?'

No, she actually wouldn't. But she did – spending the next hour listening to Audrey Young's reminiscences and looking at grey-shaded photographs of her own mother as a girl. She found it hard to associate herself with the girl portrayed, so full of laughter and fun, and even harder with her as a woman – white-gowned and gazing up at Pandora's father on their wedding-day with eyes full of awareness.

She stared at it for a long time, at the look her parents were exchanging, each so aware of the other, it left no doubt they were already lovers. Yet love had become indifference if Joy was to be believed – at least on her father's side, and they'd died together, but whether by accident or intent. . . ?

There was a small sense of loss inside her, because she couldn't remember these strangers she'd emerged from, or feel anything for them. Their masks were frozen in place, keeping her – the daughter they'd once loved – firmly on the outside.

But it wasn't until she was outside on the pavement, holding her collar up against the wind, that she remembered Bryn's words and knew the tears in her eyes were caused by self-pity and frustration.

If you imagine she's got some emotional tie with you, forget it. It was then that she understood his warning, resented it and confronted what she'd really be up against.

She drove home, left the car at the house, and taking the footpath to the edge of the cliff, stared out over the shifting mass of silver-streaked water. The wind was strong, shaping her clothes against her body with a pair of cold, sculptor's hands, so her breasts and hip bones jutted from the material.

She leaned forward and leant on the wind like she used to as a child, her arms held wide. It was exhilarating, imagining the wind suddenly dropping, imagining herself tumbling over the edge and on to the sand below.

Only she wasn't that brave, or that reckless. She'd allowed a shadow's length for error. Disgusted with herself she turned, to find Bryn standing a few feet away from her, his dark hair tossed into spikes by the wind, his eyes reflecting the turbulence she felt.

He didn't move, he just smiled at her and quoted:

> *'Here, where the world is quiet;*
> *Here, where all trouble seems*
> *Dead winds' and spent waves' riot*
> *In doubtful dreams of dreams.'*

'Who wrote that?'

'Swinburne. He was a great judge of human nature.' He gazed at her, waiting, a pulse in his jaw displaying the tension he felt. And she realized then that he thought she might have been about to end it all.

She took a step towards him and smiled, watching him relax when she said, 'You needn't worry, you know, I've got too much to live for. I was just flying on the wind.'

'And I brought you back to earth.'

'I'm still going to look for my daughter, Bryn. I don't care if it becomes an obsession, and I don't care if I get hurt. I've got to know.'

He held out his arms, and she moved inside them and laid her head against his chest, her empathy with him curiously comforting.

'Thanks for the quotation. I hope you're not going to charge me.'

A chuckle rumbled through his chest.

'Why are you here?'

'Because I knew you'd forgive me, and I couldn't stay away until Friday.'

The evening was closing around them, but there wasn't anything hushed about it. It was dark and wild, like a wind-whipped cloak settling around their shoulders. She felt as if she and Bryn were an island of seren-ity inside it – or rather, he was the island and she the shipwrecked soul clinging to his shore.

Beneath them, the sea hissed and crashed in a rapidly darkening void. The grasses sang and whipped at their ankles and the sea-birds screamed as they wheeled on the wind. The air seemed charged and threatening. The air currents pushed rags of clouds across the sky and the wind shrieked a warning at them.

'Would a woman kill herself and the man she loved, rather than face living without him?' she said on the walk back to the house.

'Why do you ask?'

'I think my mother did that. She drove them into a tree and there were no skid marks.'

'U-huh?'

'I'm glad she didn't love me in exactly the same way.'

He reflected on it for a second or two, then he shivered and his arm tightened around her. 'So am I.' A few minutes later he began to chuckle.

'What's so funny?'

'You have an inclination to dramatize a situation. Couldn't your mother simply have fallen asleep behind the wheel?'

'Joy said . . .' But Joy was an actress and *would* dramatize. Feeling a bit of an idiot, she admitted, 'That's what it said on the coroner's report.'

He gave her a sideways glance and grinned, and she grinned. They resumed their walk and a few steps further on she began to laugh and he began to chuckle . . . and then he kissed her, and then there was silence.

CHAPTER SEVEN

Something about the looming hills of Wales brought visions of Merlin into Pandora's head.

Bryn was quiet, seemingly lost in thought as his eyes concentrated on the winding road ahead. The trendy suits he usually wore had been exchanged for casual jeans and a thick, cable-knit sweater with a crew neck. Dark tongues of hair licked at the collar of his shirt. With his professional skin left behind, he looked younger and less intimidating.

They'd crossed the Severn Bridge over an hour ago and were heading for a village not far from Swansea, where Bryn's parents lived.

Plucking a comb from her bag, Pandora turned the driving mirror in her direction and proceeded to rearrange her hair.

'You did that five minutes ago. How do you expect me to get us there safely if you keep pinching the mirror?'

She hastily adjusted it. 'Sorry. Do I look all right?'

His sigh was one of mock exasperation. 'You asked me that five minutes ago, too.'

'Sorry.'

'Stop saying you're sorry.'

She gently batted her eyelids at him. 'What did you say about my hair when I asked you if it looked all right five minutes ago?'

'I have no intention of feeding your vanity with continuous compliments.'

Her laughter brought a smile to his lips. 'You've been very quiet since we crossed the bridge. What were you thinking about?'

'Merlin, mostly.'

'That figures.' He slanted her an enigmatic glance and pre-empted her next question. 'And yes – deep down in the dark, mystic pit of my little Welsh soul, I do believe Merlin exists and is buried in a crystal cave.'

'Do you think he'll ever get out?'

'I'd like to think so. The world desperately needs a Merlin at the moment.'

With the mountainous hills all around them steeped in ancient mystery and turbulent shadows, she imagined he'd been raised on Welsh myth. 'What was your childhood like, Bryn?'

'Merlin figured quite strongly in it, as a matter of fact. Some nights he roams the hills, crying out for company.'

A shiver spooked the nape of her neck. 'Did you ever hear him?'

'Never.' His hand covered hers, 'But if *you* do, call me right away. I've heard he's partial to spunky, long-legged Englishwomen.'

Which was Bryn all over, talking at cross-purposes so he couldn't be pinned down to serious conversation – and whilst she quite enjoyed the cut and thrust of such conversations. . . .

'When will I meet the real Bryn Llewellyn?' she murmured.

He pulled the car into a gravelly side road and cut the engine. 'Say again.'

Skewered by his penetrating glance, she squirmed a little, but decided he wasn't going to be allowed to intimidate her.

'You heard what I said. When will I meet the real Bryn Llewellyn? You don't have to play the learned doctor by taking the conversation into circles all the time.'

He managed to look injured and grin at the same time. 'Ouch!'

A spark of ire cut her serenity to shreds, leaving her feeling dangerously ragged. 'You're infuriating, did you know that?'

'I do now.'

'You don't give a shit about Merlin, do you?'

'Do you?' he said, in a manner designed to add fuel to her fire.

She absolutely refused to bite, and releasing her seat-belt threw open the car door. 'I'm going for a walk to the top of the hill.'

He measured the hill with a glance, then lay back in the seat and closed his eyes. 'It's only a little one, it shouldn't take you more than a couple of hours. Wake me when you get back – and shut the door, you're letting the cold in.'

She slammed the car door and stomped off, mumbling unflattering remarks about him and growing more furious by the minute as she imagined him laughing at her.

Climbing a Welsh hill – even a little one – wasn't something one should attempt on the spur of the moment, she realized fifteen minutes later. It was hard, stony and seemed to generate an icy wind, which by-passed the fibres of her garments to pluck goosebumps from the surface of her skin. Her temper cooled as fast as her body and she knew she'd been childish.

In all the years she'd spent with Gerald she'd managed to keep her temper in check, so why should she lose it over something so trivial with Bryn? Half-way up, she turned to look down at the car. The windows had steamed up with his breath, and it suddenly looked warm and inviting. Swallowing the remains of her pride, she started back down.

He was asleep when she got there. She hadn't expected him really to take a nap, and it was a bit of an ego-leveller. She realized that she'd wanted him to come after her, to bring her back to the car with softly-spoken words and laughter.

She stared at his face, noting the curving planes of his cheeks, his strong, straight nose and the way his dark eyelashes fanned his cheeks. His upper lip was firm, the lower, full and sensuous. She touched gently against the dark hairline at his temple. 'Bryn?'

His eyes opened, the black-flecked, hazel depths remaining unfocused for the few seconds it took to recognize her. His slowly dawning smile robbed her of breath and dredged all sorts of emotions up from her depths.

'Did you defeat your dragon?' he said.

She nodded, too choked up to speak, and his hand slid to the back of her head and brought her face down to his – down to his sensual mouth to be kissed with a leisurely enjoyment and mutual pleasuring.

There was no need to apologize to him for her behaviour, but when she attempted to, anyway, he placed his finger across her lips. 'Hush, woman.'

So she hushed. They drove the rest of the way in a cocoon of content-ment with each other, because Bryn had a way of drawing her into the quality of his silence.

The perfume of lavender leaked through the door. Her room was small and white-painted. The ceiling sloped downwards, the floor following suit so the black, iron bed-end had to be propped on two bricks to keep the bed level. A patchwork bedspread rioted with flame-coloured poppies.

'I'm sorry it's so small,' Bryn's mother said, standing awkwardly at the door. 'Bryn didn't tell me he was bringing a guest.' Wynn Llewellyn was a thin, wizened woman in her late sixties, the remnants of black in her hair an indication that Bryn had inherited her colouring. Her green-hazel eyes wandered over the room. 'I'm wondering now how Bryn stood up in here, so big he's grown. Just like his father.'

'It's perfect.' Pandora didn't quite know how to put this woman at her ease. 'I hope you didn't go to too much trouble.'

'None at all,' Wynn said, but with a touch of tartness, as if the quality of her housekeeping was being questioned – and if it wasn't, letting Pandora know she didn't consider her important enough to go to any trouble for anyway. 'I always keep rooms ready for the unexpected visitor. Known my boy long, have you?'

Pandora tried a smile. 'A few months.'

The woman's expression didn't soften. 'I daresay you'd like some tea. We usually have it at four. Come down to the kitchen when you're ready, we don't stand on ceremony here.'

Pandora was beginning to wish she hadn't come, when Bryn poked his head around the door and grinned. She grabbed a handful of his jumper and dragged him into the room. His head nearly touched the ceiling at the deep end. 'Why didn't you tell your mother I was coming?'

'I didn't think of it.'

'Oh, Bryn.'

'I love you,' he said, a faint smile playing around his mouth, his heart half-hidden behind eyes that were strangely defensive.

His vulnerability was all too apparent to her, the declaration entirely unexpected. 'Oh, Bryn.'

'Is that all you can say?'

'I don't know what else *to* say.'

His smile was rueful. 'I just needed to tell you.' His arm slid around her waist and pulled her close. 'How do you feel about it? And don't give me any of that, *I feel honoured, but,* crap.'

'I fancy you like crazy,' she said. 'But my life's too cluttered at the moment to think past the carnal.'

'That's encouraging, but you've chosen a good time to tell me. If we engaged in sexual fore-play, middle-play or after-play in this cottage, it would fall down around our ears.'

'And there we'd be,' she mocked. 'On the front page of the Welsh tabloids. Local psychiatrist dug from rubble with bare bum in the air. When asked what caused the disaster, he replied. . . .'

'"I was playing sex games with the gay divorcee and it all fell down around our ears. . . ."'

'"There was such a huge bang," the divorcee twittered, wiping the sweat from her eyes and plucking bits of plaster from her—'

'Bryn, my boyo,' a voice boomed and the doorway was completely filled with a huge form.

'Oh, God, a giant,' she whispered when the man ducked under the doorway. If anything, he was taller than Bryn.

Bryn gave a wicked chuckle. 'Now you know why the cottage is so crooked. When me da stands at one end the whole place tips.'

'And don't the pair of you stand in the same place at once up there,' his mother shouted up the stairs. 'The last time, a chunk of plaster fell off the ceiling into my scone mix.'

Pandora's hand flew to her heart when the floorboards creaked.

A short period of laughter and back-slapping went on, then her hand disappeared completely into a huge one.

'I'm Owen, Bryn's da. Who are you?'

'Pandora Rossiter.'

His eyebrows waggled. 'Pandora, who opened the box and released a mess of troubles for unsuspecting men to carry on their shoulders?'

'No, not that one. Pandora, who happens to think men are responsible for their own troubles – and how dare they blame their weaknesses on one woman.'

Owen's eyes flicked to Bryn. The glance they exchanged contained a wealth of amusement and rueful male insight.

'She'll do, boyo.'

'She will, that.'

'Your mam's been on to the hens. Worst thing I ever did getting the phone put on. It's peck, peck, cluck, cluck, all day now.' His glance strayed over her. 'Bryn's sisters will be here for the inquisition tomorrow, but you seem to have a well-honed tongue on you, so you should be able to handle it.'

Pandora shot Bryn a dirty look and he grinned apologetically, his hand tightening gently around hers.

'No use offering to take them all out to lunch, I suppose. They'd behave themselves better in public.'

'No use at all. The telephone lines will be melting at the moment whilst they decide what offering to bring you – and the kids will have the dirt scrubbed out of their ears and warned to be on their best behaviour tomorrow, poor little beggars. I bless the day I built that back room on the cottage.'

'It looks as if it's keeping the rest of the place upright.'

'Nothing a hammer and a few nails won't fix – or so your mam always says.' Both men laughed, and because it was so obviously an old joke between them, Pandora smiled.

They went down the narrow stairs together, father and son ducking their heads at each doorway with the ease of long practice, and the cottage shaking with every tread of foot on step.

Lunch the next day was more of an ordeal than Pandora had expected. It was noisy, and Owen's reference to hens took on new significance with six women all animatedly talking at once, scolding the many children and teasing their one and only brother. The sisters' spouses were ill at ease, their hands pulling nervously at the knots of their ties when they were called on to talk.

She soon realized Bryn was an oddity in this family, his very cleverness off-putting to his brothers-in-law. He was an object of awed, mock-derision to his sisters, who over reacted and competed in their determination to bring him down from some lofty plane they'd imagined he'd reached.

He was a reason for immense pride to his parents. Photos were unearthed. Trophies won in some eisteddfod or for a swimming race, and merit certificates earned at school and copies of reports were dragged out for inspection and discussion.

Bryn took it all with good grace, but they were all trying too hard, each claiming a little piece of him, when all they needed to do was relax and allow him to do the same.

The five sisters were so alike – Cordelia and Glenda were identical twins which made it more confusing – Pandora found it difficult to tell them apart, or match any one child to its mother.

The few times she was directly addressed, the conversation was polite, until Bryn and his father left the room, 'to inspect the runner beans' Owen said, when it was obvious to Pandora they were escaping.

One of the sisters engaged her eyes and said directly, 'I believe you're a divorcee, Mrs Rossiter.'

Pandora's senses went on alert. Bryn's mother must have overheard their exchange upstairs because she was pretty sure Bryn wouldn't have discussed her private affairs with anyone. 'I'm in the middle of a divorce, yes.'

'And do you have children?'

'Two boys.' She suddenly thought of Trinity, 'And a daughter.'

'I see.' Just two words, but they were heavy with innuendo, and when the sisters exchanged meaningful glances their husbands began to leave the room as well, emptying it of children at the same time.

There was an atmosphere. Pandora felt like a swimmer being circled by starving sharks. *I'll murder you, Bryn Llewellyn.* The only way she was going to stop a feeding-frenzy was to shoot spears into the leader of the predators, in the hope of scaring the rest of the pack off.

'What exactly is it you see?'

'Well, you being a divorced woman and all that . . . and Bryn being a wealthy doctor. It's obvious, isn't it? He'd be a good catch for someone with children to support.'

'That's enough, Olwyn!' her mother warned.

'She might as well say it, because we all think it,' one of the others said.

Pandora sliced a strip off them. 'Am I to understand you only have one brain between you to think with – and that belongs to Olwyn?' She ignored Wynn's outraged gasp. 'What's obvious to me is that you're meddling in something you know nothing about – and is none of your business, anyway.'

Olwyn coloured with affront. 'Our brother *is* our business.'

'Bryn's old enough and wise enough to take care of himself,' she reminded them gently, 'and just so you can get things straight in your collective head – Bryn and I are just friends, but if we ever decided to marry your opinion would be of no consequence whatsoever.'

Six pairs of suddenly embarrassed but hostile dark eyes stared at her, then Bryn's mother said awkwardly,

'I'm sure Olwyn didn't mean any harm.'

'I think your daughter's old enough to apologize for herself,' she said quietly.

'I'm sorry, I'm sure,' Olwyn said, her voice weighed down by sarcasm.

'Then say it as if you damned well mean it,' their father said quietly from the doorway. 'Since when did you have the right to insult a guest in your father's house? And as for you, Wynn Llewellyn, shame on you for encouraging such behaviour in your daughters. Is it out of your wits, you all are?'

'Excuse me.' Pandora rose to her feet and pushed past him. She grabbed her coat from the peg in the hall and went outside to join Bryn, who was poking around the shed at the end of the garden. There was a sick feeling in the pit of her stomach. There had been no satisfaction in the confrontation.

He saw it in her eyes at once and his mouth tightened. 'Tell me about it.'

'Your father's handling it. Let's go for a walk.'

'I suppose Olwyn started it.'

She managed a smile. 'It's OK, really, Bryn. They formed the impression I was a calculating bitch with kids to support. They thought I was after you for your money.'

'If that's all they think I've got going for me, I've got a good mind to cut the handles off their broomsticks,' he growled, and she laughed because the suggestion was so outrageously apt.

'I'm sorry this happened to spoil your weekend. I shouldn't have come.'

'My sisters are meddlesome creatures, and the product of their environment. I should have realized they'd have felt threatened by you. If you want to leave. . . .'

'With my tail between my legs? Never! Let's go for a walk. We'll leave in the morning if the situation doesn't improve.'

They walked a long way, united in the very quality of their silence, and returning only when it was growing dark and cold, their faces glowing from the exercise and inner contentment.

'I owe you an apology,' Olwen said as soon as they walked in, and Bryn crossed to where she stood and put an arm around her.

'You'd better get on with it then, you silly old girls, but before you do I'm going to tell all of you something. I'm in love with Pandora, and if she ever decides to take me on I'll consider myself the luckiest man alive.'

'And what's so wrong with you that she should be so picky?' Olwyn said tartly, then when everyone laughed, she gave a shamefaced grin. 'It's keeping my big mouth shut, that's hard, and I'm sorry I was such a bitch. God knows what you must be thinking of us all.'

Pandora could have been brutally frank, but chose not to – instead, lying a little for Bryn's sake by saying, 'I think you're as fine a family as Bryn led me to believe – and we just got off on the wrong foot.'

'Well, Bryn, you've got a good one here, and about time,' Owen boomed. 'Go and put the kettle on Wynn. It's a piece of Mary's strawberry sponge with a cup of tea they'll be having. The pair of them look as cold as the legs on a frozen chicken.'

And although the atmosphere improved considerably, the weekend wasn't at all comfortable. Pandora came to the conclusion that as far as the women of this family were concerned, no one would ever be good enough for their brother.

'You must have been spoiled rotten when you were growing up,' she said on the way home.

His smile was as jagged as his sigh. 'I'd forgotten how domineering they all are. No wonder I didn't go back there after I qualified.'

'What made you settle in Dorset?'

'A locum job which became a partnership. I really liked the place, and a couple of years later, when my partner decided to go to the USA, I bought the practice.' He shrugged. 'My parents were disappointed I didn't return to Wales.'

'They're in awe of you, I think.'

'I know, but it's simply a lack of understanding of what I do on their part. To them, a doctor stitches wounds, sets broken limbs and delivers babies. My parents supported me through my years of training, often going without themselves to supplement my scholarships. My sisters thought I should have returned home because of it.'

'You could always pay your parents back.'

'They won't hear of it. They said it was their duty to educate me.'

'Which is a kind of instinctive, emotional blackmail thing, isn't it? They're scared of losing you, and whilst you're under an obligation to them—'

'Hey,' he said in faint surprise, '*I'm* the shrink around here.'

'It doesn't need a shrink to figure that one out. What made you specialize in psychiatry?'

'Blood makes me feel queasy and I found the mind more of a challenge.'

'Do you have any hobbies?'

He threw her an amused smile. 'Why the inquisition all of a sudden?'

'Can't you just answer the question without needing a reason?'

'A good ploy, answering a question with a question. I like it. The best form of defence is attack. I bet that's what you used on my sisters – they wouldn't have expected it.'

'You're not going to side-track me this time, Bryn Llewellyn,' she warned. 'Hobbies?'

He appeared to be slightly embarrassed. 'I read a lot, and I listen to opera and classical music, and I sing.'

'Sing . . . in the bath?'

'Sometimes, but mostly in a choir. Is there something wrong with that?'

She giggled. 'Now who's being defensive by attacking? Are you embarrassed because your mother showed me all your eisteddfod trophies? I thought all Welsh men could sing.'

The faint grin he gave was loaded with irony. 'They can. It's the national pastime, along with brass bands, leek soup, rugby and pronouncing the unpronounceable.'

A tiny pulse of mischief bit at her. 'Sing something to me.'

He gazed stoically ahead at the road for a few moments, then he smiled. 'You sing something to me.'

'You're going to regret this,' she said, and opening her mouth, murdered a popular song in one fell swoop.

His frown wasn't exactly encouraging. 'I hate to say this, but that was so off-key and pathetic, you could probably make a separate hit song out of it given some new lyrics.'

'Can you do any better?'

'Sure I can, but I'm driving.'

She told him to turn the ignition off and when the car coasted to a halt, said, 'Now, you're not.'

He turned to face her, half smiling. 'You have an irresistible way with you, woman,' and he engaged her eyes to sing to her of love in a soft, husky voice that was almost mesmerizing. When the last note died away she was almost in tears, because the wealth of emotion in his eyes wasn't all that easy to accept, since she couldn't reciprocate.

'That was beautiful, Bryn. I wish. . . .'

He ran a finger down the length of her nose. 'Don't wish for anything out loud without putting a great deal of thought into it. We're not over the border yet and Merlin is still a danger.'

So she closed her eyes and wished he'd kiss her, a wish so sensationally answered she was tumbled out of the emotional into the physical – so when he started the car again she thought they were destined to end up at his place in bed together.

Yet when they reached Ashford, he took the road towards Marianna. Sam started to bark when he escorted her to the door, and stopped when he heard her telling him to be quiet.

She slid her arms around Bryn's neck and nibbled at his bottom lip. 'We should have gone to your place.'

'I'm not a mind-reader,' he growled, and taking the key from her hand, shoved it in the lock. He kissed her, then pushed her inside and pulled the door shut. 'Don't play games, Pandora,' he said against the panel. 'Goodnight.'

Play games! She'd show him who was playing games. She fondled Sam, turning him instantly from a guard dog into an ingratiating quiver of tail-wagging, licks and welcome home. Then she collected her car keys and kissed Lottie, who looked up from the television long enough to be told Pandora was going out again.

It took several attempts to start her cold car engine.

Bryn's rear lights were disappearing into the distance when she nosed out of the driveway. She followed him through town to a quiet street, where a row of Georgian houses fronted on to small, enclosed gardens. Bryn lived in the end one. She waited until the light went on and the faint sound of music drifted to her ears, then, stomach churning like a cement mixer, leaned on the doorbell.

After a few moments the door swung open. Bryn gazed at her reflectively for a few moments, then stood to one side to allow her access. He leaned against the wall, his arms crossed across his chest, his smile dangerous, his eyes disconcertingly expressionless. As the seconds ticked by, tension built up between them.

She ran a tongue over her dry lips, not quite knowing what to say, then nearly jumped out of her skin and was unaccountably and mindlessly furious with him when he said. 'You've come then, woman.'

'Stop calling me woman, you smug, Welsh . . . *chicken hypnotist!* And stop trying to be enigmatic, and staring at me and saying nothing and looking all sexy and come-and-get-me.'

'Hah! Is that what I'm doing?' he said, and, bringing his body close to hers, planted his hands under her buttocks and lifted her effortlessly against him, making her shockingly aware of the effect she was having on him. Face level with his, she received the full force of his eyes, alight with devilish laughter.

She grinned weakly at him. 'Damn you, Bryn. I'm shy.'

'I'm sure I can cure you of that particular inhibition,' he purred, and kicking open the nearest door, backed them through it.

It wasn't until afterwards – after she'd experienced the first exquisite orgasm of her life – after he'd sated her, wonderfully, sensually and she was sure, most improperly, and she thought she might die of the pleasure she was experiencing – she lifted her head and realized she was on his couch in his consulting room.

She laughed. 'Your cure was quite innovative.'

'I like a patient who co-operates.' He grinned at her, looking like a great, lazy bear who'd feasted too well and was ready to hibernate. 'And you have yet to learn what innovative means – and it's cold in here so let's go upstairs and have a spa bath to warm up before I show you.'

She followed his firm, naked backside upstairs and she realized her husband had never once wanted to see her naked, to explore her body and pleasure her as Bryn had done . . . and she'd never wanted to initiate sex with Gerald like she did with Bryn.

He quivered with repressed laughter when she gave in to the urge to place her palms against his buttocks as he walked. When they reached the top of the stairs he slid his hand around her waist and draped it over her hip bone. It dangled a mere inch from where she wanted it to be, a spot which immediately began to throb an invitation.

As if it were sending out a signal, he honed in on it instinctively, bringing her to a halt, backing her against the wall and falling to his knees. The slick, erotic caresses kept her gasping until she was quivering like a jelly. He stood up then, lifted her on to him and thrust swiftly into her, an act of possession in which she lost any thought of independence. The pounding, thrusting instrument of pleasure pinning her to the wall was her only centre of focus.

'Oh, God!' she gasped, and went over the edge a second or two before his pelvis thrust forward in a frenzy of convulsive jolts. He was breathing heavily when she gently sank her teeth into his neck.

'Careful, that's not far from my jugular,' he groaned.

'Can you imagine the newspaper headlines?' she whispered against his ear. '"Welsh shrink bitten to death by the gay divorcee. . . ."'

'"The coroner said he died in the throes of passion and with a huge smile on his face. . . ."'

'". . . and the gay divorcee has been frustrated ever since".'

He slid her down his body to the floor. 'You have a bit of a thing about newspapers. You must be an exhibitionist, at heart.'

She laughed, softly, self-consciously, because the intensity of her own passion was a discovery she wasn't altogether comfortable with. It didn't fit in with the image her upbringing had given her of acceptable ladylike behaviour, yet she'd enjoyed the discovery of every wicked moment.

When Gerald's many casual affairs stole into her thoughts, she wondered if it was possible that she might have given him reason to stray.

CHAPTER EIGHT

The following week, Joy called to say Brian had died.

Pandora travelled to London by train for the funeral, which was attended by a number of people from the entertainment industry – some of whom used the occasion as nothing more than a photo-opportunity.

A young, blonde actress rose to her stilettos, and flashing pale breasts over a black, gothic bodice breathed out a tribute.

'I wouldn't mind a set of tits like those,' a man behind them lisped to his companion before mincing up to read a Dylan Thomas sonnet, the delivery of which would have had Bryn gnashing his teeth.

Joy wasn't a big name in the industry, having spent her life in bit parts whilst chasing an elusive stardom. As a character actor, Brian was better known, but he'd never been a star. As expected, the blonde's breasts made the paper and Joy got a mention of two lines.

It was obvious Brian's death had knocked Joy for a loop. The flat they'd shared was small and dingy, full of dusty theatre memorabilia. They'd never earned enough to buy into anything, Joy said, and she had appeared vague when Pandora mentioned life insurance to her. She looked like hell.

'Why don't you come back to Marianna with me for a while,' Pandora invited.

There was an air of heavy depression about Joy. 'I can't. I'm expecting my agent to call about a character part.'

Pandora stayed a couple more days to make sure Joy didn't do anything stupid.

After Pandora left for Waterloo, she imagined Joy still sitting in her suffocating little flat with its mustard-smeared ceiling, smoking cigarette after cigarette. There was nothing she could do for Joy, yet she still felt guilty about leaving her.

'People have to help themselves,' Lottie said to her when she arrived home and told her about it.

Pandora stared curiously at her aunt. Gone was the old, timid Lottie. Day by day she was growing in confidence and skills. 'Is that what *you've* been doing, Lottie?'

The blue eyes flared with anxiety. 'Bryn is helping me.'

A void appeared in Pandora's stomach. 'Bryn is helping you? Since when?'

'Since I began to work at the centre.'

Bryn was treating Lottie and he hadn't told her? She couldn't believe it.

'It's all right, isn't it, Pandora? I said I should ask you, and he said I should if I wanted to. But then he reminded me I was old enough to make up my mind without having to ask anyone's permission?'

'So you decided you were?'

She hung her head. 'Lottie didn't want to get into trouble.'

'Oh, God, Lottie, you're not in any trouble. I want you to get better, and of course you need to make your own decisions. I couldn't be more pleased, or more proud of you.' She gave her a huge, reassuring hug, thinking: *I'll kill that damned, interfering Welshman for not telling me.*

Even though he's worked a miracle with Lottie? Even though he's your friend – your lover? She closed her eyes and grinned as another thought lodged in her mind. She loved every damned, interfering inch of him! She'd try and keep her mouth shut about any progress Lottie made, whether with or without Bryn's guidance, and even if it killed her – which it probably would.

So she said nothing the next time she saw Bryn with Lottie. She bit her tongue, watching from behind the curtains when the pair of them pushed Emily's old car out of the garage – the one she hadn't got round to selling because it wouldn't start.

Bryn hovered over the engine for half a day, twiddling this and banging that and spicing the air with the odd curse, and not once did she say anything when she took him one of the countless cups of coffee he asked for – neither did he, which was totally unreasonable of him, and infuriating!

He was patched in grease when he finished, emerging from under the bonnet with a triumphant grin on his face, and oblivious to the mean and meaningful glances she was now throwing his way. He'd forgotten he was supposed to be taking her out to lunch.

'Try it, Lottie.'

Pandora was amazed when the engine started with a backfire and a belch of smoke. Lottie was grinning all over her face when she drove off.

'Aren't you pleased she passed her test?' Bryn said, laughing and streaking her face and hands with black smears when he kissed her.

Feeling decidedly frosty, she put some distance between them. 'I am now I know she was being taught to drive. I rather like being kept in the dark, and I adore being stood up. We were supposed to have a lunch date, remember.'

'You brought me a sandwich, if I recall.'

'It was a home made Cornish pasty, but it could have been dog biscuits for all the notice you took of it.'

The corners of his mouth twitched. 'Sarcasm? Ah . . . I see. My attention was focused on Lottie instead of you, right?'

She wasn't going to let him get away with an arrogant remark like that. 'Lottie might think you're the incarnation of some deity she should worship, but I don't.'

'Come on, Pandora, don't go all mid-winter on me. Lottie wanted to surprise you.'

'Surprise or deceive?' she hurled at him, knowing she was going from bad to worse, but unable to stop pushing him. 'It strikes me that you're deliberately encouraging her to hide things from me.'

'I'm encouraging her to be herself.'

She forgot her resolve to keep quiet. 'You could have told me you were treating her. Why didn't you?'

His eyes shuttered over. 'Confidentiality is her right as a patient, and taken for granted by me as her doctor.'

'Don't bore me with that line. I'm responsible for her.'

His gaze nudged hard against hers, making her feel ashamed of her outburst – which she should be, because not only was it childish, it was also unworthy of her.

'No, you're not responsible. You only think you are because your grandmother appointed you her keeper. Lottie has never been assessed until now, and she's never been offered help, which was the worst thing that could have happened to her. She's been kept a prisoner of her own fear all these years – all because her parents allowed a criminal to be a slave to his vice rather than face the shame of exposure. She was passed over to you without consultation with her, like a package.'

Pandora was filled with consternation. Bryn was right. 'Oh, God, is that what she thinks?'

'Thankfully, no. It's what I think. Strange isn't it, that she was handed over to you, a victim of the same man? What did your grandmother think, that the crime hadn't affected you in any way?'

'It hasn't.'

His knuckles grazed down her face and his voice gentled. 'You're strong, Pandora, too strong. You can't bring yourself to love – because whenever you gave love, you became a victim, and lost something. Your parents, grandparents, and most of all, Robert Dysart – all of them deserted you.'

She felt as if she'd been punched in the midriff. 'Are you saying I don't know *how* to love?'

'I'm sure you do . . . you just go into denial and won't let it in.'

'And why should I do that?'

'So you won't have to bear the pain of losing it again.'

'Thanks for the unwanted consultation. I thought I was off-limits in that regard.' She stalked off, rage simmering inside her like a witch's cauldron full of bat stew. She took several deep, steadying breaths, knowing he'd come after her. But this time she wouldn't let him sweet-talk her into surrender, and she wouldn't let him see her cry, either. She hated it when he churned her up like this, so she had to retreat inside her Dysart façade.

She resisted the urge to slam the door in his face, and was quite calm when she reached the sitting-room. She turned to face him, nothing of her anger showing in her face. 'I think you ought to go home, Bryn.'

'You see,' he said quietly. 'You should have tears in your eyes, at least. You should be ranting and raving at me, throwing things, losing control.'

She took a step towards him. 'Is that what you really think I should be doing?'

'It would be a more honest human emotion, surely.'

Clever Bryn, his eyes full of concern, when all he wanted to do was control her in some way, like her husband had – like all of the men in her life had.

If she'd wanted to really hurt him, she'd have put much more force behind the slap she gave him. But still, it caught him unawares. Shock flared in his eyes, a denting of the ego perhaps? Whichever it was, it gave her a great surge of satisfaction.

'Is that honest enough?' she said.

His fingers investigated the reddening patch. 'I guess it is.' The hurt in his voice was almost more than she could bear.

The phone rang, the sound shocking colour into her face. It rang and rang, whilst they stared at each other, unbelieving.

'Aren't you going to answer that?'

Her voice was a snap when she snatched up the receiver. 'Pandora Rossiter.'

It was Simeon. 'There's a couple of papers urgently needing signature. My schedule's a bit tight today, but could you meet me for lunch? We could go over it then.'

'Lunch? Sure . . . where and what time?'

'One o'clock at the Baker's Arms . . . and Pandora, I've dug up a bit of information about the James family. You might be interested to know they emigrated to Western Australia five years after the adoption.'

'They took my daughter to Australia?' Australia was such a large continent, and was so many thousands of miles away, the magnitude of it stunned her. 'How on earth will I find her there?'

'I'll see if I can turn anything else up for you.'

'Thanks, Simeon, you're such a love.'

Bryn was still gazing at her, his eyes as wounded as a mistreated dog. She felt like stroking his head and fondling his ears, but that was what he was aiming for.

'It won't work, Bryn. I refuse to say I'm sorry.'

'I deserved the slap.'

If he wanted to take an uncompromising stand, he could live with it.

'I agree. All I'm sorry about is that I allowed you to goad me into losing control. I've never hit anybody before.'

His smile had a gritty quality to it. 'You can come over here and kiss it better, if you like.'

She glanced at her watch and shook her head. 'It wouldn't end there, and I'm still too annoyed with you to want to. Besides, I have a lunch date. Simeon has some information about my daughter.'

'So I gathered. You're not going to let this be, are you?'

'Would you?'

'Yes.'

'Ah . . . but you're a man.' She shook her head, trying to recall the elusive memory of the baby daughter in her arms. 'You don't know what it's like to give birth, or grieve for the loss of that child, either. Despite what you think, Bryn, I do know how to love.'

'Enough to let her go a second time?'

The life seemed to bleach from her body. 'I might not have to.'

Two steps brought him close to her, his warmth reached out to surround her. 'I don't want you to be hurt again. I could give you another daughter to love. Girls dominate in my family.'

She laid her head against his chest, the generosity of the simplistic solution humbling her, and regret for her violence sitting like a stone in her chest. He just didn't understand.

'A child should be loved and wanted for itself, not brought into the world as a substitute for another. I've *got* to do this, Bryn, however much it hurts. And it will be *with* you, or without you.'

There was a moment when she thought he'd withdraw from her. She slid her arms around his waist to keep him there, then after a few moments his arms came round her and he rested his chin on the top of her head.

'If you need me, I'll always be here for you.'

'I think I'll always need you.'

'Which gives me hope.' He kissed the top of her head and pushed her to arm's length, gazing at her with his head slanted to one side. 'You'd better go and get ready if you're lunching with the lawyer. After that, I want you to contact the organization I told you about. The people who run it have all been through some aspect of adoption trauma, and will help and support you.'

She nodded. 'You can join Simeon and myself for lunch if you'd like. I'd like him to meet you.'

Gazing down at his greasy hands and jeans, he grimaced. 'Another time, perhaps.' A brief kiss and he was gone, leaving her staring at the door after it had closed.

She wished Bryn had taken her up on the invitation when she discovered Carol Stringer was there.

The divorce lawyer was whip-thin in an ankle-length black coat. Her black hair was feathered around her face, her wide mouth was a startling line of red across an otherwise pale face. Large, dark eyes were turned towards Simeon and she was chatting animatedly.

Pandora caught her breath. It was obvious Simeon was bored with her company. It was written all over him.

When he spotted her, his mouth curved into a smile. Hardly disguised dislike flitted over Carol's face. Somehow, it didn't surprise Pandora, because the feeling was mutual. However, her upbringing wouldn't allow her to show it.

She smiled when Carol drained her glass and prepared to leave. 'You don't have to go. I haven't heard from you recently. How's my divorce proceeding?'

'I suppose it will save me ringing you later. I had a meeting with your husband yesterday. He wants a valuation of the property you own and a statement of all your bank accounts, etcetera.'

Her eyes narrowed. Carol had met Gerald? Why would she need to do that?

'I thought he'd agreed on a settlement,' Simeon said, surprise evident in his eyes. 'This will hold up Pandora's plans for the house conversion.'

Carol's eyes slid away. 'He's changed his mind. Apparently, Mr Rossiter has discovered she has a man friend.'

Simeon slid her an inquiring look and she shrugged.

'I don't see what that's got to do with anything. We didn't meet until after the marriage was over.'

He brought all his attention to bear on Carol. 'Have you told Mr Rossiter that if he goes ahead with this, he'll end up with less, rather than more?'

'I'm not sure he will,' Carol said, her attitude of studied, casual indifference and her aura of Chanel perfume, alerting Pandora's sixth sense.

Carol was as lousy an actress as she was a lawyer, and what she was trying to hide was patently obvious to Pandora. It was time to take the gloves off.

'Exactly who are you representing, Miss Stringer? And how many times have you met my husband?'

'He requested a face-to-face, first off.'

'Which you conveniently forgot to tell me about. And since?'

Carol shrugged and a shifty look came into her eyes, one Pandora had seen displayed in the eyes of Gerald's secretaries before they got over-confident.

'If you don't like my style, get someone else to handle it.'

'Consider it done – and Carol, I must warn you. If you're sleeping with Gerald, don't imagine he's attracted to you. He'll be using you as a means to an end.'

'He loves me,' she said, the conviction in her voice absolute.

Simeon leant across the table and frowned at her, his face drained of colour. 'How could you, Carol, after I gave you this chance? This could ruin your career if it gets out.'

'But it's not going to get out, is it Simeon dear?'

'It's not up to me. The client might decide to complain.'

'Then you'd better persuade her not to.' Carol rose to her feet, and stared down at them both with a smile. 'Enjoy your lunch. I'm quite sure I can persuade Gerry to go back to the old arrangement. In fact, it would be in my own interests to do so.'

'You'd better tell me what the hell's going on,' she said, after Carol had gone.

'I'm so sorry, I had no idea she'd become involved with your husband. Quite frankly, I'm appalled.'

'Don't be. Gerald's a real charmer where women are concerned, and she's welcome to him if she can catch him. What I want to know is, what has she got on you, Simeon?'

It was his turn to avoid her eyes, which was strange because he'd always managed to lie so guilelessly before.

'Several of us shared a flat while we were at law school. In our final year, we got involved with drugs. Carol was younger than the rest of us. She found the going tough, and was burning the candle at both ends to get through her exams. She got hooked on the heavy stuff, and nearly burnt herself out. She's put in some time in a private rehab – and I've been trying to help her out with clients.'

Simeon's explanation was beginning to sound iffy, and considering the furniture offer and the confidential information he was getting for her, his honesty was suspect as well. 'Why is she holding it over you when you did her a favour?'

'I guess she had a bit of a thing for me for a long time. It wasn't reciprocated.' He seemed to draw himself into his legal suit. 'I know someone who's brilliant with divorce. He'll charge more, though.'

'Another of your recommendations? No thanks.' She stood up. 'I really feel it would be better if I changed law firms. You don't seem to me to be very . . . *ethical*? I can't see how Carol could prove what you've just told me – and I don't think it's the reason, just a convenient half-truth you're trying to fob me off with.'

He gazed at her, a hint of desperation in his fine eyes. A shaft of winter sunlight came through the window, illuminating the perfect cast of his features. She saw it in him then, the secret he was trying to hide.

She placed her hand over his. 'You don't have to tell me if you don't want to, but I think I've guessed – was that why your marriage wasn't a success?'

He looked as though he was about to deny it, then he shrugged and managed a smile. 'I thought marriage was the answer to my problem, but despite doing my best to be a good husband and father, it wasn't.'

'Perhaps you should stop regarding it as a problem, then. It doesn't make you any less a person in my eyes.' She smiled at him, her annoyance forgotten. 'I'm glad I didn't fall in love with you, though. I was tempted to.'

'You'd be surprised how many of my women clients do. It's a bit of an occupational hazard.'

'You've got a way with you, Simeon, so I wouldn't be *at all* surprised. As for the real issue, I wouldn't have thought it mattered in this day and age.'

'It does to some people. My uncle would be horrified, and he's on the brink of offering me a partnership.'

'And if I withdrew my business?'

'He wouldn't like it. I'm good at what I do, Pandora, and I'm not going to beg for your business.' His eyes came up to hers, his smile so practised it could have been Gerald smiling at her if she hadn't seen the desperation behind it. 'I'd be sorry to lose you as a client and friend. I rather enjoy your company. But you must do what you feel is right.'

'You won't lose either because of your personal life.' She sighed, allowing herself to be conned because she liked him. 'Okay, ask your lawyer to ring me. Gerald's trying it on and will back-track if he thinks I'm going for the throat.'

'Why aren't you?' he said curiously.

'Because I thought I loved him once, and we had children together. That's got to count for something.'

'And now you have someone else?'

'Someone I care about very much – but I don't know whether it's the real thing, either. My immediate quest in life is to find my daughter.'

'So, you've decided to go to Australia?'

She hadn't, but the very idea of it took her breath away. Why shouldn't she go to Australia? She could ask Joy to come and live with Lottie, it would take her mind off Brian's death and make her feel useful.

So Pandora made an appointment with the organization Bryn had put her on to. She placed herself on the register for contact in case her daughter tried to find her, and attended informal meetings where adoptive parents, adopted children and relinquishing mothers talked about their experiences.

It was a painful experience, raw with emotion. She found she couldn't relate to the people involved, and neither could she bring herself to expose what was essentially private in her, to public scrutiny.

When she considered she'd gained enough helpful insight, she booked her flight and accommodation in Western Australia, choosing a holiday unit for economy's sake, because she didn't know how long she'd be there.

She chose a quiet moment and told Adrian and Michael they had a sister.

It was the wrong thing to do. She learned that mothers were expected to be slotted into the cliché 'whiter than white, and purer than the driven snow'.

'Fifteen,' Adrian said in disgust. 'You were just a child.'

'Her father was a man as old as your father is now.' Which was a reminder to them of why she'd left Gerald – and if his infidelities didn't bother them, why should her youthful folly? 'If you were to be charitable, you'd realize I was a victim – and to be quite honest, I'd expected you to be a bit more grown up and understanding about this.'

'You're our mother, so it's disgusting,' Michael said, and they both mooched off with the dog sniffing at their heels. Neither of them spoke to her for the rest of the day. Then Adrian said the next morning. 'Mike and I have talked it over.'

'And?'

'We don't mind if you look for her. It's not her fault she was born.'

Which wasn't actually forgiving her sin, but the indications were they'd get around to it.

Gerald was a little more difficult when he found out. 'You married me under false pretences,' he yelled. 'If I'd have known you were a cheap little tramp who'd given birth to a bastard I wouldn't have given you house-room. How many other men had you before me?'

'Hundreds,' she said, and hung up on him.

A few days later the settlement papers were signed and witnessed. Gerald couldn't get rid of her fast enough now.

He'd also got rid of Carol Stringer, Simeon told her with a great deal of satisfaction in his voice.

With Christmas looming, the shops were filled with lights and a flashy sort of merriment. Security guards patrolled, their eyes vigilant, because giving had to produce a profit, and every shopper was a felon in disguise.

Santas grew more jaded-looking the nearer it got to Christmas, their smiles not quite reaching their eyes, so Pandora got the impression their ho-ho-ho's were pitched to scare the children off rather than encourage them on to laps.

She bought Bryn a dark-blue cashmere sweater, wrapped it up in choir-boy paper and placed it under the tree with the presents for Lottie and the boys.

Joy had refused to come down for Christmas, saying she had a job in pantomime, and she'd see Pandora in March when she was due to fly out.

The boys were coming to Marianna for Christmas, and spending New Year skiing with Gerald in Switzerland before being shunted back to school and university to continue their education.

She'd expected Bryn to go home for Christmas, but he'd said casually to her. 'I'll come to your place for Christmas day then, shall I?'

The choral society he belonged to was carol singing on Christmas Eve in the Abbey church at Milton Abbas. She was torn between her lack of belief, and the nostalgic desire to listen to real carols being sung by a real choir, instead of the jingling Christmas blancmange being played every-where. And it wasn't as if she'd have to pretend to pray, because it wasn't an actual service.

Bryn offered to take her and Lottie with him – 'if they wouldn't mind getting there a bit early,' he'd said, which she'd thought wouldn't be a bad idea because they'd be able to get seats near the front.

Then her sons decided they might as well attend too as they had noth-ing better planned, and they squashed into the back seat with Lottie sandwiched between them.

The surprise of the evening was when Bryn sang solo. When his voice soared in all its richness to rejoice in the meaning of Christmas, it brought a lump to her throat and tears to her eyes.

She blew him a kiss when he looked her way, and he gave a faint smile. Michael was gazing at him with a rapt expression on his face. Although Bryn got on with both of her sons, he was a hero to her younger one after saving Adrian's life.

So she wasn't at all surprised when Michael announced he was going to become a doctor instead of an accountant. The surprise was Adrian, who told her he'd deferred his entrance to Oxford and was going to travel around the world with a friend, who'd also deferred.

'Have you told your father?'

'Not yet. I'll tell him when I'm up there.' He looked worried for a second or two. 'You don't mind, do you, Mum?'

'I think it's a good idea, as long as you're sensible, and don't waste your opportunity.' He knew what she meant because he kissed her cheek and whispered, 'It won't happen again, you don't have to worry. I might even see you in Australia if I get that far – and who knows, if you find my sister. . . .'

For a moment she wondered what Trinity was doing. It was hot in Australia at this time of year. Was she sunning herself at the beach? Did she have a boyfriend – or perhaps she was married. Good God, she might be a grandmother!

Bryn slid his arms around her from behind and whispered in her ear. 'You've got a faraway look in your eyes, what are you thinking about?'

'I'm wondering what Trinity's doing right at this very moment.'

'Right at this moment.' He glanced at his watch and started to count forward. 'It will be early tomorrow morning in Australia. It's Boxing Day, and she'll just be getting out of bed and leaping on to her surfboard.'

Which seemed rather an odd thing for someone to be doing when a thick frost still covered the lawn at midday, and the sun had hibernated under a blanket of unrelenting grey.

Later, when they were alone, Bryn gave her a present – a gold ring fashioned as a dragon, its claws gripping a pale-blue amethyst. Floating within the faceted crystal was a . . . she twisted it in the light to see it better . . . 'Merlin! How on earth. . . ?'

'I went to a jeweller I know and described what I wanted, and how he does it is—'

She placed a finger over his lips. 'Magic,' she said firmly, and watched his eyes change to their most enigmatic.

'So, make a wish and see if it comes true.'

Pandora wished she might be reunited with her daughter, then she wished . . . but no, she was allowed only one wish, and she was torn between the two.

But it was only a little wish extra, wasn't it . . . being certain she loved Bryn? So she smiled and left it in.

CHAPTER NINE

Trinity James shaded her eyes with her hands. On three sides of her a wash of ochre shades blended into a restless ocean of golden wheat. Beyond the tree at her back a dirt road led to Hope's End, which was dominated by several huge silos.

It was hot for mid-morning. The perspiration-soaked seams of her blue checked shirt chafed at her armpits with every movement of her pencil.

In a month or so the air would be electric with wheat-dust, and the road as busy and as dangerous as a highway, with trucks speeding back and forth.

The town of Hope's End had grown up around a railway-siding. It consisted of a church her father had built, two streets of weather-board houses, a general store and a hotel optimistically named the Railway Arms, whose bar hadn't been tickled by a paint-brush for several decades and whose rusty roof was so porous only the spiders' webs kept it intact when the wind blew.

Not that any of the town's inhabitants minded. The beer was cold, kept that way by a generator, which also managed to push the ceiling fans marginally faster than the flies circling below the pressed-tin ceiling.

As well as the church – infrequently used, because her father was unpopular, both as a man and as a lay preacher – Trinity's parents owned the general store, a place of peeling white paint, faded red lettering and cockroaches as old as Father Time. It had the look of failure, like her father after eighteen years of trying to scratch a living from it.

Not that it was Matthew James's fault. His experience of country living had only been rural England when he'd bought the place on spec from a skilful Australian real estate salesman. He'd not realized the country town was on a downward curve, due in part to the vagaries of world wheat prices.

The young people had drifted away over the years, taking with them their children and their custom. The bank had closed, the school had closed and the houses had been left for the termites. Those residents remaining in the district were the wheat-growers, the old folk who remembered better times, and those people who couldn't afford to leave – like Trinity's parents.

Her mother had a worn look, her sun-blotched face and hands a testament to the harshness of the inland climate of Western Australia.

'I wish we'd never come here,' had been a recurring theme of Mary James's over the years, and she was bitter, silently blaming her husband for their failure, her homesickness, and most of all, the allergies which made her very existence a misery.

Misery begat misery in the Jameses case – and Trinity had always borne the brunt of it. For as long as she remembered she'd never done anything right in private. Her parents were strict, religious and upright. She'd gone from being a child to be seen and not heard to a non-troublesome teenager who gained credible marks in her school exams. She was now an adult who'd been disciplined into being a dutiful daughter – a showpiece for the Jameses' archaic idea of perfection as parents, in fact.

Trinity was the core around which her parents' lives revolved. Without her they would have to face their failures because they wouldn't have her to blame for them. So they'd kept her chained to them with threats, bullying and emotional blackmail, and she was so used to it that she hadn't really noticed she was a prisoner – until a month previously.

A month ago Trinity had realized there was more to life than Hope's End. A month ago she'd met Adam Scaife, an English photographer who was on a working tour of the country. A month ago she'd made an early New Year's resolution – one that would change her life for ever.

It hadn't crossed her mind that Adam's interest might have stemmed from the fact that she was an oddity – a twenty-three year old virgin with a body and face to die for. Now, as Eve had been tempted by the apple, she'd been tempted by the first personable young man she'd met.

Her parents wouldn't have understood how innocent her short relationship with Adam was. In the four days he'd camped under the tree, he'd fired her imagination and piqued her curiosity as well as photographing her from every angle.

'If you decide to come to Perth within the next couple of months look me up. With your face and body you could be a model.'

So she'd made her arrangements, and now her parents must be told, because she didn't want to hurt them any more than she had to.

She closed her sketch-book, placing it along with her pencils in her bicycle basket. She would find the courage to tell them on New Year's Day, get it over with. . . .

'The Lord will punish you for disobeying your parents.'

Trinity threaded her fingers together in her lap and hid her thoughts behind a calm demeanour.

'I'm twenty-three years old. There's nothing for me here. I'll be able to find work in the city to support myself, and enrol in an arts course in the evenings.'

'I told you we should never have come here,' Mary James said, her mouth a thin, discontented line. 'God knows . . . I did my best. . . .'

Trinity bit her tongue as the recriminations started. She should have left without saying anything, avoiding the inevitable fuss. In the end, they wouldn't be able to stop her.

Her father tried, sending her to her room and locking her inside – a standard punishment. The window was barred – a legacy from her child-hood, when she used to climb out of the window at night to lie on her back and dream into the mystery of the night sky. They'd been shocked when she told them she'd been looking to see if God existed.

She smiled to herself. Time out, the punishment was called, which meant removing her offensive behaviour from an audience. Time out had taught her patience – it had taught her to be content with her own company – it had taught her that love had two faces, the public one, and the more elusive one she had to earn. She'd never seen the second face, no matter how hard she tried.

She sat on the bed, knowing they'd eventually leave for the store because the weekly bus was due in and they couldn't afford to lose the custom. When the door closed behind them she took a spare key from under her pillow and let herself out.

It took five minutes to throw her clothes into a plastic bag, then she went to her father's desk. There, in a document case, she found her birth certificate and extracted it. There was a piece of paper in the same enve-lope with her name on it.

She stared at it for a few seconds, then shrugged. No, it couldn't be her.

This was someone called Trinity Dysart. A distant relative she'd been named after, perhaps? She didn't have time to find out. She shoved the paper back into the document case, and placed it neatly back in place when she heard the bus rumble to a stop.

It fuelled its tank from the bowser outside her parents' store, where the passengers alighted to stretch their legs and buy chocolate, soft drinks and novels. The Jameses house was about a hundred metres further on, almost at the edge of town. The weekly bus to the city passed it.

Five minutes later Trinity stepped on to the road, and with a rapidly beating heart, held out a hand and hoped the driver would make an unscheduled stop.

When the bus slowed she saw her father on the veranda, a hand shading his forehead as he squinted up the road. He started to run, his arm raised on high, his mouth open – as if he were shouting her name.

Beyond him, and retreating into the distance, was the motherly figure of Doreen from the hotel, who was leaning on the worn millet broom she swept the veranda with.

If her father stopped her now she'd never leave! *Please God, don't let the driver see him*, she prayed. She paid her fare and hurried up the aisle to the seat at the back. The bus was already moving, the motion of its wheels disturbing clouds of cream-coloured dust.

Matthew James stopped in the middle of the road. He was panting from the effort of running, and his face was mottled red with effort. The dust swirled around him like a cloak, obliterating his feet so he appeared to be floating, like the vengeful God he'd constantly threatened her with. Then it settled, and she saw him clearly, as if for the first time. He was only a man.

She stared at him as he grew smaller and smaller until, finally, he and Hope's End were only a dot in the distance. Only then did she smile.

Trinity's affair with Adam Scaife didn't turn out quite as she'd imagined it. She wasn't as heartbroken as she would have expected, and decided to look upon the whole thing as a learning experience.

'I'm off back to London, darling,' he said one night in the rich, plummy voice she adored. 'If you ever get over there, look me up.'

She nodded, trying to appear as casual as he, but knowing she'd miss him. He was the nearest thing to a brother she'd known.

He propped himself up on one elbow and smiled down at her, handsome in his fine-boned, English sort of way. 'I've given your portfolio to the Bruno Demasi Agency. He thought your green eyes and honey-blonde hair were a delicious combination and is sure he can get you some magazine work. He wants to see you later on in the week. You will be nice to him, won't you darling?'

'Doesn't he provide models for those men's magazines?'

Adam frowned. 'I thought I'd cured you of being prudish? You've got a great body and have been photographed in the nude before.'

'Only by you. Your photographs are different – they're art, not pornography.'

Adam's eyes sharpened. 'Look, sweetie, I owe Bruno a bit of money. Just do it for my sake, will you? A favour for a favour. I taught you how to take photographs and develop and enlarge film. I also provided you with an expensive portfolio other women would have to pay thousands for.'

'I told you – I don't want to be a model.'

She'd spent a good deal of time during the last two months in being Adam's assistant, his domestic help and his source of finance – for he'd moved into her flat after he'd been evicted from his own. They also shared a bed, but purely on a platonic basis. She used it at night when he worked, and he used it during the day.

Trinity worked in a supermarket to provide a roof over their heads. She also acted as Adam's unpaid assistant when he brought clients home to film at weekends – sometimes doing the filming herself when he didn't turn up, and usually doing the developing.

And he'd thought he was doing her a favour? If there was a debt, it would have been adequately paid by now – and if women paid him thousands for a portfolio, and he had a job at Bruno Demasi's Swingers Club, why was he so hard up all the time?

One of the many things she'd learned since she'd left Hope's End was how to stick up for herself. 'And if I'm not nice to this Bruno Demasi?'

Adam shrugged and drew a finger across his throat. 'I promised him you'd help me out and if you don't, he'll come after you.'

'Why should he? I don't owe him anything.'

'He's never going to believe I didn't borrow the cash for both of us,' he pleaded, and she realized with a shock exactly what he was talking about. She took a good, long look at him. He'd lost weight and there were dark circles under his eyes.

No wonder he'd been so edgy – no wonder his eyes looked funny and he'd been too tired to offer her anything more than a platonic relationship.

'Oh, God. What are you hooked on, Adam?'

'I'm not hooked. I've been using smack, but I can stop anytime I want. I'll pay you what I owe you as soon as I get home, and I'll stop using it, I promise.' His eyes took on a worried expression. 'Look, I don't want you to get hurt, Trinity. Just do what Bruno wants, will you?'

'Like hell I will,' she spat, knowing she'd never let herself be shoved around by others again. 'As far as I'm concerned you can stay there as club photographer and pay off your debt before you go.'

'For God's sake!' he shouted. 'Bruno sacked me last night. Besides, my visa's nearly run out, so I have to leave the country.'

'So you're quite happy to run off with your tail between your legs and leave me to the mercy of a drug pusher. I refuse to let Bruno Demasi intimidate me, and so should you! Ask him if you can send him the money. If you don't, I will.'

'Okay,' he said wearily, 'I'll see him tomorrow.'

But when she woke Adam was gone – helping himself to the rent and the money she'd put aside for the electricity bill. He'd left a pawn ticket with a note in the jug.

He'd pawned his two cameras to buy his ticket home, he said, and the cameras were worth a great deal more. If she retrieved them, she might be able to sell them for more and pay off his debt to Bruno.

Then again ... if she kept them and used them, she could earn some money to pay Bruno Demasi off, she thought. It was better than being beaten up, and was worth a try. One thing she was not going to do was pose for pornographic pictures or bow to pressure. If Bruno threatened her she'd simply go to the police.

She found his number in the phone book, rang it and waited for what seemed to be an age before he answered.

'My name's Trinity,' she said.

'Hi babe.' Bruno's voice sounded thick, as though he'd just got out of bed. 'Scaife said you'd be in touch.'

'It's a pity you didn't check with me first. I understand he owes you money. I'm calling to tell you that whatever he got into, I had nothing to do with it.'

'Now, just one minute, babe—'

'No, you listen to me first, Bruno Demasi – and stop calling me babe. I have no intention of posing nude to pay off his debt.'

'U-huh? How do you intend to pay it off ... on your back? If so—'

'Don't be so insulting. I'm not a prostitute and wouldn't have the slightest idea how to go about being one. I'll take over Adam's job at the club and pay it off that way.'

There were a few moments of silence, then, 'Adam didn't tell me you were a photographer, as well.'

'I'm as good as he is,' she lied. 'How much does he owe you?'

She blanched when Bruno told her. 'I can't possibly afford to pay all that. I'll agree to pay off half.'

'Hang on a bit, doll—'

'No, you hang on ... *doll*. Adam has gone, and I don't owe you anything. He got his drugs from you, I believe.'

'*He what?*'

She ignored his affected outrage, figuring it stood to reason he wouldn't admit to doing anything criminal. 'I'll work off half his debt taking photographs, or you'll get nothing but trouble.'

'Are you threatening me?' he said, disbelief uppermost in his voice.

'Can you give me any reason why I shouldn't when you've been threatening me left, right, and centre? Adam said you'd cut my throat, so I haven't really got anything to lose.'

'He made me sound *that* tough?' Bruno chuckled. 'It might interest you to know I've never considered beating up a woman ... until now. Can I go back to bed? I had a late night and I'm not really in the mood to be hassled.'

'No you can't. I haven't finished. What about the job?'

'Okay, it's a deal.'

She took a deep breath. 'I need to get Adam's cameras from the pawn-broker first.'

'So ... get them.'

'I haven't got enough money. Would you consider lending it to me?'

His laughter had a maniacal edge to it. 'I suppose I could, seeing as how I own the hock-shop. Tell you what, I'll exchange the cameras for your portfolio. I want to frame the art shots and hang them on the wall in my office.'

They were beautiful photographs. The female form posed in all its fluid beauty – or so Adam had said.

'That portfolio is worth a lot of money.'

'Only to a model, otherwise they're worthless – on the other hand, I'm sure the woman who runs my modelling agency would be interested in having you on her books.'

So that was where he was trying to lead her.

'I have no intention of modelling for anyone. You can have the photographs on loan until the debt's paid off, then I get them back . . . and I want a hundred rolls of film as well,' she threw in as an after-thought.

'You drive a hard bargain, Trini. Do you want it in writing? I could ask my lawyer to draw up an agreement.'

'There's no need to be sarcastic. Just remember, I'm the innocent victim in this. Would it surprise you if I said I trusted you to keep your half of the bargain?'

'Not at all,' he said smoothly. 'I'm a very trustworthy person. But the thing is . . . can I trust you?'

'I could have left the country, like Adam did,' she pointed out, though how she'd have managed that with no money or passport was not even a debatable issue. 'I would actually prefer to have a gentleman's agreement with you.'

'Then I'll see you in my office at Swingers at seven o'clock, and we'll iron out the details and shake on it,' he said. 'The cameras and film will be waiting for you . . . and so will I. We'll have a man to man talk whilst we're at it.'

His voice was creamy-smooth, the amusement in it barely disguised. She failed to see what was so funny about the situation and was wondering if she was being foolish to trust him, when he ended the conversation by hanging up on her.

Bruno Demasi's office was situated above the night club, the décor of which was reminiscent of a set from an old black-and-white film, with shiny dance floor, bandstand, mirrors, chrome and smoked glass.

Trinity expected Bruno to be short, dark-haired and dark-eyed. In fact, he was tall, dark-haired, and his eyes were a vivid shade of blue. He wore black pants and a white shirt open at the neck. A tuxedo jacket was draped over the back of his chair, and hanging from the desk lamp, like a black, silk tongue, was a length of bow tie.

He was an intimidating thirtyish. Face to face with him, she lost the confidence she'd used on the phone – especially when the force of one finger stabbing at the chair nearly propelled her backwards into it without even touching her.

'Before you say anything, I want you to know something. I do not – repeat – *do not* supply people with drugs – and neither do I cut people's throats. I'm a legitimate businessman with varied interests, including a modelling agency and this club. If Adam was hooked on drugs, he got them elsewhere. Is that clear?'

His blue eyes were the colour of hyacinth petals, she thought.

'Then why did you sack him, Mr Demasi?'

'He stole money from the staff as well as from me. In short, he was dishonest. Had I known he was an addict I'd never have given him a loan.'

She found her courage. 'You *loaned* him the money he owes you?'

'He told me you were hooked on heroin and working the streets. He said he wanted to put you in a private rehab.'

Her eyes flew open. '*He what!* Thanks for the sympathy, but do I look as if I need rehabilitation?'

'You look disgustingly healthy to me.' He grinned. 'What about working the streets?'

She threw him a contemptuous smile. 'Are you offering to be my pimp, or what? If so, you're in line for a punch on the nose.'

His grin became broader. 'Tell your brother if he sets foot in Australia again, I'll wring his sneaky little neck for him.'

She stared at him. 'My brother. . . ?'

Bruno's smile faded. 'Isn't he?'

'Certainly not. We just shared a flat.' She blushed slightly under his steady gaze. The lack of intimacy in her life was none of his business. 'I . . . er . . . helped him with his photography.'

'And modelled for him?'

'But not like the women in those disgusting men's magazines you publish.'

'I'm surprised you've read them – but in actual fact I don't publish them, Bruno De'masti does. I just happen to have a similar name.'

Now she did blush. 'I only saw one because Adam left one on the couch. I just happened to pick it up and flick through it. . . .'

He raised an unbelieving eyebrow. 'And your girlish little heart was shocked to the core? That's hard to believe unless you've just graduated from a convent.'

'Not quite,' she said, with more irony than she'd intended. 'My parents were religious, and very strict. Adam sort of rescued me.'

'So you're not a hooker or a drug-addict, and Adam isn't your brother?'

'And you're not a drug-dealing pimp and porn publisher with an inclination to cut my throat?'

He shook his head. 'Correct . . . except for the inclination. That's growing stronger by the minute.'

She laughed. 'You look like a man who can adequately handle stress. Now, we'd better come to some arrangement about payment of Adam's debt.'

After gazing ruefully at her for a few seconds, Bruno shrugged. 'Under the circumstances I can't hold you responsible for his debt. I'll just keep his cameras to cover some of it and write the rest off.'

'I need one of the cameras,' she said, wondering how far she could push her luck. 'Adam took off with the rent and the cash for the electricity bill. I can earn it back with the Nikon. I'll use the other one in the club because it's got an automatic range-finder.'

He picked up the more expensive Nikon and turned it over. 'Is this the one you want? It looks complicated to me. Are you sure you know how to handle it?'

She took it from his hand, loaded it with a film, adjusted the range and aimed it at him.

'Say cheese.'

'I'd prefer not to.' He leaned back in his chair, raised an eyebrow and his lips took on a wry twist. She snapped him several times like that, going from slightly annoyed to laughing and very relaxed.

'Nice one,' she said. 'You're very photogenic, Mr Demasi.'

'Cut out the crap. The job's yours without it. You can start tomorrow night. You'll need something classy to wear, and your hair will have to be fixed.'

One hand flew to her pony tail. 'What's wrong with it?'

'It's not sophisticated enough. It makes you look about sixteen.' He came to sit on the corner of the desk, and gazed thoughtfully down at her. 'Hey, how old are you, anyway?'

'Twenty-three.'

'You're some looker,' he said softly, and her flustered blush made him smile. 'I really don't know what to make of you, babe, but I'll pick you up at ten.'

'For the last time, don't call me babe.' His grin floored her, but she mentally got up and kept slugging. 'And I'll be working at the supermarket tomorrow. I get an hour for lunch, starting at twelve.'

'Stand up,' he said, and she stood.

His glance slid down her body, absorbing it in one pass. 'Size ten. Nice and classy. Not too obvious and not too skinny. I'll pick something out myself. Shoes . . . six and a half . . . seven?'

He was close. 'Seven.'

'Be at Hair Lorenzo just after twelve. I'll make an appointment. And you might consider ditching the supermarket job. If you're a good photographer you'll earn more in one night than you will all week there, and the extra hours will prove to be too much.'

'OK.' She was at the door when she remembered her photographs. She turned. 'Where's my portfolio?'

'I wondered how long it would take you to remember it.'

The phone rang, and he snatched up the receiver.

'Bruno Demasi . . . Oh, hi Angel. I love you too.' His eyes took on a life of their own and a tender smile curved intimately at his mouth. 'Give me a minute, would you. I've got someone with me.'

He held the mouthpiece against his chest and sent a smile her way. 'I'll bring them in tomorrow, OK, Trini? And if you get stuck for the rent let me know. I'll give you an advance. How did you get here?'

'By train. City Central is only two stations from my flat.'

'From now on you use taxis to and from work. We keep late hours and the streets are dangerous. Tell the cashier to give you an employee number tag. Hang it on your key-ring and don't lose it. The club has an account, and without the tag you'll have to pay.'

'Thank you, Mr Demasi.'

His eyes and voice were laced with amusement. 'Let's come to an arrangement. I won't call you babe or doll, if you don't call me Mr Demasi. My name's Bruno.'

She felt like blowing Bruno a kiss – no not one, a hundred. But she didn't, because she remembered his smile and the way his eyes had lit up when Angel had phoned. Lucky Angel. She returned his grin with one of her own just before she shut the door, and saw his eyes widen.

She was nearly reeling when she reached the street, his aftershave still lingering in her brain like a sensual song. The fresh air brought her up to a sensible level for the moment it took the cab to arrive . . . but she was still on cloud nine when she went to bed.

It had been exactly two months since she'd left Hope's End. Her life had changed completely. It was exciting and a little scary – but she found her new independence to be exhilarating.

She'd written to her parents, but they hadn't answered, and when she'd tried to phone them she discovered they'd changed their number, and were now ex-directory.

They hadn't forgiven her for going against them, which wasn't entirely unexpected, but, until her letters were sent back unopened, she'd write now and again to let them know she was all right.

Just before she snuggled down in bed a plane flew overhead. She thought of Adam, who'd been the catalyst for change in her life.

What a waste of his talent – and how awful to be forced to steal from people to support his habit. She hoped he'd make it, and one day, when she'd made a success of her own life, she intended to go to England, look him up and return his cameras.

CHAPTER TEN

Pandora was groggy from lack of sleep, yet excited as she left Perth airport.

The wait to get through customs had been interminable. To be able to stretch her limbs after such a long and tedious journey was a relief after the cramped conditions of the plane, and the air smelled fresh after a day and a night of breathing canned oxygen.

'Good flight?' the cabbie inquired casually, as though he'd known her all her life.

'Now it's over.'

He chuckled. 'Yair, it's a bugger of a trip really and a hell of a time to arrive. Live here, do you, or just visiting family?'

'Visiting.' Whether or not family figured in the visit remained to be seen.

'At least it won't be too hot now it's April. Enjoy your trip, Australia's a beaut place,' he grunted – and, friendly as he was, she was grateful when he let the conversation lapse.

It was a fifteen-minute drive over wide and almost deserted roads to her destination. It had been raining and the tarmac glistened in the street lights.

Her accommodation was part of a motel, with doors fronting on to a strip of covered veranda, inside which was a garden and fenced-off swimming pool. An arrow pointed to a car park behind the building.

'G'day, love,' the porter said, despite the fact it was still night. With a minimum of fuss he booked her in, picked up her suitcase and strolled her across to her accommodation. 'Essentials are in the fridge and there's a supermarket just up the street,' he intoned. 'Have a nice stay.'

Feeling blissfully clean and relaxed after a shower, and not bothering to explore her accommodation, she fell into the soft, wide bed and instant unconsciousness.

It was midday when she woke.

A few minutes' drive away, a resigned Trinity was watching a man with a pair of scissors approaching her. She tried one last time to appeal to Lorenzo. 'Are you quite sure…?'

Lorenzo turned to Bruno and spoke in rapid-fire Italian.

'What did he say?'

Bruno grinned. 'He wanted to know how I can put up with a woman who talks so much – and said I should keep you under better control.'

She laughed. 'I wish I hadn't asked. All I wanted to know—'

'Lorenzo hears.' The hairdresser glared at her, picked up a length of hair and snipped it to chin length. 'I am the artist, like Michelangelo. Lorenzo says cut – you say no cut short – I cut anyway. You like, or else.' He scythed his scissors through the air, rapidly clicking them. 'Do not drive me inside out, please.'

Trinity surrendered and closed her eyes – opening one a chink a few seconds after the final click. Her hair hung in strands around her head and resembled a damp floor mop. She groaned silently, so as not to upset Lorenzo again. He attacked her with a brush and dryer. Ten minutes later the air grew cool around her and she could almost hear Lorenzo thinking.

'Mmmm,' Bruno hummed, so she could almost hear him thinking, too.

'*Bellissima.*' Lorenzo suddenly exclaimed, and she jumped and opened her eyes at the promise in his voice.

It was her, but a different her. A smooth, shining bob framed her face and curved into her jaw-line. When she moved her head it swung like silk into disarray, then back into position. Her eyes met Bruno's in the mirror.

He came to stand behind her, his hands on her shoulders. The admiration in his eyes wasn't too hard to take. 'It looks great, doesn't it?'

She might be a country girl and naive, but she wasn't stupid. He must employ several women, but she doubted if he went to all this trouble for them.

She couldn't tear her eyes away from his. 'I love it. Why are you being so nice to me, Bruno? It doesn't add up.'

'You suspect an ulterior motive?'

'Is there one?'

'Could be.' His smile was one of gentle irony. 'You have a disturbing effect on me. Just at this moment, I want to kiss you.'

Their minds had too much synergy for comfort – and she knew nothing about him except he loved someone he called Angel. He didn't wear a wedding ring, but that meant nothing either.

His eyes were a delicious blue against hers, his mouth…? Her own dried up so completely it was difficult to swallow – but she had to admit Bruno's mouth was delicious too, in a kind of way that made her feel odd.

'I … have to get back to work.'

And he removed her cape, slid a hand under her elbow and assisted her to her feet. They stared at each other for a few disconcerting seconds before she turned away, somewhat flustered. Lorenzo grinned, said something in Italian and patted her cheek. Bruno laughed.

'What did he say?' she asked, when they were outside on the pavement.

He hesitated for a moment, then he smiled. 'He says we have the look of a man and woman in love, and I should do something about it.'

'Ah … I see.' Hiding her embarrassment with a smile, she muttered, 'Italians are too romantic for their own good. Love at first sight only happens in movies and novels.'

'If that's the case, I guess I'll have to remain unmarried.' Which answered the question she hadn't been quite game enough to ask. He helped her into the car, a sleek black vehicle with a luxurious interior, a foreign name and a purring motor. 'I'll take you home.'

'I have to go back to work … remember.'

'But you've had no lunch, and you have to work tonight – for me.'

And she laughed because he was so transparent, and she decided she liked him – more than was good for her, she admitted, like an addiction to chocolate or eating a surfeit of strawberries – but she liked him.

'Okay, you've had your fun teasing me. Drop me off at the supermarket, I'll grab a sandwich on my break.'

He stopped right outside the shop in a no-parking zone, and, ignoring a tooting horn, leapt out of the driver's seat and opened the passenger door, bowing to her with a flourish, as if she was the Countess of Claremont or someone.

He pressed a large plastic bag in her hands and before she could go inside, tipped up her chin and gently kissed her mouth into trembling awareness. He smiled when she sighed. 'That's what I call teasing.'

It certainly was. She was in a bit of a daze when she started work, wondering what she was getting herself into.

*

Bruno was coming to grips with the fact that he'd fallen in love – despite the surprise of it.

Things like this didn't happen to him. He was too streetwise to be less than calculating where his love life was concerned – and avoided entanglements of any sort. Yet one look from Trini's green eyes had reduced him to rubble.

Trini James wasn't his usual type. There was no doubt she was naive. He'd never met a woman of her age so lacking in artifice or so unaware of her own attraction.

She'd twisted him into knots as soon as he'd set eyes on her portfolio. He'd eyed her artfully displayed flesh with nothing more than a carnal motive – something Adam had hinted was easily accessible – at a price.

Her husky voice on the phone that first morning had given him a serious cold-shower erection. In her portfolio, Adam had captured her sensual innocence and perfection – though her supposed habit had been a bit off-putting.

He gave a wry smile. He'd been played for a sucker – yet he'd be forever in Adam's debt because of it, *if* things went his way, which he intended they should.

Trini was delightful, she was trusting, innocent and fresh – everything a man had ever wanted in a woman. He'd never craved for anything so much as to buy her gifts, make love to her over and over again, and look after and protect her, so she'd never want to leave him.

Bruno hadn't considered marrying again. His four-year marriage had been a sham, his wife Maryanne a social alcoholic. They'd been separated for six bitter months when she'd wrapped herself around a telegraph pole so tightly, she and her car had almost become part of it.

That had been two years ago. There had been other women of course, none of them lasting more than a couple of months, because he'd never wanted permanent involvement – until now.

Now he wanted the lot. Marriage, children and love ever after – and he wanted it with Trinity James whom he'd known for exactly two days.

Despite the conviction he'd contracted a case of galloping lunacy, the only other problem as far as he could see, was Angel....

It was with some trepidation that Trini presented herself for work that evening. The gown she was wearing was short and loose, but it clung seductively to her curves – and her feet were now encased in shoes which seemed the equivalent of high-rise buildings to her.

She was assembled with the other staff in the manager's office. Bruno stayed in the background whilst Steve, the manager, issued instructions to them all. Every time she glanced at Bruno he was gazing back at her. She didn't know whether to smile at him or not, but she couldn't stop herself when he grinned at her.

'I hope you're listening to me,' Steve said, and she coloured under his scrutiny, and kept her eyes firmly fixed on him, even though Bruno was a magnetic shadow in the corner of her vision. She had such an irresistible urge to look at him again her eyes watered from the strain.

First, the bar staff came under scrutiny and inspection – then were dismissed, followed by the two doormen, the cloakroom attendants and hostesses.

'A minute, Délice,' Steve said. 'Do something about Trini's make-up, and I want you to keep an eye on her. If she gets into trouble, call me.'

'I won't get into any trouble.'

'In that dress, you've got to be kidding,' Délice said. 'It's got designer label written all over it and is a real tease. The men who frequent this place fantasize about high-class tarts, and with a face and figure like that…?' Her head swivelled round. 'Where the hell did you get her from, Steve?'

'Trini's a friend of *mine*,' Bruno said, and they smiled at each other.

'Hell, she looks too innocent to be in that dress. Have you gone nuts? They won't be able to keep their hands off her.'

'If they don't, I'll personally break their necks,' Bruno growled, which caused Steve and Délice to stare at each other, then at him.

Bruno shrugged. 'So, you're the manager, Steve. Sack her.'

'He will not. I need this job to pay the rent.' Trinity sent him an accusing look, which earned her a faint, reflective frown.

'You'll get a fair trial period first,' Steve said, his voice softer when he turned back to her. 'Your job is to sell photographs. Wait until the clientele look as though they're enjoying themselves, then go to the tables and ask. Make sure you get the names right and in the right order. Some of the clients will call you over. The films are developed outside the club and will be picked up by courier. Hand them to the cashier who'll supply you with another roll. You get to keep your tips and half of the take – the club will provide the film and keep copyright of the negatives – OK?'

'Fine,' she said, deliberately ignoring Bruno when she turned away.

'What's wrong with your feet?' Steve called out when she wobbled off towards the door with Délice.

'I'm not used to wearing high heels.'

'Well, get some practice in before it gets too busy. You look like a duck from behind. Délice, give her some tuition.'

'Lay off her, Steve. She'll soon pick it up, and with a face and body like hers, everyone will fall over themselves to pick her up if she trips.'

'And I'll be first in line,' Bruno said.

Blushing like a tomato, Trinity heard Bruno chuckle as the door shut behind them.

'I think I'll hang around and keep an eye on her,' Bruno said to Steve.

'I can do that. If she was involved with Adam, she might know who his dealer is. If the source originated from here I want it found, and the culprit out of the place.'

Bruno straightened up. 'You ex-coppers are all the same. I guarantee she doesn't know anything, and I don't want her involved in your investigations.'

Steve grinned as he poured them both a coffee. 'Got the hots for her, have you? That's not like you, Bruno. I thought you had a hands-off policy where employees are concerned.'

'This one's more than an employee. And it's more than just the hots. Hell, I'm going to marry this girl – Whoa...,' he protested, as Steve grabbed his hand and began to pump it up and down. 'She doesn't know it yet. I've only just met her.'

'Geez!' Steve stared at him and began to laugh. 'You poor sap. Couldn't you just take her to bed and get it out of your system?'

'If it were only that easy,' he said gloomily. 'I don't think she's had much experience with men – if any.'

Steve's voice dropped to an awed whisper. 'You've got to be kidding.'

They pondered on this for a while, staring at each other, then Bruno grinned a bit self-consciously. 'I shouldn't have let her start work here. She won't be able to handle it.'

'Say the word and I'll sack her.'

Which sounded like a good idea to Bruno, except Trini had taken him on trust and he didn't want to let her down. 'We'll see. I'll keep a close eye on her myself, and pull her out if she gets into any strife.'

As the evening progressed he observed that she drew respect from the clients, both male and female, and handled everything quite easily. On the odd occasion, when someone got out of line and he felt a murderous rage fill him, she simply smiled and shook her head or moved aside. Nor did she dance with anyone, or drink alcohol, despite being constantly invited.

He joined her on a break, fetching her some coffee and a sandwich. His attention drew notice, because he usually stayed here only on Steve's nights off, when the employees danced attendance on him.

His claim on her was obvious to everyone but her, which suited him, because the staff wouldn't give her any grief. To reinforce it, and because he wanted to feel her body against his, he said, 'Care to dance with me after the break, Trini?'

'I can't dance, and besides, my feet ache in these shoes.'

Her cosmetics were too thick, up close. Délice had been lavish, making her creamy skin look doll-like. Her green eyes were dramatic with mascara, her mouth was sensual, the lower lip full, and gleaming with lipstick.

He wanted to take out his handkerchief and wipe it from her face, uncover the innocent in her. 'How are you managing?' he said softly.

'Okay.' And her delicious bottom lip trembled a bit, and he saw the tiredness in her eyes. 'To be quite honest, I hate the job,' she said simply. 'I'm sorry Bruno, because you've been so kind, and understanding towards me. As soon as I've made enough money to pay my rent and electricity bill, you can get another photographer. And I'm sorry about the mix-up with the order forms.'

'What mix-up?'

'I was sure I handed nine to the cashier – but when the developed films were returned there were eleven packets. The cashier said the clients had ordered extra – but I hadn't made out an order form for extra prints. She told me anyone could make a mistake and she'd add it to their bill.'

His eyes hooded over slightly as he glanced at the cashier. So that's how Adam had managed it. It looked as though they'd have to get a new cashier – but at the moment, Trini's innocent green eyes were riveted on his and he was lost in them.

'I'm sorry to leave you,' she said again, sounding as though she meant it on a personal level, and Bruno chewed on a moment of nervousness.

'Why leave me? I happen to have fallen for you in big way.' *This was utterly crazy, he needed his head read.* 'I know we haven't known each other long, but would you consider marrying me?' He blurted it out like an adolescent in the throes of his very first love – which was exactly the effect she had on him.

She stared at him for a few interminable seconds whilst he held his breath and died a thousand deaths, then she smiled and said simply, 'My instinct tells me it would be a very good idea.'

Contrary to Bruno's expectations, Trini wasn't in the least bit reticent – just inexperienced. Her body responded to his touch and invited more with a hint of shyness that was endearing.

Her breasts were a delight, the shy little pink nubs swelling and tightening against his tongue. She tried not to make a sound, because she obviously didn't know whether she ought to or not.

He played games with her, exploring the erotic places of her gently, pushing her further and further until a tiny little gasp came, then another, then a moan, and when he could wait no longer and she was right on the brink, he pushed inside the tight moistness of her and her breath touched softly against his eardrum with, '*I love you, I love you, I love you,*' so he picked up her rhythm until he could be gentle no more and she fell over the edge with a cry that was purely orgasmic, with himself not long after.

If he hurt her she didn't show it – and he kept their union strictly conventional. Time to experiment and explore later, when she was used to his touch, easy with him and more sure of herself. Though his instinct told him to stay in her bed longer, he decided against it.

It was obviously her first time – and he wanted her to remember it with pleasure and love, not as a sexual ordeal.

It wasn't until Bruno was on his way home that he gave Angel a thought – and he wondered how he'd break it to her.

Trinity felt as though she might die of happiness when she woke. Bruno had made love to her, deliciously and gently, as if he'd known she'd never experienced love before – which of course he couldn't know, because she didn't go around wearing a label.

Now she was going to surprise him. She sprang from her bed, got a quick shower then pulling on jeans and sweater threw the photographs she'd taken of him in a folder and rang for a cab.

Bruno's home was of Spanish design, white-painted, the front wall capped by orange tiles and covered in brilliant orange-flowered bougainvillaea vine. She'd looked up the address in the phone book.

Her knock brought the patter of feet. A dark haired girl of about five answered the door and smiled at her.

'Who are you?' she said.

'Trinity James.' She thought she could smell gas. 'What's your name?'

'Angela Demasi. If you want to see my dad, you can't. He's asleep.'

'What about your mother?' she said, feeling her heart sink.

'She's dead.' Dark blue eyes achingly like Bruno's swept over her. 'Do you know how to make breakfast? I'm hungry.'

'Of course.' So this was Angel, who'd made Bruno's eyes light up with love. A little quiver of relief ran through her – and she *could* smell gas.

Angela smiled and held out a hand. 'You can come in and help me if you like. Our housekeeper isn't here today.'

They passed through several rooms with panoramic views of the river, to a kitchen big enough to hold a ball in.

The kitchen was a mess of flour and milk and the smell of gas was stronger here. Trinity turned off the gas taps and opened a window. 'What were you trying to make?'

'Pancakes – only the batter went all lumpy and I couldn't get the cooker to light.'

'Which is just as well, because you would have blown the kitchen up and yourself with it. Right, let's get this mess cleared up, then we'll start again.'

'The housekeeper does the cleaning.'

'You made the mess, you can help clean it up.'

Angela propped her elbows on the table, placed her head on her hands and issued a challenge. 'I don't have to.'

'You do if you want pancakes,' Trinity said firmly, 'and I just happen to make the best pancakes in the world.'

'With syrup?'

Her eyes darted to the sticky bottle. 'With syrup.'

Angela's smile was as heart-stopping as Bruno's. 'All right. I'll help.'

Twenty minutes later, when they were tucking into pancakes at the kitchen table and talking and laughing, Bruno walked in, his hair tousled from sleep and his lean, tanned body clad in a white towelling robe.

He stopped in his tracks, his eyes going wonderingly from one to the other, then an intimate smile touched his mouth and she found herself blushing and couldn't stop smiling.

'This is Trinity,' Angela said offhandedly. 'She makes the best pancakes in the world and I love her.'

'I know who it is. I love her too.'

His casual announcement left her feeling breathless. 'I came to show you your photographs.' *And because I couldn't stay away from you for another minute.*

His smile told her what she felt was written on her face in neon lights – and a delirious swirl of happiness flowed from her to him and back again, like an exchange of energy. She couldn't stop smiling and neither could he.

'You two look yukky!' Angela said, heaving a big sigh. 'I'm going to tidy up my room, because Trinity wants to see it, and she doesn't want to see it if it's messy.'

Bruno watched his daughter go with a surprised look on his face. 'How did you manage that?'

'She responds to reason like everyone else,' she said. 'Why didn't you tell me about her?'

'Everything happened so fast, I didn't really have time to. Do you mind?'

She took a step towards him and into his arms, nuzzling her face against his neck and loving him like crazy. 'How could I mind? She's terrific, and I want one exactly like her some day.'

'We'll probably have to take her on our honeymoon with us. I thought we could fly to Europe for a couple of months and do some touring around. Have you got a passport?'

Her face fell. 'I've never needed one, but I think I might still be a British citizen.'

'You'd better apply for one as soon as possible. I have a contact in Canberra who might be able to hurry them along.'

'When are we going?'

'Next month. I know a company who'll arrange everything. Marriage celebrant, guest list, the lot. If you'd prefer a church wedding…?'

'No … and I haven't got any guests I want to ask.'

'What about your parents?'

'They wouldn't approve – and they wouldn't come, anyway. They'd make me doubt myself and you, and I don't want to think in case this happens to be a dream and I wake up before everything I feel for you can be expressed.' Her eyes lifted to his, and he was smiling. 'I'll write and tell them afterwards.'

'Then we'll make it a small, private wedding with a few of my friends.'

'I wonder if Angela might like to be my bridesmaid when we get married,' she said, catching a glimpse of her peeping around the door from the corner of her eye. 'Do you think she'll mind sharing you with me?'

A small body hurtled across to them and Bruno scooped her up between them. Angela was all smiles and hugs.

'Are we all going to get married and go on a plane to get honey from the moon?'

Both of them laughed, exchanging glances across her head.

'Not quite – but we're going to fly across the world. First, we're going to collect Trini's things and she can move in here with us – that way, my two favourite girls can get to know one another.'

And she could get to know Bruno a whole lot better.

Four weeks later she became Bruno's wife and Angela's stepmother. As the three boarded the plane, Trinity had to pinch herself a couple of times to make sure it wasn't all a dream.

It had taken Pandora four weeks to find out where the James family were.

She was so excited she rang Bryn.

'Do you know what time it is?' he said.

She glanced at her watch. 'It's five past ten. I'm sorry, are you with a patient?'

'I'm not in the habit of taking patients to bed. It happens to be two o'clock in the morning.'

'Oh, Bryn. I'm so sorry.' She imagined his black hair sticking up in spikes and his green eyes looking all sleepy and sexy, like they did when she kissed him awake from his sleep. She smiled to herself. 'I miss you.'

'When you say it like that you give me a hard on,' he grumbled. 'But what the hell … I've had a permanent hard on since I met you.'

'Would you like me to talk dirty to you?'

She could have eaten the chuckle he gave. 'Better tell me your news first.'

'I've found the James family through the electoral roll. Trinity's on it as well. They live in a place called Hope's End.'

'*All hope abandon, ye who enter here*. I don't like the sound of the place. Be careful my darling. Use a go-between.'

Something so precious, she wanted to savour alone. 'I'll be careful.'

'Good,' he grunted. 'Now you can say something extremely dirty to me, after which I'll take a cold shower and stay awake until morning, when the patients will have to bear the brunt of my tiredness and lousy temper.'

'I love you,' she said to him, because parting from him had been like cutting herself in half, and hearing his voice had hammered it home to her. 'I love you so much it hurts.'

'There's a lovely thought to sleep on, *cariad*,' he purred, going all Welsh sing-song on her. 'Say it to me again, just so you can remember how it goes, mind you.'

'I love you, Bryn Llewellyn ... and if you think you're in trouble now, just wait until I get home.'

'I can't wait. Kiss me and hang up, woman, so I can get back to sleep.'

'Remember that cute little spot just behind your knee where I bite you?'

'Mmmm ...'

'It was reported that the longest telephone conversation took place between a severely bitten Welsh psychiatrist and his lover ...'

'... who bit him behind the knee from Australia with a pair of trained poisoned fangs.'

'... she'd extracted from a boa constrictor before she left England and fitted with a transmitter, coded to respond to a certain word ...'

'... which is?'

'Merlin.'

'Arrrrrggg,' he said, and hung up, leaving her laughing.

Using one of the business cards in the kitchen drawer she rang a car-hire company and arranged for a vehicle to be delivered. 'And could you tell me how far it is to a town called Hope's End?'

'It's in the wheat-belt, I think?' the woman on the other end said. 'I'll look it up and sent out a map with the route marked on it.'

'That's very nice of you.' Helpful people were par for the course here, even if they seemed casual about it.

'All part of the service. If it's where I think it is, it should take a couple of hours after you clear the city.'

Which was exactly how long it took, Pandora thought the next morning, when the tops of some silos appeared on the horizon of an otherwise flat, and uninteresting, landscape.

CHAPTER ELEVEN

Hope's End seemed to be an appropriate name for the place, Pandora thought. The town was tired, and seemed almost deserted, the wide, dirt road was holed and rutted from recent rain.

Her heart sank when she saw the faded green weather-board house with its wood-and-wire fence. Surely her daughter hadn't grown up here – surely she hadn't attended the dilapidated school with the sad, weed-infested playground and boarded-up windows?

Her fists tightened on the steering wheel. Robert Dysart had a lot to answer for – and for once in her life she began to hope that the myth described as hell actually existed and he was the main inhabitant.

A few cars were parked outside a hotel with a rusty tin roof. THE RAILWAY ARMS was painted above the door, though she couldn't see a railway station. Signs advertised *Foster's Beer* and *Bed and Board, weekly or nightly rates*. Next to it was a row of boarded-up shops – then a sun blistered general store. A little further on was what looked to be a church, a small white-painted place built of overlapping wooden boards.

Pandora's knock at the door went unanswered. She figured the Jameses couldn't have gone far in this place – she'd wait.

A woman came from the house opposite and pulled up a couple of weeds. She was old and withered – and her head kept swivelling towards the car. Eventually, she plucked up the courage to approach, her eyes sharp and curious in her brown-blotched face.

Why did people resort to such transparent manoeuvres instead of just approaching? she thought, winding down the window.

'You'd be looking for the Jameses, then.'

The woman's voice was loud, as if she suffered from deafness. Pandora smiled at her and raised her own voice several decibels above normal. 'That's right.'

'A relative, are you?'

It sounded to Pandora as though she was going to be subject to an inquisition. 'What makes you think that?'

The woman gave a self-congratulatory smile. 'I'm not so old I can't see the family resemblance. You're a pom, aren't you? Can't mistake that accent, either. Matthew James has been here nigh on twenty years and he's still as English as they come.'

Pandora led her gently towards where she wanted to go. 'It's hard for adults to lose the accent they grew up with, but I suppose children adapt much better and assimilate easier.'

'Some do and some don't.' The woman jerked a thumb at the Jameses house. 'That there youngster of theirs wasn't allowed to speak nothing but the proper Queen's English.' She sighed. 'They tried to bring her up as a proper little lady, they did. They might as well have stayed in England, if you ask me.'

The mention of her daughter had set a pulse fluttering in Pandora's jaw. She gently touched a finger against it.

'What's Trinity like? I haven't seen her since she was a baby.'

'A nice girl, that. Mind you, I haven't seen her for a while. I only got back from my sister's place on the coast last week. I go there every summer. This place is bad for my asthma. It's the dust, see.' She coughed and thumped a fist against her chest to draw attention to it. 'My sister has a place in Mandurah. Know it, do you?'

'I'm afraid not.' Pandora glanced at her watch. 'Do you have any idea of what time the Jameses get home?'

'About five-thirty.' Pandora's heart sank. 'They close the store about five though sometimes I don't know why they bother opening it.'

'You mean they run the store down here?'

'Have done for nigh on twenty years. You should go down there and surprise them. I expect they'll enjoy getting a visitor from England. That Mary's always going on about it. She gets real homesick, she does, but it puts people's backs up all the same, her running down Australia. They shouldn't have come if you ask me. Each to his own that's what I always—'

'Thank you, Mrs ... um.'

'Perkins ... Jean Perkins.'

Pandora opened the car door, got out and began to edge away from her. 'You've been very kind and it's been nice talking to you, Mrs Perkins.'

'I enjoy talking to a stranger for a change. Drop in for a cuppa if you feel like it before you leave, dear ... and call me Jean.' She sniffed and gazed towards the store. 'Most of us don't stand on ceremony in this country, not like some I could mention.'

How awful to be so lonely, Pandora thought. And how terrible for Mary James to be uprooted from the lushness of Dorset and transplanted to this desolate spot, especially when there was a beautiful city with a big, wide river running through it just a couple of hours' drive away.

But why was she wasting sympathy on her, when the woman had taken her daughter? She hardened her heart as she strode towards the store.

Matthew James looked up when she entered the dim interior of the shop. He had grizzled grey hair, grey eyes set in a stern, gaunt face and an air of terminal defeat.

'I didn't hear the bus come in.'

'I came by car.'

Tension gradually filled the space between them when he stared at her. 'Mary,' he said. 'Come here at once.'

A woman hurried from a back room. Her head jerked up and her eyes widened.

'Trin—' Her hand covered her mouth and she turned towards her husband, as if waiting for direction.

'Did you want something?' he said.

It was no use leading up to it. This pair had guessed exactly who she was. 'I want to know where my daughter is.'

'We don't know what you're talking about.'

'I think you do, Mr James. I'm Pandora Ross ... uh ... Dysart. Trinity is my daughter. As far as I'm concerned, you stole her.'

'Stole her? Trinity was legally adopted.' Disdain arced into his eyes. 'Her mother was a slut who tempted her father into sin.'

Having spent several years of her life shouldering the blame, and living with the shame she'd been taught to feel, Pandora had no intention of taking more of it – especially from this sanctimonious bastard. To save time, she gave it to him straight.

'Her father was Bishop Dysart. You knew that – it was on the birth certificate. He was also a paedophile, and I was just a child. The adoption was rushed through and was highly suspect. The judge, the lawyer, my grandfather and Bishop Robert Dysart conspired to deprive me of my child. Either you're a very stupid man, or you knew that too – which makes you culpable in my eyes – so don't quote religion at me, you hypocrite!'

When Mary James paled and gave a little moan, her husband quelled her with one look.

'We've got nothing to say to you.'

'I need to see Trinity and talk to her,' Pandora said. 'Don't you understand? All these years I've believed she was dead.'

'She *is* dead.'

Pandora stared at him, feeling as if the essence was draining from her body drop by drop. Her daughter couldn't be dead, it would be too cruel!

A bus drew up outside in a hiss of air-brakes.

'Get out and don't come back!' Matthew James said, and strode towards the door, tight-lipped.

She turned to Mary, tears in her eyes. 'I've come all the way from England for nothing, then?'

'Trinity isn't dead ... but I daren't defy him, like she did,' Mary whispered. Pandora's heart leaped into her throat. Years of unhappiness seemed to be etched into Mary's thin features.

'Mary, get yourself behind the counter,' Matthew James called out.

Pandora laid a restraining hand on her wrist. 'Please Mary ... she's my daughter. I must see her.'

'Come to the back of the church about seven, when it's dark,' Mary said from the side of her mouth. 'He sometimes falls asleep in his chair and I'll try and slip out.'

'Mary, come at once.' Matthew jerked a thumb towards the door. 'And you, young woman, get off my premises! We don't serve your type in here.'

Pandora booked a room at the hotel for the night.

Ignoring the astonished stares of the clientele and an approach from an obviously over-sexed truck-driver, she accepted the offer of a cool drink from the landlady and waited whilst a room was prepared.

Her room overlooked the back yard, and was reached by a flight of iron stairs and a rickety balcony with a washing-line slung between the posts.

'I've given you my best room, but I guess it's not what you're used to,' the landlady said. 'The whole place is falling down.'

Pandora remembered the cottage in Wales and grinned. Bryn would love this place. A sudden longing for him stabbed at her.

'Not much custom these days. Just a few regulars, the odd passers-by and the truck drivers come harvest time. The bathroom is at the end of the balcony. We haven't got any other guests, love, so you'll have it all to yourself.'

'It's very nice.' If one ignored the water stains on the ceiling, the worn lino and the sloping floor. The bed squeaked loudly when she sat on it and a small lizard skittered up the wall. Character accommodation, Bryn would call it.

The landlady gave a cheerful grin. 'Lucky you're not on your honeymoon, aye?'

For some reason, Pandora imagined herself and Bryn bouncing up and down on the wildly protesting bed. When she gave a peal of laughter, the landlady looked pleased that her joke had earned a laugh.

'My name's Doreen. If you want a drink or a chat just come down to the bar, love. I can fix you up with a meat pie for lunch. Help yourself to tea or coffee from the kitchen, it's down the stairs and on the left. I'll bring you up some dinner at about eight. Sausages, bacon, egg and chips do you? I haven't got anything else.'

'Fine,' Pandora said faintly, realizing – and not for the first time – that there was something very open and likeable about the average Australian. However, she felt too churned up inside to eat. 'I'm not very hungry, thank you. I'll get myself some tea later.'

'Right-oh. There's a fruit cake in the tin. Put the lid back on after, else the ants will find it. The miserable little sods carry off everything that's not nailed down if they can. I'll send my Jim up to oil that bed later on, otherwise the bloody thing will keep you awake all night.'

At least Doreen hadn't been curious about her, Pandora thought after she'd gone. She kicked off her shoes and settled herself cautiously on the squeaky bed for a think.

Trinity wasn't in town, that much was obvious. She certainly wasn't at the store, no one had answered her knock at the door of the house and the neighbour said she hadn't seen her lately. Another possibility occurred to her and the bed squealed a protest when she sat up. *What if she really was dead!*

After a few seconds she pulled herself out of her self-pity to rationalize the situation. Mary James wouldn't have told her Trinity was alive if she'd died.

But what if Mary James didn't know she was dead? What if Matthew had murdered her? It would be easy to get rid of a body in this country.

'For pity's sake, just listen to yourself,' she said out loud. 'If Bryn heard you he'd sign committal papers.'

Tears pricked her eyes. Her poor baby, how terrible to be brought up in this awful place by such dreadful parents. *Robert Dysart, may you rot in hell!*

The day ticked by so slowly that Pandora wanted to scream with frustration. By seven it was dark, and dark in Hope's End meant extra dark, with no street lights.

The moon gave no light, it was just an incandescent sliver – but what a breathtaking sky! So many stars, their beauty a definite compensation for the day.

As she groped her way past the eerie, long-abandoned houses, the wind breathed and sighed around her like the voices of spirits, and the night seemed full of faceless, whispering strangers.

Here and there an oblong of light spilled from one of the houses, where a curtain had been left undrawn. Something slithered across the road and into the long grass at the other side. Her heart began to race. She hoped she didn't tread on a snake.

The church was dark too, and locked. There was no sign of Mary James. Pandora waited for nearly an hour, her senses heightened to every rustle and snap, then she felt her way back to the hotel, trying not to break an ankle in the potholes, and with disappointment gnawing at her innards.

But she wasn't going to leave town without trying again. Tomorrow, she intended to confront the Jameses for a second time, and demand answers. She'd batter their door down if she had to!

She didn't have to. After a night of tossing and turning, she woke when Doreen knocked on the door bearing a breakfast tray. The bed gave a muted squeak when she sat up, determined not to be tamed, despite the application of oil.

Doreen threw an envelope on the bed. 'Someone shoved it under the door for you.'

It contained a letter and a full-length photograph. The subject of the photograph was obviously Trinity. Pandora devoured it with her eyes. The resemblance to herself was remarkable – the Dysart resemblance was remarkable! High, fine cheekbones, honey-coloured hair. Trinity wore an ankle-length white dress and carried three red roses. Pandora's relief and joy was such that she wanted to laugh and cry at the same time.

She was with a man of European descent by the look of him. Good-looking in a sensual sort of way; he had a nice smile, a red rose in his button hole and a possessive arm around Trinity. Between them was a small, dark-haired girl in a frilly dress, holding a basket of flowers. They were all smiling.

Laying the photograph on the bed she turned to the letter.

Dear Mother and Father,

An oddly formal beginning, Pandora thought.

> *I'm writing to tell you I'm now a married woman. Bruno Demasi is a businessman, and a widower with a five-year-old child, Angela. If you ever visit Perth you're welcome in our home.*
>
> *I hope you are both well, and have forgiven me for leaving. I would have rather left with your blessing, Father, and hope you will write and let me know how you are.*
>
> *For myself, I am well and very happy.*
>
> *Your daughter, Trinity Demasi.*

The letter was sad and very telling, with no mention of love. There was a piece of torn paper in the envelope with a few words scribbled on it.

> *This is the best I can do. He's cast her out and won't let me mention her, but that won't stop me thinking of her. When you see her, give her my love. Trinity doesn't know she's adopted. Mary James.*

'Oh, God!' Pandora groaned, knowing it made things that much harder, and forgetting Doreen was still in the room.

'Bad news, love?' Doreen picked up the photo and stared at it. 'Gone and got herself married, has she?'

'You know her?'

'Everyone in town knows Trinity. Nice kid, and good at painting and drawing. I've got a couple of her drawings somewhere. I'll look them out for you. She grew into a lovely, friendly girl, despite having parents like them as a handicap. I always knew she'd run away one day. I'm just surprised she waited so long.' A pair of friendly blue eyes lit on her. 'Your kid, is she?'

'How ... how did you know?'

'Saw the resemblance as soon as you walked in, didn't I? Besides, we all knew that miserable pair couldn't produce a beaut kid like that.' Doreen tucked her pillows behind her and handed her a cup of tea. There was a wealth of sympathy in her voice. 'You hardly look old enough to have a girl of that age. I suppose your parents made you give her up for adoption?'

'I was fifteen when I gave birth to her, and it was my grandparents.' Pandora's hands began to tremble and the brew slopped into the saucer. 'They told me she'd died. I've just found out they lied.'

'And you've come all this way looking for her, only to find she's not here.' Doreen patted her on the shoulder. 'Geez, you poor little sod. Life can be a fair cow, sometimes.'

The phraseology of this made Pandora want to laugh.

'Now, let's get some breakfast into you, then we can have a good chin-wag,' Doreen said. 'Everything looks better on a full stomach, I say. The eggs are straight out of the chook and into the pan. No battery hens round here. Poor little buggers – fancy standing in a cage all day laying eggs. It would drive you mad.'

A chicken squatting over a hot frying-pan flashed graphically into Pandora's mind. She managed to bite her lip long enough to dispel her rising hysteria.

Doreen stood over her whilst she ate bacon, eggs and sausages followed by toast and marmalade and washed down with tea so thick it resembled brown Windsor soup.

'That's better,' Doreen said when she finished. 'Now, let's be having it. A trouble shared is a trouble halved, they say, and you've got a face as long as a python's gullet.'

Which was the proverbial last straw as far as Pandora was concerned. She started laughing and couldn't stop for at least ten minutes.

Doreen handed her a packet of tissues when she almost hiccuped to a stop. She wore an ear-to-ear grin. 'Here, wipe your eyes and blow your snout, a good laugh does a body the power of good.'

When Pandora finally left town she'd almost run out of words, and, although her stomach was so distended she thought she'd burst, her body was weightless with the relief of having a sympathetic shoulder to lean on.

The best thing of all, perhaps, was lying on the seat beside her: a pencil sketch of the Railway Arms – and it was signed, *Trinity*.

She'd left with Doreen a promise she'd write, an invitation to visit if she ever came to England, and a letter to smuggle to Mary. She had the feeling Mary might need a friend – and Doreen was too big-hearted to turn anyone in need away from her door.

Mary James was outside the store sweeping dust from the veranda when Pandora drove past the shop. She neither looked up nor stopped her sweeping – but there was the merest hint of a smile on her face.

As soon as she got back to her holiday flat Pandora went through the phone book. There were only a few Demasis listed – and only one with the initial B.

She punched in the number, tapping her fingers impatiently when the phone rang out. Several more attempts brought no result.

The next morning, after another failed attempt, she looked up the address on the map and drove to the house. It was a nice area, the building overlooking the river. There was a car in the drive. She pulled in behind it and stared at the place, her heart thumping. A curtain was pulled aside and a woman stared back at her. She looked to be about fifty.

It was more than possible the B Demasi who lived here wasn't the Demasi she was looking for. But there was only one way to find out.

The door opened as she drew near, leaving a mesh security door between them. 'Can I help you?'

Pandora smiled at her. 'I'm looking for Mrs Trinity Demasi.'

A puzzled look came into the woman's eyes. 'She isn't here at the moment.'

Success! Her heart gave a tiny, elated leap. 'Oh, I see. Well, when she comes back will you tell her—'

'Mrs Demasi didn't say she had a sister, but the resemblance is too strong for you to be anything else.'

'I'm her mother,' Pandora said, claiming the distinction with some trepidation.

The woman smiled and unlocked the door. 'Come in and have some coffee. I'm Mrs Pearson, the housekeeper. Mrs Demasi did say, if you called, to give you a contact address. They're overseas, but I don't know when they'll be back. I just come over to dust, pick up the mail and keep my eye on the place whilst they're away. You were lucky to catch me here.'

Pandora hesitated for a moment. It seemed like a violation of privacy, when the mother Trinity had referred to was Mary James. But the urge to see where her daughter lived and to walk where she walked simply overwhelmed her.

Soon she was seated in the kitchen, and listening to Mrs Pearson prattle about the child called Angela and how she'd changed into a happy, well-behaved little thing since Trinity had married Mr Demasi.

'Swept him off his feet, she did – and she so nice and natural that the child took to her straight away, and if you don't mind me saying, Mrs James … you did a wonderful job bringing that girl up because she's so full of love it follows she must have been loved herself.'

Which brought Pandora to her feet, because the credit was not due to herself and conflicted with what she'd heard and knew of Matthew and Mary James. Deep inside her was such a rush of resentment, she knew she should get out of here fast before she said something to expose the farce.

But then, Mrs Pearson insisted on taking her for a tour of the house, showing her the rooms with their magical views of the river, and the bedroom where Angela slept. Next to it was the master bedroom, in which Trinity slept with her husband in the big, luxurious bed, and where she bathed in the turquoise and white *en-suite* with its spa.

When the woman went off to answer the phone Pandora slid open the dressing-table drawer and took a silk scarf, because she just had to have something Trinity had worn. After the act she felt like a sneak-thief, yet she couldn't bring herself to replace the scarf in the drawer.

She choked up to see a photo of her daughter lying on the bedside table. She'd been snapped in close-up, half-turning to laugh at the photographer. Her green eyes were both mischievous and shy. Pandora slipped it into her pocket when she heard the housekeeper return.

She had no right to be here or to take anything, even a memento, and she felt guilty that she'd deceived Mrs Pearson so easily, who seemed like a nice woman.

She held on to her tears long enough to get back to her holiday unit, then she fumbled her key in the lock because she couldn't see.

But the door was pulled open, and she was magically pulled into a pair of familiar arms. Hugged against a familiar chest she heard a familiar voice say, 'I just knew you'd need me, woman.'

He was still damp and soap-scented from the shower, and was dressed in his old, familiar towelling robe.

'Bryn, how did you know … how did you get here, you must be tired out … how did you get in?'

His laughter rumbled inside him, 'Instinct … by plane, and I slept like a top all the way so I'm not tired … and I told them I was Mr Rossiter.' He held her at arm's length and shook his head from side to side. 'What's happened, then?'

'Nothing yet. Trinity's married. I met her adoptive parents. He's horrible and mean – and a religious zealot. She's OK, I think, but well under her husband's thumb and a bit crushed. Mary James said Trinity doesn't know she's adopted, and I found out she's in Europe for the next couple of months at least. So I came all this way for nothing.'

He applied a tissue to her wet cheeks – his touch was gentle, his voice gruff. 'You know she's alive, so what are you bawling about?'

'I went to see where she lives, and the housekeeper showed me around.'

His eyes held hers. 'And you felt like an intruder in her life, and jealous of the people she loves and who love her – because you'd been denied her. Right?'

'Something like that. What I was thinking was horrible and unworthy of me – and I was just being stupid. I stole her scarf and a photograph and now I despise myself.'

'You mustn't, my darling. You were being human. The feelings you had are very natural under the circumstances – and a scarf and a photograph are hardly serious crime.'

'I didn't need you to tell me that, Bryn, but I'm glad you're here, anyway.' Her love for him seemed to pour out of her so she moved inside his arms again, and he whispered,

'I know what you're after, woman. My body.'

'Don't be so damned arrogant. You're not the only man with a torso like a god. The beaches around here are swarming with them.'

'Australian gods are ten a penny. But not everyone can snag a rare, Welsh god,' he murmured, edging back towards the bed and pulling her with him – and she mocked.

'Saint Taffy, the god of the daffodils. You've probably got a bunch growing out of your belly-button, boyo.'

He grinned, and his eyes lit up with a challenge. 'It's not a bunch of daffodils that's growing.'

She slipped her hand inside his robe and raised an eyebrow. 'Hell that's serious, Doc! If I could suggest a remedy for this strange affliction of yours … emasculation might be just the thing.'

'Shrink the shrink? How cruel can you get?' A smile appeared on his face. 'Mmmm, you've got lovely hands, and this is much nicer than your last suggestion. Less withering, in fact.'

'You have a way with words, Bryn. But the alternative remedy's not so long-lasting … and have I told you I love you, lately?'

'I've always preferred short and often, myself … and no you haven't.' His mouth captured hers, the kiss long and probing and altogether mind-blowing.

And then she came up for air and found she still had a bit of mind left. 'A pity because I've got long and often in mind.'

'I'll take that into consideration … mmmm … you might be able to convince me, but not if you keep that up.'

So she pushed him backwards on to the bed – slid out of her clothes, and did her very best to convince him.

CHAPTER TWELVE

The three weeks they'd spent together in Australia had been worth-while, Pandora's need to be with Bryn lessening her urgency to find her daughter.

'A holiday will do wonders for our stress levels,' he'd said, 'and we might as well see the place now we're here. I've heard the south-west corner is particularly impressive.'

Charmed and impressed by Perth, its surroundings and the populace, they ate too much, spent too much and made love in more places and positions than she'd imagined was possible. Her stress levels were practi-cally zero when they arrived back in England, loaded down with useless souvenirs which she suspected would ultimately end up in a church jumble sale.

They flaunted toffee-coloured tans, substituted *yair* for yes, and unashamedly carried a pair of furry koala bears for Lottie and Joy, and a didgeridoo Bryn was intent on mastering – once he'd mastered the art of carrying it safely through crowds without having to apologize every five minutes.

She was horrified to discover Bryn's car had been left in the car park at Heathrow. He grinned sheepishly at her when he paid the hefty fee. 'If I'd hung around to hire a car I'd never have made it to the airport.'

Seeing *Marianna* – the garden borders ablaze with flowers and the hawthorn trees covered in white blossoms and alive with bees, brought a lump to Pandora's throat – and suddenly her carefree holiday mood was replaced by the pressure of responsibility.

Next month the builders would move in and it would change. They'd be spared from most of the dust because their apartment would be isolated from the others, right from the beginning. But the noise and inconvenience would continue until the end of summer.

A pity Marianna had to be carved into apartments – but then, it was stupid rattling around in an oversized house, and she didn't want to end up a bankrupt old lady and leave a white elephant for her sons to inherit.

Marianna should be left to Trinity, she's more Dysart than any of you. The voice had come out of nowhere, and was so clear she almost looked around her to see where it was coming from.

Then Joy was on the doorstep, looking better than Pandora had ever seen her. Lottie came not long after, and there were hugs and kisses and Sam bounding around them all – and somehow, in the general mêlée, Bryn was forgotten.

But a man like Bryn wouldn't allow himself to be forgotten for long. He appeared in the lounge room, his arms full of koala bears, his voice rising above them all and a faint smile on his face. 'With all the commotion going on I nearly forgot these.'

Pandora hurried to his side. 'You're staying for coffee, aren't you?'

'I think I'd better get off home.' He took her face between his hands and gently kissed her. 'Thanks for the holiday. I'll call you in the morning.'

He drove off, the didgeridoo poking up through the sunroof like a decorated chimney.

Joy gave her a thoughtful look when she came in from seeing him off.

'That's a hell of a man you've got there. Are you going to marry him when the divorce is through?'

'I hadn't really thought about getting married again. It seems a pointless exercise these days. Besides, he hasn't asked me.'

'He will. I can see it in his eyes. He's ready to settle down, and if I were you I wouldn't leave it too long. Someone else might snap him up.'

'No one else would put up with him,' she said with a grin, but Joy's advice made her think. Another woman in his bed, and with or without a wedding ring on her finger, was too hard to take. To make sure of him, she rang him later that night, using the phone in her bedroom for privacy's sake.

He must have been asleep, because his foggy grunt sounded something like: 'Bin linlin.'

'This is a subliminal message so don't wake up,' she whispered. 'Do you want to get married when my divorce is through?'

'Yair ...'

She chuckled. 'Good ... now hang up the phone and go back to sleep like a good little shrink. You will forget everything I've said, but in exactly ten minutes you will wake up, ring me back and propose.'

There was a clatter and the line went dead.

She gazed at the dragon-ring on her finger, twisting it this way and that until Merlin appeared. He seemed to be smiling.

Exactly ten minutes later the phone rang. Bryn's voice was full of laughter.

'Stop trying to muck around with my subconscious. Will you marry me?'

She laughed with the sheer joy of loving him. 'Of course I will ... I thought you'd never ask.'

'For some reason, I had an irresistible urge to ... I must be in love.'

'You'd better be.' She switched off the light and snuggled under the sheets. 'Say something nice to me, Bryn. I can't sleep.'

'Neither can I ... *now.*'

It was a long time before sleep caught up with them as they discussed their future plans.

Things seemed to fall into place quite nicely.

'I was wondering,' Joy said the following day. 'Would you mind if I moved into Emily's old room? It won't be for a month, which is when the lease runs out on my flat. I'll pay my fair share of the expenses, of course.'

'What about your career?'

'There isn't much about for older actresses, but I'll stay on my agent's books. You never know in this game, something might turn up.'

Pandora considered it. Long term, she knew they'd clash if they lived together for any length of time. Joy would intrude on her life, and her age would give her natural precedence in the pecking order – which although she'd tolerate it, would result in tension. Besides, she needed the spare room for her boys.

On the other hand, Bryn had asked her to consider moving in with him. All that had been holding her back was Lottie's welfare.

'If Lottie's agreeable, you can. I know Marianna is my house, but it's *her* home, and always has been.'

'Actually, it was her idea. She said I shouldn't live alone, and she's right. She thinks I need someone to look after me – and said if I still want to act, there's an amateur dramatic company in town she's thinking of joining herself.'

'I didn't know Lottie could act?'

'She wants me to teach her. Bloody amateurs!' Joy snorted. 'They're so aware of themselves. The men swan around like Noel Coward with stupid, smug grins on their faces, and the women are terribly twee, gushing all over the place like Jessie Matthews and flapping their hands because they don't know what else to do with them.'

Pandora laughed at the bitchy remark. 'A bit before my time, really. Still, I can't imagine Lottie acting.'

'Lottie's more capable than you and me put together. I really don't know what the fuss was all about.' Joy drew her towards the open French window. 'Come outside for a few minutes. I'm dying for a cigarette and she won't let me smoke indoors. I swear, she gets more like Emily every day. I didn't think she had it in her.' She lit up with every sign of satisfaction. 'How did you manage the transformation?'

Pandora smiled to herself. 'I didn't really do anything. Lottie just needed a large injection of self-esteem and confidence. She got that through her job and the people she associates with now. There's nothing wrong with her now she's had a bit of help.'

Joy's eyes squinted against the smoke. 'Like I said, that's one terrific man you've got there. Lottie's told me all about him, and Emily's got a lot to answer for.'

'You really don't have to try and sell Bryn to me. As for Emily, she did the best she was capable of, I guess. We all work within the boundary of our upbringing.'

'I certainly don't.' Joy's expression had a provocative quality to it. 'I can't believe you've forgiven her for what she did to you.'

'Carrying emotional baggage around doesn't achieve anything.' *If much more of Bryn rubbed off on her she'd be able to write an agony column.* 'I'm close to finding my daughter. I've seen where she grew up – been to her home. Would you believe she doesn't even know she was adopted?' She closed her eyes for a moment, smiling as she visualized Trinity's face. 'She's in Italy with her husband at the moment. I've got her address and I'm going to write to her today.'

'Be careful, Pandora. You're a stranger to her.'

Her nails curled into her palms, and before she could stop herself she said, 'Oh, for God's sake, don't you start giving me advice as well, Joy. Trinity's my daughter and this is really none of your business.'

Neither was it Bryn's business come to that – and hanging her emotions out for everyone to see, like they did at the meetings he'd recommended, wasn't really her style. What did he know about mother and daughter relationships? He was a man.

She wished she hadn't been too sharp when she saw Joy's wounded expression. 'I'm sorry, Joy. I didn't mean to be so touchy.'

'Perhaps it would be better if I didn't move in.'

'Oh, don't go all huffy on me. I want to move in with Bryn. We've decided to marry as soon as the divorce is through. I know Lottie's perfectly capable of looking after herself, but I don't like leaving her alone. What if she has a relapse or something? In short, I'm being selfish. If you don't move in I won't be able to move out!'

'I thought it was something like that. We both know we wouldn't be able to live together for long. I'm too abrasive and you're too ...'

Pandora lifted an eyebrow.

'Persistent might be a kind word to use. Once you've made up your mind to something you just do things your own way, whatever anyone else says. I hope Bryn knows what he's letting himself in for, because if he doesn't, he's got a shock coming to him.'

Pandora laughed, because despite her earlier thoughts, she was quite sure her big, beautiful Bryn knew her better than she knew herself – and she'd never be able to push him too far. He wouldn't let her.

The letter to Trinity was far harder to write than she'd imagined it would be.

I was fifteen when you were born ...

It made her sound precocious so she crossed it out.

Your father was a paedophile...? A bishop...? My grandfather's brother? 'Shit!' She screwed it up and threw it into the wastepaper-basket.

My grandparents told me you were dead. Don't use excuses or emotional blackmail, and don't try to shift the blame!

When I was visiting Australia recently, I visited Hope's End and spoke to your adoptive parents. Mary said to give you her love.

The pile of paper in the wastepaper-basket grew larger and larger. It was Mollie Jackson's cleaning day. Outside the door, the whine of the vacuum cleaner grew louder and louder. She couldn't think.

Your home is beautiful – invasion of privacy. *I never stopped loving you ...*

She groaned. Letter-writing had never seemed so hard. She chewed the end of her pen and stared out of the window without seeing anything. Keep it straightforward.

Dear Trinity,

My name is Pandora Rossiter {nee Dysart}. I am your birth mother. I understand you're unaware of the fact you were adopted by Matthew and Mary James, and I do hope this letter doesn't come as too much of shock.

I have been to Australia to find you, and whilst there, met your adoptive parents. Mary asked me to give you her love.

I would very much like to meet you, and know you will have questions about your background – which I'll endeavour to answer honestly.

Yours sincerely,
Pandora.

'Yoo-hoo! Can I do your room, Mrs Rossiter?'

'Give me a minute, Mollie.' She shoved the letter into an envelope, addressed and sealed it, then stood it on the dressing-table. The contents seemed a bit stark. She wanted to think about it a bit more, soften it somehow – let Trinity know she'd always been loved and never forgotten, without getting nauseatingly maudlin about it.

Tipping the contents of the wastepaper-basket into the grate, she put a match to them and watched them flame and curl until all was ash. She wasn't leaving anything about for Mollie to read.

When Mollie's eyes darted to the smoking grate Pandora smiled and whistled for Sam, who was quite happy to exchange a snooze in his basket for a walk.

Joy was standing outside, trying to light a cigarette, and swearing each time her throwaway lighter sparked out in the wind.

Pandora took a box of matches from her pocket and threw them to her. 'Try these.'

'Thanks, Pandora. I'll be catching the afternoon train. Will you be back in time to drive me to the station?'

'Sure, it's not even lunchtime yet and I need to go into Poole anyway.'

There was a fresh breeze coming off the sea and Pandora headed for the beach. The waves were capped with rushing white foam, and the seagulls wheeled and banked on the air-currents like gliders. The bustle suited her mood, because right now she felt like punching the air with frustration.

At the same time, the pit of her stomach vibrated with a slowly growing happiness. She sat on the sand, her hair blowing in the wind, hugging her knees against her chest. Sam, like the fool he was, frenziedly ran up and down the shoreline barking at seagulls.

She wondered if Trinity would like it here at Marianna.

Her smile became dreamy and her eyes focused on a sailing-boat on the horizon. She could tell Trinity about Marianna in her letter – and tell her about her brothers. Adrian might make it to Australia one day – and it would be nice for him to have family there to visit.

There had been postcards from him waiting for her when she arrived home from Australia – postcards from France, Spain, Italy and Greece. They were heading by boat to Cyprus, then finding their way across Russia and down into India before heading through the far eastern countries into Australia.

Don't worry if you don't hear from me for a while, Adrian had written. But she would – and he knew she would, that's why he'd said it. The awful thing was, she didn't have an address she could write back to, so that she could keep up the pretence of normality.

Why did men have to be adventurers? Why couldn't they stay at home like daughters did? Like Wynn Llewellyn's daughters in Wales did – her daughters clones of her, so the woman had grown old amongst familiar faces, and surrounded by grandchildren who loved her?

Her thumb stroked across the cool surface of the ring Bryn had given her.

'*And isn't Olwyn the spitting image of you, Mrs Llewellyn? And your Bronwyn and Mary grown so fat, and the twins, Cordelia and Glenda not looking a day older. And how's your boy, Bryn keeping now?*'

She pictured Wynn's eyes lighting up like fiery Welsh coals.

'*Proud of him, I am, and him married now, Mrs Morgan. An uppity piece, his wife, and both of them too good for the likes of us,*' and Wynn Llewellyn's lips pursing in disapproval and Owen glowering down at her – looking exactly like Bryn would look at that age, so she laughed.

'Are you losing your senses, woman? Didn't you hear me?'

Strange that Bryn would appear in the middle of her musing – like magic, as if he'd been summoned to her side by Merlin himself. She knew then that she'd follow his advice about contacting Trinity. She held out her arms and he took her hands in his, pulling her effortlessly up and against him.

'You invited me for lunch last night, remember?'

'I can't remember doing that.'

His smile was something special, drawing her attention to the sensuousness of his lips, so she remembered the intimacy of their relationship.

'It's a good job I've brought a hamper, then. I hope you like champagne. I thought you might put on a floaty dress and that hat with flowers I bought you in Australia, and we'd eat romantically on the patio – just the two of us.'

'After which … like in those old films, an orchestra will start to play and we'll dance through town with the wind romantically blowing at my chiffon bits and you whirling me off my feet. Then you'll run up the walls of the nearest high-rise building and stop the traffic, whilst I stand on the head of a stone lion in Trafalgar Square and burst into song.'

'Forget the song.'

Which brought her mind back to the trip to Wales and the night they'd made love for the first time.

'Okay, you can stand on the lion and do the singing, I'll run up the high-rise.'

'Like you ran up the Welsh hill?' His eyes were dancing with laughter, as if he knew what she'd been thinking, and thoroughly approved.

Her smile reflected the love she felt for him, and she wondered what she'd done to deserve all this happiness.

Simeon was waiting for her when they got back. He winked at her when Bryn glowered at him, and kissed her impersonally on the lips in a way that reminded her of Gerald.

'I'm not intruding, am I?'

'You most certainly are,' Bryn said. 'We were about to have lunch.'

'Shut up, you macho idiot,' she said, and smiling at Simeon made the introductions before turning to Bryn. 'Simeon is my lawyer, so be careful, because anything you say might be taken down and used in evidence.'

'I know my rights," he said, his frown replaced by a smile as he held out his hand. 'Put this on record. I adore her, and any man who comes between us is likely to regret it.'

'I'll try not to then,' Simeon said. 'I've heard so much about you it's nice to meet you, at last. Didn't you bid against me for something at the auction?'

'I believe I did,' Bryn said innocently, squeezing Simeon's hand hard enough to make him grimace. 'And I believe you've just conspired with Pandora to have a piece of me.'

'You could be right. Don't bully him, Bryn. I happen to like him.' She pushed Bryn into a chair, kissed him and turned to Simeon. 'Stay for lunch. Bryn has brought all sorts of goodies in a hamper.'

'It won't stretch far, here comes Joy,' Bryn said gloomily.

'Are we going to have a party?' she said brightly.

Which Pandora thought wasn't a bad idea, and when supplemented by a tin of potato salad and a quiche Lottie had made, the hamper of chicken, caviar and salad – when washed down by a glass of champagne each – went far enough.

'What did you come to see me about?' she said to Simeon afterwards when they had a moment alone together.

'I heard you were back and just came over to see how your reunion with your daughter went.'

'It hasn't yet.' She gave him a quick run-down of events. 'I've written to her, but thought it might be better if I took Bryn's advice and used a go-between.'

'It's certainly advisable. I'd be quite happy to act for you free of charge, in this. I propose a letter would be in order first, giving her the salient facts. Then, if she's interested in pursuing it, I'll arrange a meeting with her and tell her the whole story.'

Bryn came to perch on the arm of her chair and took her hand in his when she gave an exasperated sigh and said. 'Where do I fit into this?'

'If … and only *if* she wants to meet you,' Bryn said bluntly. 'Listen to sense Pandora, and don't get your hopes up too high.'

How could she not get her hopes up after having come this far? It was like telling the sun not to rise or set. Trinity was so close to her she could almost smell her perfume and feel the warmth of her skin. She'd been born upstairs in the room Pandora still slept in. Her sketch of the Railway Arms had been framed, and was now hanging on the bedroom wall. The snapshot Pandora had stolen was in a soft leather frame on her dressing table and her scarf was kept under the pillow, because it smelled faintly of her perfume.

There were reminders of Trinity everywhere. Her daughter was so lodged in her heart and mind, she'd curl up and die if Simeon stuffed this up.

'Have you done this sort of thing before, Simeon,' she said, the anxiety in her voice clearly evident, even to herself. 'I don't know what I'd do if…?' She couldn't voice her concern in case an evil spell was cast over everything. She didn't have to rub the surface of her ring, either, Bryn did it for her.

'I have daughters myself,' Simeon reminded her. 'I'll be extra careful, I promise – and if you want me to take her a letter ... well, if she seems receptive I'll give it to her.'

'Don't go overboard on the emotional stuff,' Bryn said gently. 'You're a complete stranger to her, and it might frighten her off. It might be a good idea to mention you've met her adoptive parents. It will make her feel a bit safer.'

She smiled to herself. 'It's already written.'

But when Simeon was ready to go and she went to fetch it from her dressing table, the letter was gone.

Dread filled her as she made her way to Joy's room.

'There was a letter on my dressing-table. Do you know what happened to it?'

Joy snapped the locks on her case and hefted it to the floor. 'Mollie Jackson said she was going to the post office and would post it, so I gave her the money for a stamp.'

Pandora felt sick. In one fell swoop, Joy had managed to undo everything she'd achieved. She wanted to put her hands around Joy's scrawny throat and squeeze the breath from her body. As for Mollie Jackson, why didn't she keep her interfering nose where it belonged? She wouldn't put it past the woman to steam it open and read it first. The Aussies had a good term for someone inquisitive like her. Sticky beak!

She clenched and unclenched her fists, swallowing her ire and reminding herself it wasn't Joy's fault. She shouldn't have left the letter there in the first place.

'Is everything all right? You look a bit pale.'

She felt more than pale, because the enormity of what had happened was robbing her lungs of breath. She sucked at the air in panic, her chest feeling like a pair of overworked bellows and her head growing lighter and lighter, as if she were inhaling gas.

'Come quickly!' she heard Joy cry above the roaring in her ears. 'Get a paper bag.'

The bag clamped over her mouth smelled of mushrooms. *Flap in ... flap out ... flap ... flap ... flap.* Her eyes felt as round as flying saucers. Beyond Bryn, Simeon and Joy were anxiously gazing on. Why couldn't they leave her to expire in private instead of looking on?

Bystanders said Mrs Rossiter's eyes bulged alarmingly from their sockets whilst first aid was administered.

Bryn's hand was strong against her diaphragm, slowing her breathing down. His voice was relentless and reassuring. 'In and hold ... out and hold it … good, again … in and hold,' and a few moments later she was breathing by herself and the air was clean and sweet. Her eyes lost their bulgy feel, the panic subsided.

'Okay now?'

She nodded. 'I don't know what's happening to me lately. One minute I was all right and the next…?' *Good grief! I used to pride myself on my composure, now I'm falling to pieces.*

Bryn sent Joy to make her a cup of tea.

'You hyperventilated,' he said. 'If it happens again, you'll know what to do.' His eyes touched against hers, the concern in them making her want to cry. 'Would you mind telling me what triggered this off?'

'I wrote a letter to Trinity,' she said weakly. 'I left it on my dressing-table and Mollie Jackson has posted it.'

'Do you have her phone number? She might still have it.'

'Why didn't I think of that?' She headed for the phone, but it was a useless exercise. The letter had been posted two hours before in the main post office.

'I was only trying to do you a favour,' Mollie said, sounding huffish, 'and I did ask, so that actress woman needn't blame it on me. It were sealed, so how was I to know you didn't want it posted?'

'It's OK, Mollie,' she said lamely. 'You're not in any trouble. I just thought it might have been accidentally thrown away.'

Her face was glum when she turned to the two men.

'I think the situation needs some damage control,' Simeon said gently. 'When I write my letter, I'll explain what happened and apologize on your behalf. Can you give me a copy of yours, so I know exactly what I'm dealing with?'

She scribbled out a copy, handing it first to Bryn, who read it and passed judgement with an unconvincing, 'Well, it's not too bad, I suppose. A bit on the blunt side.'

'Don't start lying to spare my feelings now, Bryn. I've made a hash of the whole thing and you know it.'

'I only know one thing,' he said gently. 'Human reaction to certain situations is unpredictable. She might not be as sensitive or as shocked about this as I first thought. Imagine the worst and hope for the best, Pandora.'

But she could only imagine how Trinity would feel when she received the letter – how her very foundations would be pulled from under her. She should have thought of it earlier, but she'd been too focused on her own feelings to consider anyone else's.

When the letter arrived at its destination, if her daughter refused to have anything to do with her, she wouldn't blame her one little bit.

Lottie pulled her cardigan around her as she scurried into the unused part of the house. Empty of furniture now, it was full of echoes – and voices!

The workmen had arrived early. Sliding into the old master bedroom, the one with plaster cupids flying around the ceiling, her glance darted around, looking for somewhere to hide. She scuttled behind the door, her breath held tightly inside as footsteps tramped up the curving staircase.

The men paused outside the door, and she jumped as a tarpaulin was heaved into the room and thudded to the floor, her heart going a mile to the minute. Through the crack in the doorjamb she saw a tool box being lowered to the floor

'We'll have a cuppa first,' the older man in charge said. 'Mind you do that plastering around the fireplace properly, Pete. If you can't get it right, ask me or your brother to give you a hand.'

BEN SHAFTON AND SONS, *Alterations and Renovations by Master Craftsmen*, the sign on the side of the man's truck said. Lottie had met Ben before, when she'd delivered meals-on-wheels to his mother. She'd been going out and he'd been going in and he'd stood to one side, doffed his cap and smiled at her.

His sons didn't look much like him, or much like each other. One was tall and thin, the other short and stocky. She felt sorry for them because they had holes in their socks and their shirts had frayed collars. She'd already darned a hole in the elbows of a ragged jumper that had been left lying about.

As soon as they'd strolled off towards the back of the house she headed for the fireplace. Another day, and she wouldn't have been able to retrieve the photograph for Pandora.

It had been several years since she'd secreted it in the wall cavity behind the bricks. It had been her one act of defiance – for Emily Dysart would have locked her in the attic had she known about it.

She smiled to herself. Those days were over. Her mother had gone, her place taken by Pandora. Lottie had always loved Pandora, even though she frightened her a little bit. Pandora had a stillness about her when she was annoyed, and she cocked her head to one side and her eyes challenged, like a cat about to spring.

She'd arrived, a noisy bundle of squalling baby who 'resembled a rat',

Lottie's brother, Leander, had said unfairly. Lottie had thought she was the most beautiful baby she'd ever seen.

That had been just before *Lottie's dreadful accident* which hadn't been an accident at all, as the Dysarts well knew but wouldn't admit.

Robert had been summoned, she remembered. He'd come from a church service, looking like a holy angel in his robe. He'd cried, and denied it, shaking his head and looking at her with such sorrow in his eyes she'd begun to wonder if she was insane and had imagined it all.

Everyone had shouted at her at the same time, so her head went into a spin. They'd told her she was a liar and mustn't ever speak of it again. Their passion had crushed her. She'd been thrashed by her father, and locked in the attic for a week by her mother until she'd admitted her sin.

The attic had been cold and dark, and filled with unimaginable horrors at night, so she'd been forced to close her mind to what was lurking there in the darkness. She'd never been naughty again, and she still couldn't go near the attic, not even in the daylight.

She'd allowed another Lottie to take her over, leaving the real Lottie in hiding so she couldn't be hurt again. Yet, still the world had seemed a great big lie to her – adults not the trusting human beings she'd once thought they were. The real Lottie didn't want the other Lottie to grow up to be an adult who wouldn't lie and deny what they knew to be the truth.

Years later, the same thing had happened to Pandora.

'*Bullshit!*' Pandora had shouted when they'd accused her of lying about Robert Dysart, which had shocked everyone but the real Lottie, because she knew the truth.

The attic was no longer in use for punishment after *Lottie's dreadful accident*. Emily Dysart had slapped Pandora hard across the face, instead.

'You take after your mother. Blood will out, and Grace had no breeding.'

'If she had, she wouldn't have married a Dysart,' Pandora had spat out, her anger keeping her tears at bay, and determined to get the last word in. 'However much he denies it, Robert Dysart is the father of my baby.'

Pandora's baby had been beautiful, and had been the image of Robert. Her father and mother had seen the truth then, but they wouldn't admit it. They hadn't been able to stand being wrong, and had sent the baby away. Lottie closed her eyes, remembering the child in Pandora's arms, so small and dainty and sweet. Lottie had sneaked in and taken a photograph of them together, asleep.

In the morning the infant was gone, and Pandora's eyes were dead with the grief she felt. From that day on Lottie had hated her parents. She knew Pandora was looking for her child, and knew she'd never find that child – only the adult she'd become. The photograph would bring her comfort.

But the brick wouldn't come out however much she tugged. 'Come on,' she said, applying all her strength to it.

It refused to budge. Lottie took a chisel and a hammer from the tool box and began tapping. Cement chips flew from around the brick. 'Damn!' she cried out when a piece of brick hit her on the cheek. It was the most defiant word she could think of, and one everybody at the centre used when the soup burnt or the cabbage cooked before the potatoes were done – which was stupid really, because cooking was all a matter of timing and working things out in your head. She'd have rather have said something more daring and wicked, like Pandora's cry of *bullshit!* but she didn't dare.

'Are you trying to ruin my best chisel, missus?'

Colour rushed into her face and she spun around, her eyes widening at the sight of Ben, who although he was smiling had an anxious look in his eyes.

'I'm sorry … I'm sorry.' Her eyes darted to the door, seeking a way to escape. She remembered she was strong now, and she had every right to be in this room. Besides, if she ran she'd never get the tin for Pandora, and she desperately wanted her to have the photograph.

Ben hunkered down on his heels and gently took the chisel from her hands. 'You're using it all wrong, see.' He inserted it into the crack and gently tapped the end. A sizeable chunk of plaster fell out. 'Got something hidden in here, have you?'

She nodded, noticing that the navy-blue bib-and-brace overalls he wore needed ironing. 'It's a tin box. It's been there for over twenty years.'

'You're lucky it hasn't been plastered over.'

She tried to sound confident, like Pandora always did. 'Yes, I'm so sorry if I've interrupted your work. You see, I'd completely forgotten about the box, and then my niece Pandora – Mrs Rossiter, I mean – said something which made me suddenly remember it.' And although she didn't realize, she didn't sound like Pandora at all, just Lottie trying to sound like Pandora, and her eyes were blue and vulnerable and appealing. 'I'm sorry about your chisel.'

'No harm done, missus. I can soon sharpen it up again.'

'My name isn't missus, it's Lottie.' The chips were flying thick and fast now. 'I'm sorry I'm putting you to so much trouble.'

'No trouble at all.' Ben pulled the brick from the wall, leaving a cavity, into which he inserted his hand and moved it around. A rusty Oxo tin came into view. 'This it?'

She nodded, smiling at him when he placed it in her outstretched hand. His eyes were brown and kind, reminding her of Sam's – only Sam sometimes looked peeved when his comfort was being threatened and Ben definitely didn't.

'I owe you something for mending my jumper,' he said. 'The boys and I aren't much good at darning and such, and, as you know, my mother's hands are crippled up with arthritis. I don't know how she'd manage without people like you volunteering their time.'

'I enjoy it,' she said shyly, and feeling warmth flood through her because he'd remembered her from their brief encounter. 'Doesn't your wife enjoy darning?'

'My Maisie passed over when my eldest boy was ten.'

'You poor things. Goodness, you must miss her quite dreadfully.' Lottie thought how sad death was when children were left without a mother to look after them, which was followed quickly by another thought – that *some* mothers didn't give their children even the basics, like love and trust. 'If you need any mending done, just ask me. I love doing things like that. I hope your wife didn't suffer too much.'

'Maisie went real quick,' Ben said. 'It started with a cold. She wouldn't see a doctor, she said she could get over it by herself. I had to go up North for a job for a week or so.' He shook his head. 'Funny, but you never think a cold is going to turn nasty. When I got back I found the kids being looked after by my mum. Maisie had taken to her bed and didn't have the energy to lift her hand. I got her to hospital but it was too late. It had turned into pneumonia, and although they pumped her full of antibiotics she was too far gone. The doc said she wouldn't have suffered.'

'Tea's brewed,' one of the boys called out.

Ben stood up and held out his hands to help her to her feet. 'You'll be staying for tea with us, won't you, Lottie? It's not often we have the company of a real lady, and it will give the boys a chance to practise their manners.'

'Well ...' She hesitated for a moment, wondering if Pandora would mind. Then she remembered Bryn telling her she must make her own decisions as often as possible. Besides, Pandora wasn't in, she'd taken Sam out for a walk.

She smiled at Ben, pleased with herself because she'd just made another decision. 'That would be nice. I've got a chocolate cake downstairs that I've just baked. Perhaps you and the boys would like a slice to go with the tea.'

'I haven't had a piece of home-made cake for years,' Ben said, so when she scurried away she felt sorry for them all.

She thought she might make a few sandwiches whilst she was in the kitchen, and there was an egg-and-bacon tart she'd made for Bryn, but it wouldn't take her long to make another one.

She was staggering under the weight of a loaded tray when she headed back upstairs.

The three males stood up when she entered. One of Ben's sons came forward to relieve her of the tray. 'Wow! Is all that for us?' he said, and he placed the tray on an orange box and exchanged a smile with his brother.

Ben offered her another orange box to sit on, and the boys sat on the floor, cross-legged, their gazes firmly fixed on the tray.

She and Ben looked at each other and exchanged a comfortable smile, like two doting parents instead of virtual strangers. He turned the handle of a chipped, brown earthenware teapot her way.

'You be mum,' he said, and Lottie smiled, thinking she might quite enjoy that role.

CHAPTER THIRTEEN

Bruno had vowed to never come back – but here he was.

Nothing seemed to have changed. The more affluent parts of Naples were still crowded with locals and tourists, but here in the heart of the old city, in the district known as *Spacca-Napoli*, the washing still hung from the balconies, and the smell of the summer brought back the nightmare of his childhood.

The poor had always produced more babies than they could afford, and scraped a living the best way they could. Some of the babies ended up on the narrow streets, where they became fair game for drug-pushers and pimps.

Bruno had been one of them. If they were very lucky, as Bruno had been, they might find themselves in the hands of a philanthropist.

Giorgio Demasi was a widowed geography teacher, who'd plucked him from a soup kitchen at the age of seven, adopted him and educated him. To this day, Bruno couldn't figure out how he'd been so lucky, considering Giorgio had asked nothing of him except to use the brain he'd been born with.

When Bruno reached the age of eighteen, Giorgio had died, leaving him broken-hearted, but in possession of everything he'd held dear – a good education, his name, a small amount of money and a burning desire to emigrate to Australia.

Bruno had done better for himself than either of them could have imagined, and a few years ago had sent money to a priest, asking him to arrange a marble tombstone for Giorgio Demasi's grave. Carved into it were the words; *Mourned by your loving son, Bruno.*

The contrasts and beauty of Naples still astonished him. The view of the bay from their hotel balcony was breathtaking, with the islands of Capri and Ischia at the entrance. Mount Vesuvius loomed to the southeast – and the *Riviera di Chiaia*, where their hotel was situated, hogged the best view of all of it.

They'd been here a week and had done the usual tourist things, like Pompeii and the museums.

Trini was entranced by everything she saw. Amusement flitted across Bruno's face when he thought of the wonder and excitement in her eyes. He'd bought her a video camera and she filmed everything that moved – including himself and Angel. Not that Angel minded, she was as natural in front of a camera as Trini was.

Sometimes, Trini set the camera rolling without him knowing – catching them fooling around in the hotel pool, or eating breakfast or on a picnic. Between them, they'd wittingly or unwittingly posed in front of more ancient buildings than the buildings had statuary – and in Italy, that was saying something.

He took one last glance around the district he'd been born in. For all he knew, his mother could still be living amongst the cockroaches of the crowded tenements, but he didn't even know who she was – he'd never known.

He experienced a moment of real regret for that, then strode away, his legs carrying him rapidly towards the place where he'd parked the car.

'I can't shut my suitcase.'

They were leaving *Napoli* after lunch, heading for two days in Rome, then on to Lake Geneva in Switzerland. After a week spent in Paris he was looking forward to their two-week stay in England, where Trini had insisted on booking a genuine thatched cottage, and where he hoped to recuperate from the trip before they flew home.

He'd allowed Trini to plan the actual route, before placing the trip in the hand of a travel agent – and apart from Naples, because she wanted to see the city where he'd been born – he'd enjoyed every moment.

Not that he'd ever told her of his background – and he'd lied when she'd asked him to show her the house he'd been born in, taking her to a modest villa in the hills and carefully explaining his parentage away by saying they'd died in a boating accident when he'd been small, and his uncle had raised him.

She took photographs of him standing in front of the place, with her telling him it was important Angela knew of her background – and would he *please* stop looking so fierce and *smile!*

He answered her many questions with more lies, but not building himself up too much because the falseness in his voice was apparent to his own ears.

His father had been a lawyer, he said, his mother a secretary ... he'd been too young when they'd died to remember them. He'd always led her questioning back to Giorgio Demasi, or kiss her to take her mind off it altogether.

Trini was easy to fool, because she believed in him implicitly. But lying to someone he loved was hard, bringing with it guilt and a lowering of his self-esteem. Yet, much as he hated lying to her, his pride wouldn't allow him to expose his humble beginnings to her.

But even Naples had its moments for him ... like this one.

Clad in a virginal white satin slip, her face was a study of annoyance as her fingers struggled with the locks. He could have done it for her, but her moment of frustration was amusing him. She simply had no sense of direction, and was pushing the locks the wrong way.

'Where's Angel?' he murmured, his eyes running over the fluid curve of her hips and thighs.

'Gone out with young Jessica and her nanny for a farewell picnic. They'll be back about one.' She placed her knee on the case, unwittingly revealing a long length of smooth, tanned, inner-thigh and a triangle of white satin edged in lace.

He glanced at his watch, and grinning, took a step forward to circle her body from behind. Leaning forward as she was, one of her breasts felt like a plump, warm peach in his palm. His other hand bunched up the slip, then slid inside her satin briefs, splaying out and pulling her pelvis back towards him. *Two nice handfuls!*

Her husky laugh was an extra turn-on as she caressed his ego with, 'I don't think I'll ever get enough of you.'

Her buttocks gave a demanding little wriggle and his finger gently teased her, his arousal butting imperiously against the cleft between her buttocks. In the mirror opposite the bed he saw her eyes close, and his skin absorbed the ecstatic little shivers racing through her.

The mirror was a turn-on. He watched her body respond to what he was doing to her, saw the moment when she lost control and became acquiescent to him.

She made him feel powerful – she made him want something different. So he pushed the suitcase off the bed, gently placed her face down, got rid of the satin panties and lifting her buttocks against his stomach, slid deep into her moistness.

She gave an incoherent murmur deep in her throat, then whispered, '*Yes...yes*,' and her muscles closed around his throbbing penis, encouraging his slow thrusts against them, yet the resistance keeping him from ripping her apart with his strength.

But she couldn't hold off his onslaught for long, and he took her hair in his fist and pulled her head gently back, enjoying the vision of the exquisite emotions playing across her face.

There was a moment when she opened her eyes and gazed straight at him in the mirror. They were beautiful, tiger's eyes, filled with cruelty and satisfaction, as if he were her prey instead of the other way around.

He thought she was making a purring sound in her throat, but when he lowered his head to lick the moisture from the junction of her neck and shoulder, she was telling him she loved him over and over again with each thrust – until finally the words were lost in the blood pounding in his ears as he quickened inside the rushing wetness and exquisite ecstasy of her body.

His uncontrolled jerks were received with several muted groans. One half of him hoped he hadn't hurt her, the other half hoped he had, because his power had suddenly become hers ...

... as she demonstrated afterwards by joining him under the shower and performing some incredibly sexy foreplay with her soapy hands, so he was compelled to fuck her all over again – and standing up, which made his knees tremble like jelly afterwards – and made her laugh.

She amazed him with her sensuality, she turned him on. He loved her – and her adoration of him wasn't too hard to take, either. Trini made him feel ten feet tall – and when they were together his appetite for loving her bordered on greed, and his capacity to perform was impressive.

He dressed himself, and watched her dress – and was just wondering if he had the strength left to manage it all over again when Angel came rushing in.

Her eyes were anxious and her curls bobbed around her face as she placed her hands on her hips and said indignantly, despite her anxious eyes, 'Jessica said you were going to leave me behind with her nanny. You're not, are you?'

'Never. I'd fight off a thousand savage crocodiles rather than leave you behind,' Bruno said, exchanging a grin with Trini, 'and so would your mum.'

The nanny was hot on her heels, her face apologetic, her hand clutched around that of her fair-haired charge. 'I'm sorry Mr Demasi, I hope Jessica didn't upset her. She's being a bit naughty today and I've brought her over to apologize.'

'Won't!' Jessica said.

'I don't care,' Angela muttered, self-confident again now the certainty of her parents' love had been reinforced.

'I'm sure Angela will get over it,' Trini said, trying to hide a grin, then turned to Angela. 'I hope you've remembered your manners and thanked Jessica's nanny for taking you out and looking after you.'

'She's a pleasure to look after.'

Angela smiled sweetly at her and giving Jessica a triumphant look, trilled, 'Thank you, nanny.'

'It was nice meeting you too, Jessica. I've got a going-away present for you.' When Trini gave the sullen child a cuddle and a parcel to unwrap, her smile appeared.

Bruno wanted to laugh when his daughter pushed between them and his eyes met Trini's when Angel made her claim clear. 'If you come to Australia you can visit me. My mum makes the best pancakes in the world and my dad fights savage broccolies.'

Bruno was laughing when he slipped the nanny an envelope. 'Here's a little something for you. Mrs Demasi and I are very grateful.'

The girl turned pink with pleasure; as she walked away the two children waved happily at each other until they were out of sight.

'If you go and order lunch, I'll check we've got everything,' he said.

After his family had gone, he snapped the cases shut, calling the porter to convey them downstairs. The video recorder was on top of the dressing table.

'Jesus!' he whispered, grinning to himself as he picked it up. Trini wouldn't have been quite so uninhibited had she known it was still running and pointed towards the bed. He replaced the cassette with a fresh one, and slipping the x-rated one into his pocket joined his family in the hotel restaurant.

After lunch, he paid the bill, tipped the staff, and left a forwarding address for mail ... not that there was any. Steve phoned him if anything needing advice cropped up.

Trini threw him the smile of a fallen angel when she saw him coming

... and when he patted his pocket, his own smile was laced with devilment. When they got home, he'd wait for an appropriate moment, then play it to her.

Just after they drove out of the car park the mail courier arrived at the hotel. There were two letters, both addressed to Mrs Demasi.

The receptionist shrugged and readdressed them, sliding them into an empty pigeonhole awaiting mail for forwarding. Over the course of a couple of days they were pushed to the back by several other letters and a small package.

Bruno had never been to England. He was surprised to discover the sun shining fiercely down from a blue sky.

'I thought it rained all the time, here,' he said, inwardly cursing the narrow, crowded and twisting roads that had bled off the motorway.

Trini removed his tie for him, kissing the side of his jaw in the process. 'I should have arranged things better. The woman in the café told me it's the August school holidays, and this is a long weekend so everyone's going to the coast. Why don't you stop at the next roadhouse and let me take over the driving.'

He grinned at her. She'd scraped through her driving test just before they'd left Australia, but he didn't want her practising her new skills on these twisty roads, not with the late afternoon sun glaring in her eyes.

'By my reckoning, we should be there in half an hour or so.'

'It's nice down here, isn't it? Though I thought London was great with all the pomp and historical bits thrown in. Adam was pleased to get his cameras back, I thought. He looked OK, didn't he? I can't remember him being so thin – do you think he's lost weight?'

'Mmmm,' he said noncommittally to her questions. Bruno didn't know why he'd allowed himself to be talked into giving Adam the cameras back, when the man owed him money. He'd probably take them to the local hock-shop as soon as they'd left. There were signs he was still hooked – like a belt and bent spoon on a table, and the way he'd quickly rolled down his shirt sleeves so the track marks didn't show.

He bit back his irritation when he realized Adam was on the road to nowhere, whilst he had more than a man could desire. He could afford to be generous, because if giving the cameras back to Adam had made Trini happy, that was OK with him.

'It's so pretty here,' she said again.

He threw her a grin. 'I don't suppose it's anything to do with the fact that you know you were born here?'

'Quite possibly. I'm going to find my parents' house, take a picture of it and send it to them. My mother said it was a really beautiful house and she loved living there.'

'So why did she move?'

'My father got an unexpected legacy and there was a bit of a problem about it. The man who died was survived by his wife, who was in a mental hospital, or something. Anyway, the hospital tried to claim it, but the woman died before it went to court. My mother said there was some unpleasant talk, so they decided to emigrate to Australia.'

It wasn't often Trini talked about her parents.

'And?'

'And he bought the store, then built a church so he could be a lay preacher. The trouble is, no one went to hear him preach.'

The sparkle had left her eyes, as it always did on the rare occasions she spoke of her parents. His hand slid over hers and briefly squeezed it.

'Was it bad?'

'There was no love,' she said simply, and he could hear the thickness in her voice as she twisted to gaze at Angel, who was hanging limply from her seat-belt, fast asleep. Trini undid her own belt to adjust Angel's head, placing her cardigan under it as a pillow.

She was sensitive, and he didn't blame her. How could two people raise a child without love? Her vulnerability moved and troubled him. All he could do was give her all the love she needed for as long as he lived – and hope it would make up for the lack of it in her past.

'Is England as green as you imagined?' she said when she turned back, her voice over-bright as she deliberately changed the subject.

'It's exactly as I imagined.' To Bruno it was chocolate-box stuff – thatched cottages, tiny villages, patchwork fields and different shades of green. 'Do you ever wonder why the roads run right through the centre of so many villages? Why couldn't they have diverted round them? It must annoy the hell out of the people living in those cottages to have cars whizzing past their front doors day and night. I hope our cottage isn't on a busy road.'

She took out a printed brochure marking a place in the map book, and stared at it. 'It says the cottage overlooks the village duck pond and comes with all conveniences.'

Twenty-five minutes later they pulled up outside a scruffy-looking, white-painted, thatched cottage. A woman was waiting with the key. She had a face like a rabbit and a voice full of sharp angles. She stared down her nose at them.

'Aye expected you sooner.'

Bruno levelled her a look. 'The traffic was a bitch, I'm afraid.'

'It always is in August,' she said, as though he should have taken it into account. 'I'll be here on Monday week at eleven sharp. Please leave the cottage clean, or your refundable deposit will be retained. Breakages will be deducted.'

His fist bunched. The toffy-nosed bitch needed a good right hook to the jaw.

'Then we'd better do an inventory of contents,' he said pleasantly.

'Aim sure that's not necessary.'

'Ah, but I'm sure it is. In fact, I should imagine it's the law – especially since you're running a business. Records must be kept for the tax office, I presume.'

Her voice took on a more conciliatory note. 'Aye don't run it as a business, actually. It's my mother's cottage and she's in a nursing home. The holiday leases help buy her the little extras she needs. Aim sure you won't do any damage to the contents.' She scrambled in her purse and handed over some cash. 'In fact, I'll return your deposit now, and you can leave the key under the mat.'

'Where's the duck pond?' Bruno asked, gazing at the sea of nettles opposite.

'Aim most awfully sorry, Mr Dimpsea,' she threw over her shoulder as she hurried away, 'Aim afraid it dries up in the summer.' She jumped into her car and drove rapidly away.

He turned to gaze at Trini, who screwed up her face and said, 'Aim afraid that was awfully wude of you, Mr Dimpsea.'

Although they laughed, they looked at each other and grimaced when they went inside. The cottage was sparsely furnished, the ceilings festooned with cobwebs and the conveniences situated inconveniently at the end of the garden. The kitchen equipment and crockery was battered, but there was linen, a fairly modern fridge with mouldy interior, and a washing-machine of ancient lineage.

'What's that attachment on top?' he said.

'It's called a wringer. You squeeze the washing between the rollers to get the water out, I think.' She lifted the lid, recoiling from whatever was lurking inside. 'We'll need to bleach it before we use it.'

Angel pattered up and down the stairs, then opened the back door and raced into the garden with a big grin on her face. She shimmied up an apple tree, then hung herself off a lower branch by her legs.

'Shall I go up to the phone box and see if I can book us into a hotel?' said Bruno.

Trini slid her arms around him and kissed the dimple in the bottom of his chin. 'Let's just make the best of it. Angel's got a garden to play in here – and I can hear kids next door.'

She took the shopping list she'd prepared in the car from her pocket and tucked it into his. 'You wouldn't mind going to that supermarket we passed a few miles back, would you?' she said, the expression on her face an engaging mixture of apology and cajolement. 'I'll make the cottage more habitable in no time.'

'For you, my love, anything … as long as you give me a kiss.' Which lasted a lot longer than he'd intended, so she had to extricate herself from his arms and push him towards the door before the supermarket closed.

'Bring back some takeaway for tea – *and watch your head on that beam!*'

He ducked just in time, grinning at her.

Darkness fell about ten, an inconvenient hour as far as Bruno was concerned, because Angel was disinclined to go to sleep.

The cottage smelled of disinfectant and bleach, reminding him of a hospital. He'd done his bit by sweeping down cobwebs, chasing spiders outside, taping up the splits in an early model vacuum-cleaner and complaining a lot.

They bathed in what seemed to be a tablespoon of tepid water in a rusting bath with dirty claw feet.

Trini got into bed first, and rolled into a sagging hole in the middle. The mattress began to sink towards the floor. She giggled as it slowly closed over her.

'*Help!*'

He pulled her out before she suffocated, muttering, 'The damn thing's a death trap! I'm going to murder that woman if I ever see her again.'

When he stood up he cracked his head against the sloping roof. He released a string of invective, all in his native language so as not to offend her, and punched the air several times for good measure.

The curtains fell down.

Trini gazed at him, her shoulders shaking, her eyes brimming with laughter. 'Do aye know how to pick a holiday cottage, or what, Mr Dimpsea?'

He began to grin, he couldn't help it. Then they were both doubled up with laughter. Even when it died down, as soon as their eyes met, it started up again.

Too wide awake to sleep and too full of laughter to make love, he changed the mood with a bottle of champagne, enticing her into the moonlit garden.

She was wearing a white ankle-length robe that seemed to pour over her body like liquid silk in the opaque light. Hip to hip, and up to their knees in a sea of grass, they gazed up at the stars.

'You look good enough to eat in the moonlight,' he whispered against her ear.

She drained her glass and threw it into the hedge. Her arms snaked up around his neck, and he could smell the tantalizing mixture of her soap and her body.

'I love you so much,' she said, and he suddenly felt better about the cottage, despite the prospect of a night on the floor.

His glass followed hers and he scooped her up in his arms, his mouth pressing down on the softness of hers.

And later, when she was asleep, and the warmth of her breath fanned gently against his cheek, he listened to the taps dripping and the rustles and squeaks of the mice – and knew he was the luckiest man in the world.

One of the letters caught up with them on the day they vacated the cottage – dropped through the letterbox along with a card saying the electricity would be cut off if the bill wasn't paid by the weekend.

Bruno was almost tempted to leave the owner a bill for the repairs and cleaning, but it wasn't worth the effort because he wouldn't be here to enforce it.

He stared at the envelope – so scribbled over and stamped, it was hard to tell which country it had originated from.

'It's for you.'

'Me?' She was genuinely bewildered. 'I can't think of anyone who'd write to me, unless it's my parents.' She turned it over, seeming reluctant to open it.

The rarity in her life of such a common occurrence supplemented what Trini had told him of her sense of childhood isolation. He experienced a flicker of pity when he stooped to kiss her cheek.

'There's only one way to find out.'

He left her staring down at the envelope, and began to carry the cases out to the car. Angel was saying a tearful goodbye to her new friends next door.

Task completed, he went back inside and stopped inside the doorway. Trini was staring out of the window and the rigid stillness of her body told him something was very wrong.

He turned her round and stared at her. Her eyes were enormous, and wounded, and contained such a depth of shock he said roughly, 'Who's upset you?'

'The letter,' she whispered, her eyes going to the flimsy piece of paper on the table.

His brain absorbed the contents in about five seconds. At worst, he thought one of her parents might have died – but this? He could only guess what was going through her mind.

'Perhaps it's a crank letter.'

Hope flared in her eyes and just as quickly died. 'It can't be. I saw the name Trinity Dysart on a paper in my father's document case. I didn't give it much thought then. Now I know it was too much of a coincidence.'

He looked at the letter again. 'Pandora Rossiter doesn't live far from here. Do you want to follow it up?'

She gave a twisted sort of smile. 'I don't think so, Bruno. I have you and Angela. I don't need anyone else, especially someone who thought nothing of giving me away to a couple of people incapable of love. How could she do such an awful thing?'

Which was being irrational when she didn't know the circumstances, but her irrationality was understandable.

'She said she went to Australia to find you. She's spoken to your mother.'

'My mother could have phoned me … she could have told me I wasn't their child. It would have explained so much.' Her eyes shuttered over. 'You're my family, you and Angela, and I don't want anyone else.'

She walked past him, leaving the letter on the table, calling for Angel in a cheerful voice and smiling and chatting with the neighbours.

He shoved the letter into his pocket and followed, his heart heavy, and anger filling him because this unknown woman called Pandora had dared to spoil Trini's life by intruding on her happiness.

Although on the surface she remained the same Trini he'd married, the letter somehow changed her; so, once they were home, her laughter and loving seemed less spontaneous and more desperate, as though she needed to prove her worth as a person to both him and herself. He feared she might suffer a breakdown.

'I'm stronger than you think,' she said when he voiced his fears

'You need to speak to your adoptive parents,' he said to her one day. 'Do it for me.'

'If that's what you want,' she said in a neutral manner. 'Perhaps it is time you met them, but don't expect too much.'

He drove her to a desolate country town in the middle of nowhere. The place was as tired as her father was passionless – as if everything but disillusionment had been sucked from his body by the wind.

'Your mother was a whore, your father tempted into sin by the Devil. Mary and I provided a roof over your head and food for your sustenance. You repaid us with disobedience and we have no daughter now. Mary, watch the store whilst I take this woman to the house and give her what she seeks.'

To give the woman credit, she came around from the back of the counter and gave Trini a hug. He saw Trini slip something into the pocket of her apron – the photograph she'd taken of the house in Dorset.

They weren't invited in when they reached the house. The man's eyes bored relentlessly into Trini's when he placed an envelope into her hands, and the hairs at the nape of Bruno's neck stood on end. Whatever religion Matthew James embraced, it didn't extend to forgiveness.

'What you have sown, so shall you reap. The Lord will bring His punishment down upon you in His own good time.'

She said nothing, but turned towards him with a tremulous smile that nearly broke his heart in two. 'Take me home, Bruno.'

For as long as he lived, Bruno knew he'd never forget the fear in her eyes. She didn't cry, and even managed to smile a bit on the way home, but the fear lingered there whilst she examined the precious little she'd been given of her life – an order of adoption.

For a few days she was filled with sadness, until something happened to give him his old Trini back.

She rushed into his study one day, and with a smile as wide and as smug as the Cheshire cat from *Alice in Wonderland*, slid onto his lap and rained a thousand kisses on his face. He started to smile, because somehow he knew exactly what she was about to say.

'We're going to have a baby. Isn't that the most wonderful news in the world?'

The letter from Simeon Manus – dispatched two months previously from the legal chambers of Teague and Frapp – arrived in Bruno's office on the very same day.

CHAPTER FOURTEEN

Pandora hadn't expected Gerald to arrive on the doorstep. She hadn't given him much thought at all, except to feel relieved that he'd accepted the inevitability of the divorce.

'Happy birthday,' he said, and placed a bunch of roses in her hands. He was more handsome and urbane than she remembered – not a hair out of place, and wearing an immaculate suit with a carnation in the button hole.

His body was lean and well-muscled for his age – due, no doubt to his ritual of a twice-weekly workout at a gym. Habit died hard with Gerald. Something about his face drew her gaze to the smoothness of his jaw-line, and the faint wrinkles at the corner of his eyes.

Good God, he's had a face lift! She tried not to stare and stood to one side, her insides quivering with silent laughter. 'Come in. You'll have to excuse the noise. I expect Michael told you Marianna is being converted into flats.'

'No … no he didn't, I figured that out for myself as soon as I walked into the main entrance. As a matter of fact, Michael doesn't tell me much at all. He's at that uncommunicative stage.' He winced when a drill started up. 'Is there somewhere quiet where we can talk?'

'Is it important?'

'Would I have come all this way if it wasn't?'

Her hand flew to her throat. 'Nothing's happened to Adrian, has it?'

'Not to my knowledge.' Impatience rode in his voice. 'Fetch your jacket, Pandora. Let's go for a walk.'

There was a moment of rebellion, then she shrugged. Leaving the flowers on the shelf in the porch, she pulled on a long woolly cardigan and made a token resistance.

'This will do, we won't be going too far.'

With Sam darting on ahead they strolled in silence up the hill towards the woods. The trees looked splendid, robed in glorious ochre hues; the air had a nutty, autumn aroma and a stillness about it, as if the earth was slowly exhaling the last days of September.

There was an aura of tension about Gerald – it was obvious he didn't quite know where to start. Several times he cleared his throat, as if ill at ease.

'What did you want to see me about, Gerald?' she said, and he turned, his eyes filled with the little-boy-lost look she knew so well.

'I was wondering if there was anything I could do to save our marriage before the divorce is made final.'

'Gerald, I don't think—'

'Just hear me out, Pandora. I know everything was my fault – but believe me, if you come back it will never happen again. I still love you, and I'm willing to overlook your past if you'll overlook mine. We'll just start again and never mention it – as if it hadn't happened.'

She couldn't dismiss the existence of Trinity as easily as he could his women. Her lips tightened. 'I'm sorry, Gerald—'

'The boys need us – they need our guidance. Their future was all mapped out and secure. They were going to join the family firm. Now look at them. Adrian's gone off somewhere, and Michael has got some crazy idea of going to medical school, of all things. All this has happened since you walked out on us.'

'You mean, I've ruined all your lives?'

He looked taken aback for a moment. 'It's not what I meant, but I suppose if you want to put it like that ...'

'That's the scenario *you're* presenting,' she said wearily. 'Adrian and Michael are men now. What you call guidance would be considered interference by them. I'm quite sure Adrian will be back in time to take up his place at Oxford – and with the bonus of a mind broadened by travel. As for Michael – I'm as proud as hell of what he's got mapped out for himself. It's not easy to become a doctor.'

'Oh, don't let's argue,' Gerald said disgustedly. 'I don't know what's wrong with you, Pandora. We had a perfectly happy marriage before you got this damned inheritance.'

She stared at him, trying to imagine what she'd seen in him, but knowing she'd simply been looking for security and love. She would have married any man who'd shown her affection and given her a home at the time.

'No, Gerald. *You* had a perfectly happy marriage.' She placed her hand on his arm, bringing him to a halt. 'I was living a lie. All those years, when I thought I loved you ... I was actually married to a father figure.'

If she'd punched him in the midriff she couldn't have shocked him more. His mouth fell open slightly, showing a row of perfectly capped teeth, his eyes were wounded.

Recalling the fate of Carol Stringer, and Gerald's part in it, she hardened her heart and invested in an overdue dose of cruelty.

'I'm sorry, Gerald. I don't know why I didn't see it before. You didn't make many demands on my body, for which I was thankful. I'm sorry I didn't come up to the standard of your girlfriends, but it takes two to perfect a sexual act. I have to tell you – in nineteen years you never once turned me on, and I had to fake my orgasms.'

Hs mouth fell open slightly and he turned a dull red.

'Granted, you settled me in a lovely house. You guided me, told me what to wear and when to wear it. All you asked in return was that I played the role of the perfect wife and adore you – which I did for years and years, forgiving you everything. I did everything expected of me, until one day I woke up.'

'But I love you,' he said, a catch in his voice.

'You love yourself. You used me as an excuse – so you didn't have to commit to someone else. You don't want me back, it's just that your ego is dented. You can't stand the thought of me tossing you aside – when it's usually the other way round.'

'Is that your final word?' he said sadly, and she'd lived with him long enough to recognize the manipulative trick from his repertoire. His intention was to make her feel guilty, and so relieve himself of the burden.

She gave him a wry smile, faintly amused by it, and experiencing a sense of relieved finality.

'I'm in love with someone else. That's my final word.' She whistled for Sam and set off back down towards the house.

'I suppose it's that lawyer Adrian told me about,' he sneered, catching up with her. 'You disgust me, Pandora. I respected you. I could have had you without marriage, like all the others, but I placed you on a pedestal. As soon as you left, you couldn't wait to let another man get his hand inside your knickers.'

Her heart swelled with pride, because her sons had respected her privacy by keeping quiet about Bryn.

'You suppose wrong. The man with his hand inside my knickers is a psychiatrist. What's more, I enjoy having his hand inside my knickers, which is more than I ever did with you. I'm going to marry him.'

'Then there's nothing more to be said,' he shouted. He strode off ahead of her, his back stiff and prickly with the affront he felt.

She could have said plenty. She could have told him how Mare had got her revenge, and that they could so easily have lost Adrian because he – Gerald Rossiter – couldn't keep his damned fly zipped up.

She could have told him Carol Stringer had gone back on drugs after she'd been used to take revenge over the divorce. For all her brashness, the woman hadn't been able to face the contempt of her peers after word had got around. She'd slashed her wrists and was now in the mental ward at the hospital.

She could have said his face-lift was ridiculous and narcissistic, considering the destruction he'd caused – and laughed him out of sight. Against her baser instincts, she spared his feelings, slowing down to allow him time to get to the house and into his car, and to escape with what was left of his smugness and dignity intact.

Childishly, he took her birthday roses with him.

The postman had been in her absence. She shuffled through the mail. There were birthday cards, a gas bill, a brochure about computer courses she'd sent off for – and a letter from Australia! Her hands trembled as she ripped it open.

G'day, Pandora love,

I bet you didn't think you'd hear from me. Things are looking up at Hope's End. A mob of those Hari Krishnas in bells and orange robes moved into town and started buying up the place. Just our flaming luck, they don't drink.

The termites finally chewed through one of the poles holding up the balcony and the whole lot nearly fell in a heap. Jim's stuck the pole in a bucket of wet cement to prop it up for now, though it's still got a bit of a lean on it.

What I wrote to tell you was, that young-un of yours was in town a while back with her bloke. The pair of them looked as happy as two ticks on a bull's bum.

Anyhow, not long after that Matthew James up and died. He turned blue and dropped dead when he was filling up the bus. First time I ever saw Mary smile in twenty years was at the funeral, poor little cow.

> *Anyway, she sold the store and church to the Hari Krishnas and lit out of town the following month ... said she was going back home. Good luck to her, I say.*
>
> *Jean Perkins sends her best wishes. She said to tell you she's sold her house and is going to Mandurah to live with her sister, so if you visit Australia again and are down there any time, drop in for a cuppa.*
>
> *That goes double for Jim and me, of course. Bring your bloke along and try and bounce the squeak out of the bed. The pair of you might bring the whole place down, then we can claim it on the insurance and retire. Hah, hah ... only joking!*
>
> *Many regards,*
> *Doreen.*

Any news of Trinity was better than none at all, though the thought of a pair of happy ticks on a bull's bum gave her a fit of the giggles.

The death of Matthew James didn't exactly ruin her day – in fact, she experienced the relief of release for Mary James, who'd lacked the gumption to leave him – as she had herself, with Gerald.

Doreen's letter made her laugh because it was so natural. She pictured her friend hanging over the bar, her oval bosoms resembling twin rugby balls as she leaned on her folded arms to exchange gossip with her few customers.

When she replied, no doubt the letter would be read to Doreen's regulars, so she'd better be careful – and she'd send her a wedding invitation when the time came. Not that they'd come all that way, of course, but Doreen would enjoy getting it, and talking about it.

She lined her five birthday-cards up on the mantelpiece. Nothing from Adrian, which was slightly worrying, because he never forgot her birthday. She told herself that the postal services were notoriously unreliable where he was – wherever *that* was – and it would probably arrive late.

Bryn was taking them out to celebrate. Not that thirty-nine was anything much to celebrate. Another year and she'd be on the downward slide.

She'd become Pandora Llewellyn next year. She hadn't expected to fall in love when she'd left Gerald – she hadn't expected to get married again at all.

Bryn was the opposite of Gerald in every way. He didn't assume she'd become part of him. He didn't expect her to like the same people, or even pretend to. She smiled to herself. Her Welsh bear was an endearing mixture of brains and balls – and she loved him to bits.

A pity the Llewellyn women didn't really approve of her. It worried her a bit, because she didn't want to be the object of their bitchiness – and they had the advantage of numbers against her one. Their concept of a suitable woman for Bryn was a woman suitable for *them* – and since that creature didn't exist, she wasn't looking forward to reacquainting herself with them at Christmas. Yet she couldn't alienate Bryn from them, or herself, by retaliating in kind – which would place her in the same coven in his eyes.

She smiled at Lottie, who came in with a secretive smile on her face and a suspicious bulge under her jumper. Lottie hurried up to her room, returning with a little parcel in her hands and looking a lot slimmer.

'Happy birthday,' she said.

A black, fringed wrap emerged from the tissue paper. Exquisitely embroidered on it, in various shades of turquoise silk, was a peacock with its tail fanned out. Delighted with it, Pandora hugged her.

'This is absolutely beautiful, Lottie, thank you so much. Where on earth did you find it?'

'I saw it in the shop that sells all that overseas craft stuff. Bryn said you'd like it.'

'I love it … it's the nicest gift I've ever been given.' And Lottie's smile at her words was the best gift of all. She felt sad that Emily Dysart hadn't seen her daughter like this, so confident and happy.

They both gritted their teeth as an excruciating whine came from upstairs. 'This is worse than the dentist's drill,' Pandora shouted.

'Ben said the really noisy bits should be finished by the weekend.'

'Which one's Ben – the short, spotty one, the tall, unspotty one, or the medium, baldish one, who seems to be in charge, and who you keep supplied with tea and cakes?'

Lottie blushed a bit. 'Ben's the one in charge and the other two are his sons. He's a widower, and really very nice. I deliver meals to his mother and sometimes I visit her and we chat. I take them *all* tea and cakes sometimes. The boys love them.'

Pandora couldn't help teasing her a bit, because Lottie was obviously smitten by the bald little man with the cheery smile and manner.

'They'll never get the job finished because they won't want to miss out on your cooking.'

'Ben said it will be finished by the end of January.'

'Then the tenants will move in. Will you mind strangers living in Marianna, Lottie?'

'It will be nice. There's something sad about an empty house, don't you think?'

Pandora knew exactly what she meant. Sometimes the weight of it pressed against her shoulders – especially at night, when all the empty spaces above them shifted and sighed, and the Dysart ancestors – never a happy lot from all accounts – let their presence be felt.

Now they were isolated from it by the simple addition of a couple of bricked-up doorways, the servants' stairway allowing access to their second-storey rooms. The rear door with its sweetly-smelling, honey-suckled porch had become their main entrance – though it was actually at the side of the house rather than the back.

The tenants of the other three apartments would use the main hall and stairway – the three apartments leading off from it.

'It will be lovely to have Simeon living above us, and hopefully we'll get some decent tenants for the rest. The letting agent has promised to vet them very carefully.'

'Ben said Marianna could be turned into eight flats, no trouble at all.'

Pandora smiled at the way Lottie had unconsciously adopted Ben's speech pattern.

'Which would mean smaller rents and twice as many people living here. The conversion would have cost considerably more – and ultimately, the wear and tear on the building would be higher, pushing up maintenance costs. Your mother thought this out carefully, Lottie – and for once, I agree with what she planned. This is right for Marianna.'

'My mother always thought she knew what was right for everybody,' Lottie said.

Because a nervous tremor had attacked Lottie's voice, Pandora inclined her head to one side, gazed at her. 'Go on.'

There was a half-wary look in Lottie's eyes. 'I have a photograph I took of you with Trinity when she was born. I thought you might like it.'

Pandora gazed at her, astonished, but a little afraid. 'After all this time?'

'I was frightened to give it to you. I hid it in a tin and put it behind a loose brick upstairs. It's been there for over twenty years. Ben got it out for me.'

'Oh, Lottie,' she said, knowing how much courage it must have taken her aunt to do what she did. 'I can't bear it when you say you're frightened of me. Nothing would induce me to do anything to hurt you deliberately.'

Lottie took the Oxo tin from her pocket and handed it to her. 'You don't mind then?'

Pandora's hands were trembling when she prised off the lid. The photograph was as clear as the day it was taken. They were both asleep, the baby's head tucked into the crook of her shoulder. A lump came into her throat and tears scalded her eyes.

'I take back what I said about the wrap. This is the most beautiful gift of all.'

'I hope you find her,' Lottie said gruffly. They reached for each other and clung together for a few precious minutes of love. 'Oh, I do hope you find her.'

Pandora dressed carefully for her evening out, in an ankle-length black dress, pleasing Lottie by wearing the wrap. Piling her hair up on top she added lapis lazuli earrings to complement the peacock, and carefully applied her make-up.

Lottie watched her in the mirror, her eyes absorbed. 'That looks nice. Would you put some on me?'

Pandora gazed critically at Lottie's sensible dress. 'There's a blue outfit in my wardrobe with a pleated skirt. It should look good on you.'

When Bryn arrived he gazed at Lottie in mock puzzlement. 'Who's this beautiful young lady?'

Which made Lottie shy, so she hung her head for a moment. Then she realized and started to laugh. 'Oh … you know it's me, Bryn,' she said, and went off to fetch her coat.

Bryn placed the flat parcel he was carrying in her hand.

'Happy birthday, woman. You look good enough to eat.' Somehow, he'd tamed his hair into undulating waves for the occasion, except for the bit that rebelliously stuck out from behind one ear.

The book Bryn gave her appeared to be old. 'Quotes from Shakespeare, illuminated and bound in leather,' he whispered reverently in her ear – in case she couldn't see, or couldn't read the flyleaf without his assistance. When his finger stroked gently over the surface, she knew this had been one of his most treasured possessions.

'It's beautiful, Bryn.' There were tears in her eyes, because he'd made such a sacrifice for her. 'I love it, and I love you.'

She slid her eyes up to his and he held them there for a precious moment or two, murmuring, '*No sooner met, but they looked; no sooner looked than they loved; no sooner loved than they sighed; no sooner sighed but they asked one another the reason; no sooner knew the reason but they sought the remedy.'*

One finger gently lifted a tear from her lashes. 'I love you Pandora, girl,' he said, and kissed her with such tender and loving intent she thought she might die on the spot.

They moved apart when they heard Lottie coming back, their eyes filled with desire, and knowing it would be a damned long wait before they could remedy that.

Simeon rang her halfway through the next morning. 'Can you fix me up with lunch if I drop in on you?'

'Sure, if you don't mind the noise overhead. You have the choice of a chicken and asparagus sandwich or an asparagus and chicken sandwich.'

'Either will be fine, thanks.'

She knew her feeble joke had gone in one ear and out of the other for some reason. 'Are you all right, Simeon?' She wondered if Carol Stringer was OK. Simeon felt partly responsible for what had happened. 'Nothing's happened to Carol, has it?'

'No, she's fine, considering. Her parents are coming down from London, and she's being discharged into their care for the time being, on the proviso she has counselling. It's the best thing, really.'

Out of sight, out of Simeon's mind? She chided herself for being unfair. Carol wasn't Simeon's responsibility – and from what she'd seen, the woman didn't deserve to have him as a friend.

She might have been unfair to Gerald, too. If Carol had flirted with drugs at university, it was possible she'd never given them up. Her mouth tightened. No! In that she *hadn't* been unfair! Gerald had maliciously used the young divorce lawyer to demonstrate he still had the power to manipulate her. The despicable and cowardly act had ruined Carol, which had caused anxiety to her parents. Nothing could justify involving anyone else in what should have been a purely personal matter between them – and she wished now that she hadn't let Gerald off the hook so easily.

She'd asked Bryn if Carol was one of his patients, giving the reason as Carol's short affair with Gerald, and telling him she thought Gerald's motive might have been revenge. But although he'd listened to what she'd said, his eyes had remained unreadable. He hadn't answered her question either, just asked her if she'd mind making him a cup of coffee, and had gone into his study, closed the door and made a phone call.

He'd made it perfectly clear there was a line she couldn't cross with him. The privacy of the patient was totally inviolate as far as he was concerned, even from her.

She had to learn to respect that too, accepting that a part of Bryn's life would always be separate from hers, so when he came home from work she couldn't say, 'Did you fix Mrs Jones's leaking pipes?' as she could if she were married to a plumber, or, 'Is the stock market rising or falling?' which had always earned her a lengthy lecture on world economics from Gerald.

She could certainly not ask Bryn brightly over the chicken fricassee, 'Is Mrs Jones suffering from menopausal angst, or is her fascination with leaking pipes a result of penis envy?'

His spasms of uncontrolled laughter would blow the fricassee from his plate and all over the elegant, ivory wallpaper she planned to redecorate his dining-room walls with, once she'd moved in.

She was still in a silly mood when Simeon arrived, carrying the bulging briefcase that seemed to be a permanent attachment. *A placenta full of legalities attached to the umbilical cord of his arm.*

They exchanged the necessary social pleasantries – and by some miracle their lunch coincided with the lunch-break of Bert and sons, so the din overhead suddenly ceased.

Just after she poured the coffee, Simeon hauled his briefcase to his lap and opened it. She was wondering if he slept with it, and was about to ask him when he drew a letter from its depths and placed it on the table between them.

The letter wasn't a fair exchange for her beautifully-prepared and delicious lunch. It wasn't a fair exchange at all.

The sender was an Australian lawyer, who, acting on behalf of Mr Demasi, had advised Simeon to tell his client ... *her petition to establish a relationship with Mrs Demasi has been noted, but contact will not be encouraged at this time. Mr Demasi has expressed a wish that their privacy be respected in this matter.*

She hauled in a deep, shuddering breath, and her world seemed to come to a standstill. All those months of being patient, of waiting and hoping – for this! A polite little note telling her she couldn't see her daughter – her own flesh and blood, whom she'd nurtured inside her body for months, suffered through labour to give birth to, and had loved. Dammit! She *had* loved Trinity, and not for the few precious moments she'd been allowed to hold her, but for all her life.

It was so unfair ... so cruelly unfair ... and the blood began to pound in her ears and she stared around her – at the sitting-room with its stamp of Emily Dysart everywhere.

How smug and county it looked, the chintz chairs and the ceiling-high glass cabinets stuffed with delicate and expensive china: Royal Doulton and Wedgwood, even the odd bit of Minton, the treasures gleaned from the cottage sales her grandmother had frequented, where the impover-ished and elderly owners didn't know any better. There were shelves of Waterford crystal, cleaned every week, and very carefully, so it sparkled and wouldn't chip and become worthless.

'You see, Pandora, all these things are very precious to Grandma. Grandma loves her little treasures, so you must never touch them.'

And Pandora had learned to love them too – each tiny figurine had a name, like Amelia and Leticia or Eustacia, and she delighted that the sparkling crystal had the maker's name etched into the pattern underneath – so one could tell if it were genuine or not. The pinging sound when Grandma flicked it was a sign of quality. *Always flick the glass and listen to it before you buy.*

How could someone who valued delicate and pretty things so much, discard the delicate and pretty thing that was her great-granddaughter – as if she'd contained a flaw, as if she didn't have quite the right quality, or was not genuine enough? It wasn't as if Trinity hadn't enough Dysart blood in her – she'd just had too much of it for Emily's comfort.

'Thanks for letting me know, Simeon.'

Was this her being unbelievingly serene – being social and seeing to her guest's needs – watching the relief in Simeon's eyes because she was behaving in a perfectly unemotional manner? Was this her soul inside her body? Had it always been so deadened and grieving, had her stomach always ached and knotted with a tension that had never been allowed to escape?

'Must rush ... I'm so sorry about the bad news, Pandora.'

Go, go! Of course he must rush. He had paying clients with important problems. A peck of mouths at each other's cheeks, like birds of a differ-ent feather. Poor Simeon having to act all the time because of what other people might think ... poor her having to act all the time because she was a Dysart ... why didn't they just act as they felt?

She made a phone call to Bryn, her voice tightly controlled, her heart almost breaking into a thousand pieces because her daughter didn't want to know her ... and still she couldn't cry.

'Why can't I bloody well cry over this?' she yelled at him, as if it were his fault, when it was Emily Dysart's fault ... Emily, with her stupid collection of things that neither lived nor breathed nor loved nor felt either cold or heat or pain, because they were beautiful dead things – and the woman had trained her into being a dead thing too.

Her glance scanned the shelves, darting over the perfect, painted images that neither spoke nor loved. They were pretty, but useless. Lumps of inanimate clay cooked in an oven. She couldn't love this stuff like her grandmother had. It gave nothing back.

So she fetched a broom from the cupboard and knocked Amelia, Eustacia and Leticia from the top shelf. Then she fetched a mallet from the shed and smashed them into little pieces.

The pain was still there.

She looked at the rest of the china and the glass, the beauty of which was slightly dimmed because she hadn't given it the careful weekly clean it needed and deserved. She opened the doors of the cabinet, stood on a chair and pushed the broom along the length of the top shelf.

Everything fell with a top-quality musical crash to the floor. She measured the next shelf with her eye and took aim ... laughing with the pain and pleasure of destroying what Emily Dysart had loved.

By the time Bryn turned up the room was covered in broken glass and china. She sat in a chair in the middle of it, teetering on the edge of a dangerous exhilaration, but not regretting her action one little bit.

'I did it in exchange for Trinity,' she said. 'Lottie gave me a photograph holding her, taken just after she was born. I looked young ... too young to have a child. It made me think ... perhaps my grandparents had done the right thing, after all.'

'Feeling better now?' he asked.

She shook her head from side to side. 'How can I feel better? Deep down, I knew I was making excuses for them. What they did was for their own peace of mind, and nothing to do with me or my baby.'

'Try not to hate them,' he said, drawing her into his arms. 'Feel sorry for them, instead.'

She started to cry, and it was a long time before she managed to stop.

CHAPTER FIFTEEN

It struck Bryn as ironic, that a man who prided himself on his logic had fallen so instantly in love – and lately, he'd come to the conclusion he'd never been a logical man at all.

The choirmaster tapped his baton sharply on the stand, drawing Bryn's attention to the fact that the voices of the rest of the choir were trailing off. Choir practice was not going well tonight, and Rancid Rankin, the thin-bodied and thin-skinned choirmaster, was at his sarcastic worst.

'May I remind you, ladies and gentlemen, that we are singing in Latin. *Adeste fideles, laete triumphantes* – not, O come all ye faithful, etcetera, etcetera – and that means you, Miss Robins.'

Miss Robins, fortyish and long since resigned to perpetual spinster-hood, turned the same tomato colour as her jumper and stammered, 'I'm … afraid I can't pronounce it.'

'Well, we can't have you singing in English and the rest of the choir in Latin, can we? That will only draw attention to your lack of an adequate education. If you haven't made the effort to learn it, why come to choir practice?'

Poor little robin redbreast, looking so crushed, Bryn thought and frowned at the choirmaster.

'There's no need to indulge in a personal attack, Mr Rankin. Miss Robins didn't say she hadn't made the effort to learn it, only that she couldn't pronounce it. I'll teach her. We'll sing to each other over the phone until she's perfect.'

When Miss Robins smiled gratefully up at him an annoyed glance was speared Bryn's way.

'Thank you for your suggestion, Mr Llewellyn – one I was going to make myself as a matter of fact, seeing as how you're so fluent in the language. We'll listen to your solo next, then you can all go home to your firesides.'

'Will we indeed? I think you ought to apologize to Miss Robins before we proceed.' There was a murmur of assenting voices from the rest of the choir.

Rankin scowled. 'Very well then, if I must. My apologies, Miss Robins.' He tapped his baton on the stand and nodded to the pianist. 'Now, from the top.'

'It came upon the midnight clear, that glorious song of old ...'

The bloody heating was off in the village hall again! Pandora had come to collect him, because his car was in the garage being serviced. She was seated on a chair near the back of the hall. Her arms were wrapped around her body, which was encased in a long, black coat. A blue knitted beanie was jammed over her ears, her hair pouring in all directions from underneath it like a silky golden waterfall.

'From angels bending near the earth, To touch their harps of gold ...'

Her eyes caught his and she smiled, but there was nothing angelic about it ... the opposite in fact. She looked downright wicked. He took up the challenge in her eyes and sang.

'Place on the earth, good women for men and make their kisses slow ... and fill their minds with carnal thoughts so their bodies always glow.'

Pandora gave a peal of laughter.

'Mr Llewellyn! You are turning my choir practice into a fiasco.' The baton crashed down on the stand and broke in half.

When the choir began to laugh, Bryn felt like a recalcitrant schoolboy showing off in front of the class instead of a 'nice, mid-thirtyish professional gentleman of means', as his cleaning-lady had archly described him one day to someone in the next aisle of the supermarket.

He was grinning as he jumped down from the stage and swung Pandora up into his arms.

'Put me down or you might be sorry,' she cried out, keeping a tight hold on her coat.

He set her gently on to her black-booted feet, and kissed the icy end of her nose. 'You're freezing.'

'That will be all,' Rankin was shouting unnecessarily to the people diverting around him, because he didn't have the guts to bully Bryn, who was the best tenor in the choir, and whom he couldn't afford to lose. 'Same time again next week ... and make sure you learn those words, Miss Robins.'

'I'll try, Mr Rankin.'

'Never mind him, little Robin,' said Bryn when she walked dejectedly past with her wings folded tightly against her. 'I'll give you a ring and we'll have you singing like a Latin nightingale in no time at all.'

They escaped into a cold, October night, their breath steaming around them, jostling each other and laughing as she tried to unlock the car. He folded himself into the passenger seat, his knees touching the dash.

Miss Robins wobbled past them on her bicycle, then picked up speed, her red light disappearing off to the left and down Rectory Lane. Home to her mother, buttered crumpets and hot chocolate for supper – then into a pink flannel night-gown and her iron bed under the eaves with a hot-water bottle to cuddle.

'That horrible Rankin person picks on her. Why can't the Christmas carol be sung in English?' Pandora asked, drawing her coat tightly around her.

Nobody but Pandora could use *person* in that way and make it sound like a dirty word. He grinned. She could be a snooty-nosed cow at times.

Her perfume drifted across to him, and he sucked it in with a deep breath. There was nothing like a bit of scent-snorting to get the testo-sterone primed.

'It's the snob value. Rankin's heard there might be a part-time teaching position at the school at Milton Abbas, so he's out to impress. *Adeste Fideles* is actually a hymn of praise. It was written in Latin in the 1700s by John Reading – so it's better sung as it was written.'

The windows were beginning to steam up. She switched the engine on and allowed the demister to do its work before she took off.

'I heard from Joy today,' she said. 'She's been offered a part in a sitcom, so has changed her mind about moving in with Lottie.'

Bryn's heart sank. 'Does that mean you won't be moving in with me, as planned?'

'I guess not. I won't feel easy about leaving Lottie there all by herself. Will you mind very much?'

'When I hate every moment spent apart from you, when I live to hear the sound of your voice, crave to see you smile and yearn for the delicate touch of your hand against my fevered brow? Are you mad, woman? Of course I mind.'

Her eyelashes flirted a bit when she glanced his way. 'I'll have to find some way of making it up to you.' Her coat slipped when she changed gear, exposing a pale length of bare thigh above a black stocking attached to a frilly suspender. His throat dried up and he closed his eyes for a moment. Surely she wasn't...? When he opened them he thought he must have been mistaken, until he caught her glance in the mirror, full of bright laughter and faked innocence.

'Oh my God,' he whispered. 'What have you got on under that coat, you seductive little hussy?'

'Just a saucy little something made of black lace and satin. My divorce was finalized today, so I thought we'd celebrate in your spa. I have a bottle of bubbly on ice in the back seat, and have learned a new massage technique from my handbook, *How To Please A Welsh Psychiatrist By Becoming A Sexual Goddess*, written by that well known oriental sheep farmer from Glamorgan, Look Yoo, Boyo.'

The car swerved when he slid a punishing cold hand into the warmest spot inside her coat. After giving a delicious little squeal, she wriggled, slid him a sideways glance and began to sing: 'Your tiny hands are frozen ...'

Laughing, and suddenly feeling as hot as Hades, he couldn't wait to get her home.

His workload the following week was busy because he'd rescheduled some appointments to deal with Pandora's crisis the week before. That would have come sooner or later, and he was pleased it was sooner – before the pressure really blew the lid off.

Her choice of retribution had been simple and direct – all her frustration and anger efficiently metamorphosed into a pile of broken glass and china, her disappointment over Trinity washed away in an ocean of tears.

He'd held her until she'd cried herself out, then unwisely pointed out something she'd missed in the wording of the lawyer's letter – *contact will not be encouraged at this time*.

'This means they haven't completely shut the door on contact in the future,' he'd said to her. 'Just be patient.' Hope had flared in her eyes, and trust, which had made him uneasy with himself, because he wasn't as confident of his people-skills as she was.

What if the wording of the letter had been a polite way of saying no? He'd met Australians. On the whole they were warm, friendly people with a laconic sense of truth, but no desire to hurt people unless pushed to it. What if *at this time* meant, *not at any time*?

And now there was a new sense of optimism in Pandora – an air of expectancy and waiting ... for the phone to ring ... a letter to drop on the mat saying something like *I miss you mummy ... please come*.

It would never happen that way. The relationship between the two women was vegetable and mineral ... the emotional aspect one-sided.

He could only imagine how Trinity had felt when she'd received Pandora's letter. Her very foundations would have been pulled from under her. Self-esteem and a sense of worth would have been replaced by self-doubt – if she hadn't shut her mind down on it completely – and possibly some resentment.

Yet, now the seed had been planted it would slowly grow. People were curious. Trinity might have a child, and would then understand what the pain of parting would be like ... or she might see something in that child and puzzle over it. *I wonder why her eyes are that colour ... or shape ... or where did she inherit her musical ability*, and she might think of the mother who gave her life, and might make enquiries.

And it *might* take years before she was ready to commit to such a step. Everything was a mess of ifs and mights.

It was unlikely that Trinity needed her, but Pandora needed to let her daughter know she'd been loved. That a nurturing, maternal bond had surfaced when she'd first seen her baby, and was now programmed into her psyche.

He hoped it would happen for both their sakes, but mostly for Pandora's, because he didn't want it eating away at her for the rest of her life, didn't want to see the sadness in her eyes when he caught her unawares and knew she was thinking of her lost child. So between patients he rang her and told her he loved her, because he had his needs too, and one of them was making her happy.

Later, he went down to the centre, conducting a group-counselling session for juvenile offenders as part of their probation. A complete waste of time as far as he was concerned, because juveniles would always make and learn from their own mistakes, the way they always had.

He enjoyed their company, their colourful language, and their boisterous and total disregard for convention. He joined them in a lively game of basketball afterwards, the fresh air and exercise charging him with energy.

Just as he was about to leave the centre, Lottie hurried out of the kitchen, untying her apron.

'Can I talk to you if you're not busy?'

Lottie was the least complicated person he knew. Her sessions with him were no longer needed now she'd undergone hypnosis. He'd brought in a female associate who specialized in child abuse and regression techniques. Being the docile person she was, Lottie had responded marvellously to the power of suggestion, though he'd experienced one of those moments of murderous rage when he'd learned exactly what she'd been through.

Thank God, Pandora had been made of tougher material. She was far more complicated than Lottie – not really aggressive, but honest with herself and a fighter when the chips were down.

'I was just going for tea and scones at the café up the road. Fetch your coat and I'll treat you.'

Lottie's news nearly knocked him off his seat. He stared at her, unbelieving.

'You're getting married?'

'I thought you might tell Pandora for me.'

'Hang on a minute.' Although Lottie's diffidence was understandable, he wasn't going to be made the meat in the sandwich. 'If you can make a decision like this, you can certainly tell her yourself.'

'You know what Pandora's like. She'll only worry about it.'

'That's because she cares for you, Lottie. Surely you can understand that.'

'Of course I understand it.' She sighed. 'That's part of the trouble. She'll interfere, and want to make sure Ben's good enough for me.'

'That's natural. Didn't you want to satisfy yourself I was good enough for her? In fact, I remember you coming into my office and asking me what my intentions were.'

Lottie managed a smile. 'Ben works with his hands and lives in a small house in Poole with his two sons. My mother would have considered him unsuitable. Pandora might think the same.'

'I think you're worrying unnecessarily. Pandora isn't a snob.' If she was, he hadn't seen any sign of it with his own family. In fact, a reversed kind of snobbery had been evident, something he'd keep his eye on at Christmas, otherwise his sisters would make her life a misery.

Yet Pandora was no slouch at verbal sparring when pushed to it. Lottie wouldn't stand a chance if Pandora decided to take her on over the issue, so he could understand her reticence.

'Tell you what, Lottie. Ask your Ben to put on his best suit and face up to her with you. About seven. I'll be there if it will help.'

Her face lit up in a smile. 'Thank you, Bryn.'

He placed a hand over hers. 'There's one thing we should perhaps talk about, Lottie. In view of what happened to you in the past, there are certain aspects of marriage you might wish to consider.' He cleared his throat, knowing he sounded pompous, and for once, his natural gift of the gab deserted him. He couldn't even think of a quote to cover the situation, at least, not for Lottie's tender ears. 'Perhaps it would be better if you consulted Pandora about that side of things.'

'If you're talking about the physical side, Ben and I are quite … compatible.' Her smile had a certain contentment to it, despite her faint blush. 'I never thought my mother's death would bring such freedom from loneliness for me, and I never dreamed I'd meet someone nice like Ben, and be married like a normal woman. I'm really looking forward to having a family to care for.'

The relief Bryn felt was all-encompassing. Perhaps the ability to shed the past and move forward was a Dysart trait. A pity Lottie hadn't had the gumption to do it sooner. His mouth twitched as he tried to contain his smile. 'Tell her that, if she argues – and stand up to her, Lottie my love.'

Her eyes came shyly up to his. 'I'd really like you to give me away, if you wouldn't mind.'

'Mind? Of course I wouldn't mind. In fact, I'd be damned annoyed if you hadn't asked me.'

Pandora took the news calmly, as if she'd been expecting it, but not quite yet. The expression on her face was a mixture of disbelief, of happiness, and of affection whenever she looked at Lottie's happy face.

That's my girl, Bryn thought, as proud of Pandora's attitude as he was of Lottie's stand.

Ben was subjected to several assessing sideways glances from Pandora, as if she was trying to satisfy herself he didn't eat with his mouth open, or wear odd socks or dribble food on his tie. *Poor sod!* He was sweating a bit under her silent scrutiny.

Pandora insisted on opening a bottle of champagne for the occasion.

Ben sat on the couch with his knees together, appearing awkward and out of place in his navy-blue suit, and staring into his glass as if he didn't quite know what to do with it.

'Would you prefer a beer?' Pandora asked, and he started at being directly addressed.

He placed the glass carefully on the table and fiddled with the knot of his tie. 'I'm not much of a drinker, I'm afraid.'

Bryn smiled when Pandora put out another feeler. 'Where were you thinking of living after your marriage? Lottie's grown up here, she's used to the place.'

'I have a house in Poole.'

'I know, but if you lived here you could act as caretaker.'

Admiration came into Bryn's eyes. *The crafty little cat!*

Ben drew himself up and looked her straight in the eye. 'I have no intention of becoming a caretaker. I have my own business to run. My house isn't as grand as this, of course, but it's good enough – and though the business will never make me rich, it brings in a decent living. Lottie won't lack for anything, and she'll get proper respect from my boys, or they'll hear it from me.'

Bryn wanted to applaud when Lottie cut in:

'And just because I've spent my life here, it doesn't mean I want to stay here until I die. This house doesn't hold many happy memories for me, and I'd much rather live in Poole.' She smiled lovingly at Ben. 'That's settled then. I'll go and get my coat, otherwise we'll be late for the pictures.'

Ben shuffled from one foot to the other. 'You don't have to worry about Lottie, really, Mrs Rossiter. I'll look after her better than her own family could.'

Which was a mouthful, if ever Bryn had heard one!

There was something awesomely feral about the smile Pandora gave him. 'Of course you will, Ben. If you don't, I'll bloody well cut your throat.'

A huge grin spread across Ben's face and he began to laugh. 'I knew you were a bit of all right the minute I set eyes on you, missus.'

'So did I,' Bryn said.

'What do you think?' she said after the couple were gone.

'I think she's got a good man there. I think she deserves to be happy … and she will be.'

'When did you know about it?'

'About two hours before you did.' Lottie's confidences to him always annoyed Pandora, but he wasn't about to spare her that.

The glance she slanted up at him was uncertain. 'Why didn't she tell me first? What's wrong with me?'

'She's in awe of you because you were able to stand up to her mother when she couldn't … and I guess your strength is off-putting to her, for the same reason.'

The laugh she gave had a slightly bitter edge to it. 'Standing up to Emily Dysart cost me heaps. I lost my home, my security and my nerve. I married the first man who asked me, and for the wrong reason. I spent nineteen years frightened to open my mouth at all, in case I lost my security all over again.'

'What was the wrong reason?'

He could see the hesitation in the depths of her eyes, the bewilderment and the pain of self-understanding. He wanted to take her in his arms and shield her from herself, and he winced when she blurted out. 'He reminded me of Robert Dysart.'

'And you can't understand why you loved a paedophile in the first place?'

'Of course I can. He was the only person who showed me love … but why didn't I see what he was, even though I knew what he was doing was wrong?'

'Think about what you said before about your marriage to Gerald.'

She thought, puzzling at first, then the answer came suddenly to her. She snapped her fingers.

'I thought Robert Dysart loved me, which gave me a sense of security.'

'Expand on it a bit, if you can.'

'Certainly, doctor.' Her smile was a bit self-conscious. 'As soon as my grandmother died and I knew I was secure, then there was no reason to stay married to Gerald – and don't bother sending me a bill, I figured that out for myself.'

Most people did figure things out for themselves if given the right sort of encouragement from a good listener.

Consternation flitted over her face. 'Hey, there's a downside to this self-analysis business What if I see *you* as a father figure??'

He threw her a smug glance. 'That's hardly likely, seeing as how I'm four years younger than you. I've got to admit, you're not bad for an old broad, though.' This brought a cushion down on his head, and before long they were wrestling on the floor, laughing like idiots and with Sam leaping all over them.

One thing led to another, and the rest of the evening contained enough excitement to satisfy them both – once Sam was sent off to sulk in his basket.

October moved into November, and the smoky smell of bonfires was replaced by odours of damp leaf-mould and mist.

Choir practice, with Rankin growing more agitated the nearer the performance came. He was a scholarly-looking man whose own voice was mediocre, but whose ear for pitch was deadly accurate. One off note would have him almost tearing his hair out.

Miss Robins gave him no cause for complaint, now being word perfect. As an added bonus for Bryn, she knew the part of the schoolboy soprano he was singing a duet with, allowing him to rehearse it.

She had a nice, clear voice, reaching the high notes with no strain at all. Rankin gave her an assessing glance when they finished.

'Not bad at all, Miss Robins.'

Bryn thought she might faint with the excitement of receiving praise.

Rankin turned his way, his smile stretched to its sarcastic limit. Stress had made him more courageous. 'Mr Llewellyn ... we are not standing on the Welsh hills bringing in the sheep, we are praising the birth of our Lord. A little less fortissimo if you please.'

Then, when they'd rehearsed to his satisfaction, he told them: 'The next two rehearsals will be in the abbey with the school choir, after which will be the performance.' Which brought a buzz of excitement all round. He beamed round at them all, suddenly genial. 'The performance will be attended by the parents of the boys this year, so the seats will have to be reserved – and for immediate family only, please, because we expect a good turn out.'

And that was where Bryn ran into trouble, with Rankin arguing that as he wasn't married yet, he couldn't book a seat for Pandora – and *he* hadn't made the rules, the school had.

To which Bryn answered, that he – Rankin – wasn't on the school staff yet, so he could drop his airs and graces. He also threatened he'd book seats for every member of his family in Wales if that were the case, which would take up half the church. And how would the school know if he was married to Pandora or not?

After a bit of verbal sparring, Bryn triumphantly carried home four tickets, in case Lottie, Ben and Michael wanted to attend as well.

Before then, though, he had Lottie's wedding to attend, Christmas presents to buy and his woman to love. All of which would take up a great deal of his time.

He made a list of all his nephews and nieces, then realized to his surprise that he didn't have any nephews, bought his nieces a Barbie doll each, so they couldn't squabble. Five boxes of chocolates for his sisters, five bottles of whiskey for their husbands and one for his da, a gold horse-shoe brooch for his mother with tiny diamonds for nails – she could show it off in church on Sundays. He had all the parcels gift-wrapped in the shop to save him the bother.

He bought Lottie a toaster for a wedding present, agonizing for five minutes over which colour to choose. Taking advice from the salesgirl, he settled on chrome, which she assured him would go with anything.

He knew exactly what he was getting Pandora for Christmas. He paid for it, arranging to have it delivered to his home the following week.

Christmas shopping done, he concentrated on loving his woman. She'd be home now, sitting in front of the fire with her knees tucked under her chin. She and Lottie were probably going over arrangements for the wedding.

It was to take place at the church. Lottie had already told him her suit was pale blue with a flared skirt, and she was going to wear a hat with violets around the brim. He decided to wear a violet waistcoat with his grey suit, to match.

Grabbing up a bottle of white wine, he headed out into the evening. A chilly mist rose from the ground as he headed out of town. If it got much thicker he'd have to stay the night. He hoped it got thicker.

There was a niggling worry in his head as he turned into the driveway of Marianna. After Lottie married at the weekend, Pandora would be out here alone. It was an isolated spot, the neighbouring houses standing aloof in their own grounds.

The sitting-room light was on, the curtains drawn back so that an oblong of light spilled down over the garden. He saw shadows moving across the light – Pandora's instantly recognizable from the shape and the way she moved, sinuous and graceful.

He let himself in, giving the investigative Sam a pat of reassurance.

Two women looked up when he walked into the sitting room. One was Pandora, the other was someone he didn't know.

His eyes took in the photograph album open on the table ... and something about the scene made his heart sink a little.

Perhaps it was Pandora's over-bright welcoming smile, or the way her eyes flicked guiltily to the photograph album, then to the woman. Then he thought he might have imagined it when she walked across to kiss him.

'Mary, this is Bryn Llewellyn, my fiancé.'

He walked to where the woman stood, taking her hand and shaking it. Her face had a life of hardship and worry etched into it, and her smile was cautious, as if she hadn't smiled much and was just learning how.

He gazed down at the photo album, his gaze caught by a stunningly beautiful girl. It was either Pandora a few years ago, or...?

His glance of enquiry was met with such a blazing challenge he took a step back, wondering what he'd done to earn it.

'Mary is Trinity's ... *adoptive* mother. She's been telling me about Trinity's childhood.'

She'd been filling in a void ... fuelling Pandora's need with hunger and envy, because Pandora was desperate to see her daughter, and any information was a crumb to build up a picture.

The air was thick with Pandora's resentment now. He'd interrupted. A mere male had dared to tread on hallowed ground.

When he silently questioned her hostile attitude, he realized he didn't know a thing about mother-love. He only knew he'd openly opposed her quest to find Trinity, and now understood she was desperate enough to sacrifice their relationship – if he got in her way.

What also came as a surprise was the thought that his motive to oppose might have been jealousy in case Trinity came between them.

Physician heal thyself, he muttered under his breath, then, plastering a smile on his face, he said with as much assurance as he could muster. 'That's absolutely wonderful, I couldn't be more pleased.'

CHAPTER SIXTEEN

Trinity had never been happier, and she'd never felt better. In five short months her baby would be born. Just that morning she'd learned from an ultra-scan that their baby was a boy, and she couldn't wait for Bruno to come home so she could tell him.

Angela's head was resting lightly against her stomach, a nightly ritual now. As soon as she finished reading her a story, Angela whispered, 'Good-night, baby, good-night, mum.' Then she settled down to sleep.

Trinity kissed her cheek, then went through to the kitchen. Bruno would be home soon. She set the table, adding a couple of candles because she always tried to make their time together romantic and special.

Half an hour passed before he arrived. A smile lit her face when she heard the garage door rumble open. He came up behind her and cuddled her, looking over her shoulder and resting his palms gently on her stomach. He kissed her behind the ear, and because she couldn't wait to tell him, she snuggled herself back into his body.

'Guess what? I had an ultra-scan today and the baby's a boy.'

She could almost feel him grin. 'Hey, that's great … that's fantastic … a boy, huh?'

He'd have been equally pleased with a girl, because Bruno was far from being an egotist.

'I thought we might call him—'

'Not an Italian name, please, Trini.' He gave her a pained laugh, as if he'd known she intended to name the baby after him.

She swallowed her disappointment and turned to face him. 'Our son's on track for the middle of April, so he must have been conceived in Naples. One day we'll take him back and show him the house his family used to own.'

He frowned for a moment, looking as though he didn't quite relish the thought of it, then he shrugged and his eyes narrowed in on her. A wicked smile slowly spread across his face and he took her face between his hands and kissed her.

'I know exactly when he was conceived, and I'll show you after dinner.'

It turned out to be a video. It started innocuously enough with her filming the bay from the balcony of their hotel room in Naples ... there was a blur, then the picture steadied to show her folding clothes into a case. She was wearing her slip.

Her hand went to her mouth. *Oh God ... she couldn't possibly have...?*

Bruno came in from the other room just after she closed the lid. 'I can't shut my suitcase,' she'd obviously said, and she'd knelt on it. His eyes wandered along the length of her body, and when he grinned she could almost read his thoughts.

... She had left the video running!

'Oh no...' she said, heat rushing to her cheeks as everything came back to her, and she picked up a cushion and held it over her eyes.

He was laughing when he took it from her. His hand slid around hers as he teased. 'Come on, Trini. Watch it with me, watch our son being conceived.'

Seeing them making love together made her blush a lot, and she was pleased she had Bruno's shoulder to hide in from time to time. She appreciated the video was not pornographic, just an erotic account of two people expressing their love for one another, and completely unaware they were being filmed.

Bruno was very much the instigator, she acquiescent in her enjoyment of his touch, and made available to his demands by his skill in arousing her ... though she'd since learned to be bolder.

And when the climax came – when the powerful, thrusting, triumph of his orgasm combined with the exquisite, shuddering surrender of hers – then she knew that moment must have been the catalyst for the conception of their son.

'That was quite beautiful,' she said, still blushing and because being voyeur to their own lovemaking had aroused them both, and because Bruno had tenaciously exploited the erogenous zones of her body whilst they were being visually stimulated, they were already hot for each other.

She slid her mouth around to his, her whole body energized with the deep, aching sense of the urgent love she felt for him.

*

Bruno was a happy man when he left his lawyer's office.

He had good news for Trini – the adoption of Angel had gone through.

He was on his way to Posers, the modelling agency he'd started out with – though it hadn't been a modelling agency when he'd bought it, but a combination of modelling and escort. It hadn't been called Posers, then either, but Cassandra's Companions.

He'd met his first wife there. Maryanne had come in looking for work as a model. She'd been gorgeous, and he'd married her, making sure she got the best jobs. She'd soon become popular, but the rot had set in when she found out she was pregnant. Throughout her pregnancy, Maryanne had whined and complained, and as soon as Angel was born she'd disappeared back into the night-club scene like a worm down a hole.

She'd kept late hours, sleeping through most of the day and missing jobs she'd been hired for. Soon, she'd begun to look like hell and the job offers had trailed off. She'd been a lousy mother, and an unfaithful wife, and he'd been on the brink of divorcing her when she'd died.

Bruno had reorganized the business into a legitimate modelling agency by then, and had raised a loan to buy Swingers, a club he'd changed from a tacky disco into a theme club to attract a wealthy clientele. It was doing well, and in the future he intended to open an interstate chain of clubs.

He also owned half of the hock-shop in partnership with Steve, and a half-share in an undertaker's business, which no one but Steve and his accountant knew about, and which he'd now transferred into Trini's name. The other half belonged to the woman who managed it. Davinia Roger's father had been an undertaker, and she knew the business inside out.

Apart from Trini, Steve and Davinia were the only two people Bruno trusted.

He'd met Davinia in a bar when he was out with Steve one night. She'd been with a man and had quickly become inebriated – too inebriated for one drink. When the man had half carried her out, he'd winked at two others and they'd followed after them.

She'd been trying to fight them off, and to even things up he and Steve had joined in the fracas. Although older than himself, Davinia had been a looker. One thing had led to another, and they'd set up in business together, remaining friends long after the affair had run its course.

He'd spoken to Davinia before he'd transferred ownership, assuring her nothing would change. She'd still have complete autonomy, as per their agreement – and to be quite honest, being a silent partner suited him fine; he had no interest in the procedures accompanying death.

Because of the nature of the business it brought in a steady income – and would continue to do so. Death was predictable – unpredictable only in its selection of victim.

Bruno had seen his accountant the previous day. His finances just covered his existing loans. He'd made an appointment with his bank-manager for the following week, with the intention of renegotiating them.

He'd also increased his life insurance. If anything happened to him he wanted his family to be secure, he thought as he took the elevator down to the ground floor and strode into the lobby and out on to St George's Terrace.

The day was overcast, but so far the rain had held off. He strolled through the arcade to a jeweller's shop and picked up a bracelet he'd bought for Trini. It was a simple, eighteen-carat gold band with hearts etched into it. He'd had a message engraved inside. *To my wife, Trini – I'll love you forever, and forever after – Bruno.*

So Angel wouldn't feel left out he purchased a silver heart hanging on a chain, and had engraved on it *Love to my favourite Angel* whilst he waited.

He passed a baby wear shop on the way to the car park. There was a life-sized doll in the window with staring pale-blue eyes and a stupid grin. He grinned back just as stupidly … and by the time he reached his car he was piled up with parcels of all things blue. A son! He hoped Trini would give him a couple more children over the next few years … then he'd be somebody. A man needed a family.

He joined the traffic flow, increasing speed when he reached the outskirts of the city. There was a sense of completion about him now he'd taken a few simple business steps to safeguard them all.

He whistled along with the radio, feeling relaxed, despite the headache he'd been carrying around with him for the past couple of days. It wasn't until he turned into his own driveway that he realized he'd gone home instead of on to Posers.

Trinity was delighted when Bruno arrived home.

'I'll make you a cup of tea before you go on to the club, you've been looking a bit pale for the last couple of days.'

'It's a tension headache, that's all.'

She set the tea before him and smiled. 'What's in the parcels?'

'Open them and see.' He pulled Angel on to his lap and two pairs of matching eyes watched her examine the things he'd bought for the expected son and brother.

She cuddled a cute blue suit against her cheek. 'He'll look so sweet in this.' And she stared at Bruno, thinking dreamily, *He'll be the most perfect baby in the world. He'll inherit his father's looks, those beautiful hyacinth-blue eyes of his and his dark hair.*

He should have a family name. 'I know you don't want him named after you, Bruno, but what about your father or grandfather?'

His gaze shifted sideways, then back to her face. Different emotions flitted across it. He seemed to be struggling with something, and she held her breath.

'It's not a good idea.'

'Why not? Are they awful names like Caligula or Tiberius?'

Bruno didn't even crack a smile. He just put Angel down and watched her scamper off. His eyes came up to hers, went past her. For a moment he stared over her head out of the window, then his gaze came back to her and he said flatly. 'I lied to you.'

Her heart gave a little leap. 'Lied? I don't understand.'

'That place I showed you in Naples wasn't my family home. I was born in the slums, ended up on the streets and never knew who my parents were.'

'And Giorgio Demasi you talked so much about?'

His smile was edged with sadness. 'Giorgio existed. He plucked me out of a soup-kitchen and gave me his name and an education. So you see, Trini, you're married to a nobody.'

She slid her hand into his across the table and said fiercely, 'If you're a nobody, then so am I. That makes us equal.'

'Not quite,' he said carefully. 'You have ways and means of finding out about your background. That's something to hang on to.'

She remembered the letter from some woman claiming to be her mother, remembered with clarity the awful sensation of panic she'd felt, and throwing the letter away without noting the details. She'd also thrown away the adoption order her father had given her.

Now he was dead, and her adoptive mother, Mary James had gone back to England – or so Doreen had told her over the phone. She'd felt completely deserted when she'd heard that, her feelings crushed, as if she was an expendable item.

She'd never bring her children up without love, she'd never make them feel less than worthy. The fierceness of her love for them both rose up to overwhelm her. 'I don't need them, Bruno. I have you and Angel, and soon the baby will be here. We don't need anyone else.'

'You should at least contact your birth mother.'

'If that woman wanted to be my mother she wouldn't have given me away.'

'Perhaps she had no choice.'

'Perhaps ... perhaps....' She sprang to her feet and walked to the sink, to aimlessly pick up cutlery and dishes put them down again. 'People always have a choice. She made hers when she gave me away.'

'She said you had two brothers.'

'I bet she didn't give them away,' she muttered, then turned, already dismissing it from her mind, because although she didn't want to argue with Bruno, she would if they continued on the same track. 'Can we drop the subject?'

His smile was a little worn. 'Of course. I didn't mean to upset you.'

'You didn't.' She crossed to where he sat and slid on to his lap to prove he hadn't. 'Thanks for the bracelet. It was much too expensive, and you shouldn't have, because I don't need jewels to make me happy. I only need you.' She feathered several tiny kisses all over his face. 'I'll love you for ever, too.'

Which was the absolute truth, for here was a man who made her feel loved, and needed, and cherished.

It was Steve's night off, so Bruno was obliged to stand in at the club for the evening.

There were problems with a couple of men trying to gatecrash. Drunk and abusive as they were – neither he nor the bouncer could pacify them. In the end he was forced to call in the police to eject them. As they went off, hurling threats over their shoulders, Bruno ruefully debated whether the rewards of the hospitality industry were worth the effort.

Right at this moment he could sell the club at a profit and invest elsewhere. He winced as the band struck up a catchy number to take the clients' minds off the fracas. His headache had grown worse over the course of the evening.

He should invest in something more peaceful, he thought – the irony of which didn't escape him as he went to his office in search of some aspirin. He managed a grin. He already had the most peaceful business on earth – he just didn't want to learn how to run it.

Délice poked her head around the door and gave him a big smile. 'How's Trinity going?'

He couldn't help but smile at the thought of her. 'Beautiful, and pregnant, and perfect.'

'I've got to hand it to you, boss. You're a fast worker. A typical male as well. I bet you intend to keep her barefoot and pregnant.'

'There's something to be said for that,' he said, throwing her a grin. 'You should try it yourself.'

'Don't hold your breath.' Délice laughed and moved on.

He closed the club just after two, placing the take in the safe, and checking that the main doors were secure.

With the two abusive drunks in the back of his mind, he checked out the alley, then let himself out – a time-switch allowing him enough light to unlock his car and secure himself inside. Within twenty minutes he was home, sighing with relief.

Sleep, that's what he needed. He swallowed a couple more aspirin and slid into bed. A sigh trickled from Trini's mouth and she moved against him. He gently kissed her cheek and spooned her into his body. She fitted as if she belonged there, which she did.

Tears filled his eyes as he felt the absolute depth of his love for her. He couldn't understand why he was experiencing this moment of melancholy, when life had never been so good. He was too tired for sex, too tired for anything. All he wanted to do was sleep, and to sleep curled around the woman he loved.

Two hours later he woke. A pulse was pounding inside his head and he felt sick. When he tried to sit up he had no control of his limbs and everything spun.

Something was wrong! His words were slurring as he tried to call Trini's name. A stroke perhaps…? Not at his age … it was ridiculous! … it was unfair when he was so happy.

There was a click.

'Bruno?'

The sudden light hurt his eyes but he couldn't shut them, and the voice came from a distance.

'Oh, my God! What's the matter, Bruno, my darling?'

He saw her then, her head haloed in the light, as though she were an angel or something. Her mouth was forming his name, but he couldn't hear the words. Her eyes rounded in panic as she reached across him for the phone. He wanted to reach up and touch her face. *Such beautiful eyes*

... so green and anxious now. Ah ... how he loved her. Heat prickled inside his head, spreading ripples into his skull. He thought he heard the bell of an ambulance.

I'm dying ... not when I've found the love I've always craved for.

Trini's face was wet with tears. He didn't want to make her cry, he loved her. He tried to say her name and her face faded into a wave of redness which grew dimmer and dimmer until finally he could see nothing but the dark space inside his head ... there was a moment of incredible anger in him, then peace....

'*Oh God! ... oh God! ... oh God!*' Trinity stuffed her bunched fist into her mouth to stop herself screaming.

'If it's any consolation, he wouldn't have felt anything,' the doctor said.

No consolation at all ... Bruno was dead ... nothing would ever console her. She wanted to die herself.

Her whole mind was a mass of disjointed emotions. They attacked each other like piranha fish in a feeding-frenzy – the razor-sharp teeth peeling away the hastily erected defences of denial layer by layer, leaving her raw.

'He was alive when he got here, which was lucky. He's on life support at the moment.'

Her head jerked up as if it was on a string. The hope in her voice was pathetic. 'But you said he was dead.'

There was compassion in the eyes behind the glasses. 'He had a brain aneurysm, and the haemorrhage was massive. Even though we clamped it off, nothing could have saved him.'

'Then why...?' She stared at him, her eyes widening in horror as the reason seeped from inside the rawness. 'You want his body parts, don't you? That's why you're keeping him alive.'

Panic rose inside her like a tidal wave. *Bruno's beautiful body, so warm and alive, cut to pieces?* It didn't bear thinking about. It was macabre. She shook her head from side to side so she didn't *have* to think.

'It was what he indicated on his driving licence, but we need your permission, Mrs Demasi.'

How could this doctor be so persistent in the face of her grief?

Because his job is to save life, not to agonize over a life already expended.

But she couldn't be sensible yet. She just couldn't imagine Bruno being dead. She had to see for herself.

'What if you made a mistake? I want to see him, first ... before ... I sign anything.'

He nodded, obviously used to it. 'I'll get the sister to take you in. As soon as your friend gets here, she'll let him know where you are.'

She'd got the hospital to ring Steve, she couldn't think who else to call ... and she'd called in the next-door neighbour, who'd promised to care for Angela until the housekeeper came in. Mercifully, the child had slept through all the clamour.

First light was coming through the window, tinting the room a pale yellow. It was too happy a colour for death. Bruno lay under a sheet, looking for all the world as though he were asleep. His skin was warm when she took his hand in hers. Around them, the machinery bleeped and wheezed – relentlessly breathing for him, keeping his heart pumping blood – the heart they wanted to cut from his body.

'Please give us some privacy,' she said to the nurse, who'd started checking the equipment, and seemed to be there to keep an eye on her, *in case she picked up her husband's body and absconded into the night with it.* She knew she was being paranoid when the woman silently left.

He would want someone else's life to be saved.

Bruno looked as if he would wake up any moment, kiss her and tell her he loved her. The bracelet he'd given her was still on her wrist. *I'll love you forever, and forever after.* Bruno's *forever after* would be longer than his for ever.

She spent twenty minutes with him, telling him she loved him, willing him to open his eyes, to wake, to speak to her. The machine pumped air in and sucked air out. His chest rose and fell, his hand was warm inside hers, without a response, without life.

Eventually, she admitted defeat, and standing, tucked his hand back under the sheet. She leaned over and kissed him, her heart breaking into a million tiny pieces when he didn't respond. Her beautiful Bruno was gone from her, without even having the time to say goodbye.

Then the baby stirred inside her, a fluttering of life ... her son ... Bruno's son, conceived from their love. Inside her was a boy who'd never know his beautiful father, only through her eyes. And she'd build Bruno into a legend for him and for Angela – and to hell with the truth!

'Goodbye, my darling, husband,' she whispered. 'You'll live on in our baby, because whether you like it or not, I'm calling him after his daddy – and I'll make your children so proud of you.'

Then Steve was leading her away. She gave the still form behind her one last agonized look, then signed the form, because Bruno would have wanted her to and she had to believe the doctor was competent enough to recognize death when he saw it.

Receiving into her hands the wedding-ring she'd placed on her husband's finger those few short months ago, she slid it on to her middle finger next to her own. *Till death us do part!*

Steve took her to a house that suddenly felt so empty it wasn't like a home any more. He stayed with her whilst she broke the news to Angela, his face haggard with shock.

Angela wasn't old enough to totally comprehend death, but she instinctively understood that something momentous had happened, something that would prevent her father from ever coming home again. She grizzled a bit, clinging tightly to Trinity, as if frightened she'd leave her too.

'It's all right, darling.' Trinity held her close, glad she didn't have only herself to think about. 'I won't leave you and we'll have the baby to look after soon.'

'I'll give Bruno's lawyer a call,' Steve said. 'Oh God! I can't believe this has happened … not to Bruno. Would you like me to make arrangements?'

She stared at him, uncomprehendingly. He crouched down beside her. 'For the funeral. Davinia Rogers will have to be told, anyway. She'll arrange everything for you.'

'Davinia Rogers?'

'Bruno's partner. Your partner now, I suppose, since he transferred his half of the undertaking business over to you.'

'I don't know what you're talking about, Steve,' and she didn't really care. 'Thanks, I'd be grateful if you could take care of the business end. I can't seem to think.' All she wanted to do was sleep for a week, then wake up to find it was all a nightmare.

'Listen, Trini,' Steve said. 'I know this has hit you hard, but it's going to get worse when word gets out. The sharks will start circling.'

She still didn't know what he was talking about.

'Bruno had debts, and they'll be called in. You'll most certainly lose the club and the modelling agency … and you'll most likely lose this house as well if Bruno used it for collateral for a loan. He had his fingers in a lot of pies, you understand?'

He looked relieved when she nodded. 'The thing is, you need to cover yourself as best you can. Bruno always kept a reserve of cash in his safe. Shall we see what can be salvaged?'

'I don't know the combination,' she said dully.

'I do. Will you trust me on this?'

She nodded. Whom else could she trust, when Bruno so obviously had trusted Steve.

The safe was set in the floor in Bruno's study. Steve removed a bag and rifled through the contents. He smiled up at her, then dropped a small roll of notes and some gold coins back into the safe. 'They'll expect to find something in there. I'll hang on to the rest until things die down.'

He opened a flat box he'd taken from the safe. Diamonds glittered in a sea of black velvet and he gave a wry smile. 'Bruno was going to give you this when the baby was born. If the creditors see it they'll claim it as part of his estate. Is there any other jewellery he's given you?'

'Only my wedding-ring and this bracelet.' A faint smile touched her lips as she handed the bracelet to him. 'I don't want to lose this; look what Bruno had engraved in it? He only gave it to me last night.'

Steve slid it back on to her wrist. 'Wear it. They won't touch anything obviously personal like that.'

She thought Steve was probably doing something illegal, but she didn't really care. Angela had recovered enough to ask for breakfast, and although Trinity didn't feel like eating herself, she was going to try and force herself to. One thing she was determined about – baby Bruno was going to be born healthy.

It was the day of the funeral, and Trinity hadn't realized her husband knew so many people.

Some she recognized from the club, others she'd never seen before. She'd decided on burial. Cremation had seemed so final, and she knew she needed the comfort of visiting his grave – and of bringing his children to this peaceful place in the future, so they'd have a sense of connection with him.

It was a day full of life. The breeze made the shrubs and tree branches dance and shake, and the sky was filled with scudding clouds. Shadows raced across the grass, across the yawning grave.

The coffin was lowered, a bed made for a prince, gleaming black mahogany with silver handles and a silver nameplate. A sob choked from her as she imagined Bruno inside, his hands crossed on his chest.

She'd seen him before they'd closed the lid. He'd been cold and remote, not looking like the warm, sensual man who had made love to her just a few days before. His smell had gone, his lovely, warm, olive skin had a yellow, waxy look. He'd looked dead, and that had surprised her.

She'd tried not to think about the wounds where they'd removed parts of him, and tried not to think of his organs warm and pulsing inside someone else's body, giving them the life that had been snatched from her.

Davinia Rogers had been good to her. 'This isn't Bruno, it's just his body,' she'd said. Now Davinia slipped an arm around her waist in support and handed her a red rose.

'I love you, Bruno,' she whispered, and there was a sense of finality when she dropped it on top of the coffin. 'Safe journey, my darling.'

Soon the house was full of people ... people who'd never been there before, walking around with glasses of wine in their hands, and talking about Bruno as though they'd been the greatest of friends with him.

Condolences were offered. *So sorry ... sorry for your loss .... if there's anything I can do...?*

There was. They could all get out of her house and leave her to mourn Bruno in peace.

And they did, making their excuses one by one, then in trickles, then a flood, until there was only herself and the housekeeper remaining.

They silently gathered up the glasses and plates to stack in the dishwasher, and the housekeeper dissolved into tears when she picked up Bruno's favourite cup. Trinity sent her home. 'I'll do this. I need something to keep me busy.'

When she'd gone, Trinity suddenly became aware of Angel chattering away to someone. A man's voice answered.

My God! ... my God! It couldn't be! Her hand flew to her mouth as a tall figure stepped from Bruno's study. When he moved into the light, she saw that the only resemblance to Bruno was his height. Her heart slowed to its normal pace.

'I'm sorry if I startled you, Mrs Demasi,' he said. 'Your daughter insisted on showing me her daddy's study.'

She took Angela's hand in hers and brought her protectively to her side. 'I didn't see you at the funeral ... who are you?'

'My name's Richard Stowe, and I'm acting on behalf of your husband's bank. I'm here to tell you an application has been approved on behalf of your husband's creditors, to freeze and investigate his assets.'

She went to the door and opened it, smiling at him. 'I'm sorry, Mr Stowe, you're too late ... you see, my husband's already given his heart to someone else.'

'I'll be back in the morning, Mrs Demasi,' he murmured as he went past her.

'That would be the decent thing to do,' she agreed, and closed the door on him.

CHAPTER SEVENTEEN

Pandora enjoyed Lottie and Ben's wedding.

Joy had come down from London, arriving straight from the railway station in a taxi. She left her overnight bag in the porch and strode confidently into the church, looking stunningly vampish in black crushed velvet, a red beret slanted stylishly to one side of a black dye-job.

'Darling!' she cried out, pecking at Pandora's cheek with scarlet lips. For a few moments she posed theatrically at the end of the pew, her eyes roving over the congregation. When nobody recognized her she slid into her seat, took out a powder-compact and examined her face. With a frown she snapped the compact shut, muttering, 'It doesn't seem so long ago that I was young.'

'How's the taping of the television show going?' Pandora said, thinking how animated Joy looked now she was working.

'It has the makings of a smash hit. I play an upper-crust and eccentric grandmother to a couple of stuffy establishment types, whom I totally embarrass. My character rides a motor bike, plays a guitar in a pop group, and involves herself in protests and such whilst she's trying to restore the family fortunes. It's a load of rubbish, really, but good fun. The premier episode is in January. You will watch it, won't you, Pandora?'

'I wouldn't miss it. What's it called?'

'*The Honourable Grandmother*.' Joy laughed when she raised an eyebrow. 'I'm not joking. I'm being interviewed for a magazine next week to publicize the show ... and talking about shows, here comes the bride.'

Lottie looked lovely in a blue suit and hat, and Ben had bought himself a grey, off-the-peg suit for the occasion. Bryn wore a rather eye-catching purple waistcoat and not for the first time, she wondered if it was vanity on his part, or eccentricity. He winked at her when he walked past with a self-conscious Lottie on his arm.

We are gathered together in the sight of God ...

After the ceremony was over, Lottie half turned and glanced at Robert Dysart's window. She turned a bit more, her eyes seeking Pandora out. There was a new resolve in Lottie's expression, and they exchanged a smile of understanding.

A reception was held in the centre for them, with everyone making a fuss of Lottie, and Ben standing by her, with a proud and proprietorial smile on his face. Lottie had bloomed over the past year, but Pandora hadn't realized how well-liked she was.

We'll miss you Lottie ... don't do anything I wouldn't do ... don't forget to come back and see us ... and, how are we going to get along without you? As if she were moving a thousand miles away.

Ben's elder son blushed and stammered when he made his best man's speech, in contrast to Bryn – who, acting as father of the bride, had Lottie blushing and everyone else in fits of laughter.

Then off Lottie went, with Ben at the wheel of Emily's car, all polished up for the occasion, and both of them looking as proud as peacocks. Michael and Ben's two sons had tied a heap of cans, ribbons and an old boot on the back, and they clanged and bumped all the way down the road with everyone cheering and laughing.

Bryn had to go straight off to Milton Abbas for choir practice after the reception, so they kissed goodbye in the car park, with a merry bunch of onlookers wolf-whistling at them.

'Our turn next,' he said, gazing down at her. 'Have you decided when?'

Pandora realized she hadn't given it much thought, even though she'd done the proposing. She fobbed him off with some excuse about the alterations, which he must have seen straight through because his smile turned into a bit of a frown and his eyes assessed her just a fraction too long and too strongly.

Something inside her was holding her off from a final commitment, and it wasn't because she didn't love Bryn enough – in fact, she couldn't imagine her life without him.

She recognized there was a restlessness in her, the need to resolve the dilemma of her daughter. It seemed inconceivable to her that Trinity didn't want to see her, and she couldn't seem to find a way around it except to sit and wait for something to change, which went very much against her nature.

So she kissed Bryn's frown away, and said, 'As soon as Christmas is over we'll set a date. Perhaps I'll have a bit of breathing space then.' Which wasn't much of a promise, but one Bryn accepted without comment.

The night was cold, the air misty. The nearer they got to the sea, the thicker the mist got, until she had to slow almost to a crawl, and Michael was forced to hang his head out of the window to help her navigate. Joy didn't seem to notice the mist, talking animatedly as she was about the television show.

'It's going to be funny not having Lottie here,' Pandora said a little later as the lights of Marianna emerged from the mist. 'Once the tenants are settled in I'll be marrying Bryn, so I'll be gone too.'

'For the first time since the house was built there will be no Dysarts in residence,' Joy said. 'Trust you to break with tradition. Emily will turn in her grave.'

A shiver raced up Pandora's spine. It was odd how much this place had meant to her when she was alienated from her grandmother. Now it was hers, it didn't have quite the same nostalgic feel. In the normal course of events, Marianna should have gone to Lottie, and once the tenants had taken up residence she was going to arrange for Lottie to have income from the rent.

'I suppose you'll let this apartment?' Joy said. Her eyes widened when they saw the empty shelves. 'Hello ... where's Emily's prized china and glass collection gone?'

'I ... um ... smashed it.'

Michael and Joy both turned to stare at her, chorusing. 'Smashed it?'

She gave a short, uneasy laugh. 'I had a bit of a crisis, I'm afraid. I got a letter from a lawyer, telling me my daughter didn't want to know me, and I just let rip.'

'Poor Mum,' Michael said, so obviously choking back his laughter that she grinned. His eyes had an unbelieving look to them. 'I can't imagine you losing your rag. I mean, all that time we were growing up I never heard you raise your voice once. You always seemed like Dad's well-trained pet or something. Wait till I tell Adrian.'

'A well-trained pet!' She didn't know whether to laugh or cry at the description, and Joy snorted with laughter.

'Well ... not a pet exactly, but you were sort of contained and a bit obedient. If Dad wanted you to jump through a hoop, you automatically jumped.'

'You mean I failed you as a mother?'

'Hell no,' Michael said hastily. 'We thought you were a great mother. You never fussed about things like grass stains on cricket whites, scuffed shoes, or whether a tin of biscuits was scoffed in one go, and you never, ever lost your temper.' Mischief rode across his face. 'What happened to you ... a bout of retarded adolescence?'

She grinned at that. 'Could be, and it sounds to me as though you've been mixing with the wrong company. I must have words with Bryn Llewellyn.'

'Did you break my mother's vase as well?' Joy spluttered.

Pandora smiled at her, deciding to put an end to the long-standing farce. 'I don't know why you're sounding so indignant, when you know it's a fake.'

Blood seeped under Joy's skin. 'I know nothing of the sort.'

'Nice try, Joy, but it was valued by the antique dealer who conducted my auction. The vase is worthless, and is in the cupboard if you'd like to take it home with you. Otherwise it will go to a jumble sale when I move out.'

Joy's eyes slanted sideways at her. 'Did you consider that the antique dealer might be wrong?'

'Not for one moment. Is he?'

The laugh Joy gave was bravado layered over embarrassment. 'Hell, no – it wasn't even the same pattern as mother's vase. Emily didn't notice, and it was the one thing I had over her all these years.'

'What happened to the original?'

'I broke it over my first husband's head.'

The three of them dissolved into laughter, which set the stage for an enjoyable evening of reminiscences from Joy, who related some of her marriage and theatre experiences with a lavish measure of abrasive wit.

'Television isn't the theatre, but this show will make me a household name and provide me with a comfortable old age,' she said as a final wind-up. 'I've waited a long time for it, and Brian wouldn't expect me to grieve.'

It wasn't until after she'd gone to bed that Pandora realized Joy hadn't lit up a cigarette once.

Joy left on the morning train, and for once Pandora was sorry to see her go. Now she was gainfully employed in what she loved doing best, Joy had proved to be a delightful companion, her eccentricity endearing.

She spent a lazy day with Michael, and they discussed his plans for his future.

'I have a good chance of getting into medical school. I'm getting top marks in all my subjects, and distinctions in the sciences. You won't see much of me if I do get in, I'm afraid. It's a long, hard slog to qualify.'

'I'm very proud of you, Michael, and I'm sure your father is.'

He shrugged. 'Dad's still disappointed I'm not joining him in the firm, but he'll have to get used to the idea. I have my own life to lead. Adrian will join him, eventually, I suppose.'

'Have you heard from your brother, at all?'

'I got a postcard last week. He was in Bangkok. He said they're going to bypass Malaysia and Indonesia and fly straight over to Sydney.'

Pandora heaved a sigh of relief. 'It's ages since I heard from him, I was worried.'

'You know what postcards are like. They usually fall through the letter-box after the sender arrives back home.' Michael appeared thoughtful for a moment, an expression which reminded her forcefully of his father. It was odd how she rarely thought of Gerald now, unless she saw him mirrored in his sons. 'You know what you said about your daughter not wanting to see you?'

Her smile faded.

'What if Adrian went to see her when he gets over to the west coast of Australia? She might not feel so threatened by him, and agree to see him out of curiosity. Once she's met one of us she'll realize we're not a complete wipe-off as a family. It's just a thought, of course, but wouldn't it be less intimidating for her, than to actually meet you, first off?'

Which was exactly what Bryn had counselled her to do in the first place – use a go-between. Still, she was dubious, Adrian was too young for such a responsibility. *He's nineteen, just five years younger than Trinity. They'll have a lot in common.* The more she thought about it, the more the idea appealed to her.

'Do you think Adrian would agree to it?'

'He is her brother, you know, we both are, and *we're* curious about her. If you're interested I have a list of the youth hostels where Adrian will be staying. He said he was going to ring you on New Year's Day, anyway.'

A smile slowly inched across her face as she thought about it. 'Do you know, Michael, I never really appreciated what wonderful sons I had until I left home.'

The quiet moment of pride and satisfaction she felt was tempered by a humbling thought – despite being a lousy husband, Gerald had probably been a better father to them than she'd been a mother.

Living alone at Marianna wasn't an option Pandora had considered when she'd moved in to care for her grandmother.

It wasn't so bad during the day, when Ben and his sons were about. And sometimes Lottie came along as well, to sweep away the wood shavings, scrape plaster from windows or remove bent nails and tacks from the floorboards.

She seemed to have been incorporated into her husband's business as general handy woman. Ben and his sons gently teased her if she didn't go about a task the right way, and taking the scraper or claw-hammer from her hands would patiently show her the right way to do it. There was an enviable sense of closeness about the four.

Night time was the worst, when she felt like a small embryo in a very large shell. Then the memories of her childhood came rushing down around her, threatening to crush her. Mostly they were small hurts that had made small wounds, like the time her grandfather had screwed up the picture she'd painted of the house and thrown it into the wastepaper basket, or the bunch of bluebells she'd picked for her grandmother, later found wilting in the bin.

But it wasn't just one or two hurts, there were thousands of small hurts piled one on top of the other – and they'd all added up to general lack of interest in her.

Robert Dysart had understood her pain – and had used it for his own pleasure, but in the process he'd made her feel loved and wanted, something her grandparents never had.

Her mouth twisted into a wry grin. No wonder Bryn didn't like her being isolated at Marianna by herself. He must have known the past would come back to haunt her. But then, it wasn't a bad thing. The more she uncovered of her feelings the more she found herself able to rationalize and cope with them.

Sometimes Bryn stayed the night, but more often than not he was caught up in the Christmas festivities, with children's parties, and carol-singing and choir practice.

She knew she should get involved with something herself, apart from the computer course. Her life seemed a bit futile when related to Bryn's, but until the issue of Trinity was resolved she couldn't manage to apply herself properly to do anything else.

Of late, she'd been toying with the idea of getting a dog to replace Sam – who now rode around in the cabin of Ben's truck with a stupid grin on his face, and who wrestled with Ben's sons and chased balls across the lawn for them.

Sam only tried to ingratiate himself into her life now when he smelled something cooking, totally ignoring the fact it had been she who'd rescued him from the pound. She grinned to herself. Sam had a selective memory, and anyway, she'd got him for Lottie. She decided a dog as big as Sam might not suit Bryn's house, and as she wasn't fond of yappy little lapdogs, she dropped the idea.

Even with Christmas so close, she didn't see the need to decorate. She'd sent out cards, including one to Trinity, which she'd only signed with her initials, in case her daughter felt threatened by her whole name. Silly really, because how could a name on a Christmas card threaten anyone … and wasn't she getting a bit paranoid about the whole thing if she was resorting to stupid measures like this?

They were going to Wales the day after the Milton Abbas performance, to spend two days with the Llewellyn family. She was not looking forward to it.

Her glance went to the big box of wrapped presents. She still wasn't sure she'd done the right thing in buying everyone a gift – not that she'd bought anything expensive – just scarves and chocolates and such, gifts that couldn't embarrass anyone.

Because she couldn't wait, she gave Bryn his present on the eve of the Christmas performance at Milton Abbas, sliding the initialled gold signet ring she'd bought him on to his little finger.

They were driving through the picturesque village at the time, on either side of them an avenue of thatched cottages, the alms house and St James's church, sign posting the way to the fourteenth century abbey. Bryn could discover for himself the inscription inside, later.

'You're not getting my present yet,' he said. 'It was too big to carry in my jacket pocket.' And when she asked him to give her a clue, the smile that touched his mouth chased the winter evening from her soul. 'It's grey and has got buttons.'

'A cardigan?'

His eyes were enigmatic, and although she played a guessing game for the rest of the journey, he wouldn't say another word. As he nosed the car into a parking spot right near the abbey, she snuggled her head into his neck and whispered against his ear. 'I love you to pieces.'

'I feel like beating on my chest and hollering whenever you say that.'

'Save your hollering for the performance.'

His smile faded. 'The boy soprano has suddenly caught a galloping case of laryngitis, and so has his understudy. I'll be singing the *Ave Maria* by myself.'

'What about Miss Robins? She sings it beautifully with you.'

'Now, why didn't I think of her?' A smile flooded his face, then just as quickly fled. He slowly shook his head. 'Rancid Rankin wouldn't allow it.'

'Then don't tell him.'

He reflected for a moment, his eyes distancing into space. A big, beautiful smile slowly spread cross his face. 'She might be willing to buck Rankin, at that.'

'I'm sure she will. From what I've seen of her she's one of those capable people who get overlooked or picked on all the time, and just because they're quiet-natured. All she needs is a confidence booster. You're the expert in that department; persuade her.'

And Bryn was good at that, because when the last, vibrating note of the *Ave Maria* faded, the reverential moment of hushed silence was broken by a burst of spontaneous applause.

Rankin postured a bit, then graciously passed the accolades over to Miss Robins and Bryn, by indicating they take a bow – holding his arm towards them, palm flat and facing towards the audience, as if it had been all his idea, when the amazement on his face had been almost laughable when it had begun.

The performance ended with a rousing *Good King Wenceslas*, after which the choirs, parents and teachers refreshed themselves with mugs of cinnamon-spiced hot chocolate and mince pies, served by the boys.

Mr Rankin beamed and smiled as he accepted the congratulations, and introduced Bryn and Miss Robins around. 'Mr Llewellyn is our leading tenor, and Miss Robins,' he gazed at her with a new light in his eyes and said, sort of surprised, 'is a most accomplished soprano. The acoustics here brought out the quality of her voice quite wonderfully.'

Miss Robin's smile had an air of *I told you so* about it, but still, she turned quite red at the compliment.

'Have you ever thought of teaching, Mr Llewellyn?' somebody said. 'I believe there's an opening for a choirmaster at the school.'

Panic gave Rankin's voice a breathless edge. 'Mr Llewellyn's a psychiatrist, not a professional musician ... not much time for anything else in his life, I should imagine. Oh look, Mr Llewellyn, I do believe some of the boys are waiting to talk to you, I shouldn't keep your fan club waiting.'

Before too long Pandora and Bryn were warming themselves in front of the fire in his sitting-room. It was the one room that had an open fireplace. Shadows danced across the ceiling, and a log spat out a shower of sparks as it shifted. As she sipped at the Irish coffee he'd made her, Pandora eyed the three wrapped presents dwarfing his Christmas tree.

'Are they all for me?'

He nodded. He was sitting at the opposite end of the couch, not saying much, but just looking at her. His eyes were dark against hers, reflective, and she could almost read his thoughts. Her smile contained enough mischief to whet his appetite. Finishing her coffee she set the cup on a side-table, kicked off her shoes and slid herself on to his lap.

'How much Irish did you put into that coffee?'

'Enough to knock out a rhinoceros.'

'Odd,' she mocked, 'because I feel quite frisky.'

'That's because you're not a rhinoceros. I have it on good authority that Irish coffee has a detrimental effect on rhinos.'

'The RSPCA was called in to capture a drunken rhinoceros ...'

'... who was found ringing doorbells at midnight. When asked what the hell he was doing ...'

'... he said he had an appointment with—'

'Let's stop playing games, Pandora,' he said abruptly. 'How much longer do you intend to keep me dangling on a string?'

'Only as long as you'll let me.' She traced a line down his nose to his mouth, watching his lips quiver as she outlined them. 'Don't go all prickly on me, Bryn Llewellyn. You've been wearing the answer on your finger all night. The date's inscribed inside.'

A smile softened his mouth. 'What does it say?'

'Valentine's Day.'

'But that's only eight weeks away.'

'Uhuh! Now, what's in those packages?'

'I told you, something grey with buttons.' He slid down the couch with her on top of him and pulled her close. 'Come here, first; I've got something I think you'll enjoy.'

And that something had some really heart-stopping moments ... and a long time afterwards she got to open her Christmas present, and she thought she'd rather enjoy the computer as well, especially since she was now learning how to use one.

Snow had visited Wales, the mountains were iced in white, and loomed cold and imposing above them. She gazed at the ring on her finger. The stone picked up the winter light, making it seem an icy blue. Merlin was frozen inside.

'I've booked us into a hotel,' Bryn told her. 'I thought it would be easier all around.'

There was a sense of relief in her, and a sense of shame too, as if she were somehow responsible for causing a division in his family. 'You didn't have to do that for me, Bryn.'

'It's not all for you, darlin'.' He slipped her an exaggerated leer. 'My mother's a bit straight-laced, and I'd rather we shared the same bed. We'll stop in on the way for a cuppa to let them know we've arrived.'

Wynn Llewellyn's pursed lips said it all, but she didn't stop at that. 'Is it getting too good for us, you are?' She slid Pandora a look that clearly told her where the blame was to be placed.

'Nothing of the sort, and here's some good news. You're the first to know. Pandora and I are to be married on Valentine's Day.'

There was another sniff, then a grudging, 'Married is it ... are you indeed? Well, it's about time, with you being as old as you are, and Pandora not getting any younger. Soon the pair of you will be too old to have a family, then where will you be?'

'Married and childless, like lots of couples,' Bryn said.

Having a family was something neither of them had really discussed, except for a fleeting remark Bryn had made once about giving her a daughter to replace Trinity. Birth control hadn't been on their agenda, but she'd been taking precautions for years, which Bryn knew, and she'd seen no reason to stop. For herself, it didn't matter. She had children. Her heart gave an anguished squeeze as she thought of Trinity. But yes, she'd like to share a child with Bryn and he'd be a wonderful father, so it was really up to her.

'We should have a grandson to carry on your da's name.'

'Llewellyns are twenty to the dozen in Wales, so any offspring we might have wouldn't make much of a difference.' Bryn's hand slid around his mother's waist and pulled her against him, making the three of them one. 'And before you go any further, you can congratulate us and give us a kiss, else I'll be thinking you've turned your back on your son, and his future wife's not welcome in your house.'

To which Wynn got very indignant, and flustered about and pecked and hugged and nagged, until she finally disappeared into the kitchen, coming back with a determined smile on her face and a tray loaded down with tea and scones.

It was obvious the Llewellyns took Christmas very seriously. There was a huge Christmas tree loaded up with presents, and the house smelled of a mixture of pine-needles, mincemeat pies, boiled fruit-pudding and brandy.

Pandora thought the phone lines must have been running hot that evening. On Christmas Day it was very obvious that Bryn's sisters were all on their best behaviour. Even Olwyn thanked her for the silk scarf, but couldn't resist taking her aside and chiding her for buying something so expensive.

'Not that it's not lovely, mind,' she said wistfully, and her work-worn fingers stroked over the filmy silk. 'It will spruce up my best blue dress a treat, but you shouldn't have spent so much.'

There was a flicker of pity in Pandora's heart, that the woman should think such a cheap gift expensive, and she should have a dress she kept for best. Of the sisters, Olwyn was the one least well off. Her husband was out of work and she spent every evening cleaning at the local school to earn a little extra to supplement her benefits. No wonder she was sharp.

'I was wondering ...' Pandora said on impulse, and without allowing herself time to think about it and change her mind '... whether you'd like to be my matron of honour at our wedding.'

A pair of dark eyes gazed sharply at her. 'And why should you want me?'

For a moment, Pandora thought Olwyn might prove to be difficult, then she saw the need for acceptance in her eyes and laid her cards on the table. 'For Bryn's sake, I don't want to come into this family with ready-made enemies. Just because we didn't hit it off when we met, it doesn't mean the situation has to continue.'

Olwyn nodded, but her chin lifted a fraction. 'I can't afford to come fancy, mind you.'

'You won't have to pay for an outfit. Bryn will take care of it.' She hadn't consulted him about that yet, but knew he'd agree. Olwyn had her pride, and coming from Bryn, the gift would be more acceptable. 'I thought we might wear suits. I'll send you some patterns and materials to choose from, and I'll have them made up. Something pretty, but serviceable, so it can be worn again. And you could come up the day before, so we could get our hair done ...'

Olwyn's eyes began to sparkle at the thought, then she gazed at her. 'I thought you said you had a daughter? Won't she want to be matron of honour?'

Again that lurch in the region of Pandora's heart. 'She lives in Australia. I haven't seen her for many years.'

'How old is she?'

'She'd be twenty-four now ...' She realized her mistake when Olwyn sucked in a scandalized breath.

'Oh, my God. You'd have only been—'

'I was fifteen, and I was sexually abused by someone. The baby was taken from me.' She sucked in a deep breath, mortified by what she'd said, and trying not to let the pain of the past show in her voice. 'They told me she was dead, but I recently discovered she'd been adopted. I'm trying to establish contact with her, but so far it's not working.'

She'd expected Olwyn to sneer, but instead she found the woman's thin arms around her in a hug that was strangely comforting. 'You poor old thing. Does Bryn know?'

'Of course he does.'

Owen walked in just at that moment and smiled at them both from his lofty height. 'That's nice, seeing the pair of you friends at long last.'

'Pandora has asked me to stand up with her at her wedding to Bryn,' Olwyn said proudly.

The approval in Owen's eyes wasn't too hard to take. 'That's a lovely gesture, Olwyn. Mind you're on your behaviour, then.'

'Oh, Da, stop treating me like a little girl. I'm a married woman with children.'

He gave her a hug and kissed the top of her head. 'You'll always be a little girl to me, Olwyn love ... you and all your sisters.'

His eyes met Pandora's over Olwyn's head and his smile was filled with the knowledge of what she'd done, and was grateful for it. 'Pandora, Wynn wants to know if you'll be coming to church with us, tonight. Bryn said you were an unbeliever, but even if you don't believe in God, the birth of Jesus Christ, or any child, is a miracle to celebrate.'

Pandora had no intention of alienating herself just as she'd made some headway with this family.

'I'll be happy to attend.' She might even pray for a small miracle of her own.

And later, after a large dinner of turkey and Christmas pudding, and when the whole family of Llewellyns were gathered in the small church together to worship in the spirit of Christmas, the feeling of unity was so strong in her she could almost believe her miracle would come about.

CHAPTER EIGHTEEN

Adrian's back-pack thumped to the ground outside the hotel, sending up a puff of dust.

'Thanks for the lift, Don.'

'Any time, mate,' the truck driver said. 'Nice to have a bit of company on the road for a change, even if it were a pom. Well, I'd better get on, the missus is expecting me home. Give Doreen my regards. Tell her she's got the best pair of knockers I've ever laid eyes on.'

And mindful of what was the done thing in Australia, Adrian offered: 'Why don't you let me buy you a beer before you go, then you can tell her yourself.'

Don beamed him a smile. 'Never thought you'd ask, mate. I wasn't goin' to, mind, not with the bloody breathalysers hidin' up every tree these days, but what the hell! A man doesn't wanna be unsociable.' He leaped from the truck and disappeared through the door of the hotel.

The size of Australia had impressed Adrian. He'd left his travel-weary companion in Sydney, determined to see something of the outback whilst he was here. He'd made his way up to Townsville in Queensland, trucked to Alice Springs in the centre, and had managed to scrounge a lift in a one-engined plane across the Great Sandy Desert to the iron-ore shipping town of Port Hedland in the Pilbara.

There, he'd met Don, who'd given him a lift down the inland road to Hope's End. His next stop was Perth, where he'd attempt to see his sister before eventually flying home to take up his place at Oxford.

'You must have a good reason to visit a place like Hope's End, unless you're going to join the beads and bells mob,' Don had said. 'They've taken over the place from what I hear.' When Adrian had explained his mother's friend lived there, Don had laughed.

218

'Yair, I remember your ma. Nice little blonde piece, she was. A real little lady who wouldn't have much to do wiv the likes of me . . . and who can blame her, eh? Doreen's right fond of her. A born mother, that woman, a pity she didn't have any kids of her own, she's built for it.' An elbow caught Adrian in the ribs and he'd grinned, '. . . if you know what I mean.'

Adrian looked around him. Don had been right, anyone would need a good reason to visit Hope's End. The town hardly seemed inhabited, though he could hear hammering going on somewhere. The sun blazed down from an endless blue sky and the street was a cream-coloured glare in the midday sun – even through the tinted lens of his sunglasses. Sweat trickled down his back and soaked through his clothes.

He'd never imagined heat such as he'd encountered on this leg of the journey, had never realized the energy could be sapped so easily from his body. The outback Australians did it tough, and were judged by their deeds, not their education. In comparison, Adrian felt like the privileged young man he was – though he knew the trip had broadened his perspectives considerably. He'd never again look down on his fellow humans as he had in the past.

The thought passed through his mind that Australia might have also changed his mother. It was out of character for her to have made a friend in such a town. He'd never imagined she'd live in such a ramshackle place, either, though it was no worse than most of the outback hotels he'd seen.

A bald-headed man in an orange robes, Jesus sandals and beads drifted past. The man flicked him a friendly glance. 'Peace, brother.'

'Happy New Year,' Adrian said, his eyes already scanning the hotel. His skin was shrivelling from the blistering heat of the sun as he headed for a door leading off the veranda. The interior of the pub was dim, and as his eyes adjusted, Adrian saw Don at the bar, tossing back a glass of lager.

'Fill 'em up again, Doreen, the young fella's shoutin' this round.'

Adrian's eyes were drawn to Doreen's breasts, two smooth, perfect ovals quivering against her pink T-shirt. He remembered a well-endowed girl he'd spent a couple of days with in Townsville and tried not to grin when Don caught him looking, and winked at him.

'He's come all the way from the old country to see you, Doreen. Could be, the fame of your knockers 'as spread far and wide.'

A scowl was winged Don's way. 'You leave my knockers out of this, unless you want your wife to find out what a dirty-minded old bastard you are.'

Don cackled as he drained his glass. 'She already knows it . . . which reminds me, I'd better be off before she invites the milko in. See you matey, ta for the drink. Not many poms puts their 'ands in their pockets.'

'Take no notice of him, love. Come to see me, 'ave yer? 'fraid I haven't got any work on offer. Hardly enough to keep meself occupied these days, in fact we've just sold the place to some fool from the city who thinks he can make a go of it. Me and Jim's going to buy a nice little house by the seaside.'

'My mother . . . Pandora Rossiter, told me to drop in and give you her regards.'

'Well, strike me lucky, you're Pandora's boy.' Her smile was as wide as the desert. 'You must be Adrian, the one that's going to Oxford. Your mum said you'd be visitin' Australia the last time she wrote. Great little place, ennit?' She turned, bawling out. 'Jim . . . come out here, we've got a visitor . . . and you'll never guess who.'

Before too long word must have got around, because people began to drift in, eager to see a new face in town. Soon, Adrian was suffering from a surfeit of goodwill and the evening became a bit of a blur. The last thing he remembered that night was scaling a rickety set of iron steps, followed by a loud squeak when he fell into the middle of a bed.

Morning brought a large cooked breakfast on a tray. Doreen handed him a glass containing a couple of fizzing Alka Seltzer.

'Here, get this down you while it's active. Haven't had much practice at drinking, have you?'

'I'm afraid not,' he croaked, wondering how long his head would keep up its thumping.

'Ah well, at least you kept it down, and you'll get over the effects eventually. Eat your breakfast whilst it's hot, and don't you spin me a yarn about not being hungry. A good breakfast is the best cure for a hangover.'

By the time he'd finished eating he did feel a bit better, and the mug of tea she handed him washed it all down nicely. She sat on the end of the bed and smiled at him.

'I like a bloke with a good appetite. Now, I didn't have a chance last night, but when you get to Perth, if you visit young Trinity you be sure to give her my love. I heard a whisper she's had a rough time of it lately.'

He nodded.

Doreen's breasts quivered when she leaned forward to pinch his cheek. He quickly looked away when she caught him staring at them. She winked at him. 'Geez, young as you are, youse blokes are all the bloody same, ain't yer? Still, just because you sound like a poofter, doesn't mean to say you are one, eh?'

He felt himself turn brick red and she chuckled.

'I've arranged a lift for you with the brewery truck. He'll be leavin' in an hour and he's a real sticky-beak, so don't tell him nuthin' you don't want broadcast around the rest of Australia.' Her hand waved in an arc. 'Bathroom's at the end of the veranda. The water's cold because the boiler's given up the ghost, but I daresay you'll manage.'

'Thanks, you've been very kind.'

When she reached the door, she turned. 'Tell Pandora thanks for the wedding invite. Jim and I are planning a trip to the old country, but not until the weather warms up a bit. Tell her I'll drop in for a cuppa then.'

An hour later, Doreen shoved a bag containing a couple of hot meat-pies into his hand. 'Here, get your choppers round this. I don't want your mum thinking I didn't look after you.'

'Good sort, Doreen,' the driver commented as the truck pulled away. 'Known her long. . . ?'

It was one of Trinity's better days. She ironed all the clothes and put them neatly away, then she helped Angela draw a picture, got her some lunch and took her to the local play-group for the afternoon.

Mrs Pearson had said she'd pick her up. The housekeeper was the only person who hadn't deserted them during the last few troubled weeks, and even though Trinity couldn't afford to pay her, she dropped in to give her a hand.

Pandora knew she should really start looking for somewhere else to live. The house had been sold, and the new owners wanted possession of it in a couple of weeks. Half-heartedly, she looked down the columns of houses to rent, but she didn't seem to have the energy to follow them up, nor the required deposit.

She'd been allowed to keep most of the furniture, except for a couple of pieces classed as antiques. The estate auditors had carefully gone through everything, including her personal belongings. Everything had been listed. Bruno's car, all the art pieces and his Rolex watch had been taken away, as well as other bits and pieces. Every item of clothing had been examined in case anything had been concealed in pockets; all their private papers had been perused and, as Steve had guessed, the makers had been called in to open the safe. They'd removed the roll of money and the coin collection Steve had left there. She'd received receipts for it all, but she felt her privacy had been totally violated.

Richard Stowe had quizzed her about Bruno's business. *Why did your husband transfer the undertaking business to your name . . . was it a tax-avoidance scheme . . . did he know he was ill and could die at any time? Did you know he'd doubled his life insurance the day before he died?*

Trinity signed a release so her husband's medical records could be examined, she signed everything they set in front of her, just to get rid of them. She could tell them nothing – she knew nothing except her husband had been gloriously alive one minute and now he was dead.

An injunction had been filed, claiming the undertaking business as part of the estate. She could draw no income from it until the issue was settled one way or another. All she had to live on was the pension she'd applied for and a small amount of child support.

The money and the necklace that Steve had taken from the safe had disappeared into thin air.

'You can't touch that yet,' Steve had said evasively when she'd inquired, though he'd slipped her some cash. 'It will look suspicious if you've suddenly got money. Later, when things are sorted out, perhaps. Just trust me.'

Since then the club, the modelling agency and pawnshop had been sold. Steve had left town, taking the cash and the necklace with him. Because Bruno had trusted him, Trinity had trusted him too, and his betrayal saddened her.

She couldn't report him to the police, because the theft was only her word against his, and besides, it would involve her own complicity in the affair. If she went to prison, Angela would have to go into care, and her baby might be taken from her when he was born.

Even Bruno's lawyer had deserted her once his fee wasn't forthcoming.

She slumped into an armchair and gazed out over the river, recognizing that she was depressed, but unable to think clearly enough to do anything about it. Her life was shattered. She was incapable of making a decision for herself, was hardly capable of doing anything much at all, except miss Bruno and cry herself to sleep every night. If it wasn't for the baby she carried inside her, and dear little Angela, so lost and bewildered, she'd have considered ending her miserable life.

What had her father said to her the last time she saw him? *What you have sown, so shall you reap. The Lord will bring His punishment down upon you in His own good time.* She shivered, wondering why she should be punished for falling in love and getting married, and why Bruno's children should be punished as well.

The doorbell penetrated her grim thoughts. The baby kicked inside her as she lifted herself from the depths of the chair. If only he knew. He was going to be born into a life of poverty with no father to guide him. She managed a tired smile. What she needed at this moment was to find a fairy godmother on the other side of the door – and the first thing she'd wish for was to have Bruno back.

What she got was a tall, brown-haired young man, with a lovely smile and a voice that reminded her very much of Adam Scaife – the man who'd encouraged her to escape from Hope's End in the first place.

'Mrs Trinity Demasi?' he said. 'I'm so sorry to bother you, and if you don't want to talk to me I'll quite understand . . . but I rather hope you will.' His eyes appealed to her. 'I'm Adrian Rossiter.'

The name had a familiar ring to it, but she couldn't think why.

'Yes, what is it you want?'

'I'm your brother. Pandora Rossiter is my mother . . . our mother, actually.' His eyes sharpened as he gazed at her and an affectionate smile touched his mouth. 'It's unbelievable, you look so very much like her.'

Because he reminded her of Adam Scaife, and because just at that moment she fell very vulnerable and needed someone to lean on – especially a brother – she began to cry. Through her tears she managed to blurt out, 'I'm so glad you're here, because since my husband died I haven't got anyone to turn to. Will you help me?'

Though he was obviously embarrassed, and awkward in the role of saviour, he put a comforting pair of arms around her and led her back to the chair. After placing a pillow behind her head, he said. 'If you'll tell me where the kitchen is, I'll make you a cup of tea, then when you've composed yourself you must tell me all about it.'

Adrian admitted to himself that night that he was a bit out of his depth. The sight of Trinity, looking so much like his mother, had shocked him somewhat. But where his mother had always been capable and calm, this young woman was a mess.

It was obvious she was grieving deeply about the recent death of her husband. He'd learned from her disjointed explanation that she had to vacate the house the following week. She had nowhere else to go, and even if she did, she had no money to get there with.

She was also pregnant, her baby due in ten weeks' time.

Her plight had touched him, her appearance shocked him. Her thinness indicated she wasn't eating properly. The dark smudges under her eyes were a dead give-away, so was the way her voice trailed off in midsentence. She'd stare into space, her eyes full of pain, and forget he was there. She triggered off some deeply felt emotion in him, and although he didn't quite know how to handle the situation, he could no sooner walk out on her than fly to the moon.

Then there was the child, Angela. A pretty little thing with large, blue eyes who clung to Trinity's skirt, and, from his limited experience, seemed too quiet for a child her age.

He tossed the problem over in his mind for a bit, kept awake by the moonlight coming through the window and the muffled sobs from the other room, his heart aching for what she was so obviously suffering. Finally, the crying trailed off. She'd fallen asleep.

He glanced at his watch: 2 a.m. It would be early evening in England and he badly needed advice. Pulling a T-shirt on over his shorts he padded out to the lounge and picked up the receiver, then he cursed under his breath – the phone had been cut off.

He remembered he'd passed a public phone box on the way here. Five minutes later he was making his call while staring at a panoramic view of the river. It was all so serene with the moonlight playing on the water and the air warm and balmy. He smiled to himself. He might come back when he'd earned his degree, because now he'd seen some of the world he wasn't at all sure he wanted to join his father's firm.

He could move into this phone box, which had a million-dollar view.

'Adrian!' His mother's voice was full of love, and he felt a rush of homesickness. 'I'm so glad you've called. How are you?'

'I can't talk for long, Mum, I haven't got enough coins. There's a problem I desperately need help with.' When she gasped, he knew she'd recalled his pill-popping episode and the rough justice meted out to him by Bryn Llewellyn, something he'd be eternally grateful for. He smiled, and proceeded to give her a brief summary of what had happened to Trinity.

She didn't waste any time, furnishing him with the first solution that came into her mind. 'Call me tomorrow at 4 p.m. your time, and let me know,' she said quickly when the warning bleeps began, 'and reverse the charges so we can talk longer.'

Trinity didn't take much convincing. She felt curiously deadened now she had a brother to lean on. She didn't want to think or to plan her future, she just wanted to be told what to do and when to do it, like she used to do as a child.

She tried not to think of Bruno, in fact she panicked a bit when she did, because sometimes she couldn't quite recall what he'd looked like. Her whole marriage was beginning to blur, as if she'd been one person before it, and was another after. Trinity James – Trini Demasi, her marriage an intermission in between.

On Adrian's instructions she visited her doctor for a check-up and a certificate of health. Her son was healthy, the doctor said, but her iron-levels needed boosting. She could feel baby Bruno protected inside her, moving and growing in the confined space of her womb. Her lethargy she'd put down to depression – but now she committed herself to a daily course of injections to keep her precious infant healthy, and soon she began to feel a bit better.

She allowed Mrs Pearson to pack Bruno's clothes and take them away. She hadn't been able to do it before. Somehow, she'd managed to convince herself he wasn't really dead, and had expected him to walk in, his blue eyes alight with laughter and love for her.

The intensity of what she'd felt for him sometimes took her breath away. She'd never known love before she'd met him, never known emotion could be so uncontrolled and consuming. Deprived of Bruno's love, she'd been reduced to nothing, and although she tried to cling to the memory, it kept slipping away from her.

Life intruded, telling her body she couldn't love a dead person, that the memories her flesh retained of the caress of his hands, and his mouth so tender, yet demanding of hers, were just that. Her body reacted to those memories, waking her with its need for love, but torturing her by remaining unfulfilled.

The day after Adrian had arrived she'd abandoned any notion of Bruno coming back. She'd woken up to the fact that his home had been sold. Now his possessions were gone, his wardrobe doors opening on to empty spaces haunted by a lingering smell of leather belts and cologne.

All Pandora had left of him was his wedding-ring, some photographs and his children . . . and she wondered now and again if their son would look like him, and sometimes gained pleasure by imagining him born, and his dark head nuzzling at her breast. Bruno reborn in their son.

Adrian found Mrs Pearson's help invaluable. It was she who advised him how to sell the furniture at the best price, who helped him pack his sister's personal belongings and arrange for their collection.

Then there was the woman from the undertakers. Her name was Davinia Rogers, and although she proved to be hard-minded, the interview gave him a better insight into Bruno Demasi than anything anyone else had said.

'The transfer of Bruno's share of the business into Trinity's name has affected the cash flow,' she told him. 'I've got a lawyer breathing down my neck, and all the accounts have to go through the auditor for payment. By the time they've finished, and the legal eagles take their cut ... well, you can tell your sister we'll be lucky if there's a business left.'

She scribbled the forwarding address on a notepad, saying grudgingly: 'Bruno was all right, despite his toughness. He helped me out of a hole once and I was grateful and we had a bit of a thing going.' She shrugged a little angrily. 'But you needn't tell Trini that, it was before her time and he was a different person with her. He really loved her, you know, worshipped the ground she walked on. In fact,' she stared into space for a moment, a smile trembling on her lips, 'I'd never seen Bruno in love before. It was a real eye-opener, I can tell you. Once he met her, he lived and breathed only for her. Tell Trini I'll do my best to stop the buzzards picking the bones clean.'

Mrs Pearson directed him to the various authorities. He cancelled the electricity and gas services and arranged a forwarding address for mail. He dealt with the bank, left a retainer and contact address with Trinity's former lawyer, paid her bills with his credit card and informed Angela's school she'd be leaving. It had been two weeks crammed with unexpected activity.

'I'm so glad you came along when you did,' Mrs Pearson said to him on the last day. 'I was just about at my wits' end. Poor wee thing.' She sighed. 'It's hit her really hard.' She wiped her eyes on the corner of her apron. 'Mr Demasi was a real gentleman and thought the world of her. He was good to me, too.'

The last thing Adrian really needed was another blow by blow account of Bruno Demasi's goodness from her. Mrs Pearson reminded him of an older Mollie Jackson, always handing out advice and trying to overstep the mark. Bruno's demise seemed to have turned the man into a saint in her eyes, even though he'd left his family so deeply in debt they were practically impoverished.

'My mother is very appreciative of your support of Mrs Demasi, and she intends to write to you herself.' He smiled at Angela and stooped to pick her up. 'Shall we go to the corner shop and buy ourselves an ice-cream?'

'Her father would never let her have ice-cream in the evening. It keeps her awake at night.'

'Daddy's dead and he's not coming back, so he won't know,' Angela said practically, and slipped her hand into his. 'Uncle Aidy's looking after us now.'

When Mrs Pearson looked away and tears began to trickle down her cheeks, Adrian realized she wasn't a bit like Mollie Jackson, she was more motherly and caring and had been good to his sister. He slipped his arm around her shaking shoulders and held her for a little while.

'I'll ask my mother to let you know how they're all getting on, and I'm sure Trinity will write once the baby is born and she's over things a bit. It will work out for the best, just you wait and see.'

The plane took off late the following afternoon. As her back pressed into the seat a strong sense of reality hit Trinity, and she wondered what she and Angela were doing on a plane.

Then she remembered she was going to England . . . going to meet her mother, the woman who'd given her away. Her brother had arranged it. She doubted if they'd have much in common. She gazed across at Adrian. He had his eyes closed and his knuckles were gripping the armrests.

'You shouldn't worry, Adrian. Bruno told me the chances of a plane crashing are almost non-existent.' She smiled when he opened his eyes, seeing him clearly for the first time. He was really very handsome, his hair was ruffled into wavy curls and his grey eyes had a cool and astute honesty to them. He looked surprised that she'd addressed him directly, and physically uncomfortable, his long legs just fitting the space between him and the seat in front.

They'd flown first class with Bruno. *And Bruno had left them almost destitute*. She buried the treacherous thought of Bruno back in her subconscious. 'I haven't thanked you for all you've done for us. I'd never have managed without you. Have I been much of a nuisance?'

'Not at all.'

She was surprised to hear herself laugh, though it had an expendable ring to it, as if it was just an odd, mistaken note blown from the flute of a beginner into the air. 'A slight exaggeration, I'd say. Your mother must be very proud of you.'

She saw with great clarity that the note had indeed been expended, for his face closed up with the hurt he felt, and she suddenly realized how very young he was. So she placed her hand across his and gently squeezed his fingers.

'Forgive me, please, that was insensitive and inexcusable. Sometimes I don't know what I'm saying. It's hard for me to think of a stranger as being my mother, but I'm very glad you're my brother.'

But she had known. She'd used him up, then deliberately alienated herself from him. She was moving away from all that was familiar and into the unknown – and that scared her.

There was no reason to blame or punish Adrian for what his mother had done to her, and she suddenly began to despise herself.

CHAPTER NINETEEN

The plane was late.

It had been dark when Pandora arrived at Heathrow two hours earlier. Now, a grey dawn was breaking and shifts were changing. Night-workers wandered off weary-eyed, whilst fresh ones took their places, wearing cheerful smiles.

Morning brought a clamour with it. There was a general shifting going on around her – businessmen coming and going with bulging briefcases, seasoned travellers casual and relaxed, a sheik or two, wearing sunglasses and with a retinue of robed staff.

An excursion of animated middle-aged ladies passed by, all dressed in brightly coloured track-suits. Pandora wondered where they were going as she sat and waited – waited for Trinity.

Seen passing through Heathrow today, The Widnes women's snowball-throwing team on their way to the winter games? Or. The Bournemouth ladies' formation team of lawn bowlers, straight from their triumphant uphill tournament in Gibraltar.

She'd waited for over twenty-three years to see Trinity. What was a few more hours, especially when filled with flippant thoughts to disguise her nerves?

An eternity!

'Would you like to join us for a coffee?' The voice close to her ear made her jump, even though she recognized it. She turned and automatically smiled, looking up into Gerald's familiar face. Oddly enough, she was pleased to see him. 'I take it you've come to collect Adrian.'

'Yes. I didn't expect to see you here as well.'

So Adrian hadn't told him Trinity was travelling with him.

'He's my son, too, and I haven't seen him for a year.'

'Of course.' Gerald slid a hand under her elbow, assisted her from her seat and steered her towards the café. 'We're over here.'

She admitted surprise. 'Is Michael with you?'

'Michael? How can he be? He's in Edinburgh.'

'You don't mind do you ... Michael deciding to become a doctor, I mean? He's so keen.'

'I did mind at first, especially when everything I had planned for him was tossed aside without further discussion.'

That would have miffed him!

'Actually, I thought he was being too ambitious when he first told me, but his tutors have assured me he's more than capable of realizing his ambitions. He did extremely well in his A levels. I'm really very proud of him, you know – of both of my sons. You were a good mother to them, Pandora, and I hope you can forgive me for what's been said in the past, and we can remain friends.'

His sons, indeed! As if he'd hired her to bring them up in his image! Had Gerald's ego been less inflated, he might have realized his urbane little speech was more of an insult than a compliment. Yet, the speech was so unlike him it was a surprise in itself – until she saw the woman waiting at the table, tall, blonde and elegant and a few years older than herself.

'Selena, this is Pandora, my former wife,' Gerald said smoothly, and she noted the slight anxiety in his eyes.

Selena's gaze was self-assured and direct as she held out a hand. 'I'm very pleased to have this opportunity to meet you. I don't know if Gerald told you, but we've just become engaged.'

She squeezed Selena's hand and kissed Gerald on the cheek, determined to be as civilized as he'd expect her to be. She nearly laughed at her train of thought. Old habits died hard, and she remembered Michael's remark about her being Gerald's trained pet. A performing seal, perhaps? She felt like clapping her hands and barking, *uff, uff.* 'I'm very pleased for you both.' *And relieved.* 'Where did you meet?'

Selena smiled, as if unable to believe her luck. She twisted the engagement ring on her finger so the diamond sparkled in the light. It was almost a replica of the one Pandora had been given twenty years previously.

'I took the job as Gerald's secretary after I was widowed, and we fell in love.' The smile she gave him was faintly accusatory. 'He's so sweet and old-fashioned. Would you believe he wants me to give up work and stay at home when we're married?'

Pandora managed to turn her laugh into a cough. 'Really, and will you?'

Selena's glance met hers in a moment of wry cognition. 'Why pay some young secretary for her services, when I can do the work better, and for nothing?'

Selena was no fool, and Pandora thought she could get to like her. She couldn't resist the opportunity to taunt Gerald with a pitying grin.

'I'll get you some coffee,' he mumbled.

Selena was exactly Gerald's type, Pandora realized a few minutes later. She was of good family, elegant and socially aware – a complete contrast to his affairs on the side. She hoped they'd be happy together, but knowing Gerald's deviousness, it was debatable whether Selena would cure him of his fondness for a smorgasbord of women. They spent a pleasant half-hour talking generalities, then the plane landed.

'Are you coming through to Arrivals,' Pandora said, the roof of her mouth drying up at the thought of meeting her daughter with an audience in attendance.

'It's too crowded. Adrian has arranged to meet me here, so you can greet him in private.' He gave an easy laugh, all at once in charge of the situation now he'd sensed the absence of tension. His hand took possession of Selena's. 'I expect he thought there might be a scene if we ran into each other, and he doesn't know about my engagement yet, so I'd prefer it if he was introduced to Selena without you present. More civilized that way.'

'I can't imagine why, he's all grown up and should be able to cope with most things now.' She knew exactly how well Adrian could cope, but she blessed her son for his foresight anyway. She smiled at Selena. 'It's been lovely meeting you. If I'm ever up your way I'll give you a ring, perhaps we could do lunch or something.'

'Don't keep Adrian too long, Pandora,' Gerald said, just before she hurried away, his frown totally disapproving of her suggestion. 'I have our weekend planned, and we don't want to hang around here all day.'

There was a sense of a door closing behind her and another one opening when she caught sight of Adrian coming through from customs pushing a trolley piled high with suitcases.

He wasn't looking in her direction, so she look the opportunity to observe the woman beside him. Her heart began to thump when a pair of wary green eyes gazed directly at her, as if her daughter had sensed the perusal and homed in on it. There was an odd expression of shocked recognition, then a shutter seemed to close over her eyes, leaving them blank.

At last, at last! There was a momentous shifting of jubilation in her, and a sense of completeness, as if she'd just been made whole. So why did she feel like something had just begun?

The exhaustion layered on Trinity's face couldn't hide its aesthetic delicacy, or make the high, taut cheekbones appear gaunt. Her mouth was wide and exquisitely shaped. The resemblance to herself was obvious – the resemblance to Robert Dysart, startling. The child holding on to her hand was dark-haired, wide-eyed, and skipping now she was free of the confines of the plane.

Sucking in a deep breath, and hoping her elevated heartbeat wasn't noticeable, Pandora pulled a smile to her face and took a few, tentative paces forward. Trinity watched her progress, unsmiling, her head inclined a little to one side, like a wary and untrusting bird. It was a bit disconcerting to be put on the defensive so easily.

'Mum!' How tall and tanned Adrian looked as they embraced. He swiftly introduced them, and she stepped forward to hug her daughter.

There was an attitude of resistance in Trinity, a stillness that rejected. She picked the child up, fussing over her and creating a physical barrier between them, so the hug was never realized. She extended her hand.

'How do you do, Mrs Rossiter. I do hope my visit hasn't put you to too much trouble.'

'Not at all,' Pandora said, letting her free arm drop to her side as they barely touched fingers with the other. 'And do call me Pandora. Mrs Rossiter is too formal, and to refer to me as mother might prove to be a bit embarrassing to us both, all things considered.'

'You're right, of course. We wouldn't want to be embarrassed,' Trinity said vaguely, which disconcerted Pandora even more because there was no malice in the words. She busied herself making friends with the child, who proved to be much more responsive.

There was more warmth in Trinity's voice when she turned to Adrian. 'Thank you for everything, I really don't know what I would have done without you.' Her eyes were suddenly anxious. 'You will visit when you can?'

'Every chance I get, sis.' Adrian hugged her for a moment, then kissed Angela. 'I've got to go now. Be good, and look after your mum for me, huh!'

'Bye-bye, Uncle Aidy,' Angela piped up.

'Sorry I have to rush off, Mum,' he said, giving her an apologetic look and another hug. 'I'd hoped to spend more time with you, but with the plane being late Dad will be waiting for me. You know how he hates hanging about. I'll be down to bore you with the photographs of my holiday as soon as I can.'

He swung a hold-all off the trolley and called over a porter to handle Trinity's luggage. There was a sense of relief about him now his responsibility had been discharged. A final kiss and a wave and Adrian was gone, his long legs carrying him through the crowd in search of his father.

'Shall we go?' Pandora said brightly to the silent and dejected-looking younger woman, and they all trooped after the porter.

The journey to Dorset was agonizingly awkward. Angela fell asleep on the back seat, huddled in Pandora's coat. Trinity stared out at the frost-bitten landscape, speaking only when spoken to, and then mostly in monosyllables.

Pandora felt woefully inadequate, and didn't quite know how to deal with the situation. But then, she hadn't expected it to be easy. She concentrated on her driving, and was relieved when the congested roads around the airport had been left behind. The grey dawn had become a grey, depressing morning, but the spatters of rain against the windshield never became more than a threat.

She tried to make conversation, talking about the weather in the way the British did when they were breaking the ice with a stranger, but eventually she gave up in the face of her daughter's indifference. To her relief, Trinity finally fell asleep as well, her head lolling against the window.

She pulled the car into a lay-by, using the break to slide a cushion gently under Trinity's head and to cover her legs with a tartan car-rug. The girl wouldn't be used to this cold weather and she was inadequately dressed for it.

Something tugged at her heart when she saw the rounded stomach. According to Adrian, the baby was due in April. Her daughter looked so thin and frail, and she choked up inside as a thought struck her. The infant Trinity carried was her grandson, and Pandora was going to make sure she and Angela were looked after properly from now on. Somehow, she was going to find a way to get through the barrier Trinity had erected around herself.

When she gently kissed her pale cheek, Trinity murmured a name under her breath. Remembering Bruno was the name of her daughter's dead husband, Pandora nearly burst into tears.

*

For the next couple of days, Pandora encouraged Trinity to rest as much as she could. Angela adjusted with ease, and proved to be a charmer, chattering to everyone. Trinity remained distant, though polite. She was curiously compliant, as if she had no will and was drifting along in the hands of fate. Although it made things easier for Pandora, they were like strangers living in the same house, not mother and daughter.

Trouble loomed the minute Mollie Jackson laid eyes on Trinity, and the animosity that had been brewing between them suddenly came to a head. She and Pandora had never really liked each other, and Mollie had become more disagreeable and more familiar over the past few months. If she hadn't been such a good worker, Pandora would have got rid of her.

Mollie's nose twitched like a bloodhound's when she first set her avid little eyes on Trinity. 'Gave me quite a turn seeing her, it did. Your daughter, isn't she. . . ? Yes, she'd got to be, she's too like you to be anything else. I knew that photo on your dressing-table wasn't you.'

'I don't recall ever saying it was,' Pandora said coldly. 'Mrs Demasi's recently widowed, so I'd be grateful if you'd be sensitive to her feelings, Mollie.'

'I ain't daft, you know. I've been widowed myself.'

And because the situation with her daughter had made her tense, Pandora snapped at her. 'Also, I'd prefer it if you didn't talk to me in that tone of voice, or discuss my business with anyone,' which sent Mollie into an immediate huff.

'I've never gossiped in my life, and anyway, there's nothing here people don't know about.'

'What do you mean?'

'Your grandmother must have thought everyone was blind, deaf and dumb, and her acting like the lady of the manor and all hoity-toity Dysart and all, as though they were born gentry instead of trade. I knew about the bishop and his dirty little ways. He should've been locked up, if you ask me.'

Pandora gave a shocked gasp when Mollie turned on the vacuum cleaner and attacked the carpet with unusual verve, her face twisted with anger. The engine died and Mollie rounded on her again, her face aggrieved and flushed. 'I've always done my best for this family, me and my mum before me, and I never once gossiped about what went on. What do I get for it? Insults. The old woman was too mean to even leave me a little something in her will, and after all I did for her.'

'I didn't mean to insult you . . . and please stop shouting. Mrs Demasi's trying to rest.'

But Mollie's face was livid. 'Does she know who fathered her, or haven't you got around to telling her yet? Gossip? I'll give you gossip, because you're no better than you oughta be, what with both the doctor and the lawyer hanging around. I know enough about the Dysarts to keep the tabloids in print for a year if I wanted too. Flora Selby is a friend of my mother and she told me plenty – in confidence mind, though it doesn't have to stay that way, does it?'

'Be very careful you don't get sued for malicious slander, Mrs Jackson,' Simeon said, appearing at the doorway.

Mollie stared at him, her face blanching as she suddenly realized she'd overstepped the mark. 'I never meant anything by it,' she whined. 'It's my age. I'm having one of my bad days. The doctor said I should rest more.'

'Then I suggest you take his advice.' Sick at heart, Pandora fetched her purse from the dresser. 'Your services are terminated, Mrs Jackson,' she said, sliding her wages across, 'and I would suggest you adopt a less familiar manner with anyone who employs you in the future.'

Mollie's hands went to her hips. 'I never meant anything by it. How am I going to manage without my wages, and what about payment in lieu of notice and a reference? There's nothing wrong with my work, and I'm not going to have anyone saying there is.'

Pandora turned her back on her and moved away when Simeon opened his briefcase and look out a pad and pen. 'Before you go, Mrs Rossiter will require you to sign an agreement of non-disclosure, after which we'll discuss a reference and extra payment.'

Trinity was in the sitting-room, and staring out over the garden in much the same way as Emily Dysart used to towards the end. Angela sat at her feet, intent on colouring in a seaside picture with fat, coloured crayons.

'I've never seen trees without leaves on them before,' Trinity said, her voice strained.

Pandora knelt by her side and took her hand. It was cold and unresisting. 'You overheard, didn't you? I'm so sorry.'

'I'm not. I think she's been prying into my personal things.'

'You should have told me.'

'I couldn't have proved it. It's just a feeling you get when your privacy's been invaded.'

This sent a rush of colour to Pandora's face because she'd been guilty of doing exactly the same thing when she'd taken a scarf and photograph from her daughter's house.

Trinity slid her hand away. 'You must have been very young when I was born.'

'I was fifteen.'

Her mouth tightened a fraction. 'Was that why you gave me away?'

'I had no choice.'

Trinity's head swivelled towards her; her eyes were a cold, green glitter. 'Everyone has a choice. My father used to say, *You've made your bed, now you have to lie on it*. You must have known what the outcome of a sexual relationship was likely to be, even at that age.'

Shock ripped through Pandora. 'You don't understand the circumstances, Trinity.'

'You're right, and I don't really think I want to know,' she said. 'Tell me about the men that woman was talking about? I know you're divorced from Adrian's father, but who's the lawyer and the doctor? I need to know because I have Angela to think of. Bruno wouldn't have wanted me to place her in moral danger.'

Pandora's nails dug into her palms. Trinity certainly knew how to go for the jugular. The accusing eyes pierced her to the core. Tempted to retaliate, she found herself biting down on her tongue. She refused to be prodded into an argument.

'You can meet the lawyer in a moment. As for the doctor, he's coming to dinner tomorrow night especially to meet you. I'll be marrying him in three weeks.'

The heat went out of Trinity's eyes. 'Ah yes, I'd forgotten. I believe Adrian mentioned it. He seems to like the man.' It was apparently of as little interest to her as yesterday's news.

'If there's anything else you want to know, just ask. In the meantime, I'll fetch you some tea. Lottie brought round a strawberry sponge she made for you. I hope you'll try some of it, because I'd hate to see her feelings hurt.'

'Lottie's lovely. I wouldn't dream of hurting her feelings,' Trinity said – a statement which struck at Pandora's heart again, so she had to tell herself to stop being so sensitive. 'I'm sorry I was so rude.' It was said as a formality, but at least it was said.

'I understand how hard this is for you, I really do.'

'Do you?' Trinity folded her hands in her lap and went back to staring out of the window, her shell back in place.

*

Over the week, it became apparent to Pandora that Trinity was making an effort to get on with everyone but herself.

'I can't understand it,' she said to Bryn one evening, when she took time off to spend a couple of hours with him. 'I'm bending over backwards to please her. What am I doing wrong?'

'You're doing nothing wrong. Deep down, she's angry about the death of her husband, and she needs someone to expend that anger on. Once she's recognized that fact, she'll begin thinking more rationally.'

'It's not my fault he died.'

'I didn't say she was blaming you, Pandora.' A tiny smile inched across his face. 'She blames herself, when she really wants to blame him.'

'I don't understand. He didn't die on purpose.'

'She knows that. She loved him and she's angry and shocked that he left her so suddenly. Deep down, she has a sense of betrayal.'

'That's illogical.'

'We're not dealing with logic, only with emotion, the part of the brain that makes us human. The shock of sudden bereavement has changed her perception of things. Anger does that.'

'Can't you just tell her what's wrong with her, so she can start thinking straight?'

'Write it down, you mean?' He chuckled, and his arms came around her, pulling her against him from behind. 'It would be nice if it were that simple. Grief affects people in different ways. Trinity's an intelligent girl, she'll eventually figure it out for herself. . . when the baby's born, or perhaps before. She's dealing with her pain the only way she knows how. Encourage her to talk about it if you can, but go easy on her.'

'A lot of help, you are. If I paid you, could you come up with a better solution?'

'Sorry.' He chuckled, as if enjoying the thought immensely. 'You brought this on yourself, now you've got to handle it.'

'So, now you're saying it's my fault?'

He laughed when she turned her head to glare at him, and ignoring her struggles, kissed her into a rebellious submission. 'Psychoanalysis of your problem isn't on the menu tonight, Pandora. Let's find another way of easing your tension . . . and mine. I've had my mother on the phone.

complaining because we're having a small, informal wedding . . . and she said Olwyn's suit is the wrong colour.'

'It's our wedding, and Olwyn likes her suit, that's all that matters.'

'You know you're marrying my whole family when you marry me, don't you?' His eyes were full of laughter because her fingers had found their way inside his shirt and had touched on a ticklish spot. 'They'll never keep their Welsh noses out.'

She closed her teeth around the end of *his* beautiful Welsh nose and nipped it. 'I'll cut their damned noses off, then they'll *have* to keep them out. You change the subject quite beautifully, Bryn. As a reward I'd suggest a mutual massage in the spa followed by my Celtic special number seven – taken from *Doctor Braithwaite's Bonking Book for Welsh Garden Gnomes.*'

'You have quite an amazing library, woman. But first, I'd suggest you find your gnome.' He laughed and began to wriggle when her fingers explored a likely spot.

'Ahah! I've found him,' she growled a few seconds later, 'now, let's get you out of there, you cheeky little devil. . . .'

Trinity heard Pandora come in. She couldn't sleep. The baby had twisted into an uncomfortable position and was pressing into her bladder.

She waited until she heard Pandora go to bed, then crept to the bathroom, shivering a little, because the central heating cut off at midnight, and didn't come back on again for six hours.

In need of a drink, she headed for the kitchen and heated some milk up. She found some chocolate biscuits in a tin to go with it. She'd developed quite an appetite over the past few days. As a result, she had more energy and an urge to get out into the fresh air.

There were several things she needed to do, and she drew Pandora's shopping pad towards her and began a list. Pension entitlements, schools for Angela, find a doctor for them both and book a hospital bed for the birth of baby Bruno. Warm coats. They both needed winter coats and boots for an English winter. (Charity shops?) She made a face, but the little money she had left from the sale of her furniture couldn't be wasted, and she owed Adrian money.

When the baby stirred inside her she placed a hand against her taut stomach and smiled. 'That's right, you move over a bit – and take your foot out from under my ribs so I can get some sleep.'

She thought she heard a noise outside. She turned off the light and went through to the sitting-room to gaze out of the window. A heavy frost lay across the lawn and a moon sailed brightly in the sky, making the frost glitter. It was really quite pretty.

Marianna was peaceful, and at night she could hear the sound of the waves shushing against the shore. When her mother married she'd live in this apartment by herself, and was looking forward to it. Not that she'd be entirely alone. Simeon Manus would be moving in upstairs next week, and the other tenants shortly afterwards.

She'd taken quite a liking to Simeon. Bryn Llewellyn, the man her mother was going to marry, was easy to talk to and made her smile. She felt ashamed that she'd been so willing to believe Mollie Jackson's accusation of Pandora.

The noise hadn't been repeated, and she was about to go back to bed when she suddenly saw the trail of footprints in the frost. They were heading towards the house. Her heart jolted in her chest, and she swiftly padded towards Pandora's room.

Pandora woke in an instant and sat up 'What is it, are you ill?'

'I think there's a prowler.' Then she remembered Angela was asleep in the other bed, and alone, and felt a bit frantic. 'I must see if Angela's all right.'

'Switch the lights on going through,' Pandora said calmly. 'It might frighten them off. They haven't got inside yet, else the alarm would be triggered.'

The lights did the trick, because when the garden floodlight was switched on they saw a shadowy figure hurrying off across the lawn. Pandora put down the poker she'd snatched up.

'There's no point in phoning the police now. By the time someone gets over here he'll be long gone. You're not too scared to sleep, are you? I doubt if he'll come back.'

'I'd like to sit up for a little while. I'm wide awake now.'

'Would you mind if I kept you company? I feel a little bit keyed-up myself.' She gazed at the poker she'd snatched up. 'I'm glad I didn't have to use this.'

'Would you have?'

Pandora's laugh was a little unsteady. 'If I had to, I suppose, though I admit I wouldn't like to be put to the test.'

'I wish I had that much self-assurance,' Trinity said. 'Bruno said it was because I never learned to make my own decisions when I was growing up.'

'You must miss him dreadfully.' She was taking a risk, deliberately treading on difficult territory. 'Was his death an accident?'

'He died of a brain haemorrhage. It happened quite suddenly. The doctor said he didn't suffer.'

'I'm so sorry.'

Trinity couldn't seem to stop herself from talking. 'They took his body parts. It's odd to think that bits of him are still alive in other people, and quite disconcerting as if he's become a jigsaw puzzle or something, and all I need do is collect the pieces and fit him together again . . . if you see what I mean.'

'Yes . . . yes, I do see. It was a wonderful, unselfish gesture you made, and one that would have been hard.'

'If Bruno hadn't stipulated it on his driving licence I probably would-n't have allowed it to go ahead. It seemed . . . oh, I don't know . . . cannibalistic at the time, I suppose.'

'There's nothing cannibalistic about saving another's life.'

'No, I suppose not.' Although she didn't know it, her smile was small and sad and infinitely tender. 'We came here on our honeymoon. We rented a little cottage not far from here, sight unseen. It was such a hovel. Bruno complained a lot, but I made him fix everything and cut the lawn, and it was such fun, much better than the hotels in Europe. That's where I received your letter. It was a shock, you see . . . as if Trinity James suddenly didn't exist . . . as if I was nothing . . . a piece of trash that had been dispensed with.'

'It wasn't like that.'

Trinity ignored her words, she was cold and her teeth were chattering. 'Bruno is the only person who's ever truly loved me. My father said God would punish me for being disobedient . . . and He did, you see. He found me unworthy of being loved.' She shot to her feet and headed towards her room before she burst into tears.

'Don't you dare say that,' Pandora shouted at her. 'I loved you. They told me you were dead. All those years I thought you were dead and grieved for you! Do you hear me?'

Trinity shut the door in her face.

'Listen to me,' Pandora said, her voice a furious whisper against the door. 'You're talking crap if you think some mystical being is directing your life. Your husband died because he had a weakness in his body. It could have happened to anyone, and often does.'

Trinity got into bed and pulled the pillow over her ears, refusing to listen because deep inside her she knew Pandora was telling the truth, and as yet, she didn't have the courage to face that truth.

CHAPTER TWENTY

Pandora scrubbed at the graffito with unrelenting fury. The word was blurred amongst the black smears on the dining-room window, but was still noticeable.

'What an odd word to put there,' Trinity said from behind her.

Pandora's heart sank as she whirled around. Odd wasn't a word she'd use for it. It was venom sprayed from a can labelled deluxe enamel. She kicked the can against the fence. She'd hoped to remove the graffito before Tninity got up, but it was proving to be stubborn.

'I've just looked at the footprints before the frost melts. They're too small for a man.

'I think it was Mollie Jackson out for revenge. We don't need to involve the police. I doubt if she'll risk coming back. I'll fetch a scraper from the shed.'

A detaining hand was placed on her arm before she could move off. 'Why would she write *incest* on your window?' Trinity waited for an answer, her eyes calm. When one wasn't evident, she said. 'Who was my father? Was it that man called Bishop she was talking about?'

It had to come eventually, but Pandora had expected to work up to it, not be asked such a bald statement. Although she'd sorted it out satisfactorily in her own mind, she'd been reminded on several occasions in the past that other people didn't regard things in exactly the same way as she did.

There was a prickly tension building up in her, an uneasy thought that Trinity would see through any half-truths she could dream up. 'Would you rather I was bluntly honest, or should I try to sugar the pill a bit for both our sakes?'

For the first time, Trinity gave her a glimmer of a smile. 'Who was it accused me of talking crap last night?'

The tension between them eased a fraction. 'At least wait until I get this off the window, after which I intend to ring Mollie Jackson and warn her off.' She smiled when Angela ran towards them in her pyjamas and bare feet, her teeth chattering through her smile. 'Would you like to go into town after breakfast? I really think we should shop for some warm clothes for Angela and enrol her in infant school.'

She swung the girl into her arms and hugged her tight. Because she'd seen Trinity's list, and because her daughter seemed to respond to honesty, she engaged her eyes and said gently, 'You won't mind if I buy her something warm to wear, will you – and yourself, perhaps? It would be silly to freeze for the sake of your pride.'

Mollie was all bluster and denial when she rang her. 'You've got no right to accuse me of property damage, Mrs Rossiter.'

'I have every right. You were seen running away by both of us.'

'It would be your word against mine.'

'Not really. You left footprints in the frost and we took photographs of them. I'm sure the police would soon fit them to your foot . . . besides, you dropped the spray-can. I should imagine your fingerpnints are all over it.'

'You haven't called the police in, have you? Oh God, it wasn't much. I wanted to get my own back, that's all.'

'All you did was draw your own wrong conclusions from something that wasn't your business anyway, and hurt the feelings of someone who didn't deserve it – someone who's got enough troubles of her own at the moment without you adding to them. I'm disgusted with you, and if you ever step foot on my property again I'll have you arrested. Is that clear?'

'Yes, Mrs Rossiter,' Mollie said, and burst into tears.

Pandora hung up on her.

'Did she jump to the wrong conclusions?' Trinity said from the kitchen doorway.

'No, but she's only guessing, and really, it's not quite as bad as she made it out to be. However, I'll not give her the satisfaction of knowing she was right. Sit down, would you. I'll make us some tea and we can talk.'

A few seconds later, when they were eyeing each other over their teacups, Pandora gave it to her straight. 'A man called Robert Dysart was your father. He was a bishop by calling and a paedophile by nature. He's been dead for a long time.'

A nerve twitched in Trinity's jaw.

'He was my grandfather's brother, and without going into detail, because I came to terms with this some time back, I needed love at the time. He sensed that and used it.'

Trinity nodded, the expression in her eyes wary now.

'Again, without going into detail. You were born upstairs in the room I sleep in. I held you for a short time, then fell asleep with you in my arms. When I woke you were gone, and my grandparents told me you'd died. I didn't question it, I had no need to because I thought they were decent, upright people. I found out you were still alive, and there had been a conspiracy to push the adoption through.'

'When did you find out I was alive?'

'About eighteen months ago, just after my grandmother died. It started with a remark Lottie made. Then I couldn't find your grave or a record of your death, and I got suspicious and started to make enquiries.'

'Why didn't you ask Lottie about it?'

'There were reasons. Lottie had her own problems at the time, also related to Robert Dysart. Mine seemed weak by comparison. I would ask you not to pursue this with Lottie. She's had counselling and is happier now than she's ever been in her life. I don't want that spoiled for her.'

'Of course. There's just one more thing,' Trinity said, her voice as unemotional as before. 'Do you have a photograph of Robert Dysart? I'd like to see what this monster looked like.'

'Actually, he looked like an angel.'

She fetched the box of photographs and fished out one of Robert Dysart. It was black and white, and taken when he was a young man in his early twenties. She'd used it deliberately because he'd been close to Trinity's age when it had been taken. Robert lounged nonchalantly in the main doorway of Marianna in tennis whites, a sweater tied around his shoulders and his racket under his arm. An aesthetically handsome young man, fair-haired and wearing a bright smile – he looked to be his daughter's twin.

Trinity slowly sucked in a breath. 'What a beautiful-looking man. I wonder what made him deviate from the norm.'

'Academically, he was brilliant, earning several distinctions at Cambridge in English literature, history, philosophy and theology. He was also bilingual. You'd have liked him if you'd known him. He had a most charismatic personality.'

Trinity's eyes sliced into her. 'You don't have to sell him to me.'

'I'm not. I'm telling you the facts. The family treated him like someone special and he gloried in his popularity, even though he appeared saintlike and unpretentious. The family were in total awe of him, and they closed their eyes to his faults, though they must have known what he was like. They nearly ruined Lottie's sanity, and made me feel shame and guilt for his wrongdoing.'

She threw the photo back on top of the others. 'That's one of the areas I don't want to get into, but I'll try to explain it in a way I think you'll understand.' She issued her daughter with a challenging glance. 'Last night, when you said Bruno was the only person who ever loved you? I felt exactly the same way about Robert Dysart at the time.'

'Thank you for telling me,' Trinity said dispassionately. 'You've given me something to think about, and I hope it wasn't too painful for you.'

Everything about this is painful. What are you, a damned robot who doesn't feel, cry or think?

But that was unfair. Her daughter was coping in the only way she knew how, by instinct. Whether Trinity knew it or not, she'd survive her bereavement – because the Dysart women had a history of challenging adversity and emerging from it strengthened.

'If there's anything else you want to know, just ask,' said Pandora feeling curiously light-headed after unburdening herself 'Now, we'd better find young Angela and make sure her shoes are on the right feet. I think we'll go into Poole. It's further away than Dorchester, but the shopping is better there. We can pop into the local school on the way back.'

There was method in her madness. Mary James lived in Dorchester, and she didn't want to risk running into her – not until she'd established a strong relationship of her own with Trinity.

Over the next couple of weeks the relationship gained a bit of ground. Mother and daughter didn't exactly become friends, but there was an atmosphere of tolerance.

Bert bought Lottie a new car for her birthday, so Emily's old car was returned to Marianna for Trinity to use.

'I've just had her overhauled,' Bert said. 'Apart from a bit of rust in the doors she runs a treat. She can get a bit cantankerous on a cold morning, but if you give her a bit of stick she soon settles down.'

Simeon moved in upstairs, giving them a sense of security at night. He told her that one of the other applicants for a tenancy was an architect, and a particular friend of his – did she mind? But of course, she didn't, and she blessed him for his confidence and discretion.

With her mind mostly focused on Trinity, Pandora's wedding day crept up on her, and she was involved in a last minute flurry of perfecting arrangements. Olwyn had arrived the night before, and Pandora woke on Valentine's Day with a sense of churning excitement.

The Llewellyn tribe had hired a bus and, much to the annoyance of Bryn's neighbours, it took up three parking spaces in the street. The women and children had taken up residence in every nook and cranny of Bryn's home, whilst the overflow of husbands were housed in a bed-and-breakfast house around the corner.

Olwyn had stayed the night in Grandmother Dysart's old room whilst Michael and Adrian shared a put-you-up in the sitting room. Her eyes had darted over the place when she arrived.

'Rent this flat, do you?'

'No, it's mine.' And before Olwyn asked, she said, 'The whole place is mine. I inherited it.'

Olwyn nodded to herself 'We were stupid thinking you were after Bryn's money. I don't know what you must have thought of us.'

'Better to let bygones stay bygones in this instance.' She watched Olwyn give a faint smile. 'Even if I didn't have any money of my own, you'd still have been wrong. I'm marrying Bryn because I love him.'

She turned and headed for the kitchen just as the phone rang.

It was Joy saying she might be a bit late. She was coming down for the ceremony and would stay for the speeches and toast, then catch the afternoon train back to London so her shooting schedule wouldn't be interrupted. The television series was proving to be a hit with viewers, Joy's newly discovered flair for comedy giving her the recognition she'd always craved.

The morning suddenly became busy with the hairdresser and beautician arriving almost on top of one another. Everyone seemed to want to use the bathroom at once. Finally they were all dressed and ready to depart.

Olwyn's glowing, rose-pink suit and flower-covered hat warmed up her complexion. She had a nice figure, and the softly gathered skirt and cropped jacket suited her. Pandora's outfit was made of the same softly flowing material, but in pastel pink. She'd decided on a straight dress with a knee length jacket, and a jaunty little hat made up of pale pink flowers, with a small veil over her eyes. A single strand of pearls and matching earrings set it off.

The day was bright, with just a faint, teasing breeze as they emerged into the porch. It was one of those unseasonably warm days that some-times occurs in late winter, as though the weather was in rehearsal for spring.

'You take Mum and Olwyn in Mum's car, and I'll bring Trini and Angela,' Michael said. 'That way no one will get crushed.'

'But the heater's stuffed in your car. They'll freeze.'

'Well, what about taking Great-Grandma's old bus?'

'It's got a gear-stick on the column, I've never used one of those. I'll take Mum and Olwyn and you take Trini and Angela in the bus.'

'I've never driven a steering-column gear-shift either, you blithering idiot.'

Trinity gave an unexpected peal of laughter, and they all turned to gaze at her, grinning like idiots. 'What if I drive it?'

Michael and Adrian gazed at her stomach, looked at each other and shook their heads. 'Too fat.'

Luckily, Simeon knocked on the door to see if he could give anyone a lift, and because he had a luxury car all to himself, he shuffled things around so all the women arrived at the venue in his car, with him as chauf-feur, and the boys by themselves in Pandora's car.

'Nice going, Simeon,' the boys joshed him when they got there. 'How is it you managed to end up with all the women?'

'Managing women is something you'll learn as you get older,' he said loftily. He raised his head to smile at Pandora and they exchanged a poignant glance.

They were ten minutes late, and the Llewellyn women surrounded them outside the registry office like a flock of gobbling Christmas turkeys.

'I didn't think that outfit would suit our Olwyn, but now I'm not so sure.'

'Don't be daft, Mum, she looks a treat. I'll be after borrowing it myself to go to Thommo Lewis's wedding in May.'

'It won't fit your backside, our Cordelia, look how slim Olwyn is, like a bean-pole. Besides, what am I going to wear if you borrow it?'

'Stop clacking and come away in, the registrar keeps looking at his watch and frowning. Siân,' Olwyn said to her daughter, 'go and tell your father to get everyone seated. They've arrived. . . .'

Then they were all in the ante-room, and Bryn was standing in front of her, grey-suited and wearing a pink rose to match his rose-pink waistcoat. She noticed someone had tamed his hair when he smiled down at her.

'You're the most beautiful bride in the world, *cariad*, and I've been going through hell wondering if you were going to turn up.' He drew her against him and kissed her so lovingly she ached with the tender feelings it evoked in her.

'Will you look at that,' someone said, and everyone went quiet.

'And here was me thinking your Bryn hadn't a romantic bone in his body.'

'I'd be kissing her too if she was marrying me.'

Then Bryn was gazing into her eyes, wearing a half-smile and some of her lipstick on his mouth, so she had to wipe it away with a tissue and renew her own.

'Ready, woman,' he said softly, and she nodded.

Then they had to wait again, because Joy made her entrance, looking very much the celebrity in a faux-fur coat with matching Cossack hat and black, high-heeled boots.

'Darling Pandora,' she cried, and sweeping her into a hug said reproachfully, 'you didn't intend to marry without your great-aunt present.'

Young Siân's mouth dropped open and her eyes became as round as saucers. 'You're the honourable grandmother,' she whispered. 'Did you come on your motor bike?'

'I'm afraid not, my Harley is being repaired so I came on a train. You can show me where to sit if you like, young lady.' She blew Bryn a kiss. 'You look quite the dandy today, darling. I'd marry you myself if you were a bit older.'

Olwyn got into a bit of a stew then. 'You're supposed to be inside, waiting, Bryn, away with you. Where's that lump of a best man? Gareth, stop goggling at the bride, now, and take our Bryn in. The rest of you, get in there after them and find a seat, but not at the front, mind. No, not you two! Come back here. You're supposed to be escorting your mam and me in. . . .'

Lottie, Ben and the boys all turned to smile at her when she entered the office between Adrian and Michael, and everything seemed to click into place. Somehow, they managed to exchange their vows, and Pandora became Mrs Bryn Llewellyn.

They all retired to the small function-room upstairs at the Carrington, where a substantial sit-down meal had been arranged, mainly because

Pandora couldn't imagine the Llewellyn family appreciating being fed canapés and having to make small talk.

'To Mr and Mrs Llewellyn, and I'd like to hear the bride say her new name,' the best man challenged when he made his speech.

'*Thlwllyn*?' she stuttered, and she could feel waves of silent laughter coming from Bryn beside her. There was a quivering silence when she daren't look at him because she couldn't stop grinning, and from the variety of expressions she thought they all might laugh, until Owen banged his knife on the table.

'Not bad at all. On the strength of that, I now declare my one and only daughter-in-law an honorary Welshwoman.'

'In return, I confer British citizenship on my new family,' she said gravely, and a great shout of laughter went up from Bryn. Across the table, Trinity caught her eye, and her mouth twitched into a spontaneous smile.

During the evening they slipped away, leaving their guests to it. Simeon would look after Trinity and Angela. She had no idea where they were going as the car purred off, and she didn't ask Bryn. A few days off was all the time he could spare from his practice, so they wouldn't be going far.

So when she found herself carried over the threshold of the honeymoon suite at a top London hotel a couple of hours later, she was pleasantly surprised. Bryn set her on her feet and his eyes filled with love and satisfaction when he pulled her into his arms.

'Happy Valentine's Day, Pandora my love.'

'The best I've ever known. I love you,' she whispered, and ruffled his neatly arranged hair into spikes.

A grin spread across his face when he eyed her hat. 'A daft thing that is on your head, Mrs Llewellyn, but you look a proper picture in it, mind.' His fingers gently dislodged it from her hair, then slid under her chin.

Her face lifted to his, their glances joined, and when his mouth gently grazed against hers, a cloud of confetti drifted down around them.

It was the end of March, and rags of clouds chased across the sky.

The days had passed quickly for Trinity. She was pleased to be independent at last. She liked living at Marianna by herself. Not that she was alone all the time. Lottie and Pandora called in often, and Simeon, Bryn or Ben dropped in now and again – obviously a conspiracy, but that was fine with her, because it stopped her from dwelling on the past too much.

Her life had regained some normality. Angela had settled happily into infant school, and Trinity regularly attended antenatal classes to learn about the birth and the breathing techniques to help her though her labour. Now Angela had settled into her new life and wasn't so clingy, she was about to move her into Pandora's old room, and herself into the bigger room, so she could turn the small adjoining sitting-room into a nursery.

She'd bought the cot in a second-hand shop. It came with a built-in changing table and set of drawers. She'd derived a simple pleasure from hand-hemming some small sheets from cheap remnants. The drawers were already full. The first to go in had been the clothes Bruno had brought home for his son. She'd added to it over the past few weeks – impossibly small vests and nighties, matinée jackets, bonnets and bootees Lottie had knitted for her.

A beautifully hand made layette had arrived from Bryn's sisters shortly after the wedding. Everyone's kindness had overwhelmed her – except Pandora's, which always left her feeling slightly resentful, but she couldn't think why.

Pandora wouldn't hear of her rearranging the rooms alone, and was coming to pack the things she'd left behind into a box. Their relationship had improved a little of late. Living under Pandora's constant scrutiny had been uncomfortable, and her natural mother had tried too hard, obviously needing something from her she couldn't provide.

Trinity had undergone change, and she thought it might be because her physical condition had improved. The dead, hopeless feeling had been replaced by emotion, some of which she hadn't expected to feel again. It wasn't all happy. The tiny flaming excitement in her when she thought of her baby's imminent birth, brought with it the remembrance of Bruno's smile when she'd told him she was pregnant. She wished he could be with her for the birth, and to share the antenatal classes like some of the other fathers did.

She stared into space, smiling a little, yet with tears pricking at her eyes as she talked to Bruno – something she often did when she was alone. 'Three more weeks, Bruno. Our son is strong, and you'll be so proud of him.'

Baby Bruno no longer kicked, he surged against her womb, sometimes at sharp angles so her stomach changed shape and it caused her pain. The weight of him had pulled her stomach lower, and she had the feeling if he grew any larger she'd split open and he'd fall from inside her like a ripe pea from a pod. Her breasts had swollen, the nipples growing larger and darker the nearer she got to her time.

She looked up from her sewing when she heard a car, hoping Pandora hadn't brought anything with her today. She brought something every time she came, usually practical things like paper nappies, bibs, bunny-rugs, baskets with lotions, potions, powder and pins.

After she knocked, Pandora let herself in, looking incredibly beautiful and happy with a smile on her face. Behind her came a delivery man with a large parcel, and Trinity's heart sank. He placed it on the floor, smiled and tipped his hat when she thanked him.

'What have you brought this time?' she said, trying not to sound ungracious.

'A pushchair.' Pandora knelt and began to rip the cardboard off. 'Wait till you see it, you'll love it.'

Which she did, because it was a top of the range product she'd coveted, but knew she couldn't possibly afford. The rush of anger she felt made her feel uneasy. Pandora would take over her life if she wasn't careful.

'You shouldn't have,' she said, but her token effort at resistance was brushed aside.

'Nonsense, and I've got some blankets and a sheepskin rug in the car. I'll go and get them whilst you put the kettle on. I'm dying for a cup of tea.'

Later, when they went into Pandora's room, she simply tipped all the drawers on to the bed in a big heap, then turned a photo-frame face down and slid it towards her. She stared at the rest critically. 'Most of this stuff can go to the charity shop, unless there's anything you want . . . except for that.'

Pandora reached for the silk scarf at the same time she did. Trinity got there first. 'I used to have one like this, I lost it ages ago.' Her eyes darted to a small label, and as she shook it from its folds a soft photo frame containing a snapshot of herself fell out. They both snatched at it at the same time, but Pandora beat her to it this time.

They stared at each other. Pandora looked slightly wary, and Trinity took the opportunity to slip under her defence.

'This is my scarf, my initials are written on the label, and that snapshot is of me,' said Trinity. 'Bruno took it. Where did you get them?'

Pandora looked away, saying casually, 'I expect you brought them with you and it got mixed up with my stuff.'

'No. I specifically looked for the scarf because Bruno bought it for me. I couldn't find it anywhere.'

Pandora shrugged. 'All right. I went to Australia last year. I was trying to find you, and your housekeeper said you were away. She showed me round the house, and I took them.'

The sense of her privacy being invaded was almost overwhelming.

'When Mrs Pearson said my mother had visited, I never dreamed it was you . . . I thought . . . then when I discovered my father had died, I tried to ring my mother, only to find she'd sold the house and store and had gone.'

'I'm sorry.' Pandora's hand was on her arm. 'I needed to have something of yours, and I just couldn't help myself. I went to Hope's End first and spoke to your parents. Your father called me names and sent me away. I felt sorry for your mother, for Mary. It was she who told me where you lived. Look, perhaps we'd better talk about this. Perhaps I can make you understand how I feel.'

'It would be better if you tried to understand how I feel instead,' Trinity said slowly. 'I'm grateful for your help, but the fact that you're my natural mother is uncomfortable. Until a few weeks ago you were a stranger. It's bad enough that I'm forced to live on your charity, but now you're showering me with gifts, and I get the feeling you're trying to buy me.'

When Pandora's face paled she turned the screw a bit tighter because she had to get something through to her. 'You can't expect me to accept you as a mother when I have no memory of you. Mary James is my mother. She might not have been perfect, but she's always been my mother and always will be.'

If she'd hit Pandora, the effect couldn't have been more dramatic. The smiling, generous and friendly woman who'd walked in a few moment ago was suddenly reduced to a wreck, and it was all her doing. Pandora stared at her, her eyes so wounded that Trinity fell like an utter shit.

'I'm so sorry,' Pandora whispered. 'I didn't realize I was being so pushy and intrusive.'

Trinity wanted to call Pandora back when she turned and walked unsteadily away, but she didn't have the guts. The outer door shut, and when she heard the car drive away she knew it was too late.

She threw Pandora's things into a cardboard box. The frames contained more pictures. One was the wedding photograph she'd sent her mother, the other was a sketch she'd done of the hotel at Hope's End, and given to Doreen.

Her face blanched. 'Oh, my God,' she whispered, realizing the significance of these pathetic mementos to Pandora. 'What have I done?'

She fetched her coat and walked slowly down to the cliff edge. Quite by accident she'd discovered a spot where the wind channelled up a groove in the cliff-face and created a strong up-draught. When the wind blew strongly enough, if she held out her arms and leaned into it, she felt as if she were no longer earthbound, and all her problems seemed to melt into nothing.

But it wasn't blowing hard enough today. It was coming in gusts and the sea was full of strands of brown seaweed, which bubbled in the barrel of the small bay like fermenting beer. The air smelled of salt and iodine and the seagulls shrieked and wheeled around her in case she had scraps for them.

She wondered if Bruno was looking down on her, and she suddenly didn't feel quite so lonely. He would have wanted her to get to know her family and would desperately have wanted his children to know their background, however humble. He'd even invented one for Angela.

There was nothing humble about her own background, though the circumstances of her parentage filled her with disgust. No wonder they'd got rid of her and told Pandora she'd died.

But they hadn't got rid of her, not really. There could have been an abortion. A quick visit to a doctor and her existence would have been snuffed out before it had really begun. If that had happened she'd never have been born, or adopted. She'd never have met Bruno and discovered what love was all about. Her hands protectively covered the child she was carrying. She'd never have conceived this beautiful child who would bear Bruno's name – and Pandora would never have suffered her loss in exactly the same way.

She asked herself: what if someone took this child she loved, gave him away and told her he was dead? How would she act twenty years later if she found out he was alive? How would she feel?

Exactly how Pandora acted and felt. The act of stealing a scarf and photograph suddenly didn't seem so pathetic after all.

And just as the thought left her mind, an ache started in the pit of her body, built up, then slowly rolled into her back. It didn't have much strength, but she knew exactly what it was.

Slowly, she made her way home, stopping to accommodate a couple more contractions. She picked up the phone when she got home and rang Pandora, relieved to find she was home.

'Can you pick up Angela from school and come over, the baby seems to have started?'

'Oh my God! This is all my fault.'

'It's no one's fault,' she said. 'He's just decided this is his time to be born.' She rejoiced in the fact. Although the relationship Pandora was seeking was impossible for her to contemplate at the moment, at least she could give her a grandson to love, and that might help heal her hurt.

'Would Lottie mind looking after Angela whilst you help me through the birth? I would really like you to be with me,' she said.

CHAPTER TWENTY-ONE

Watching her daughter suffer through childbirth was the hardest thing Pandora had ever done.

By comparison, the birth of her own sons had been short, and easy, though she couldn't really remember what she'd gone through producing her first-born – it was as if her mind had buried it with the trauma of her loss.

'The birth's going well,' the midwife assured her, something she seemed to do on a half-hourly basis. 'It shouldn't be much longer.'

Trinity was clearly exhausted. Her face was slicked with sweat and her hair was damp and sticky. Yet there was a dogged determination about her as she panted her way through her next contraction.

Picking up a damp towel and panting with her, Pandora mopped the sweat from Trinity's face. She needn't have bothered, because the next contraction swamped her almost immediately, leaving in its wake the same result.

'Try not to push,' the midwife said, glancing up from between Trinity's spread thighs.

Trinity groaned with the effort of not pushing.

The doctor came in and the midwife whispered something to him. Pandora closed her eyes when the saw the small, shining instrument in his hand.

'I'm going to make a small cut, but you won't feel it,' he said.

When she opened her eyes again the doctor had lifted his head and was gazing over his mask at Trinity; his eyes were blue and twinkling, his voice calming. 'Everything's going well, and the baby's head has crowned. I want you to push hard with your next contraction.'

It came almost immediately. Pandora slid her arm around Trinity's shoulders as she strained to birth her baby. She winced when Trinity's fingers dug deeply into her other arm.

Then she gave a long, drawn out, shuddering groan and gasped, 'Nobody told me . . . this was going to be . . . such . . . bloody hard work.'

The doctor chuckled. 'It's nearly over. Another push . . . good, good . . . and again.'

Trinity moaned and sweated over the next one.

'You're doing just great . . . the head has presented, have a breather whilst we wait for him to turn. Now, just one more little push . . . good girl, great . . . that's it, wonderful! There, you have a beautiful son, Mrs Demasi.'

To which announcement, young Bruno gulped in his first breath of air, gave a tentative, quavering squawk, then began to bawl.

Trinity stretched her neck as far as it could go to catch a glimpse of her son. She was laughing and shivering and crying with expended effort and relief. She looked as though she couldn't believe her eyes when the baby was placed in her arms. Tears trembled in her eyes and a smile so tender chased over her face that Pandora's eyes filled with tears too.

'Look at his little hands,' Trinity whispered. 'Isn't he absolutely perfect?'

Bruno chose that moment to gaze up at the sound of his mother's voice. His eyes opened and he stopped crying. Trinity looked entranced at him.

'Look, Pandora. His eyes are blue, just like I imagined they'd be.' She stared at the wisp of hair flattened against his skull. 'Oh my God! I think his hair is ginger. I wish Bruno was here to see him.'

'I'm sure he'd be proud of his son, dear. It's going to be a nice, dark chestnut colour when it's dried out,' the midwife said. 'He's a lovely baby, a good weight considering he's a bit early. Now, I'm just going to clean you up, then doctor will put in a couple of stitches. I'll take you up to the ward so you can rest afterwards. I bet you could do with a nice cup of tea.'

Trinity kissed her infant, and presently he gave a yawn and fell asleep. She was still trembling from the effort she'd been through, yet she looked up and managed a smile. When she was ready for the ward, Trinity grabbed her hand and held it for a moment. 'Thanks for helping me through it, Pandora.'

For an aching moment, Pandora wished this girl she loved so much would call her mother, and she wondered if she ever would. What was it Bryn had said when she'd assured him she knew how to love?

Enough to let her go a second time?

She had an awful feeling it had come to that.

'Bruno's adorable,' and she felt the tears trembling in her eyes. 'I'll probably spoil him rotten, whether you want me to or not.'

'I know,' Trinity said, and briefly bore her hand to her cheek in a caress.

Surprised by the tender gesture, Pandora bent to kiss her daughter's forehead. 'I'll bring Angie in to see you every day after school so she won't worry.'

When they wheeled her off to the ward, Trinity had her son cuddled against her, and was gazing down at him with an intensity of love in her eyes and a smile of wonder on her face.

It was a beautiful expression. Pandora wondered if she'd worn it herself when she'd looked at Trinity. Unexpectedly, her subconscious rewarded her with the moment, and it came back to her in all its emotional exquisiteness. Only a mother could feel this way just after the safe delivery of her baby, and nothing, not even a parting could take it away from her. Love flooded through her body so strongly she almost choked on the unbearable pain of what she must do.

Trinity had been right in what she'd said earlier. Pandora could never be a true mother to her, and had thought only of her own feelings, imagining it would make Trinity happy too. Love was supposed to be giving, not taking, and she could have so easily driven her daughter away.

Realistic enough to know she hadn't the nature to be totally self sacrificing, Pandora decided to act fast before she thought it through and found reasons to change her mind.

She blew her nose and went through to Reception, surprised to discover it was still day. There was a pay-phone in the corner. When she picked up the receiver and began feeding coins into the slot, she realized it was actually the following morning.

'Hello,' she said, when the voice at the other end answered. 'There's something I think you should know. . . .'

Later that evening, when Mary James approached the bed, Trinity's unbelieving and totally welcoming smile nearly tore Pandora's heart from her chest.

'Mum!' she cried out, her face lighting up. 'I can't believe it! What on earth are you doing here? How did you know?'

The two of them embraced, laughing and crying and both talking at once. Pandora picked up her bag and crept away. When she looked back, the two women were still chattering and laughing, and didn't seem to notice she'd gone.

She told Bryn what she'd done later that evening, when Angela was tucked up in bed.

'I'm proud of you,' he said, drawing her into his arms and holding her tight.

'You shouldn't be, Bryn. I'm really not the self-sacrificing type. I felt so jealous when I saw Trinity hug Mary James. I wanted to rush over to the woman, strangle her and shout: *She's mine. I gave birth to her, not you.*'

'What stopped you?'

'I've put my case, and now I have no right to interfere. I should have listened to you in the first place. Mary James is the only mother Trinity's known. She couldn't choose who gave birth to her and she had no say in who brought her up, so why did I imagine she'd prefer me?'

'*But what am I?*' he murmured. '*An infant crying in the night: An infant crying for the light: And with no language but a cry.*'

'Who wrote that?'

'Tennyson.'

'And are you referring to me or Trinity? because that's exactly how I feel at the moment, as if I'm crying out to be heard. But I haven't got the words to express my frustration, and anyway, no one's listening and I've run out of china to smash – except yours, and you haven't got much to smash.'

'I'm listening – Trinity's listening – Mary James is listening . . . and I get the feeling you're also listening, now.'

'But I'm not hearing the things I want to hear. I keep thinking that Mary James didn't deserve to have her and she stole her from me. Then I think of her horrible husband and how miserable she was with him, and then I think worse things – like how glad I am she had a miserable life, because then she was punished for stealing my child. I hate myself for thinking horrible things.'

'Wasn't Mary punished enough by not being able to have a child of her own?'

Pandora hadn't even considered that.

'Perhaps having Trinity to love made her otherwise miserable life bearable. Would your daughter's life have been any better being brought up by your grandmother? What if Robert Dysart had lived longer?'

And he didn't have to spell it out for her because she shuddered at the thought.

'Stop trying to make me feel glad she went from my life. What if I'd jumped off the cliff with her? What if I'd run away with her and we'd both starved to death in a London back alley? What if. . . ? What if. . . ? What's the use of using hypothetical what if's?'

'Exactly. The thing is, my darling, you have to realize you *can't* change things after they've happened. Trinity is part of your future, and you mustn't allow excess baggage from the past to spoil that. Leave it on the station where you caught the train.'

'I hate it when you've got an answer for everything,' she muttered.

'I've got the feeling you've come up with the same answers and just want confirmation. When I said you were listening, I meant you were listening to your intuition. . . . Why else are you questioning your own motives when it's such a damned uncomfortable pastime?'

'It is, isn't it?' She snuggled herself against him and stared into the flickering firelight, feeling totally at one with him. 'I'm pleased she asked me to be with her for the birth. She was so brave and Bruno is so sweet. He has red hair, and he doesn't look in the least bit Italian . . . Bruno's hair was dark, like yours.' She turned her glance up to his, wondering what their baby would look like if they were lucky enough to have one. 'I've never seen an Italian with red hair and blue eyes, have you?'

His eyes caught hers and he smiled as though he knew what she'd been thinking, and he stopped her words with a kiss.

When Trinity went home to Marianna, it was her adoptive mother who picked her up from the hospital.

Mary James had changed in the time they'd been apart. She smiled more, her eyes were brighter and she'd lost her dried-up look. She was still timid, but not as much as she had been.

'I've bought a small cottage with the insurance money, and I've got a pension to keep me going. It's nice having a garden where I can grow vegetables, and I've got a little dog for company. Remember how you always wanted a dog when you were small? I used to hear you praying for one.'

'I did a lot of praying, then.'

'So did I.' They gazed at each other. 'We really had no choice,' Mary said slowly. 'I still go to the church on Sundays, and I help out with the flower-arranging. I've made friends in Dorchester and have joined the Women's Institute. What about you?'

'I don't pray now. I associate it with pain and punishment after a childhood spent on my knees praying for my sins. Besides, if God existed, I don't believe He'd have given me Bruno then snatched him away so cruelly.

'Pandora's a non-believer, yet she's been good to me. Just because a person's an atheist it doesn't mean they're sinners. I don't know what I would have done without her.'

Mary looked uncomfortable as she gazed around her. 'I came here just before your father arranged for us to go to Australia. I wanted to see her, to tell her you were all right. Her grandmother told me she'd married, and wouldn't want everything dragged up again. I've since found out she'd been told you were dead.'

'Yes, that was a cruel thing to do to her.'

Her mother seemed to be holding something back. She was twisting her handkerchief in her hands, a sure sign she was agitated. Trinity was sick of the secrets surrounding her birth.

'If there's anything else you want to tell me, let's have it.'

'The Bishop and his brother were on the board of a church orphanage, so was the judge and the magistrate. Matthew did some voluntary work there, and the adoption was pushed through quickly.'

'Didn't you think it odd?'

'I knew something wasn't quite right about it, but at the time I was desperate to have a baby. We'd tried the usual channels, but had been turned down. I don't know why, when we had a nice home and Matthew had a good job. We went to interviews, and did all those psychological tests and things, but still we got turned down. We'd discussed it with the bishop, you see, so when you were offered to us I thought it would be my last chance.'

'You didn't question why he wanted to give his own daughter away?'

'I didn't know he was your father then. He said it was a private adoption, that the mother was too young to care for you and we were to regard you as a gift from God, and keep you pure in His name. I discovered that the bishop had fathered you when we signed the papers . . . and then I saw Pandora had the same name. At first, I thought you were his wife's child – she was a bit funny in the head – then I realized she was too old, and I saw how young Pandora was . . . and knew what he was. It shocked me to the core a man in his position doing something so dreadful.'

'Yet you didn't report him to the authorities . . . you left him to prey on other children?'

'Matthew said it was none of our business . . . and that the clergy often named themselves as the father of a child when the father was actually unknown. He said Pandora was a whore who didn't know who'd fathered you. After the bishop died it didn't seem to matter.'

Trinity squeezed her eyes shut for a moment. She'd more or less accused Pandora of the same thing.

'And you chose to believe him?'

'It was easier than believing what I suspected. Matthew threatened to leave me and take you with him if I said anything. Robert Dysart had left him some money, and there was a bit of a dispute about it, and when he learned I'd visited Pandora's grandmother, he beat me up. I ended up in hospital with cracked ribs, and I had to tell them I'd had a fall. I was terrified I'd get home to find you gone if I said otherwise. He told me he was putting the house on the market. He said he'd had a divine vision, and Robert Dysart had left him some money to found a church in Australia – as if they didn't have any churches. And that was that, until Pandora came looking for you.'

'Oh God! He hit you? I never realized.'

'Matthew often hit me,' Mary said quietly, 'but not when you were home, and not where the bruises were obvious. Now it's over and I'm freed from his tyranny, I'm convinced he was insane. Over you, he exercised a different type of power, that of fear and complete obedience. I'm glad you were strong enough to oppose him, and got out when you did.'

Trinity took her mother in a hug. 'Thanks for telling me the truth.'

'I just didn't want you to blame Pandora for any of this, when she was the one who was wronged in the first place.'

'I'm not blaming anyone.' Trinity took a peek at her son, lying peacefully in his pram. He looked a bit like Bruno, but more like her, and she guessed that was because of her Dysart genes. His eyes were going to be a lighter blue than his father's. His skin had a faintly olive hue, but his hair was definitely and gloriously chestnut.

'All I want now is to bring up Bruno's children and leave the past behind. I've decided to stay in England. I want my children to know Pandora is their grandmother, and I want them to have a background. I need to give back something to her for what she lost. As for me, you'll always be my mother, despite the circumstances.'

Mary's eyes filled with tears and Trinity smiled. 'I've done more than enough crying lately to last me a lifetime. Go and make some tea if you're going to cry, whilst I sort out the bedroom. I didn't have time to do it before I left.'

To her surprise, everything she'd planned had been done. Angela's new room had been redecorated with pink flowered wallpaper. New furniture had replaced the old, with frilly white hangings on the bed to match the curtains, and a wicker chair had a rag doll sitting on it. It was a room designed to gladden a little girl's heart.

The cot had been made up and was in the small sitting-room, her bed and belongings moved.

'I didn't want her to feel left out when the baby arrived,' Pandora said, when she brought Angela home later that day. 'It was great fun doing it. Bryn's a dab hand with wallpaper, and wants to help you decorate the nursery when you're ready. Is there anything I can do for you, or would you rather be alone to sort yourself out?'

She sounded so eager to please that Trinity's heart nearly broke.

'If you wouldn't mind holding Bruno for a while I'll prepare some dinner. If you can stand it, you can check his nappy. He's nearly due for his feed, and is getting a bit stroppy. I can see I'm going to have to learn to manage my time around his demands.'

'You'll soon get the hang of it.' Pandora's eyes were on the baby, and Angela ran over to stand by her knee to smile adoringly at him. Pandora slid her arm around Angela's waist when she said proudly:

'That's my baby brother, Grandma.'

'He's beautiful, just like you, Angela.'

Trinity snatched up her camera and look aim, clicking it just as Angela bent to kiss her brother. When Pandora looked up and smiled, she snapped another one.

When her family grew up, she wanted all their moments to be happy ones like these. She experienced a moment of sadness when she thought of Bruno, but she knew she had to go on without him, because she couldn't waste her life grieving for the dead when she had the living to care for.

A month later, when Trinity was firmly in her routine, and the lawns of Marianna were covered in spring flowers, she had an unexpected visitor.

It was nearly lunch time. She'd heard the car pull into the drive, which was nothing unusual because the tenants often had visitors, or came and went during the day. She'd just finished hanging out the washing when a voice shouted out her name.

'Steve?' she said, shock spearing through her. 'What are you doing here? I thought. . . I thought I'd never see you again.'

He bounded towards her, laughing. 'Liar! You thought I'd taken off with the booty, didn't you?'

'No, of course not,' she said unconvincingly.

'I'm sorry I didn't contact you before, Trini.' He looked her over and grinned. 'You look bloody fantastic.'

'Would you like some coffee?' she said.

'What I'd like first, is to see my goddaughter. Where is she? I've got a present for her.'

'Angie's at school. You'd better come in and meet the new addition, and if you can stay a few hours she'll be home about three-thirty.'

'I can stay all the hours you want, and we need to come to some arrangement about the cash I took from Bruno's safe. I sold the necklace to a private buyer, by the way. No problem there. I forged Bruno's signature on the receipt and back-dated it a few months.'

Her smile faded at the mention of Bruno's name and she felt a little guilty about doubting Steve's integrity – at least, where her own welfare was concerned. Her husband had thought highly of him as both friend and employee.

'Sorry,' he said awkwardly, 'I forgot how you two were with each other.'

'It's all right, Steve. I don't expect people to walk around me on eggshells. In fact, I'd rather they didn't. Come in, and I'll get us some lunch.'

'Will you look at that kid,' he said a few moments later as he gazed into the pram. 'He's the spitting image of you, except for his smile. That's pure Bruno.'

'What smile? He hasn't begun to smile . . .' Her eyes flew open, because young Bruno was staring at Steve, seemingly fascinated, and with a gummy grin plastered on his face. She laughed. 'That's the first time he's smiled.'

'He must have thought I was funny, or something. What's his name?'

'Bruno.'

'That figures.' He gave her a sideways grin and a quick hug. 'His dad would be chuffed if he knew.'

'Bruno told me he didn't want the baby named after him.'

'Yeah, but that was just Bruno talking. He'd be as pleased as a dog with two tails to wag if he knew. 'That babe of mine has a mind all of her own,' he used to say, 'and I wouldn't have it any other way.'

'I told him not to call me babe,' she said, and they joined together in a moment of laughter – the first time she'd shared laughter with anyone about Bruno since he'd gone. But then, Steve had known Bruno a long time – so it was different and natural, because they'd been more like brothers than friends.

'I miss him, Steve,' she said suddenly. 'You've got no idea how much I miss him.' She moved into the circle of his arms. Gently he stroked her hair, and the few empathic moments they spent together were comforting.

'Yeah, babe, I do know,' he said when the moment was spent. 'If you need a friend to talk to, who better then me? You never did get to show me those honeymoon videos, you know.'

Which she did, later, when the children had settled down to sleep. 'That was in Naples. See that house behind them?' She choked on a teary smile when Bruno and Angela started clowning around in a dance routine. 'He told me it once belonged to his family . . . and that's Mount Vesuvius, and the bay, which was the view from our hotel balcony.'

'U-huh!' Steve said cautiously. 'Impressive, isn't it? Did he say much about his family?'

She slid him a smile. 'It's OK, Steve, Bruno told me the truth later. He was trying to impress me, and he needn't have bothered. Funnily enough, I'd almost decided to invent a background for Angie on his behalf, but have decided against it. You can't build a strong family relationship based on lies. It's love that counts. Angie and I both loved him just as he was. . . he was quite a guy.'

'And you're quite a gal. He adored you, you know. The day he brought you to the club I knew you were special, and so did he. I never expected Bruno to be hit so hard, or so suddenly, especially to some skinny chick who hadn't even mastered the art of walking in high heels. He always liked his women stacked.'

His eyes widened when he glanced at the video, and so did hers when she followed his gaze. 'Oh, God . . . oh no!'

He choked back a laugh, got up and casually turned it off. 'If I were you, I'd hide that little gem from the kids.'

She was blushing all over. Snatching the video from the machine, she stammered. 'The camera was left on by mistake . . . I'd forgotten.'

'Hey, you don't have to explain.' He was trying not to grin at her embarrassment. 'Bruno would laugh if he knew.'

She placed her hands against her heated face. 'Bruno might, but if *you* dare laugh, I'll never speak to you again.'

But Steve was finding it hard not to, and so was she, and the small, nervous giggle she gave was her undoing, and his. They both began to laugh, and they laughed until tears rolled down their cheeks, which seemed a natural thing to do with Steve.

Finally, they calmed down, except for the odd outbreak when their eyes met. It was gone midnight, and she felt happier and more relaxed than she had for a long time. 'Would you like some more coffee?'

He stood up. 'No, I'd better be getting back to the hotel. I'll drop in tomorrow and we'll sort out this cash business. You could do worse than invest in a small, but discreet club in London, with someone you trust . . . something along the line of Swingers.'

Her eyes sought his and she smiled. 'I see you have it all planned out. I'll sleep on it and we'll discuss it tomorrow. Thanks for being such a good friend, Steve.'

His knuckles grazed gently across her chin. 'Forget it. Bruno would have expected me to look out for you, babe, and even if he hadn't . . .' He gently kissed her before he walked away.

After he'd gone, Trinity slid the Naples video back in and watched it through from beginning to end. It was bitter-sweet to watch herself with Bruno, to see love expressed so beautifully and graphically. Her body responded to it now, as it had then but now it found no release. Their love-making would have to remain a beautiful and sensuous memory, a memory that would fade in time unless she watched this act of love between them over and over again.

With real regret, she erased the tape and removed it from the machine. It would be unfair to herself, and unhealthy to crave for the touch of a dead man. She ripped the tape from the cassette, threw it into the fireplace then held a match to it, squatting on her haunches to watch it flare into brightness, then bubble and burn before the flame finally died.

Perhaps their relationship would have ended up like that, the instant passion between them flaring up to burn brightly, then spluttering out.

Young Bruno gave an agitated cry from the other room. A few moments later she cuddled him to her breast and gazed down at his chestnut hair. She fancied it might be a statement, that hair – that this child was saying, 'Hey, I'm going to be my own unique person, not a substitute for my father as you imagined I'd be.'

The love she felt for him was almost as overwhelming a pleasure as his mouth taking sustenance from her breast, and her grief seemed to fall away from her.

It was as though a weight had been lifted from her shoulders.

CHAPTER TWENTY-TWO

April had become May, but it was not the benign ending of spring Trinity had heard so much about.

An unexpected storm had blown in from the sea overnight. It had whipped and lashed around Marianna in a fury of maniacal moans and groans. It had rattled the windows, and, getting a grip on the door, had shaken it so firmly she'd thought it would he ripped from its hinges and the house would be torn to pieces around her.

But Marianna had resisted the assault. It was a house built to last, and was as resilient as the family it had been built for.

The storm had abated slightly with the dawn, but had not yet blown itself out. The trees and shrubs whipped back and forth and the wind sang a wild song over the rise. There was a flavour of sea-salt on her tongue and the fragrance of pine-resin in her nostrils.

Trinity closed her eyes, imagining the waves pounding at the shore and the wind whistling over the cliff face. She had an urge to launch herself on to the wind and fly, but she couldn't leave the children by themselves.

She should be unhappy. She'd just heard that Bruno's creditors had won their case for control of his share of the undertaker's business. She hadn't expected to win the case, anyway, and had let it go undefended because she couldn't afford to fight it.

To balance that was an unexpected bonus. The Public Trustee, who'd been handling Bruno's estate had awarded her half of his life insurance. It wasn't a vast amount, but there had been enough to pay Adrian back and give her a nest-egg. The children had been given a quarter each, and that had been invested for them.

Life, of late, seemed to have imposed its own series of checks and balances and provided her with paths to take. They'd led her back to where she'd begun.

Her last tie with Australia had been severed – except for the small patch of earth where her husband's body lay. She didn't need a shrine to Bruno when she had the living memory of him inside her heart, and the gift of his child in her arms.

It was her birthday, and for the first time in her life there was a quiver of expectation inside her. Yet the morning's post brought her nothing. She'd half expected a grand gesture from Pandora, but not even a phone call had come her way. It had become obvious her birthday would remain uncelebrated – as it always had in the past.

She told herself that Pandora was busy these days. Bryn had persuaded her to teach the art of computing to some of the youth who went to the centre. Initially, Pandora had done so with trepidation, but she was fairly enthusiastic about the task now she'd found some confidence.

Trinity's daily routine took her mind from the forgotten birthday. Feeding and playing with her son and daughter took priority. Then came the cleaning and washing, after which any spare time she had was spent with her sketch-book, a hobby she'd recently resumed. She was happy with her children, and wanted for nothing else.

Pandora came late that afternoon with Bryn.

Angela squealed with delight when she saw them and aimed herself like an arrow at Bryn. When he swung her up in his arms she rained kisses all over his face. From her vantage point on his shoulders, she beamed at Pandora.

'Brad Hershaw kissed me at school, Grandma. It was yukky, so I punched him and he cried.' She patted Bryn on the head. 'Will you help me build a castle with my Lego?'

'Exactly what I came over to do, pippin. Let me say hello to your brother first.'

'He's had his feed and he's asleep.' A worried look crossed her face. 'He won't grow up to be yukky like Brad Hershaw will he? My teacher said boys are all the same, when I told her what Brad did.'

Bryn choked back a laugh. 'No doubt, young Bruno will knock spots off them when he gets a big bigger.'

'Sarah Denison can't come to school because she caught spots from the chickens.'

Bryn glanced up and the three of them exchanged a smile. Bryn's glance became more meaningful at the sound of a car pulling up outside. 'Didn't you want to show Trinity something?'

Pandora suddenly seemed charged with excitement. 'Yes, conditions should be just right now, and on today of all days. Fetch your coat, Trin, I want to show you something special. Bryn will mind the kids for an hour or so.'

'I might need the practice,' he said, trying to sound casual, and his smile broadening when Pandora threw a cushion at him.

'You weren't supposed to say anything until we're *sure*,' she said.

Trinity heard more cars arriving as Pandora hurried her across the lawn; she looked back to see Lottie and Ben carrying parcels and dishes into the house, and, oddly, a couple who resembled Doreen and Jim from Hope's End.

I must be imagining things.

It was transparently obvious what Pandora was up too, and also what she wanted to show her in the meantime. Trinity smiled to herself . . . and she'd thought it was her secret!

At the edge of the cliff the wind was so strong it blew the breath back into their bodies before they could exhale – and left them gasping. Her hair whipped about her head in strands and the air was charged with so much ozone it made her blood fizz.

'I discovered this place as a child,' Pandora shouted over the din of the waves, wind and wheeling seagulls. 'I want to give it to you as part of your birthday present.'

Trinity's grin matched Pandora's. Of course Pandora wouldn't have forgotten her birthday. She was her daughter, and as cherished by Pandora as baby Bruno was by herself. This place had been something special to Pandora as a child. It had been her place of healing, and she wanted to share it with her.

It was a very special gift, she realized, and she wasn't going to spoil this moment for her. Today, she was seeing a different Pandora, a part of her mother that had always been childlike and free – not the serene and carefully-controlled being she presented to the world.

Arms outstretched, they joined hands and leaned into the wind. It was stronger than anything Trinity had ever experienced before. It cradled her body, so she closed her eyes and imagined they were gliding together over the turmoil of white-crested waves.

There was a moment when she felt herself joined in spirit with Pandora, when the pain of her birth and moment of her bonding was very clear to her . . . then she gently floated back to earth, her soul at peace with the universe.

They exchanged a glance of mutual understanding.

Pandora was gazing at her, her eyes full of tears.

'Bryn said that you'll always mean more to me than the other way around. I'll try not to push the relationship further than you want it to go – and you must tell me if I overstep the mark.'

Trinity nodded, appreciating her mother's honesty. 'We're too alike as people for comfort. You do realize we're going to hurt each other at times?'

A rueful smile flitted across Pandora's face. 'What matters is that I know you survived – that you're well, and as happy as you can be at this moment. Whether you want me to or not, Trin, I love you,' she said. 'I can't change the way I feel, and to be quite honest, neither would I want to. Love is far too precious.'

Pandora was right. 'I think . . . I *know*, I do want you to love me,' she said, and she moved into her mother's arms, where they hugged for a long, long time. . . .